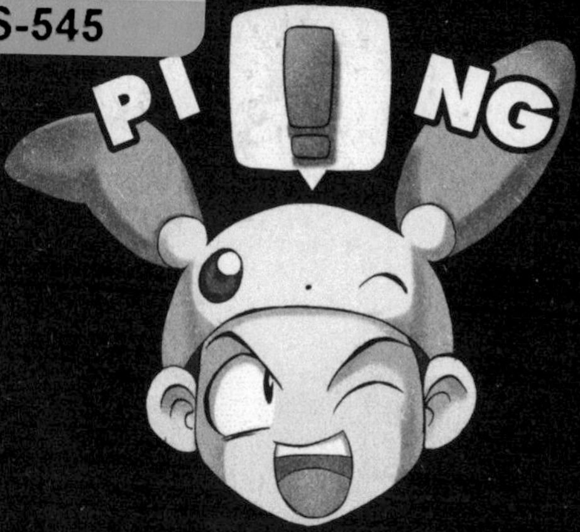
PI!NG

The battle reaches its climax!

The action moves from Team Galactic headquarters to the Distortion World, where Hareta finally meets the Legendary Pokémon Giratina. The time for the ultimate showdown has arrived!

Plus, this volume has another special bonus episode.

I enjoyed this series all the way to the end… I hope you did too!

– *Shigekatsu Ihara*

Shigekatsu Ihara's other manga titles include *Pokémon: Lucario and the Mystery of Mew*, *Pokémon Emerald Challenge!!* and *Battle Frontier, Dual Jack!!*

Pokémon DIAMOND AND PEARL ADVENTURE!
Vol. 8
VIZ Kids Edition

Story & Art by SHIGEKATSU IHARA

© 2010 Pokémon.
© 1995–2010 Nintendo/Creatures Inc./GAME FREAK inc.
TM and ® and character names are trademarks of Nintendo.
© 2007 Shigekatsu IHARA/Shogakukan
All rights reserved.
Original Japanese edition
"Pokémon D•P POCKET MONSTER DIAMOND PEARL MONOGATARI"
published by SHOGAKUKAN Inc.

Translation/Kaori Inoue
Touch-up Art & Lettering/Eric Erbes
Graphics & Cover Design/Hitomi Yokoyama Ross
Editor/Annette Roman

VP, Production/Alvin Lu
VP, Sales & Product Marketing/Gonzalo Ferreyra
VP, Creative/Linda Espinosa
Publisher/Hyoe Narita

Printed in the U.S.A.

Published by VIZ Media, LLC
P.O. Box 77010
San Francisco, CA 94107

10 9 8 7 6 5 4 3 2 1
First printing, November 2010

www.vizkids.com

www.viz.com

POKÉMON®
DIAMOND AND PEARL ADVENTURE!

Volume 8

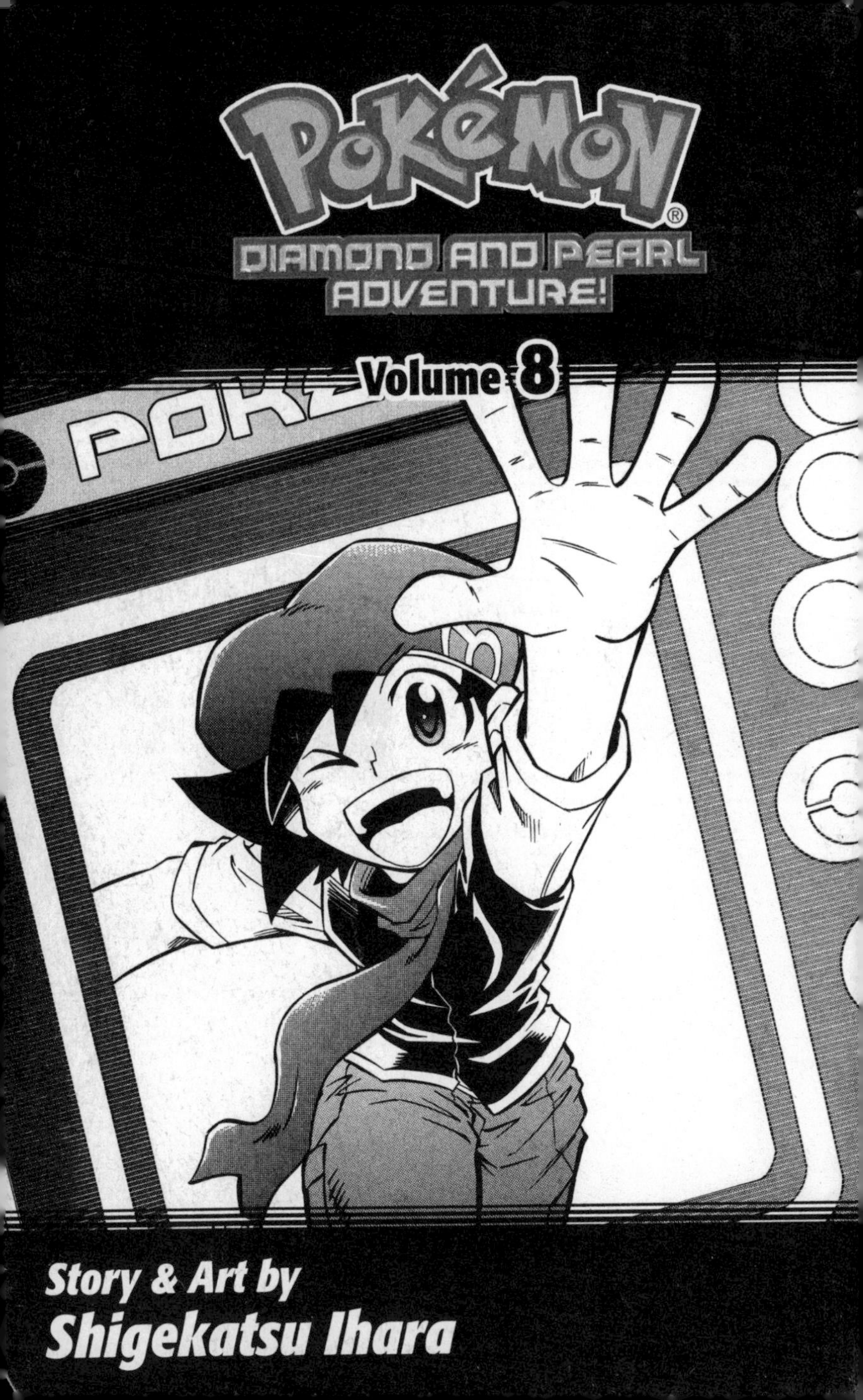

Story & Art by
Shigekatsu Ihara

MAIN CHARACTERS

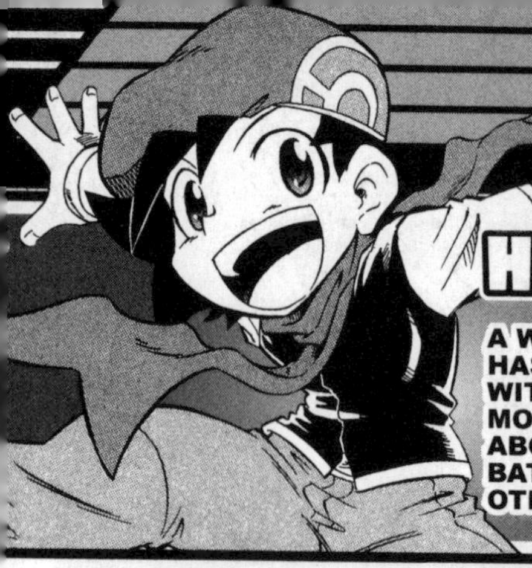

HARETA

A WILD BOY WHO HAS A SPECIAL BOND WITH POKÉMON! HE'S MORE ENTHUSIASTIC ABOUT POKÉMON BATTLES THAN ANY OTHER TRAINER!

MINUN

HARETA'S NEW PARTNER! MINUN IS A SUPER CUTE POKÉMON WHOSE CHARM MOVE IS IRRESISTIBLE.

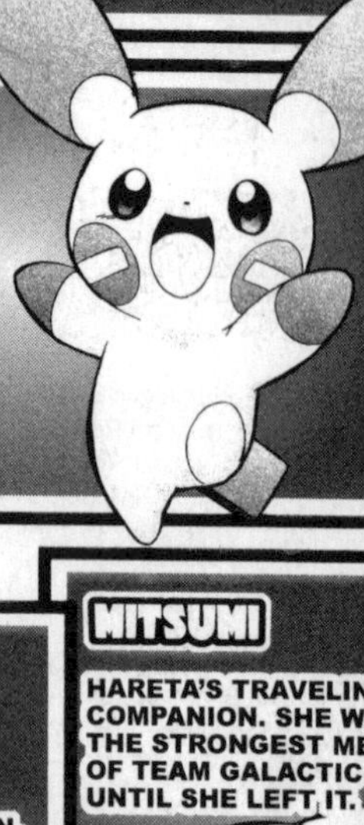

KAISEI

HARETA'S LONG-LOST FATHER, WHO LOVES TO TRAVEL THE WORLD.

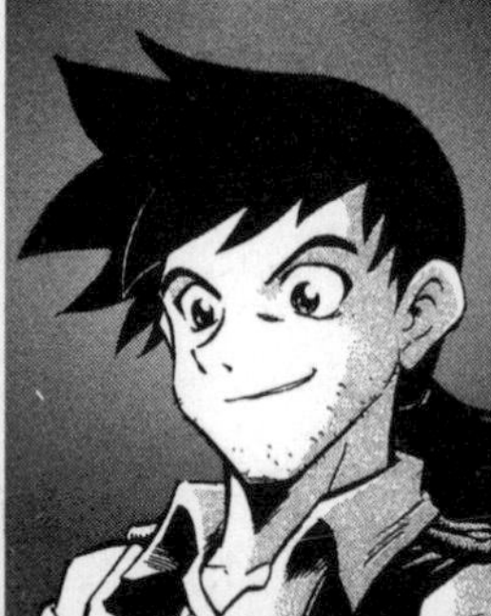

KOYA

A YOUNG MEMBER OF THE INTERNATIONAL POLICE. A COLD AND CALCULATING TACTICIAN.

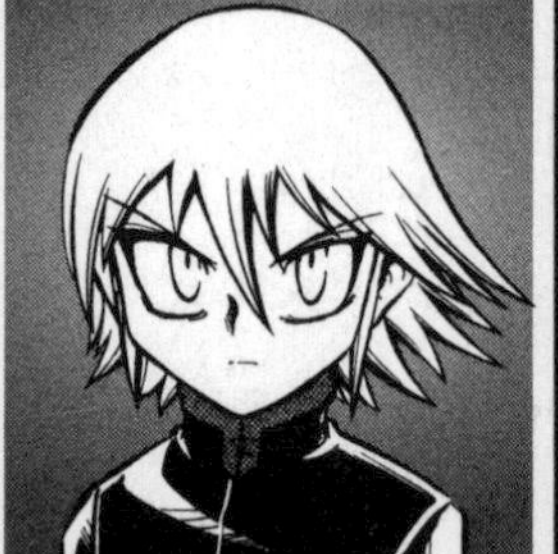

MITSUMI

HARETA'S TRAVELING COMPANION. SHE WAS THE STRONGEST MEMBER OF TEAM GALACTIC—UNTIL SHE LEFT IT.

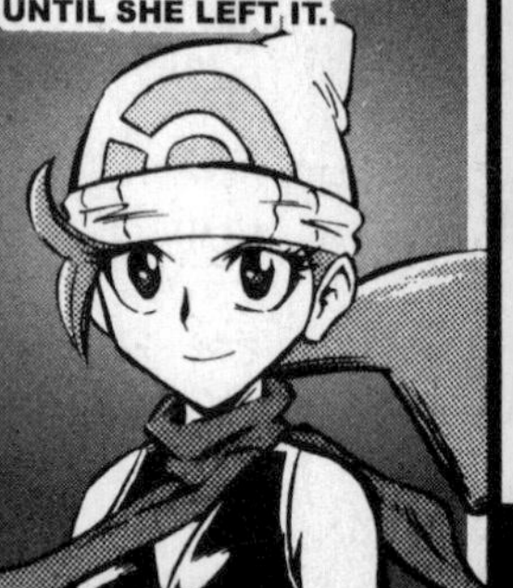

TEAM GALACTIC

AN EVIL ORGANIZATION THAT SEEKS TO EXPLOIT POKÉMON.

CHARON ▷
THE LEADER OF NEO-TEAM GALACTIC. HE'S SEARCHING FOR GIRATINA.

MARS ▽

SATURN ▽

◁ JUPITER

△ **CYRUS**
FORMER LEADER WHO WENT MISSING AFTER LOSING HIS POSITION TO CHARON.

▽ **LOOKER**
AN INTERNATIONAL POLICE DETECTIVE COMMITTED TO BRINGING TEAM GALACTIC TO JUSTICE.

PROFESSOR ROWAN
THE POKÉMON RESEARCHER WHO RAISED HARETA.

JUN ▷
A TRUE FRIEND WHO ALWAYS RUSHES TO HARETA'S AID.

THE STORY SO FAR

Hareta and his friends are in search of the Legendary Pokémon Giratina. They hope to find Hareta's father, Kaisei, with the rare Pokémon. During their journey, they find out that Neo-Team Galactic intends to capture Giratina. To stop the team's new leader, Charon, our friends head for Team Galactic's headquarters. There they discover that Charon is turning Pokémon into *living weapons!* Hareta is furious and confronts Charon...

TABLE OF CONTENTS

Chapter 1   The Birth of the Greatest Tag Team?! 7

Chapter 2   Koya's Sad Reunion 37

Chapter 3   Enter the Distortion World! 71

Chapter 4   Hareta's Fierce Battle! 106

Final Chapter: Gathering of the Legendary Pokémon! 140

Pokémon Diamond and Pearl Bonus Story:

Hareta's Future 175

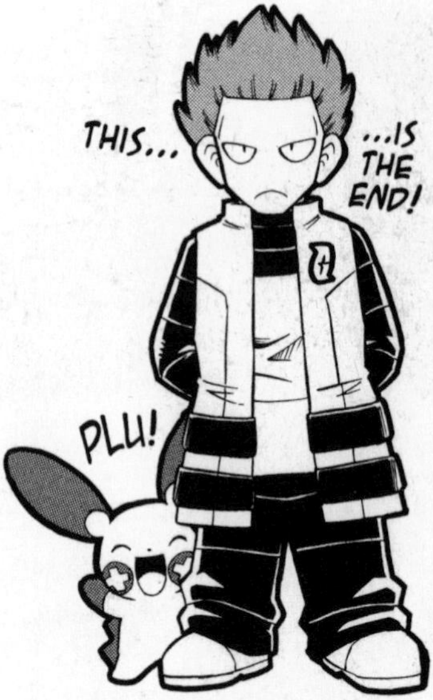
THIS...
...IS THE END!
PLU!

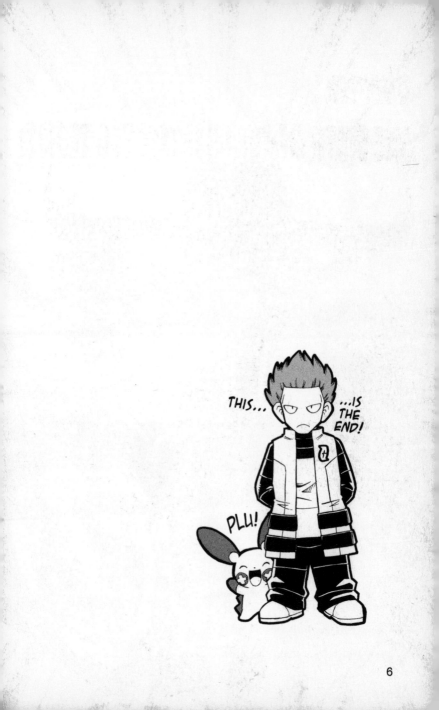

CHAPTER 1
THE BIRTH OF THE GREATEST TAG TEAM?!

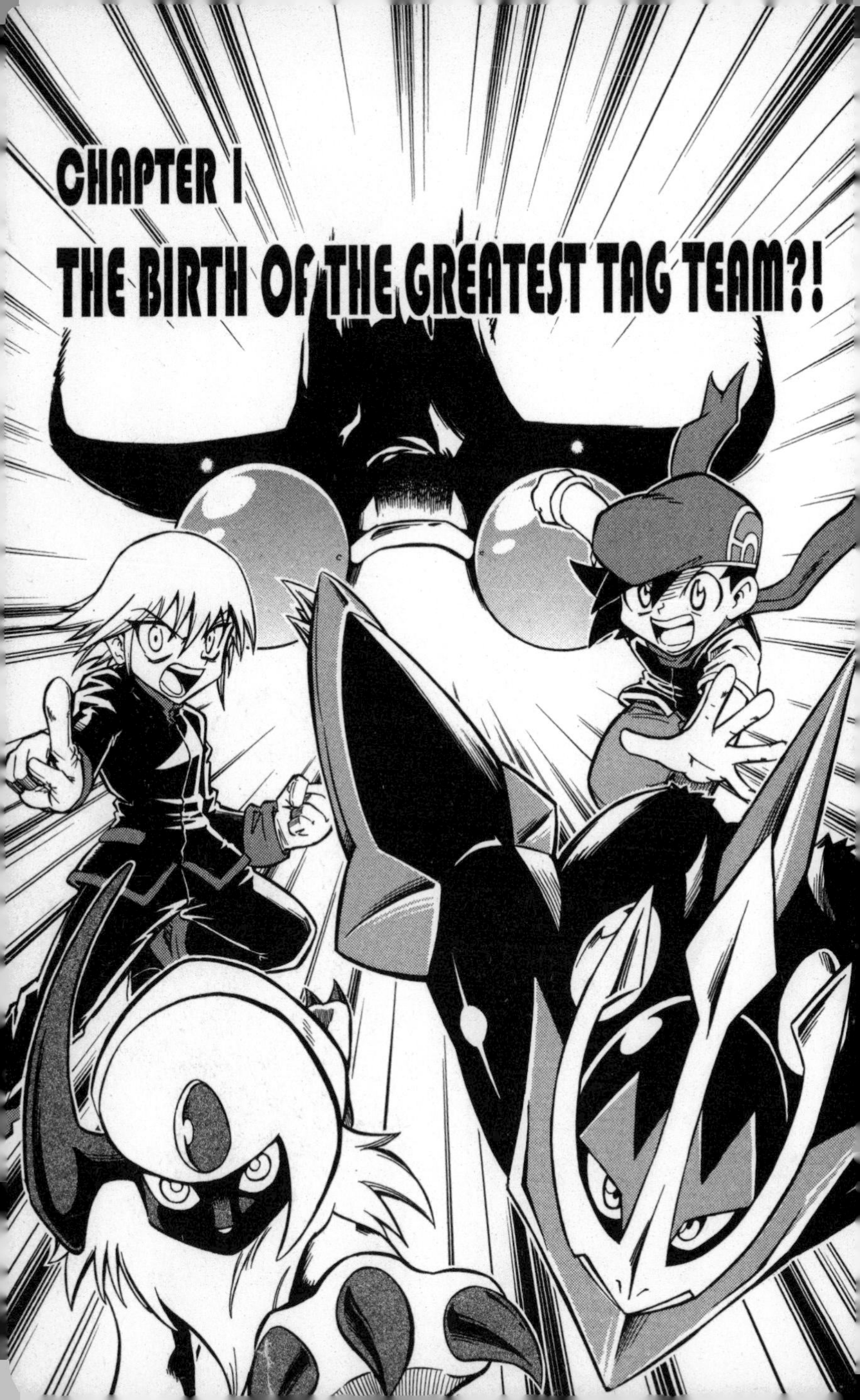

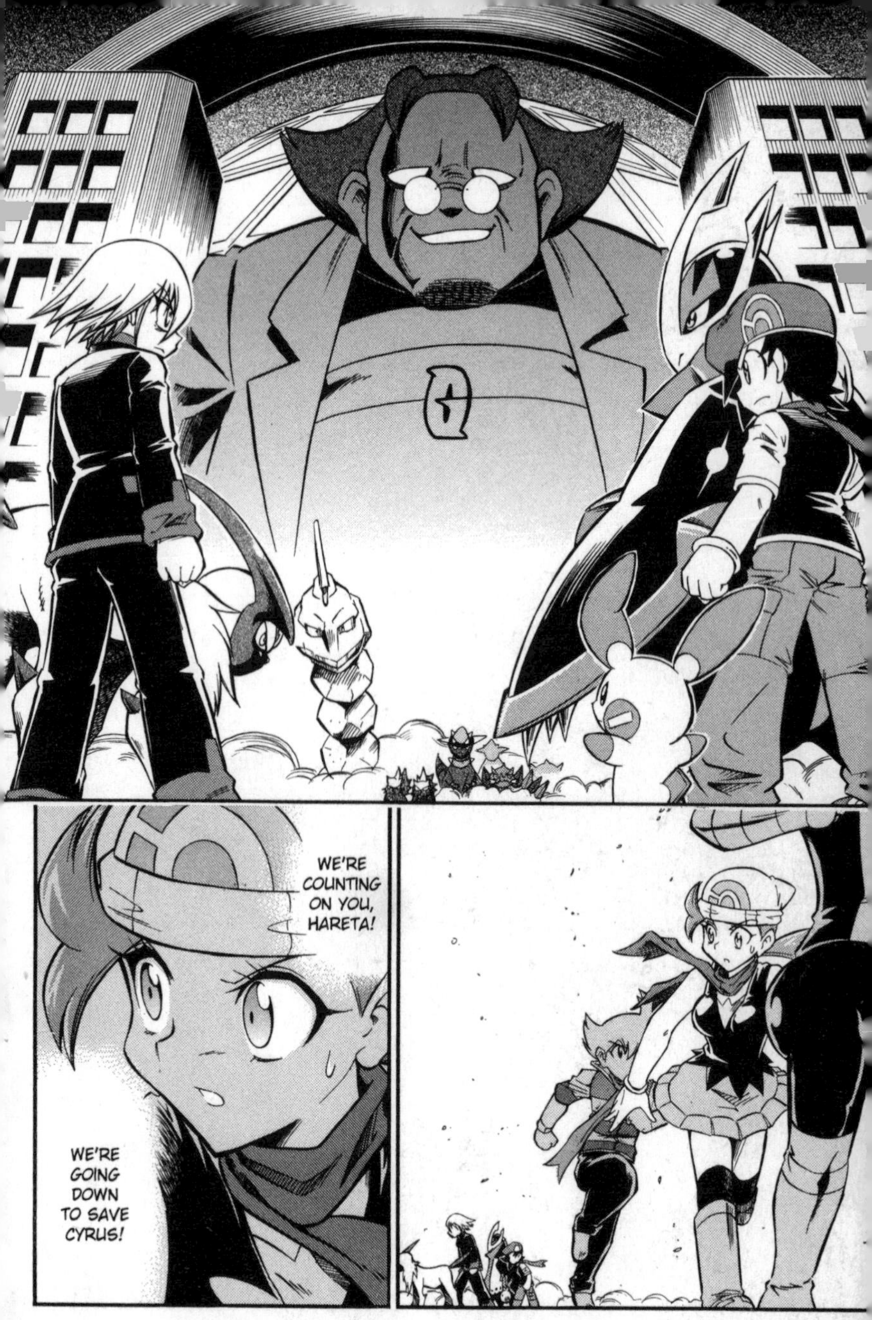
WE'RE COUNTING ON YOU, HARETA!
WE'RE GOING DOWN TO SAVE CYRUS!

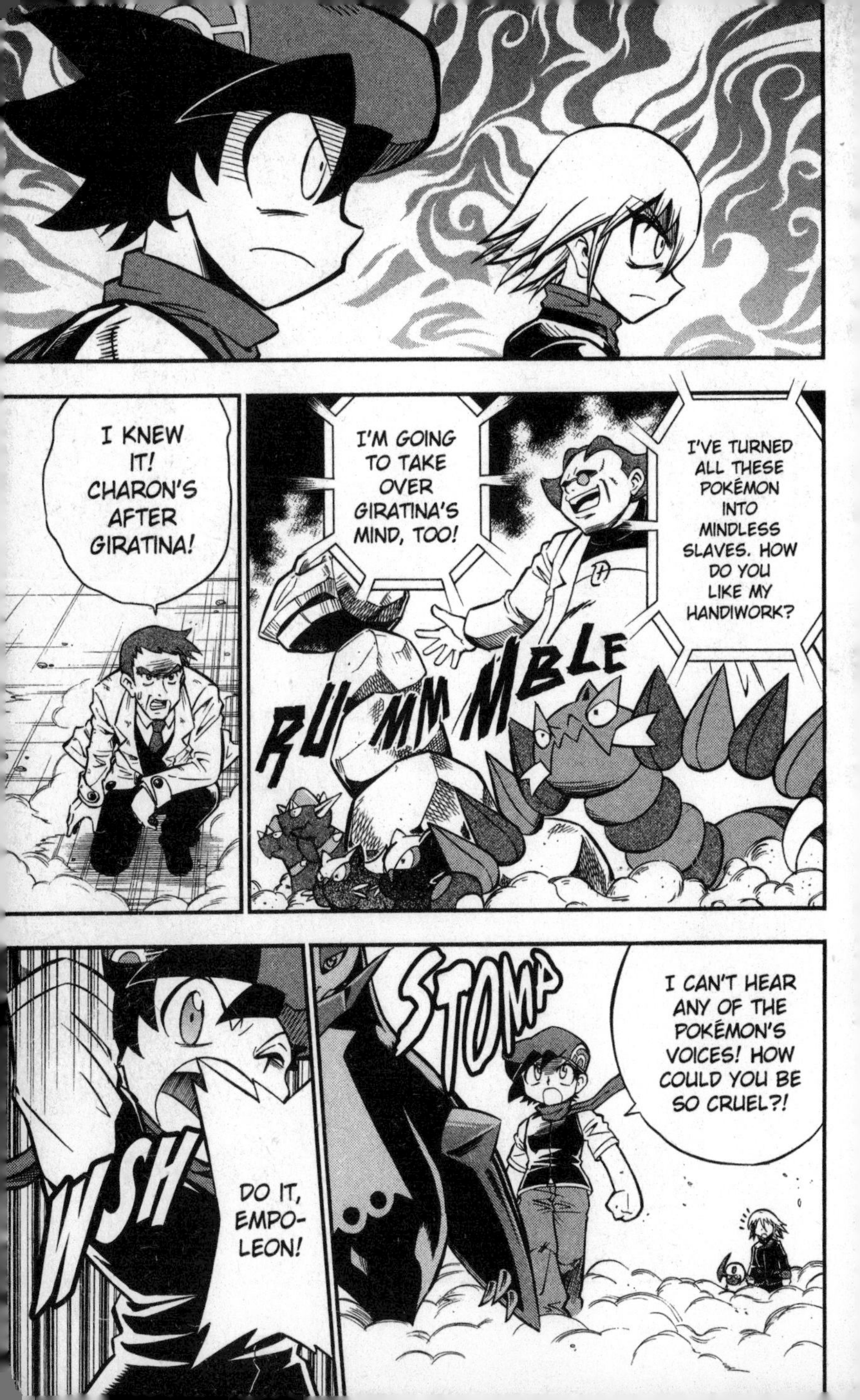
I'VE TURNED ALL THESE POKÉMON INTO MINDLESS SLAVES. HOW DO YOU LIKE MY HANDIWORK?
I'M GOING TO TAKE OVER GIRATINA'S MIND, TOO!
RUMMMMBLE
I KNEW IT! CHARON'S AFTER GIRATINA!
I CAN'T HEAR ANY OF THE POKÉMON'S VOICES! HOW COULD YOU BE SO CRUEL?!
STOMP
DO IT, EMPOLEON!
WSH

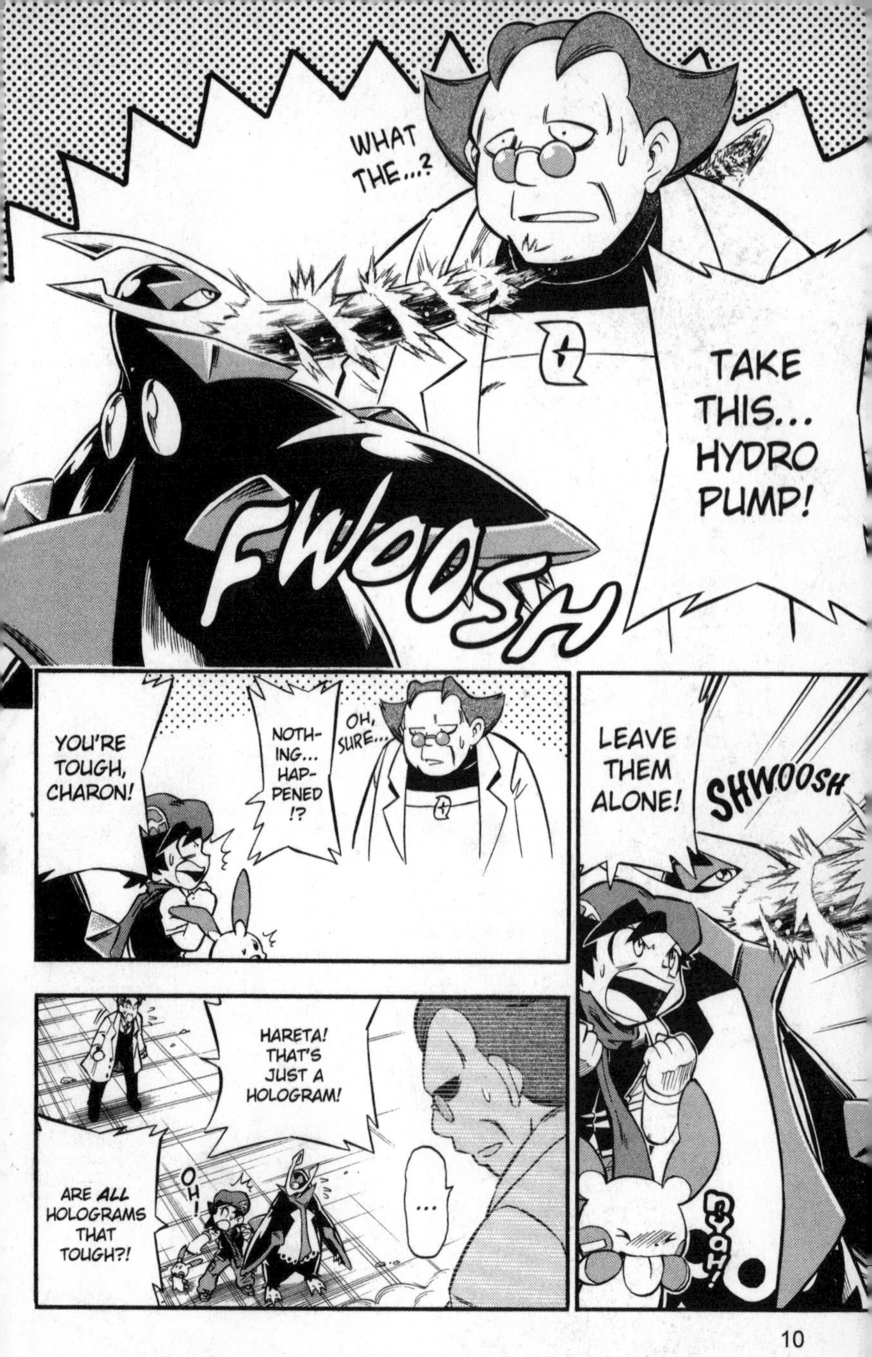
TAKE THIS... HYDRO PUMP!
FWOOSH
WHAT THE...?
LEAVE THEM ALONE!
SHWOOSH
NYOH!
OH, SURE...
NOTH-ING... HAP-PENED!?
YOU'RE TOUGH, CHARON!
HARETA! THAT'S JUST A HOLOGRAM!
...
OH!
ARE ALL HOLOGRAMS THAT TOUGH?!

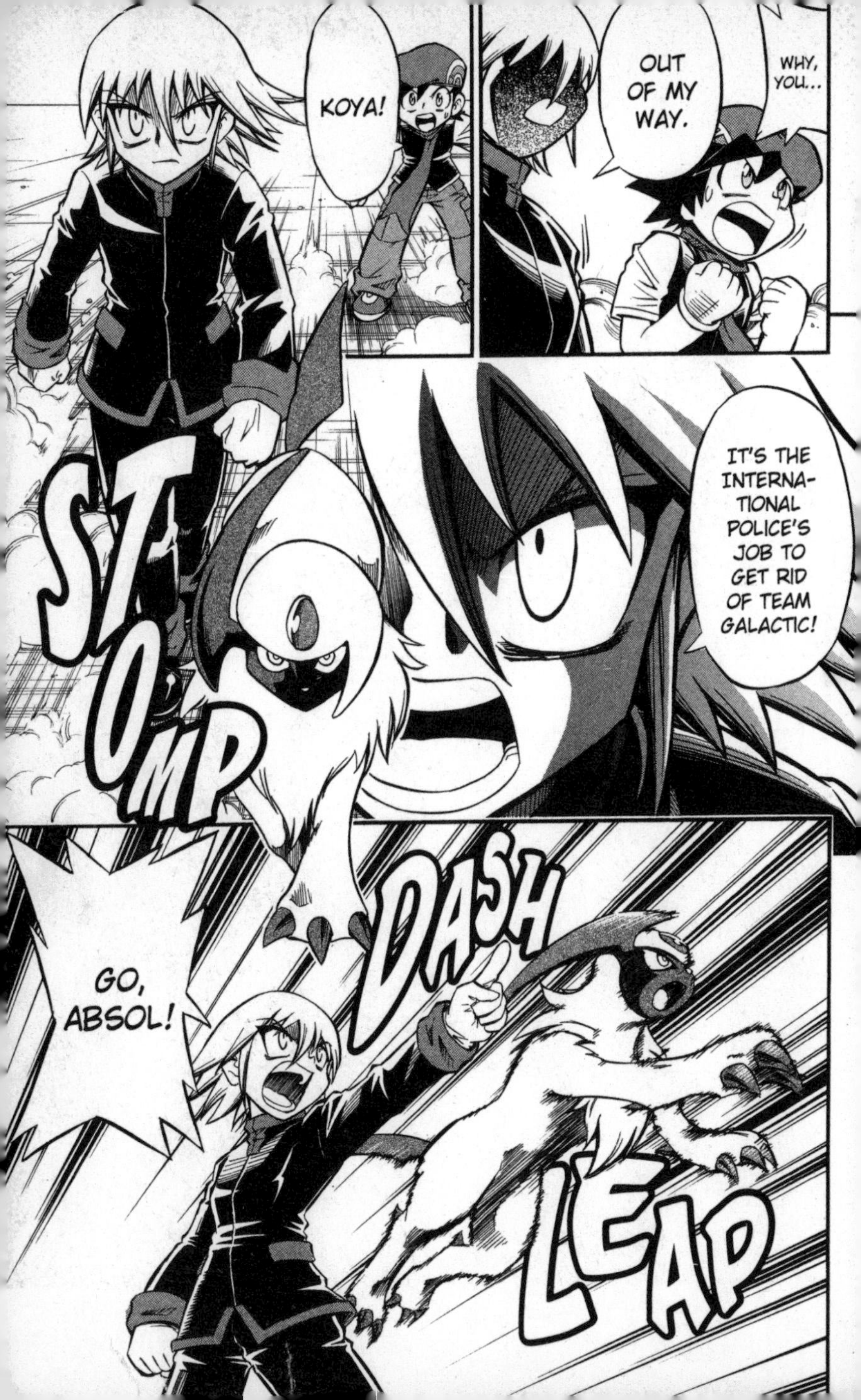
OUT OF MY WAY.
WHY, YOU...
IT'S THE INTERNATIONAL POLICE'S JOB TO GET RID OF TEAM GALACTIC!
KOYA!
STOMP
GO, ABSOL!
DASH
LEAP

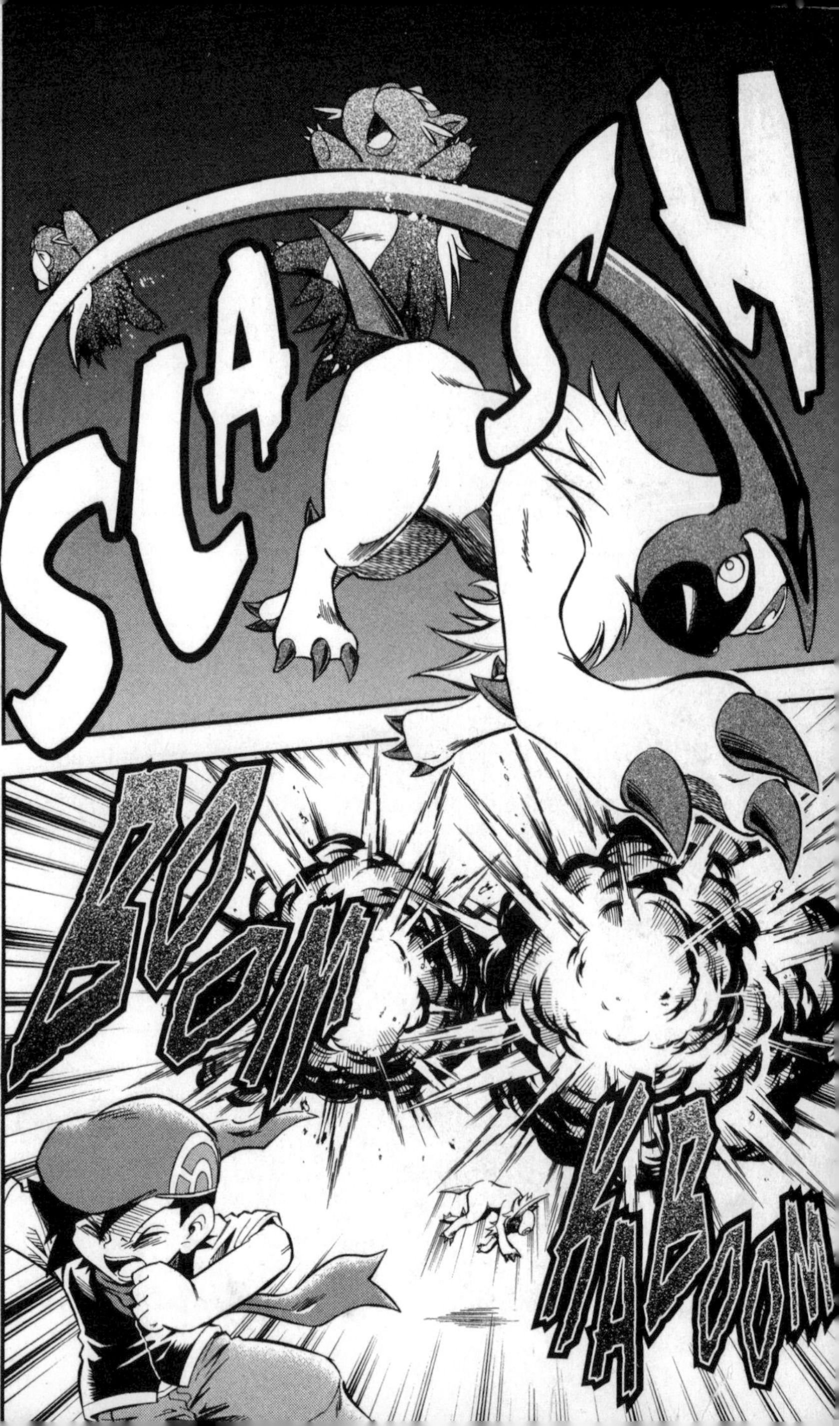
SLAM
BOOM
KABOOM

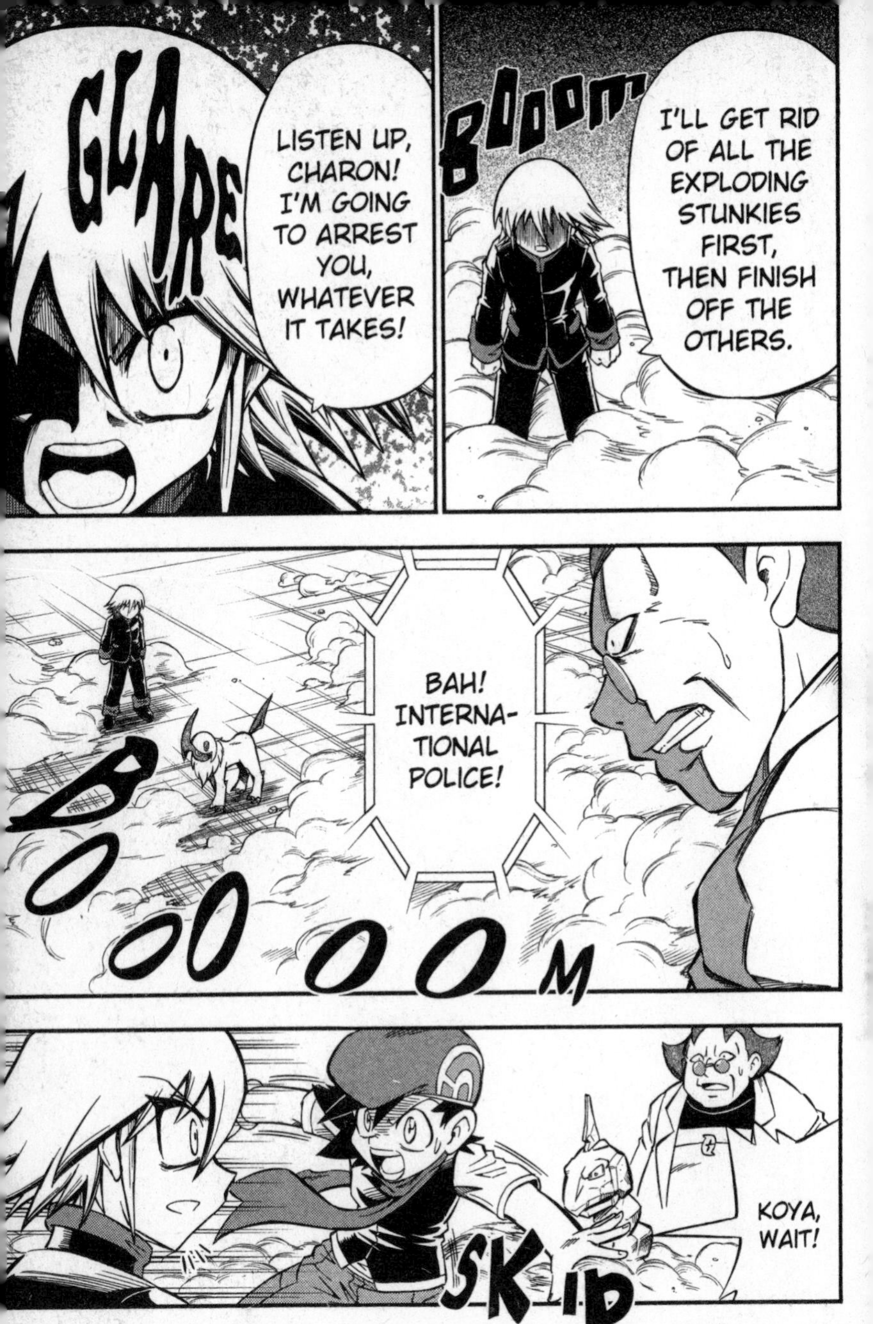
BOOOM
I'LL GET RID OF ALL THE EXPLODING STUNKIES FIRST, THEN FINISH OFF THE OTHERS.
GLARE
LISTEN UP, CHARON! I'M GOING TO ARREST YOU, WHATEVER IT TAKES!
BAH! INTERNATIONAL POLICE!
BOOOOOOM
KOYA, WAIT!
SKID

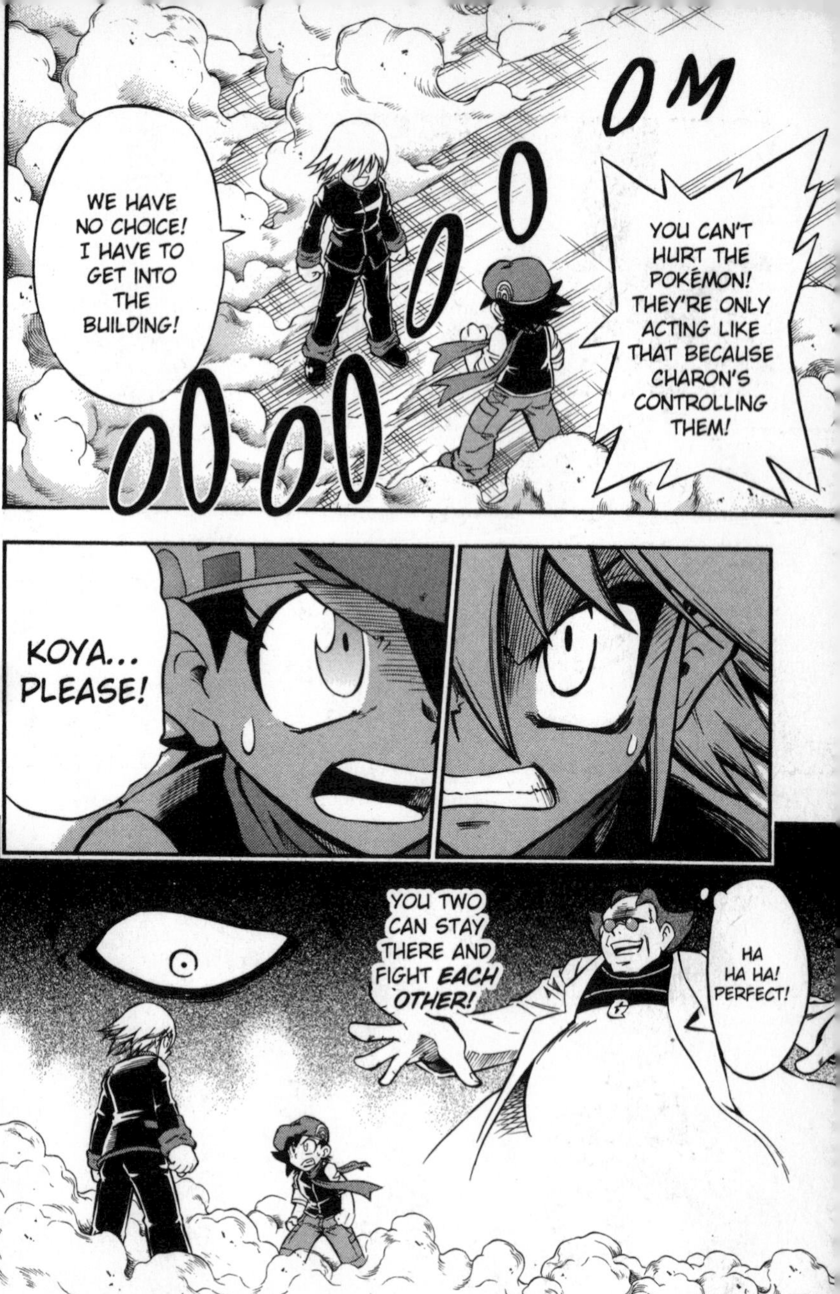
YOU CAN'T HURT THE POKÉMON! THEY'RE ONLY ACTING LIKE THAT BECAUSE CHARON'S CONTROLLING THEM!
OOOOOOOM
WE HAVE NO CHOICE! I HAVE TO GET INTO THE BUILDING!
KOYA... PLEASE!
HA HA HA! PERFECT!
YOU TWO CAN STAY THERE AND FIGHT **EACH OTHER!**

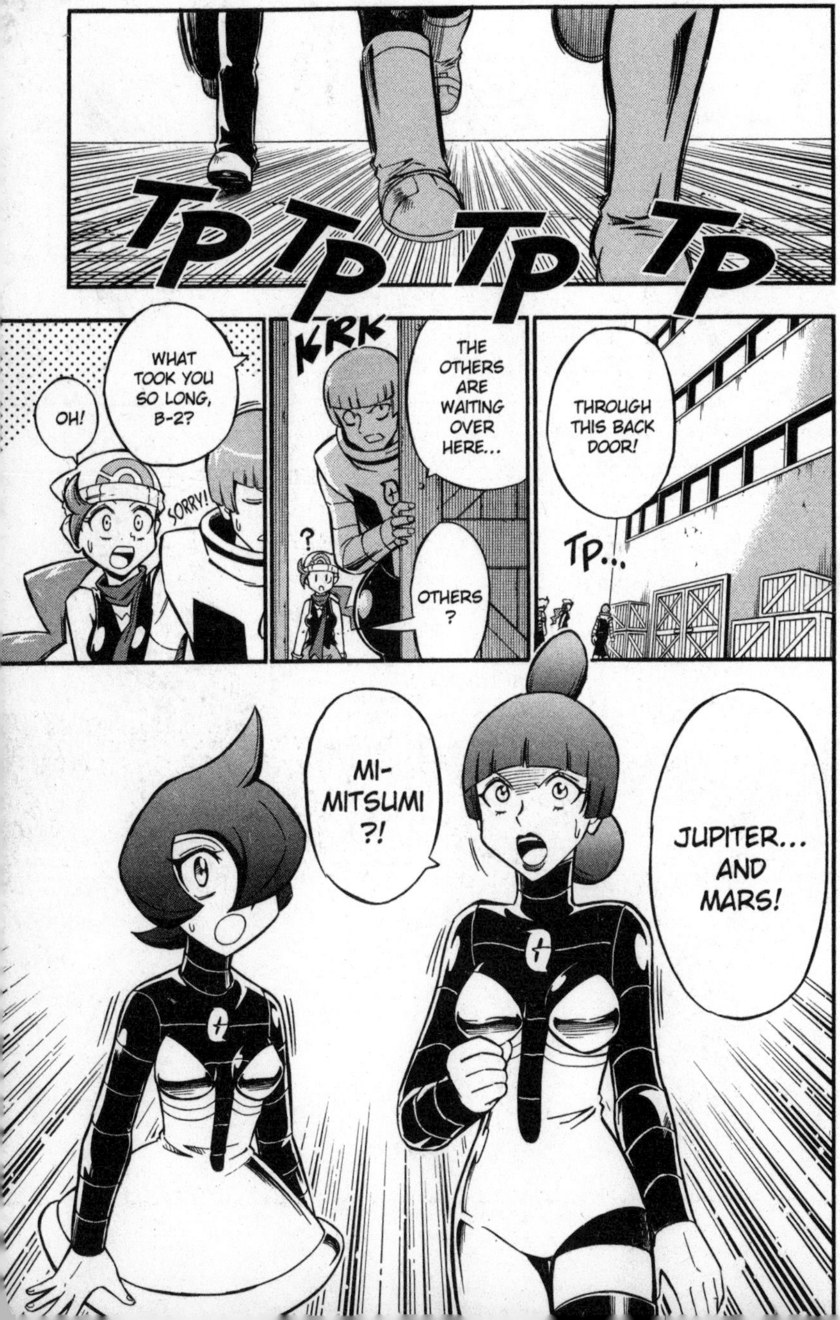
TP TP TP TP
THROUGH THIS BACK DOOR!
TP...
KRK
THE OTHERS ARE WAITING OVER HERE...
?
OTHERS?
WHAT TOOK YOU SO LONG, B-2?
OH!
SORRY!
JUPITER... AND MARS!
MI-MITSUMI?!

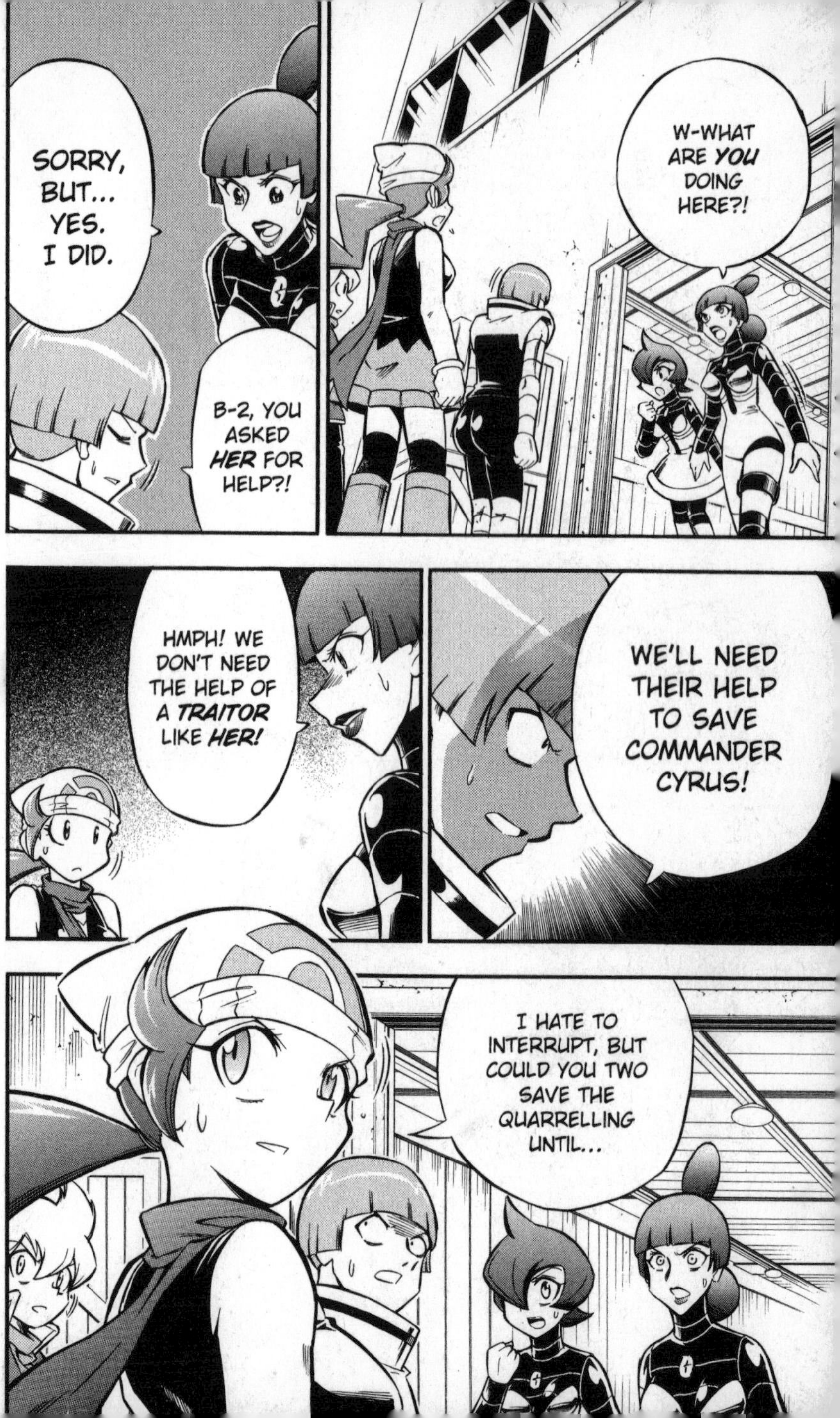
W-WHAT ARE *YOU* DOING HERE?!
B-2, YOU ASKED *HER* FOR HELP?!
SORRY, BUT... YES. I DID.
WE'LL NEED THEIR HELP TO SAVE COMMANDER CYRUS!
HMPH! WE DON'T NEED THE HELP OF A *TRAITOR* LIKE *HER!*
I HATE TO INTERRUPT, BUT COULD YOU TWO SAVE THE QUARRELLING UNTIL...

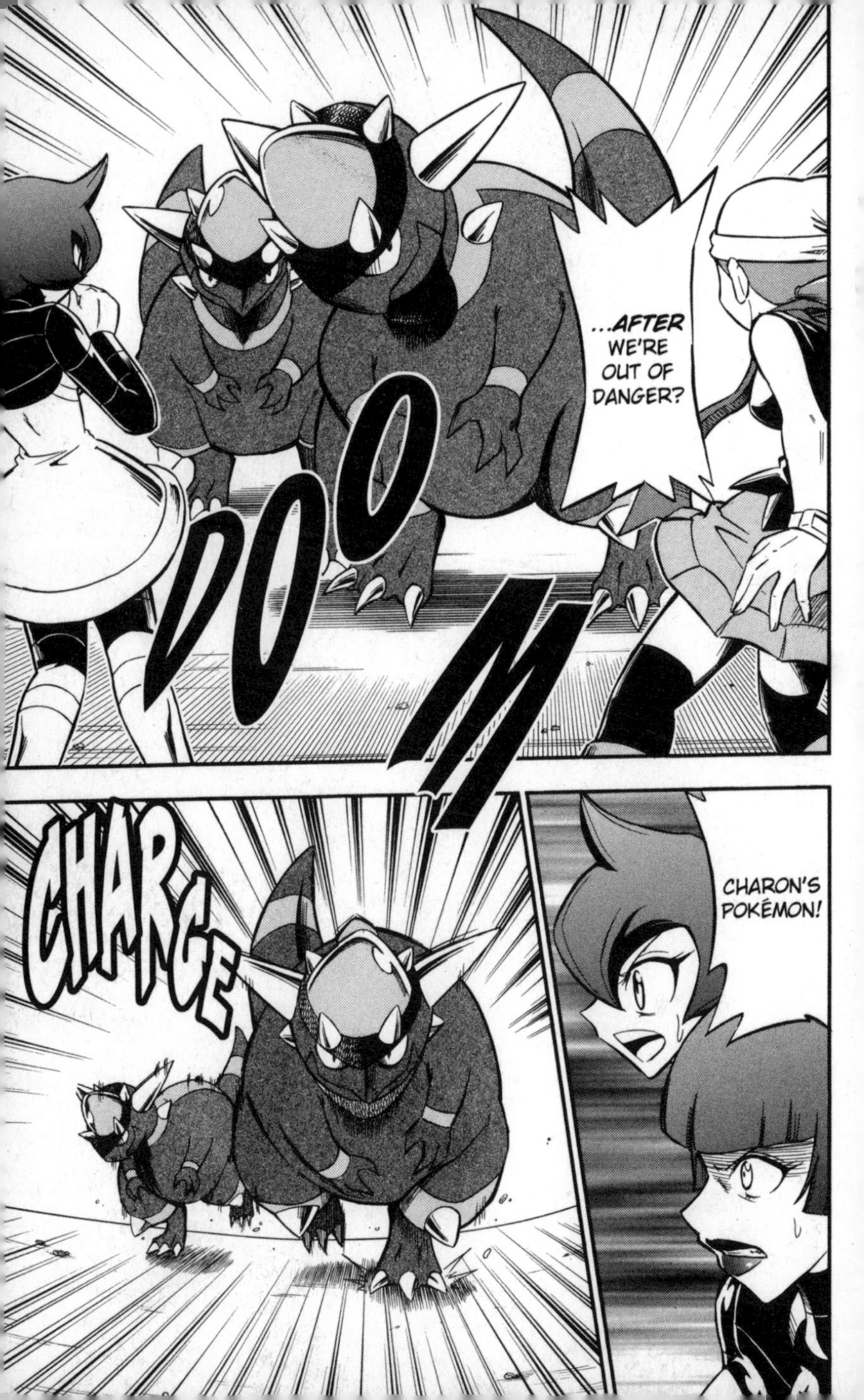
...AFTER WE'RE OUT OF DANGER?
DOOOM
CHARON'S POKÉMON!
CHARGE

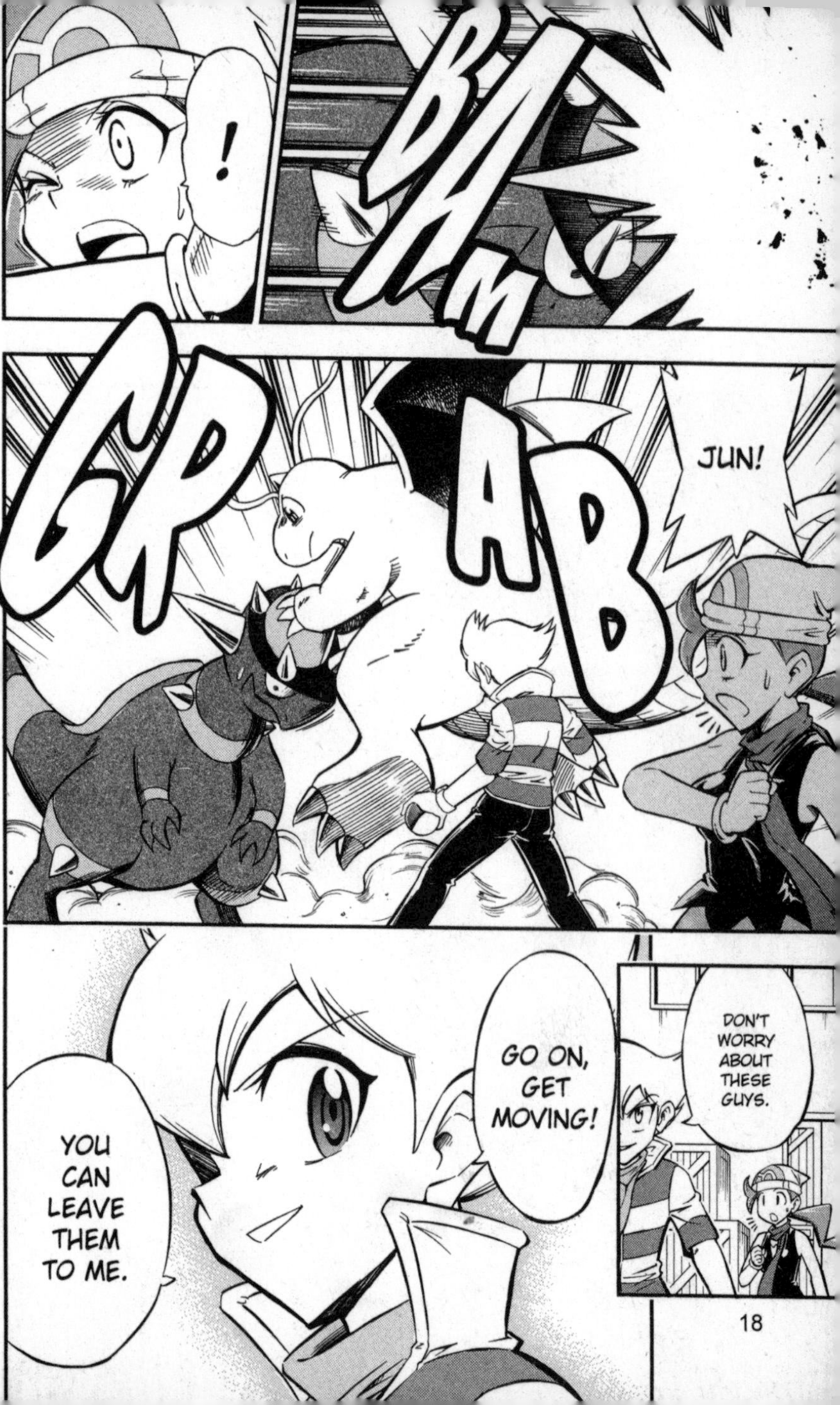
BAM
!
GRAB
JUN!
DON'T WORRY ABOUT THESE GUYS.
GO ON, GET MOVING!
YOU CAN LEAVE THEM TO ME.

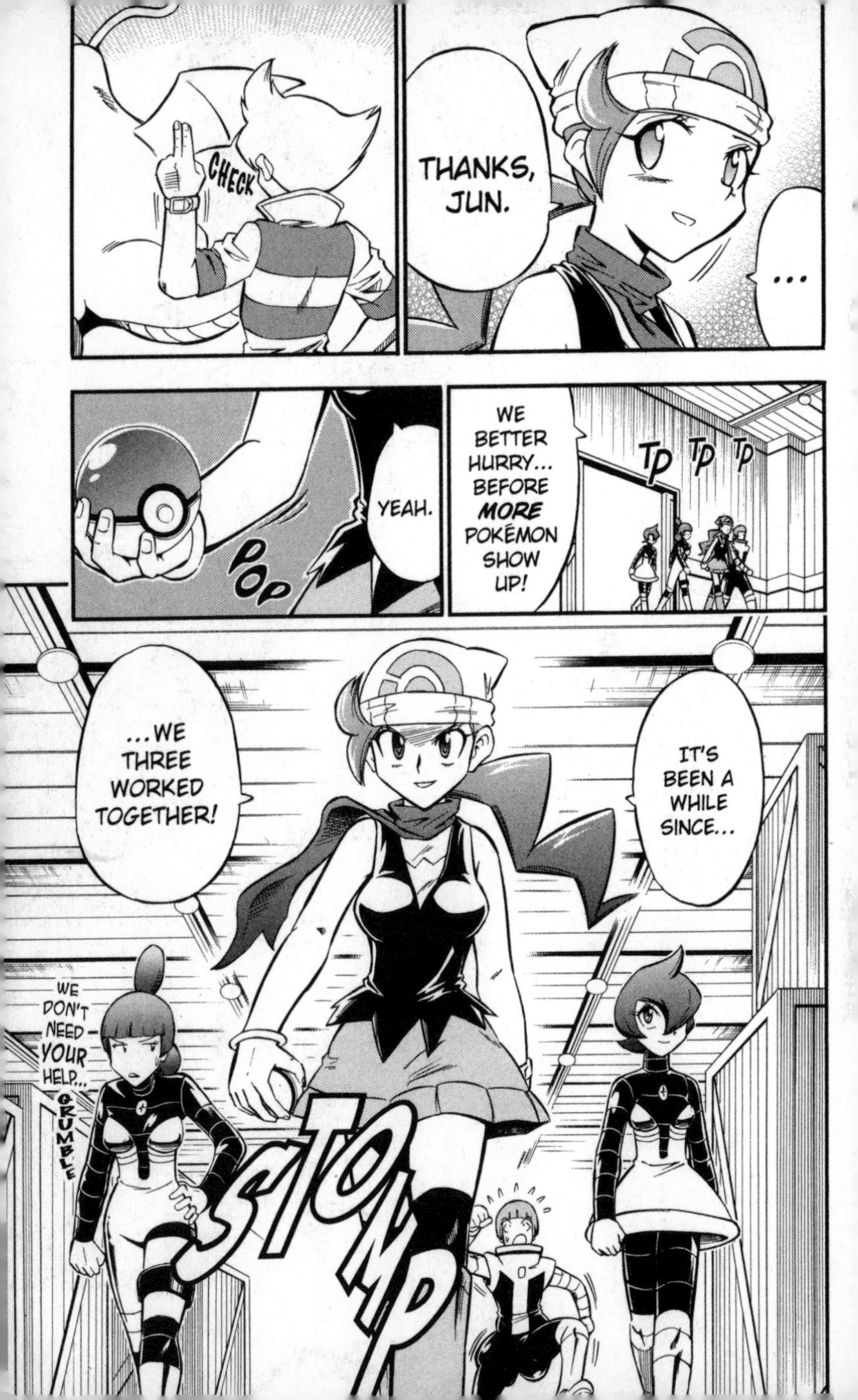
THANKS, JUN.
...
CHECK
WE BETTER HURRY... BEFORE MORE POKéMON SHOW UP!
TP TP TP
YEAH.
POP
IT'S BEEN A WHILE SINCE...
...WE THREE WORKED TOGETHER!
WE DON'T NEED YOUR HELP...
GRUMBLE
STOMP

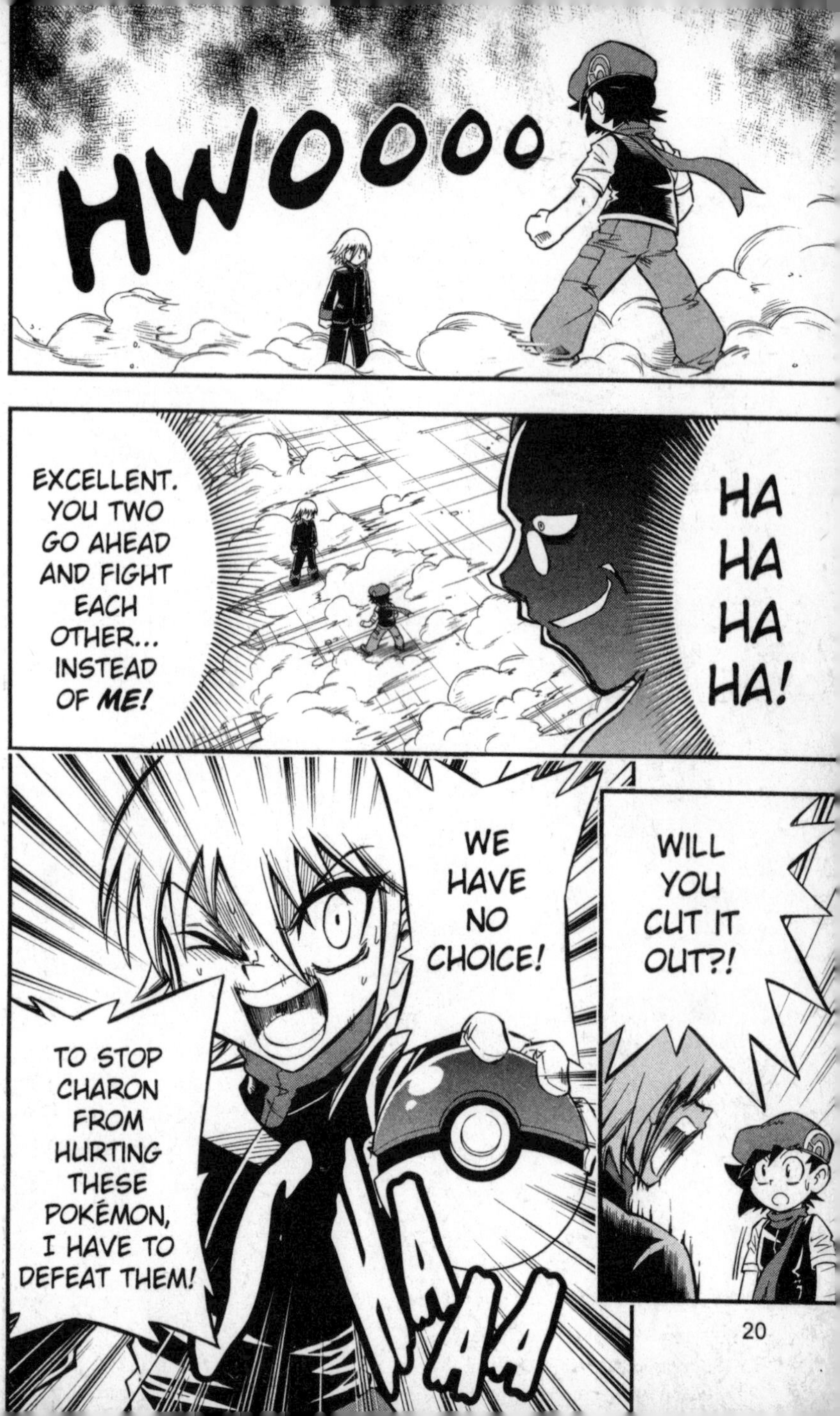
HWOOOO
HA HA HA HA!
EXCELLENT. YOU TWO GO AHEAD AND FIGHT EACH OTHER... INSTEAD OF *ME!*
WILL YOU CUT IT OUT?!
WE HAVE NO CHOICE!
TO STOP CHARON FROM HURTING THESE POKÉMON, I HAVE TO DEFEAT THEM!
HAAAA

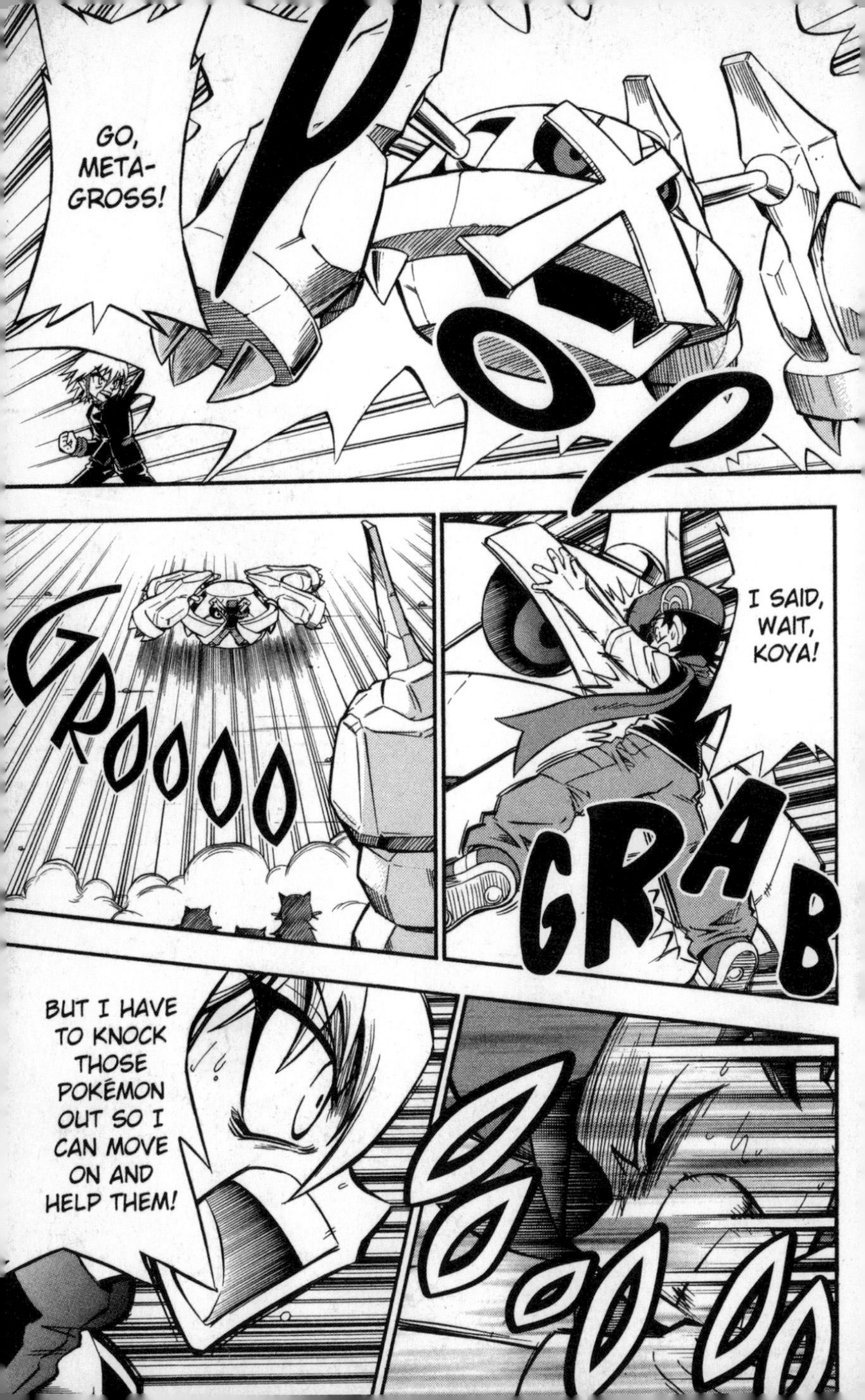
GO, META-GROSS!
POP
I SAID, WAIT, KOYA!
GRAB
GROOOOO
BUT I HAVE TO KNOCK THOSE POKÉMON OUT SO I CAN MOVE ON AND HELP THEM!

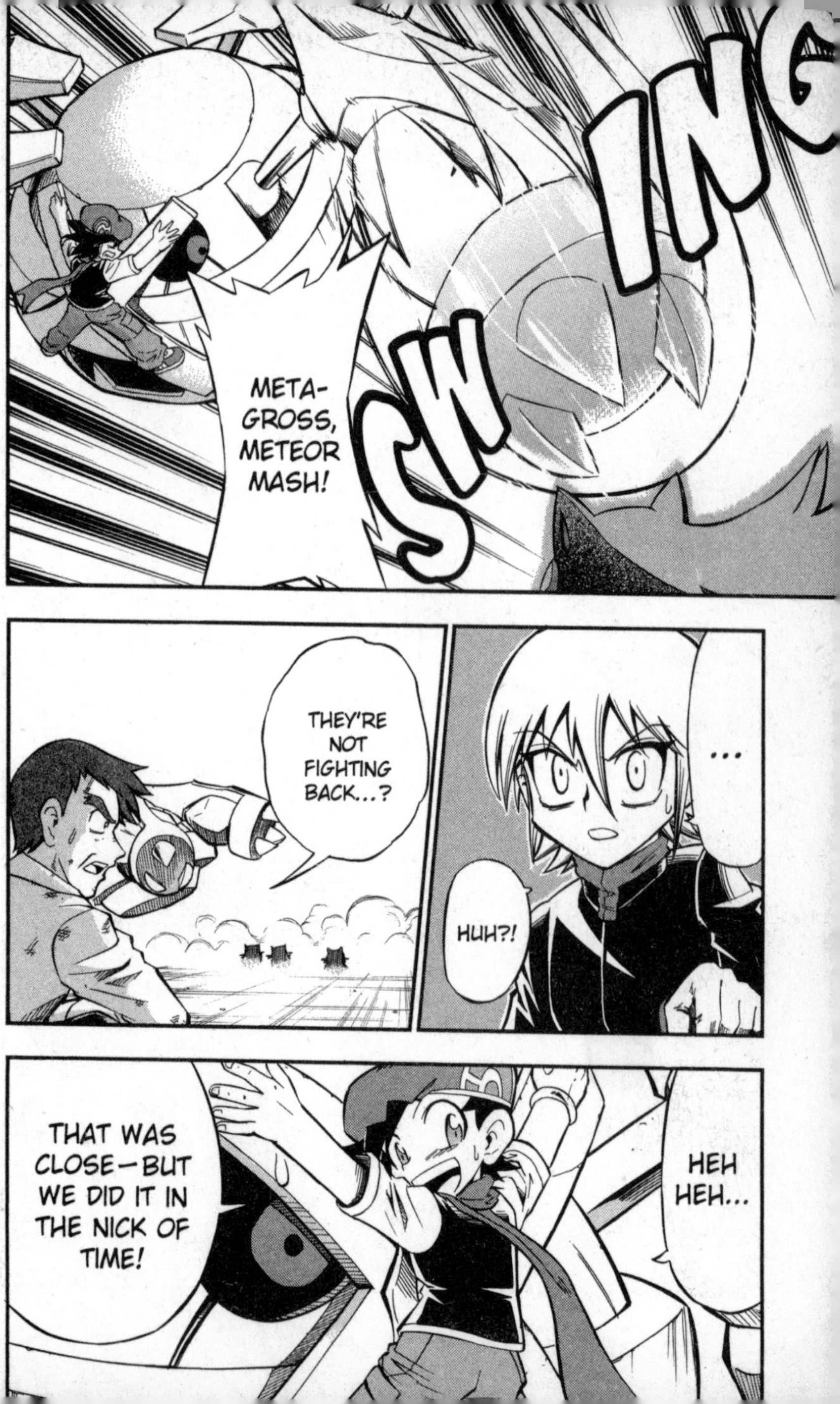
SWING
META-GROSS, METEOR MASH!
...
HUH?!
THEY'RE NOT FIGHTING BACK...?
HEH HEH...
THAT WAS CLOSE—BUT WE DID IT IN THE NICK OF TIME!

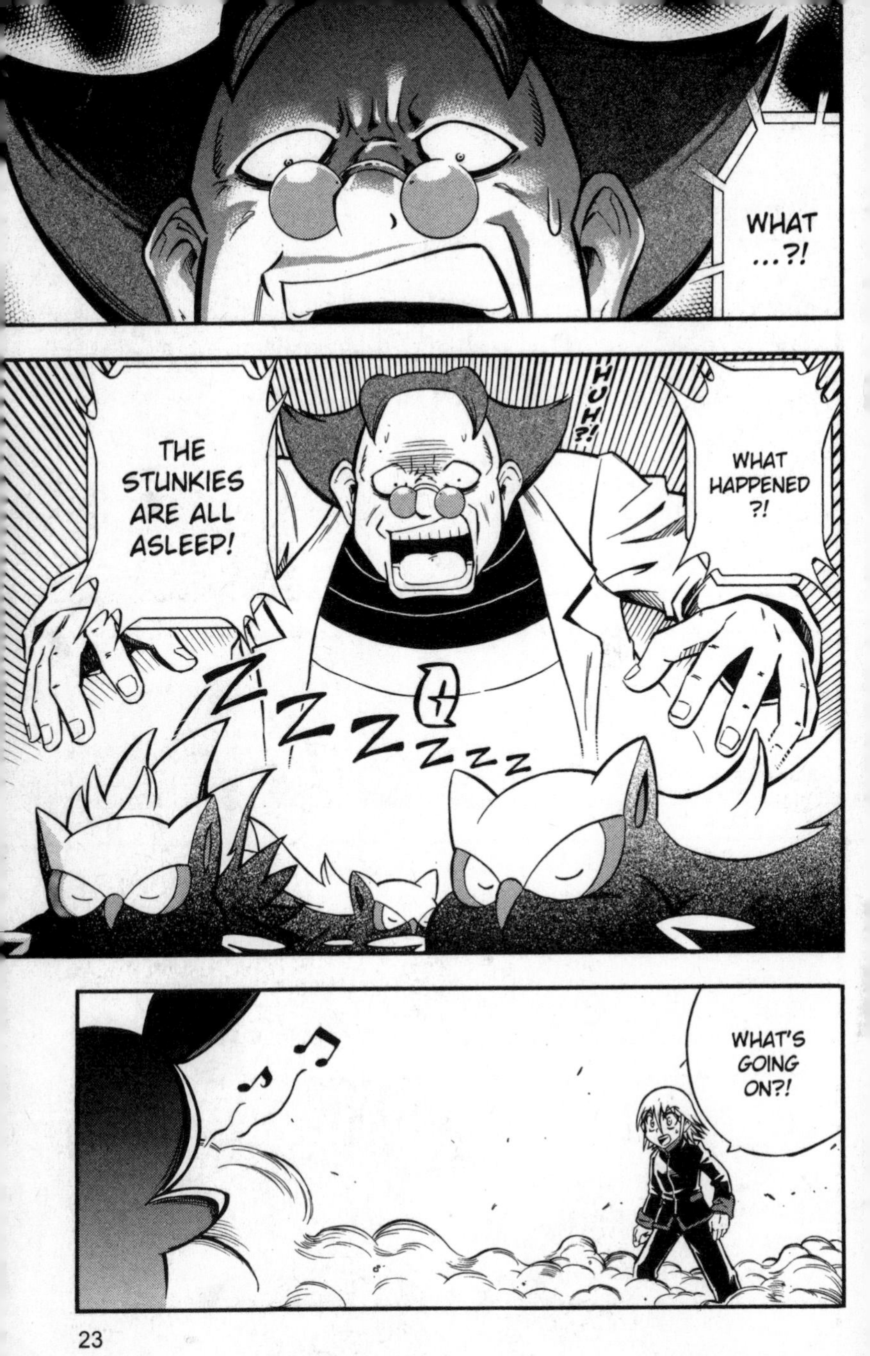
WHAT ...?!
WHAT HAPPENED ?!
HUH?!
THE STUNKIES ARE ALL ASLEEP!
ZZZZzzz
WHAT'S GOING ON?!

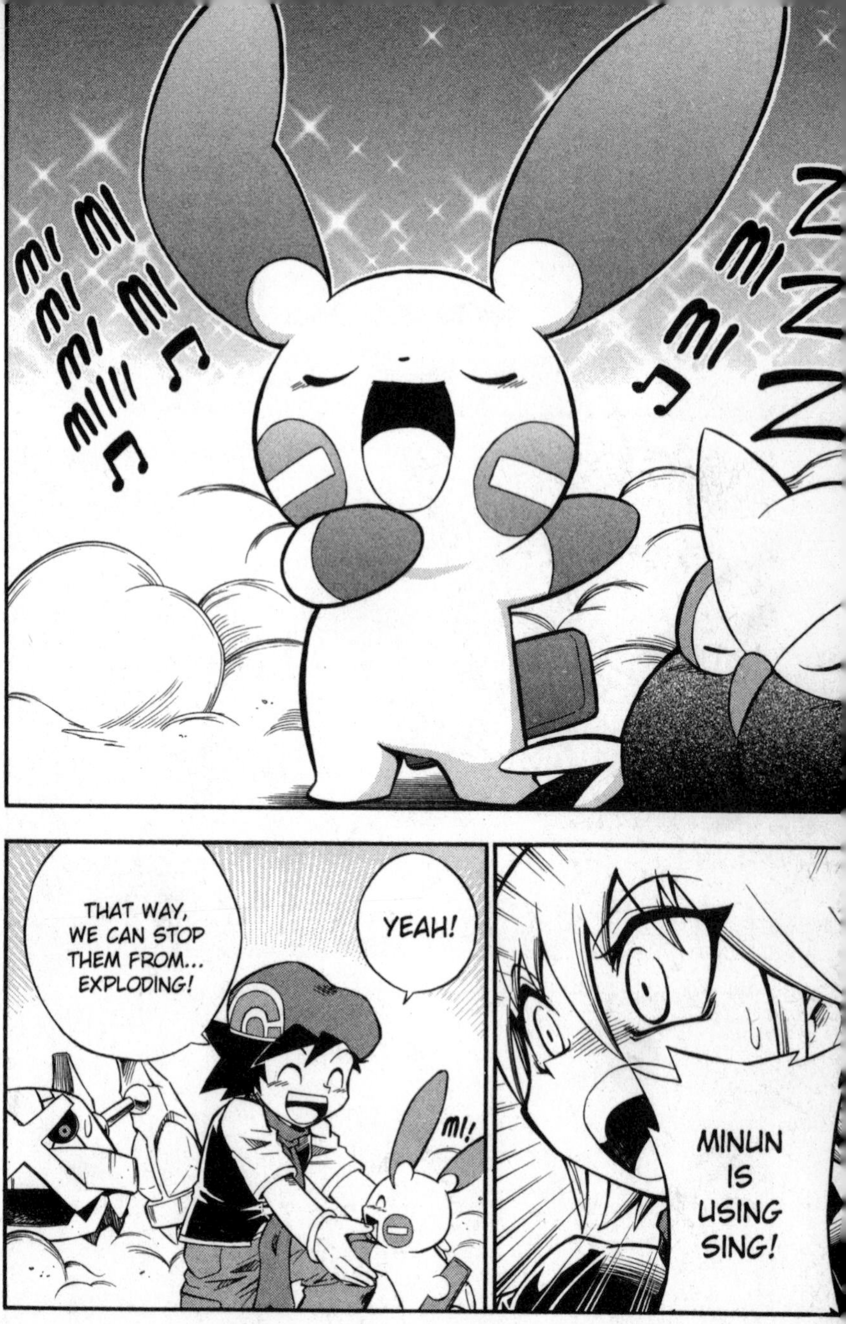
MI MI MI♪
MI MI MI MI MI MI MIIII♪
MINUN IS USING SING!
THAT WAY, WE CAN STOP THEM FROM... EXPLODING!
YEAH!
MI!

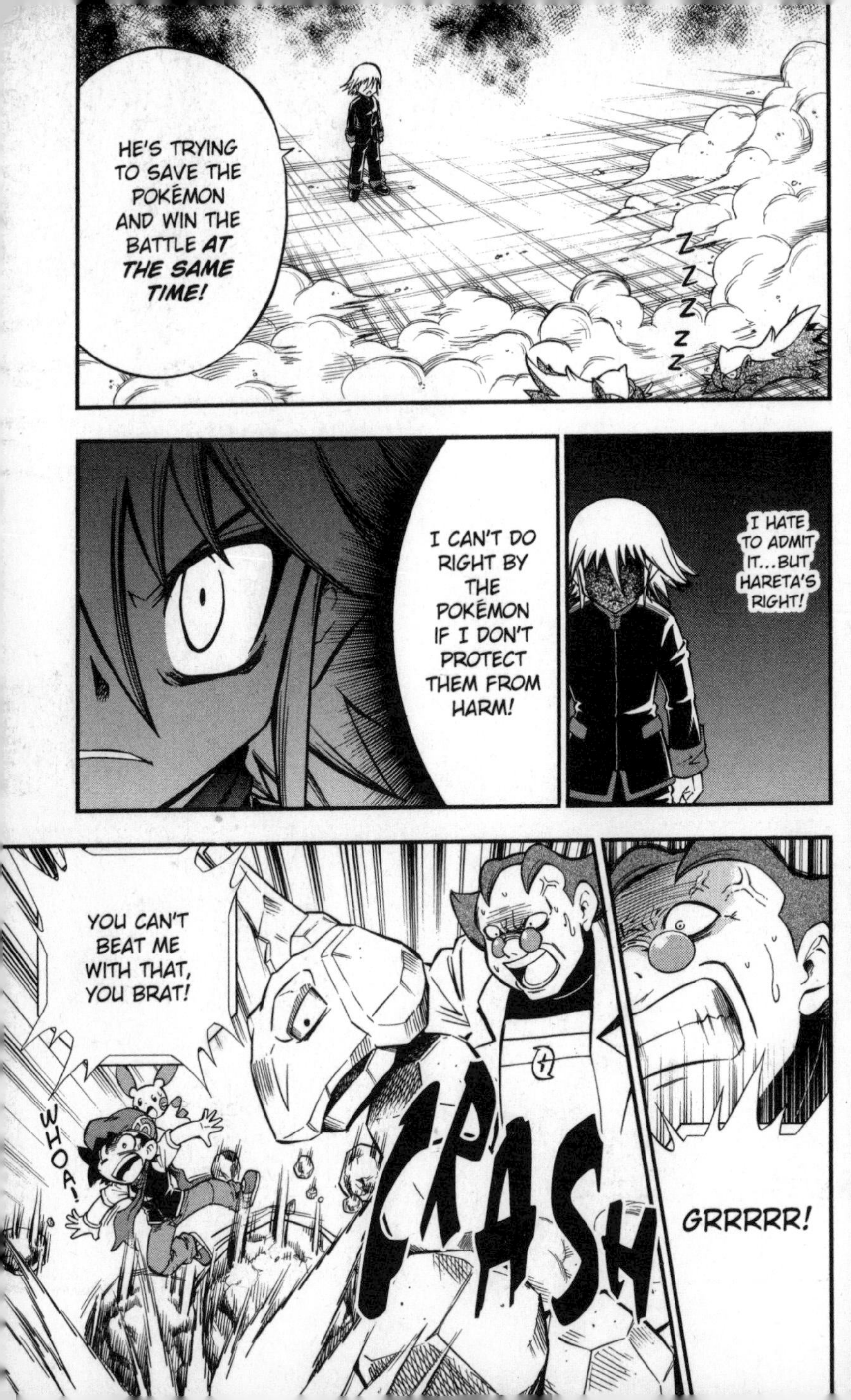
HE'S TRYING TO SAVE THE POKÉMON AND WIN THE BATTLE AT THE SAME TIME!
ZZZZZ
I HATE TO ADMIT IT...BUT HARETA'S RIGHT!
I CAN'T DO RIGHT BY THE POKÉMON IF I DON'T PROTECT THEM FROM HARM!
GRRRRR!
YOU CAN'T BEAT ME WITH THAT, YOU BRAT!
CRASH
WHOA!

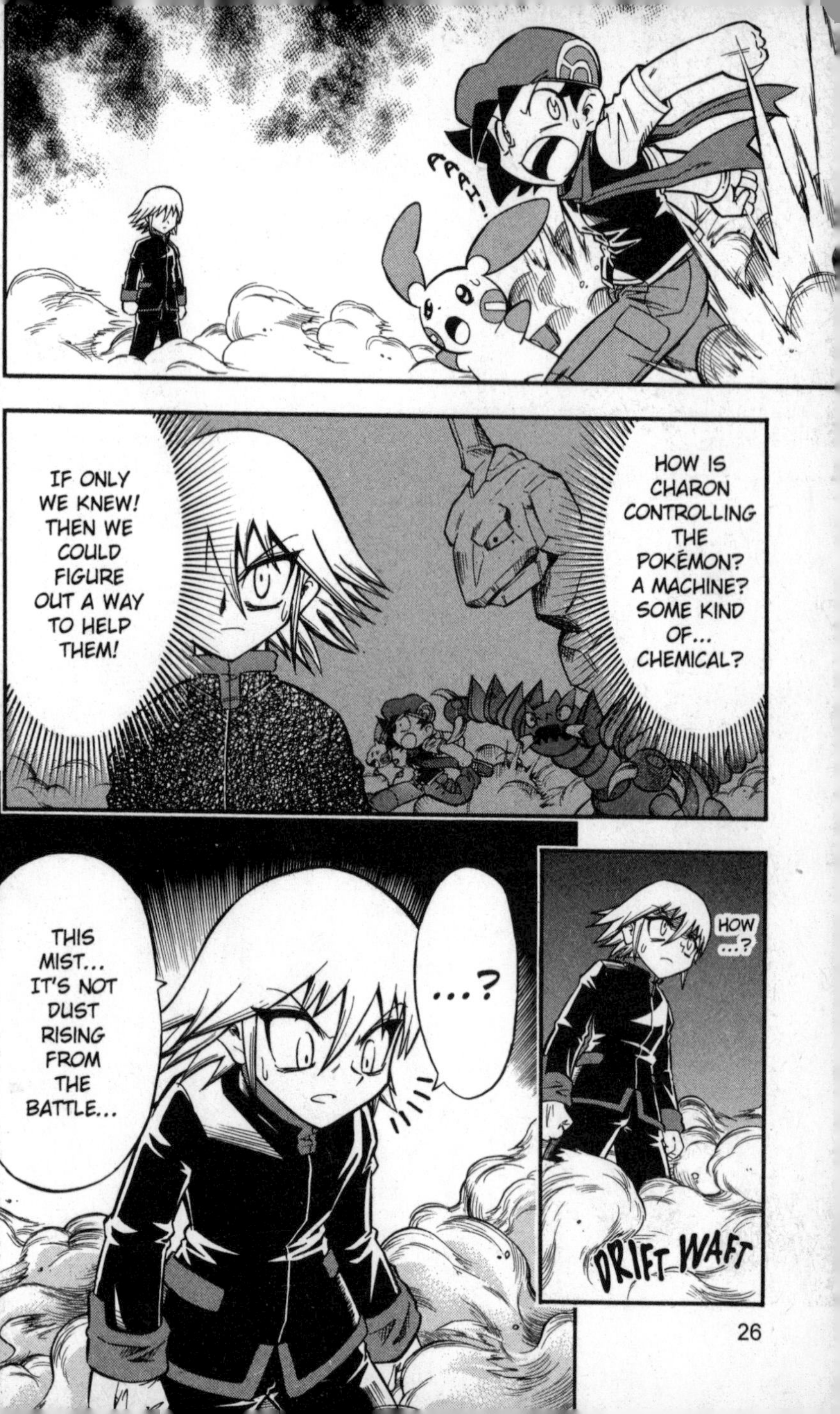
AAAH!!
HOW IS CHARON CONTROLLING THE POKÉMON? A MACHINE? SOME KIND OF... CHEMICAL?
IF ONLY WE KNEW! THEN WE COULD FIGURE OUT A WAY TO HELP THEM!
HOW ...?
DRIFT WAFT
...?
THIS MIST... IT'S NOT DUST RISING FROM THE BATTLE...

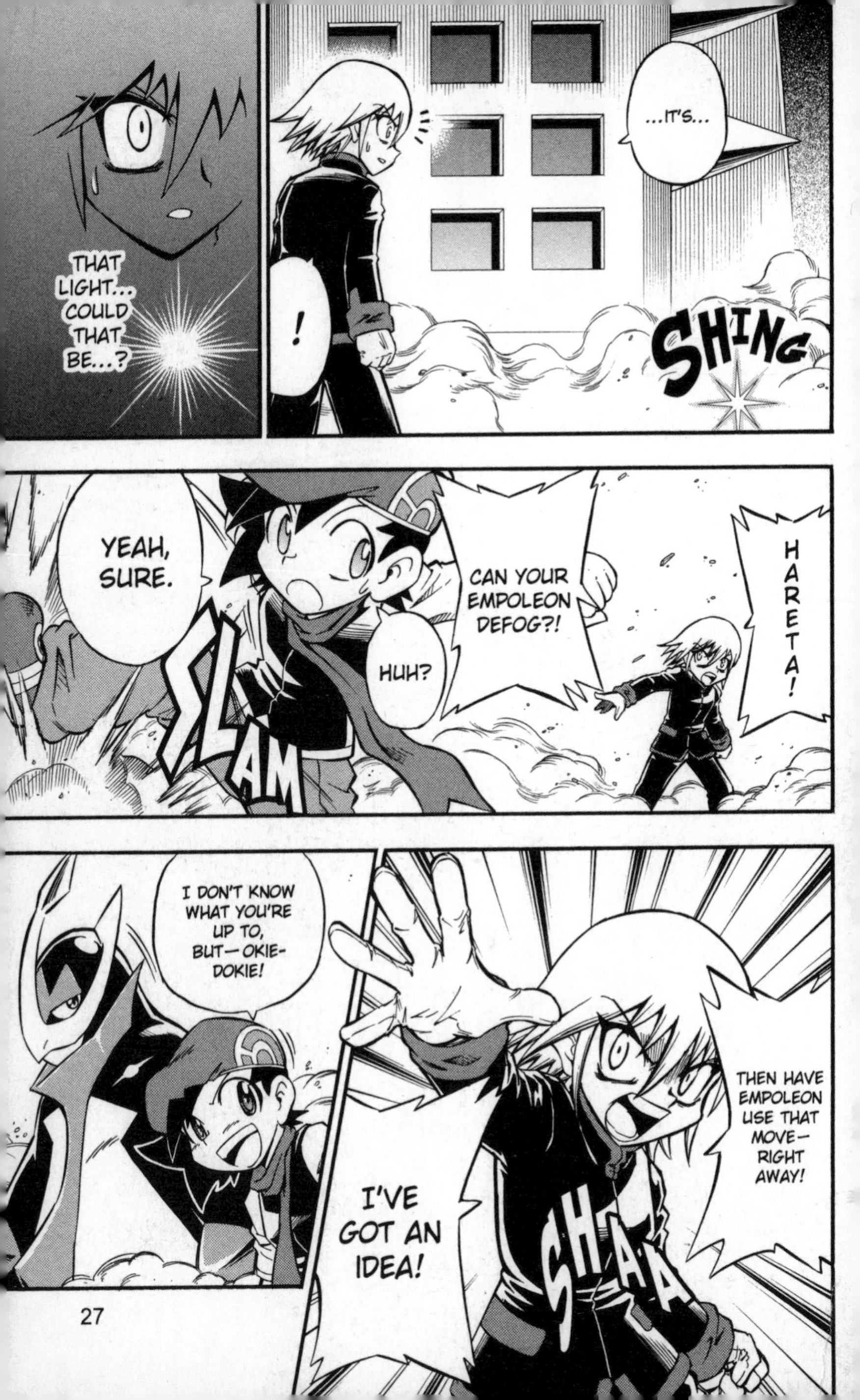
...IT'S...
!
SHING
THAT LIGHT... COULD THAT BE...?
HARETA!
CAN YOUR EMPOLEON DEFOG?!
HUH?
YEAH, SURE.
SLAM
THEN HAVE EMPOLEON USE THAT MOVE—RIGHT AWAY!
I'VE GOT AN IDEA!
SHAA
I DON'T KNOW WHAT YOU'RE UP TO, BUT—OKIE-DOKIE!

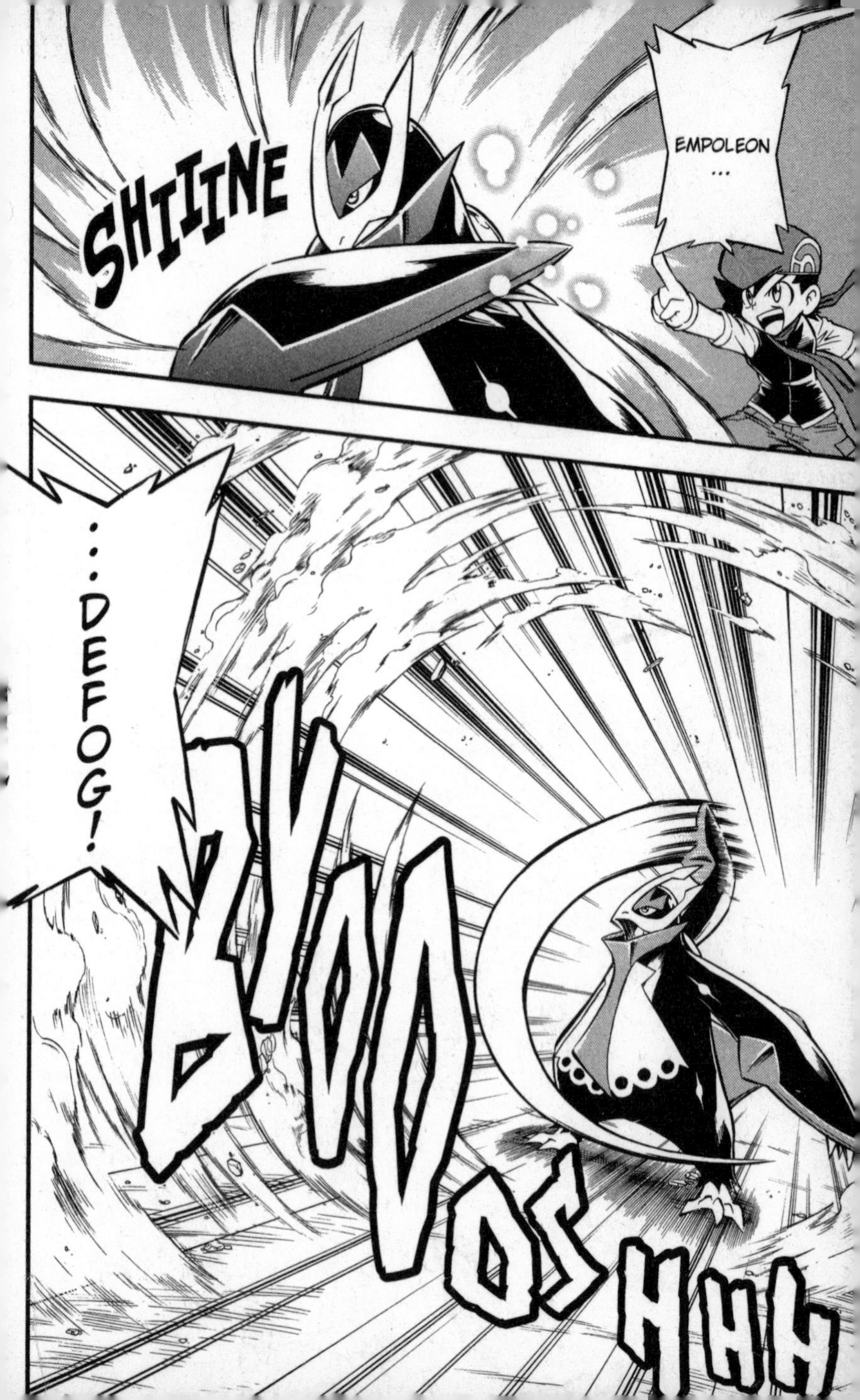
EMPOLEON
...
SHIIINE
...DEFOG!

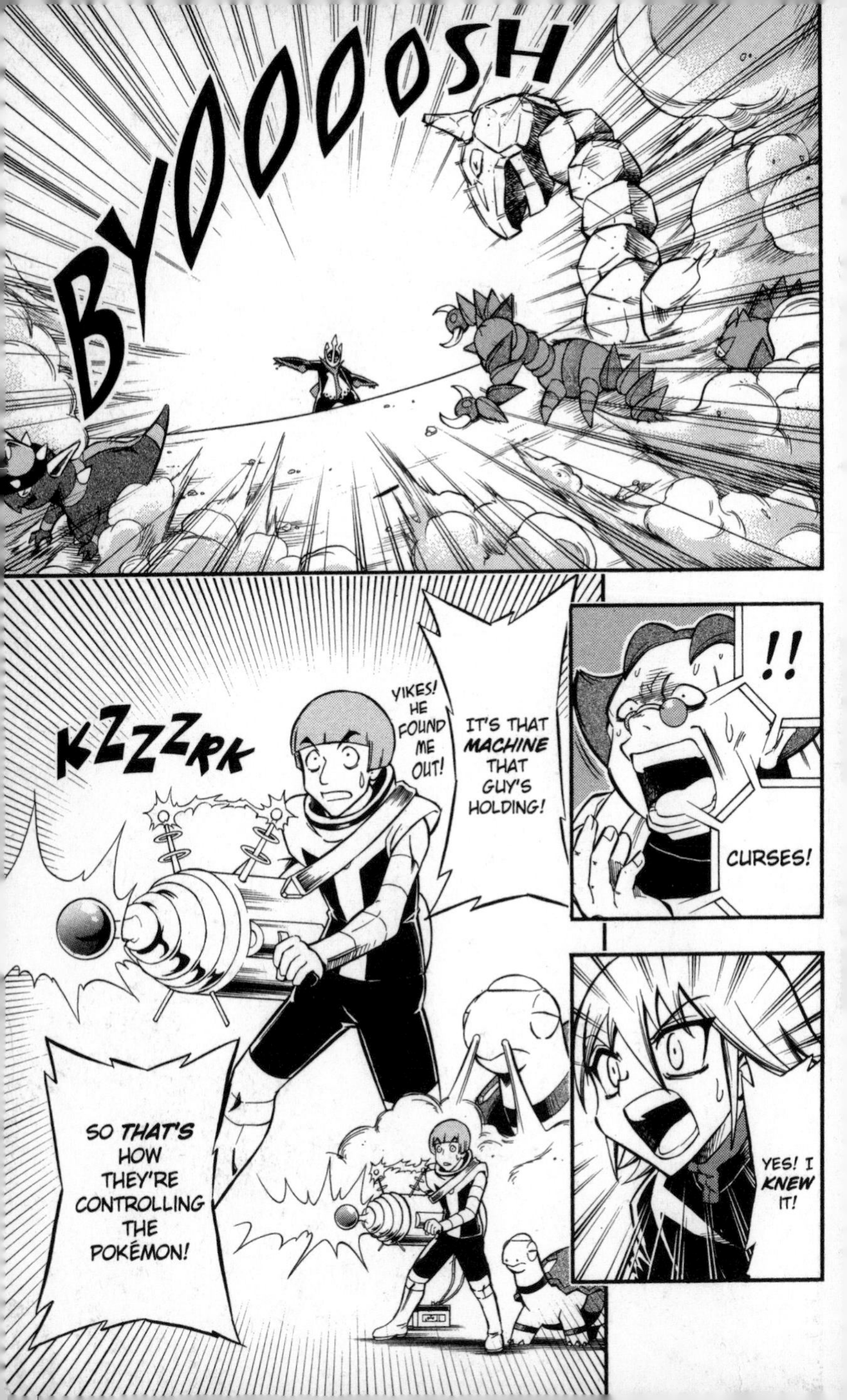
BYOOOOSH
!!
CURSES!
YES! I KNEW IT!
IT'S THAT MACHINE THAT GUY'S HOLDING!
YIKES! HE FOUND ME OUT!
KZZZRK
SO THAT'S HOW THEY'RE CONTROLLING THE POKÉMON!

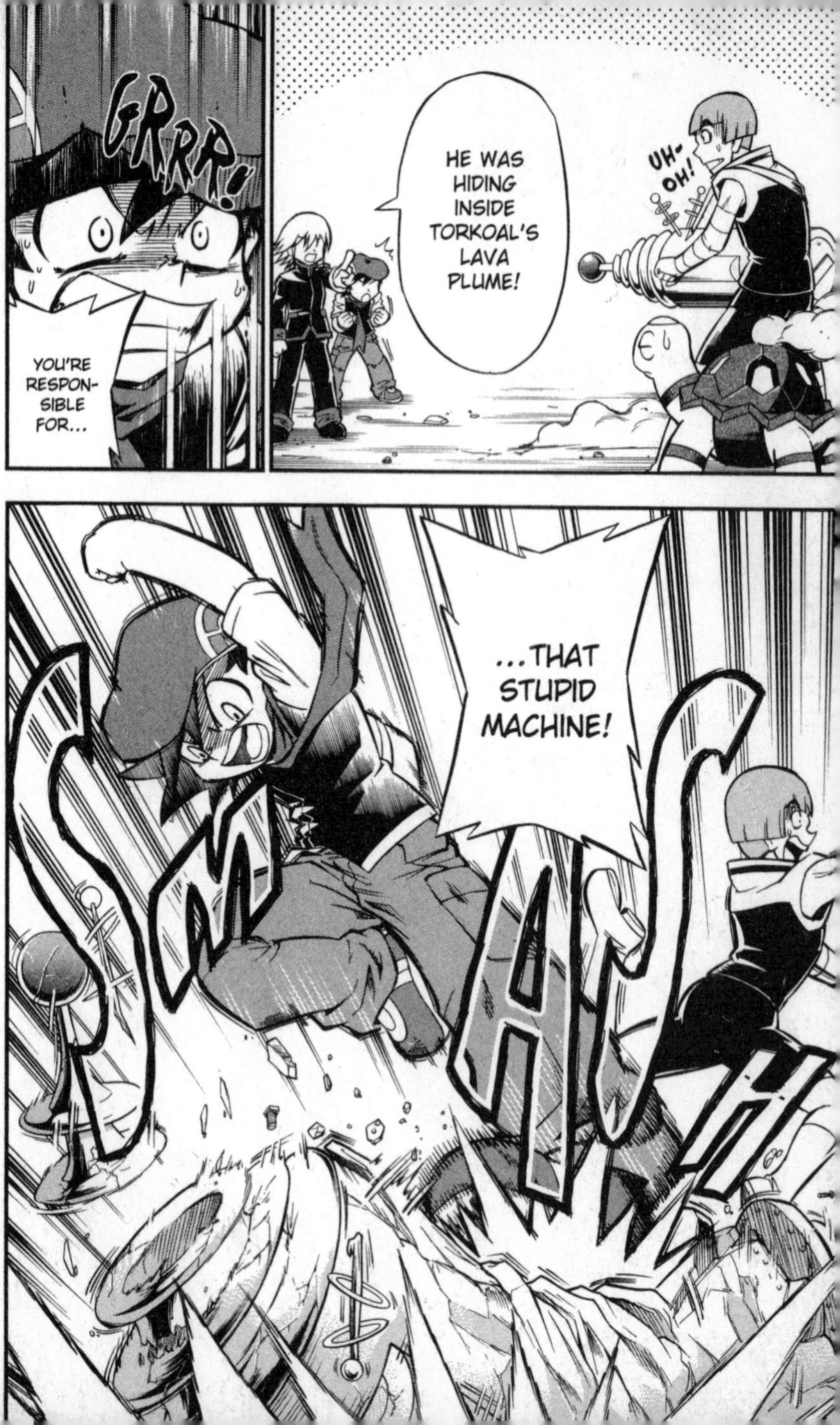
UH-OH!
HE WAS HIDING INSIDE TORKOAL'S LAVA PLUME!
GRRR!
YOU'RE RESPONSIBLE FOR...
...THAT STUPID MACHINE!
SMASH!

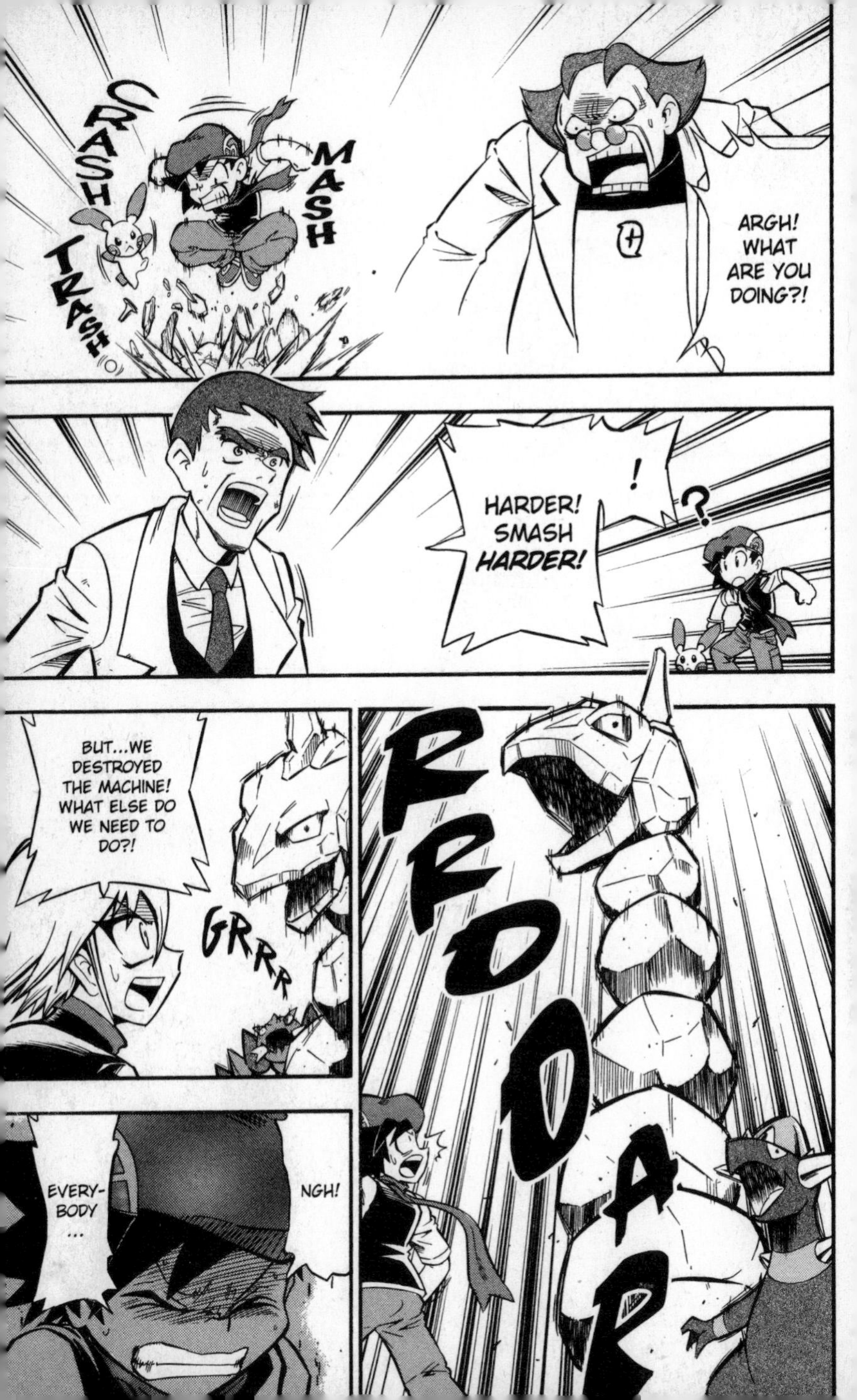
ARGH! WHAT ARE YOU DOING?!
CRASH
MASH
TRASH
!
HARDER! SMASH HARDER!
?
RRROAR
BUT...WE DESTROYED THE MACHINE! WHAT ELSE DO WE NEED TO DO?!
GRRRR
NGH!
EVERY-BODY ...

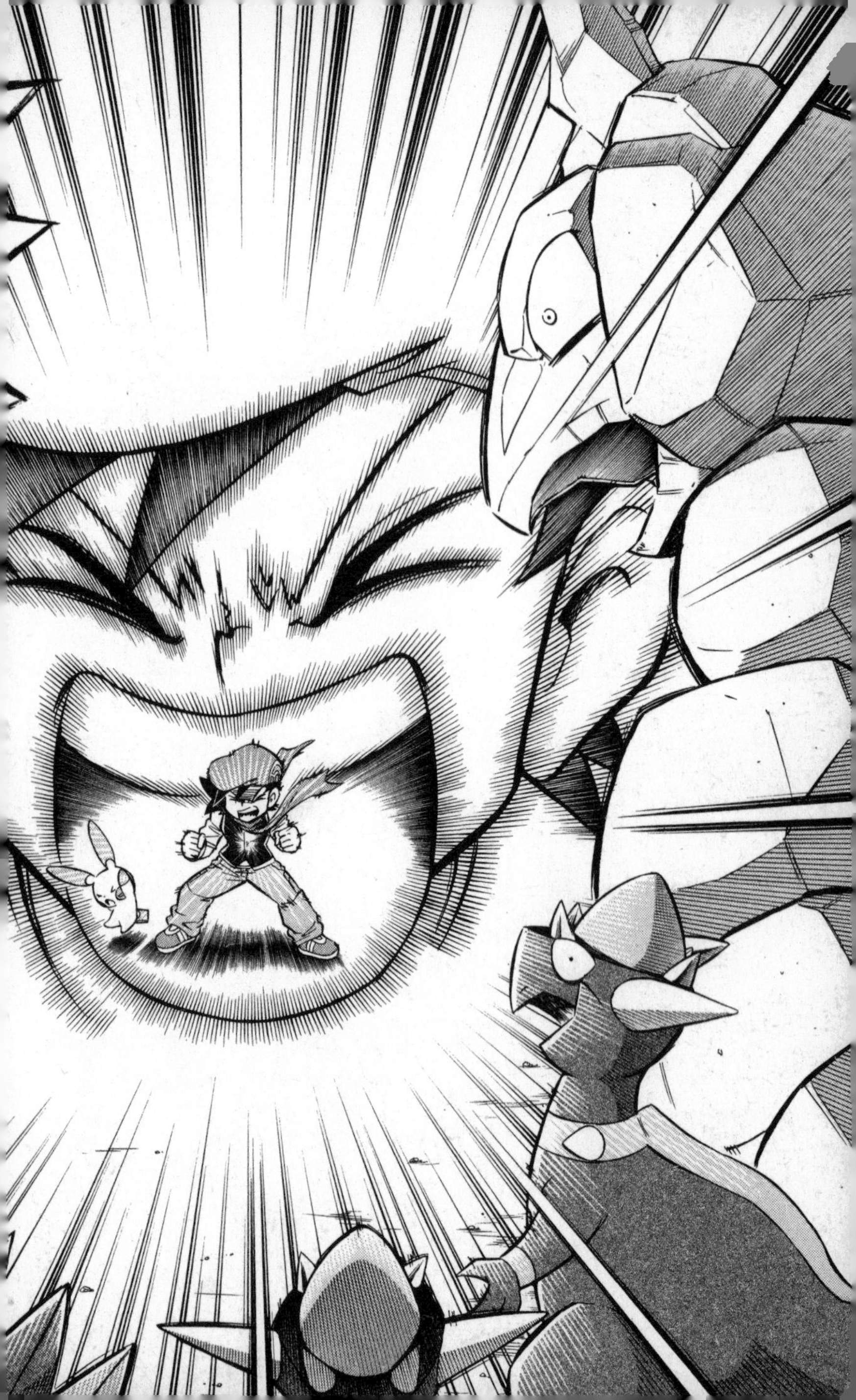

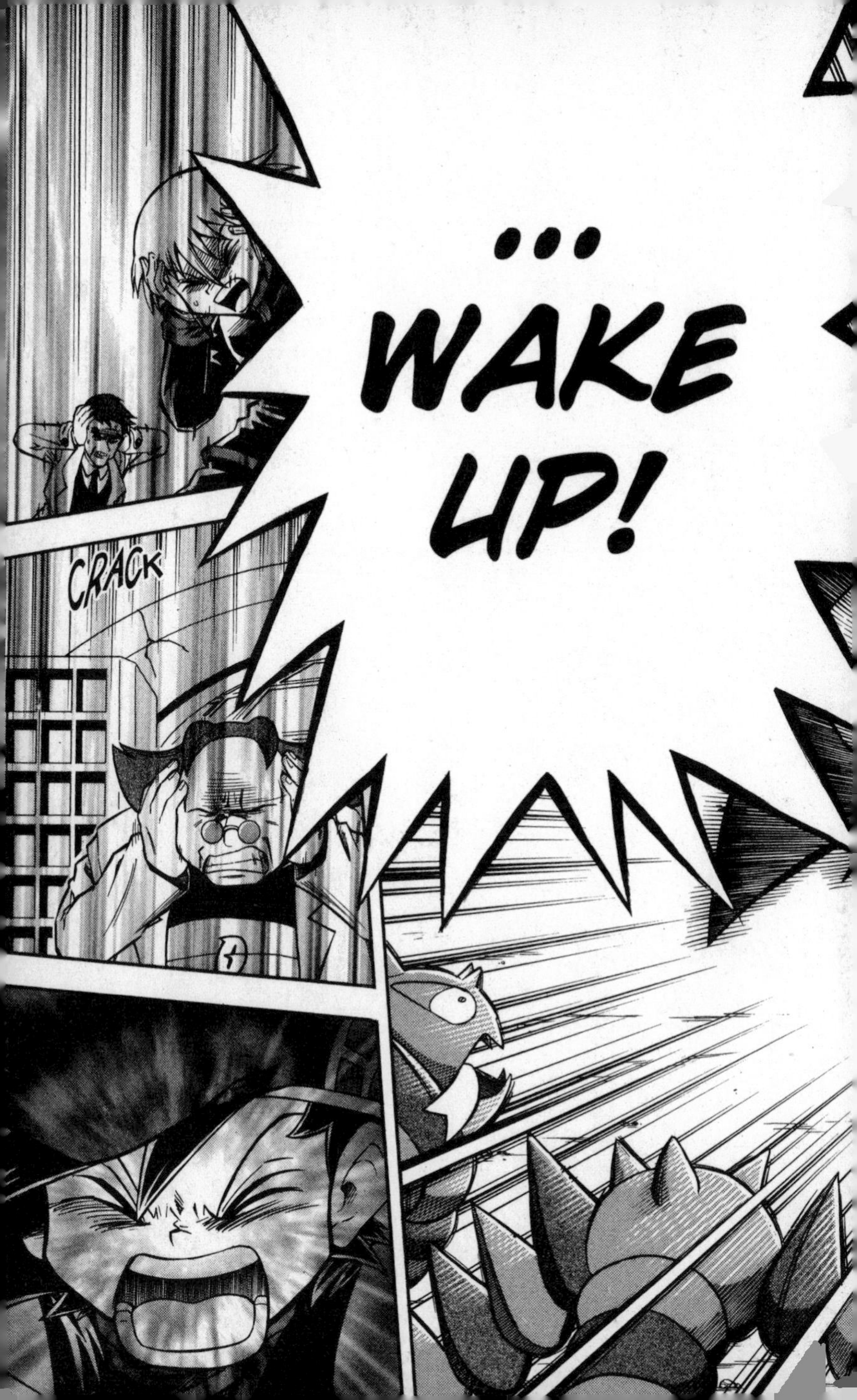
...WAKE UP!
CRACK

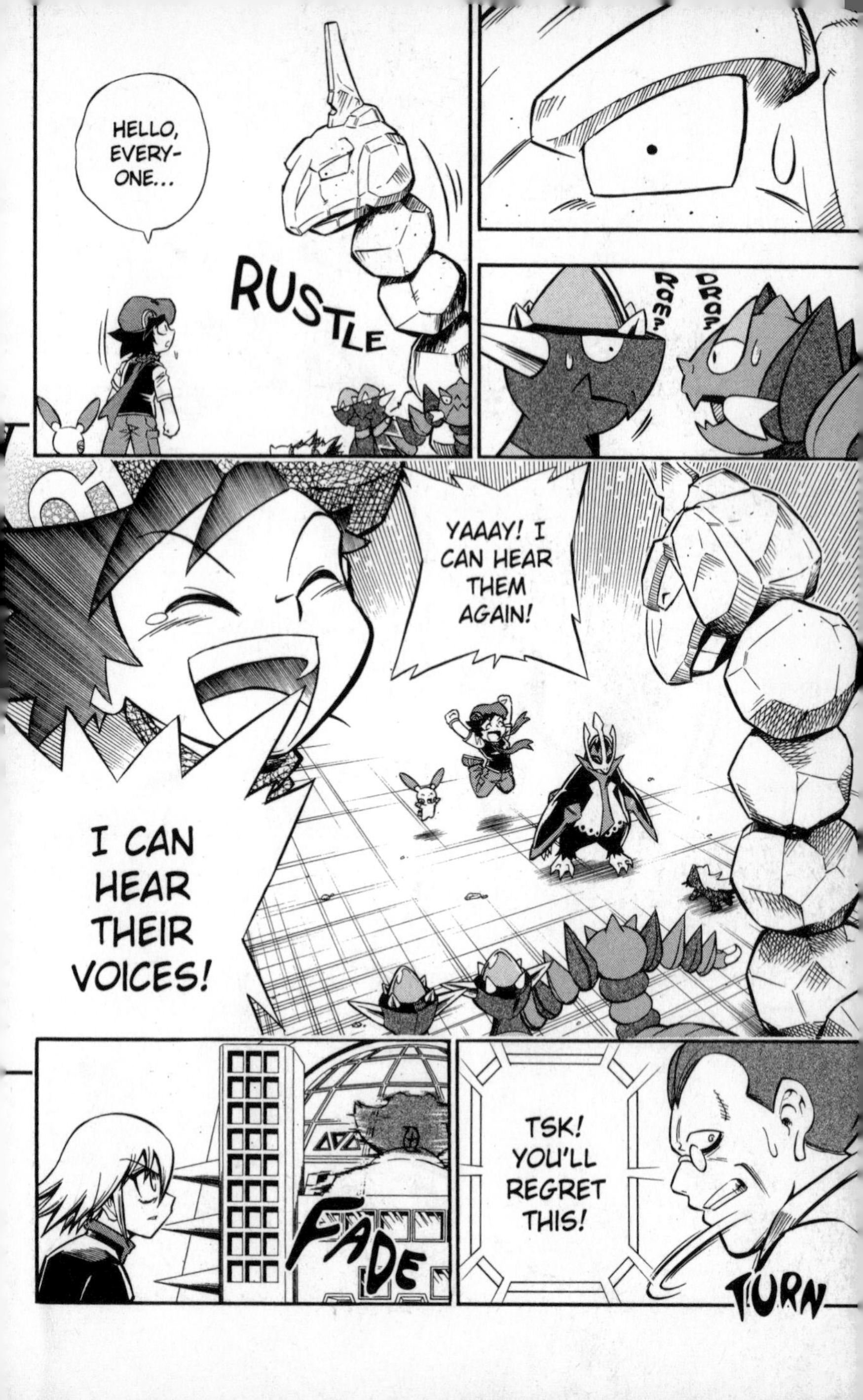
DRA?
RAM?
HELLO, EVERY-ONE...
RUSTLE
YAAAY! I CAN HEAR THEM AGAIN!
I CAN HEAR THEIR VOICES!
TSK! YOU'LL REGRET THIS!
TURN
FADE

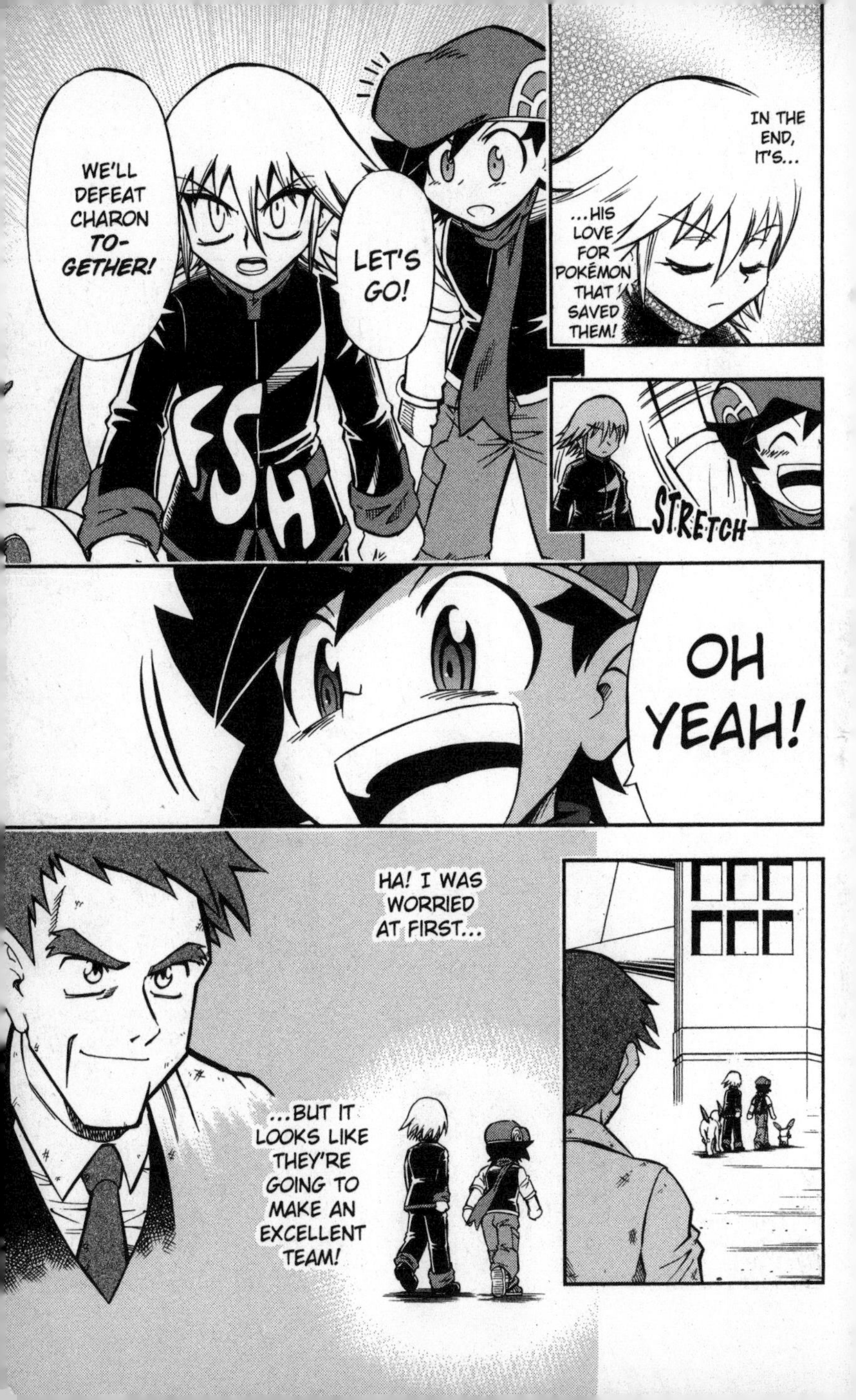
IN THE END, IT'S...
...HIS LOVE FOR POKÉMON THAT SAVED THEM!
STRETCH
LET'S GO!
WE'LL DEFEAT CHARON TO-GETHER!
OH YEAH!
HA! I WAS WORRIED AT FIRST...
...BUT IT LOOKS LIKE THEY'RE GOING TO MAKE AN EXCELLENT TEAM!

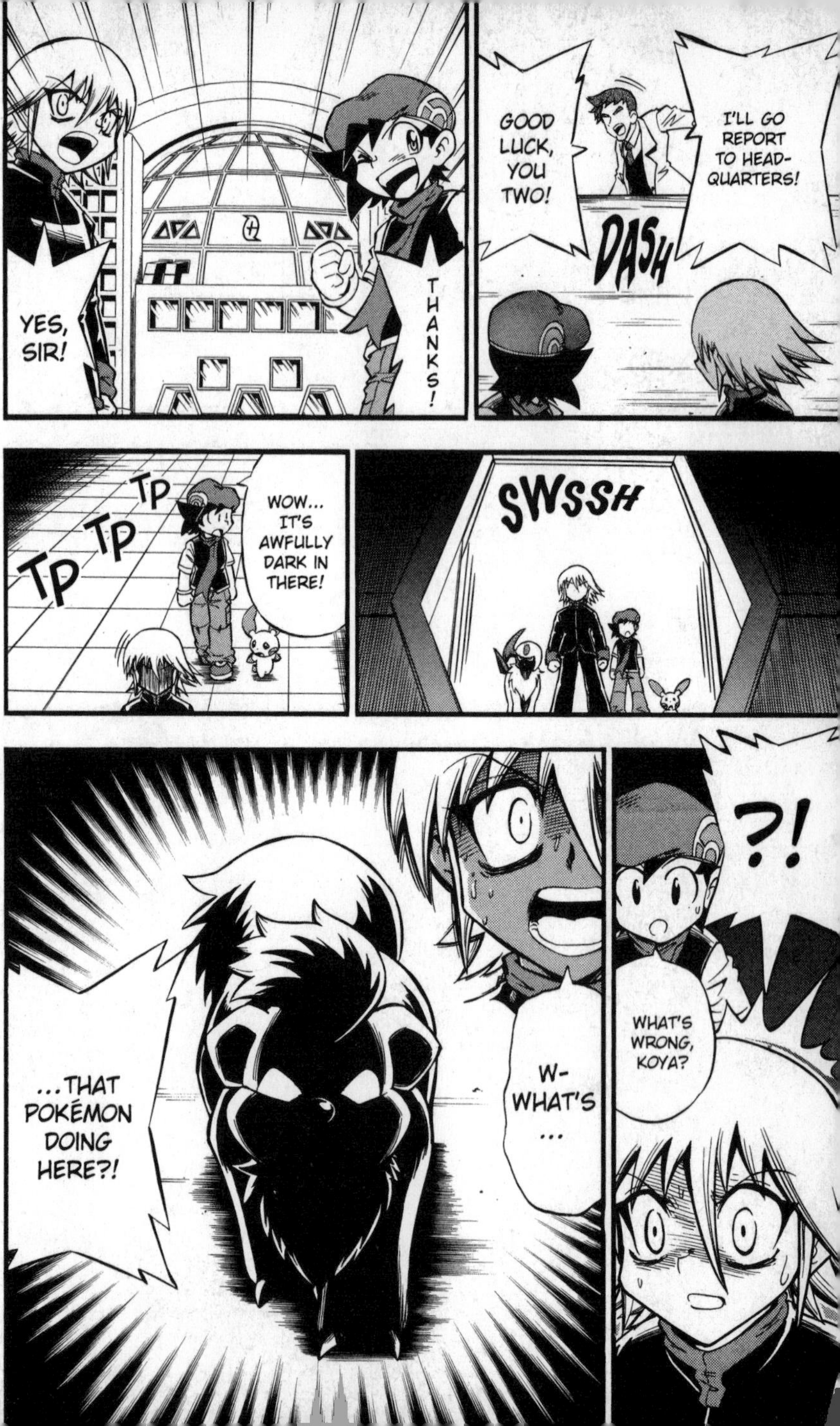
I'LL GO REPORT TO HEAD-QUARTERS!
GOOD LUCK, YOU TWO!
DASH
THANKS!
YES, SIR!
SWSSH
WOW... IT'S AWFULLY DARK IN THERE!
TP TP TP
?!
WHAT'S WRONG, KOYA?
W- WHAT'S ...
...THAT POKÉMON DOING HERE?!

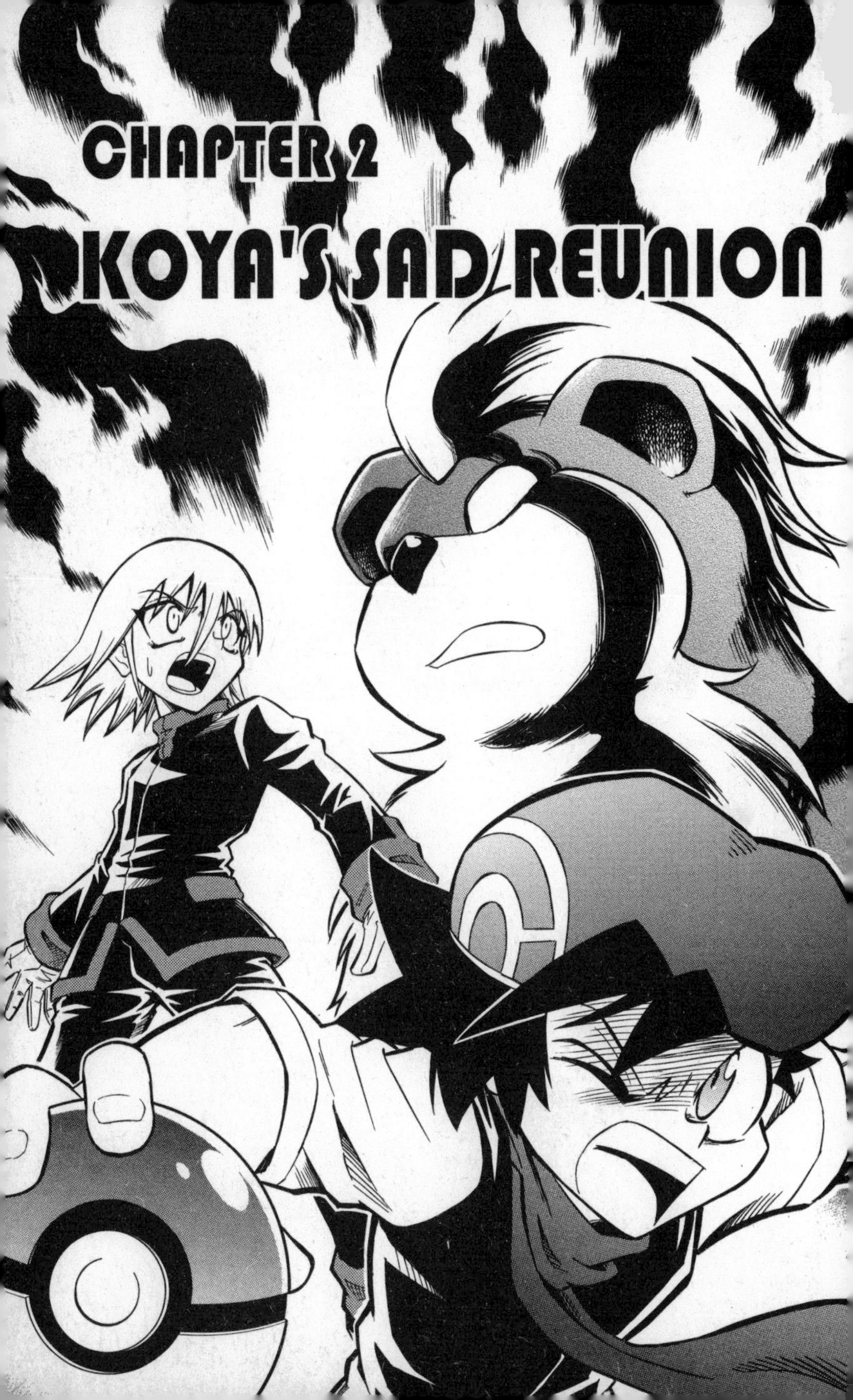
CHAPTER 2
KOYA'S SAD REUNION

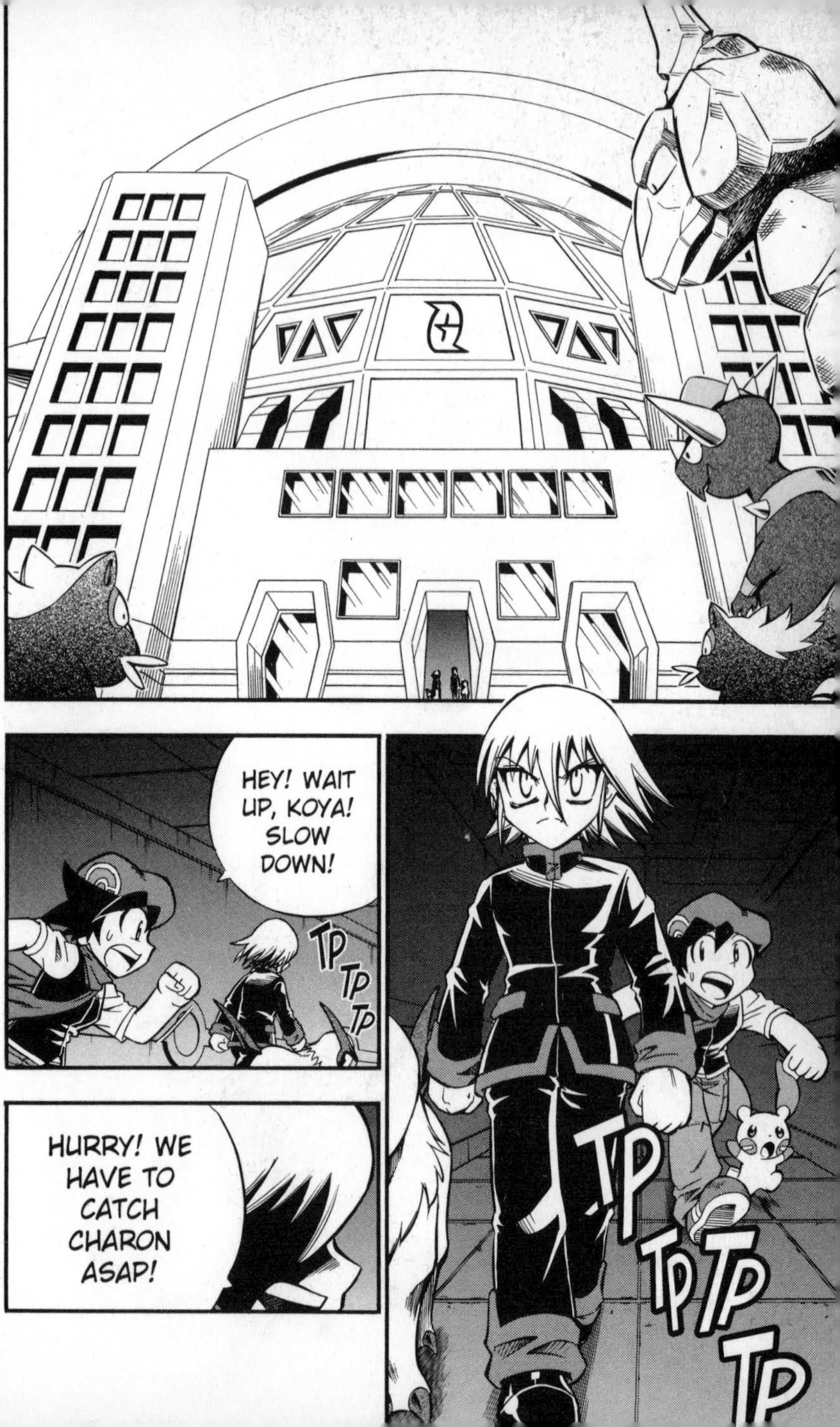
TP TP TP TP TP
HEY! WAIT UP, KOYA! SLOW DOWN!
TP TP TP
HURRY! WE HAVE TO CATCH CHARON ASAP!

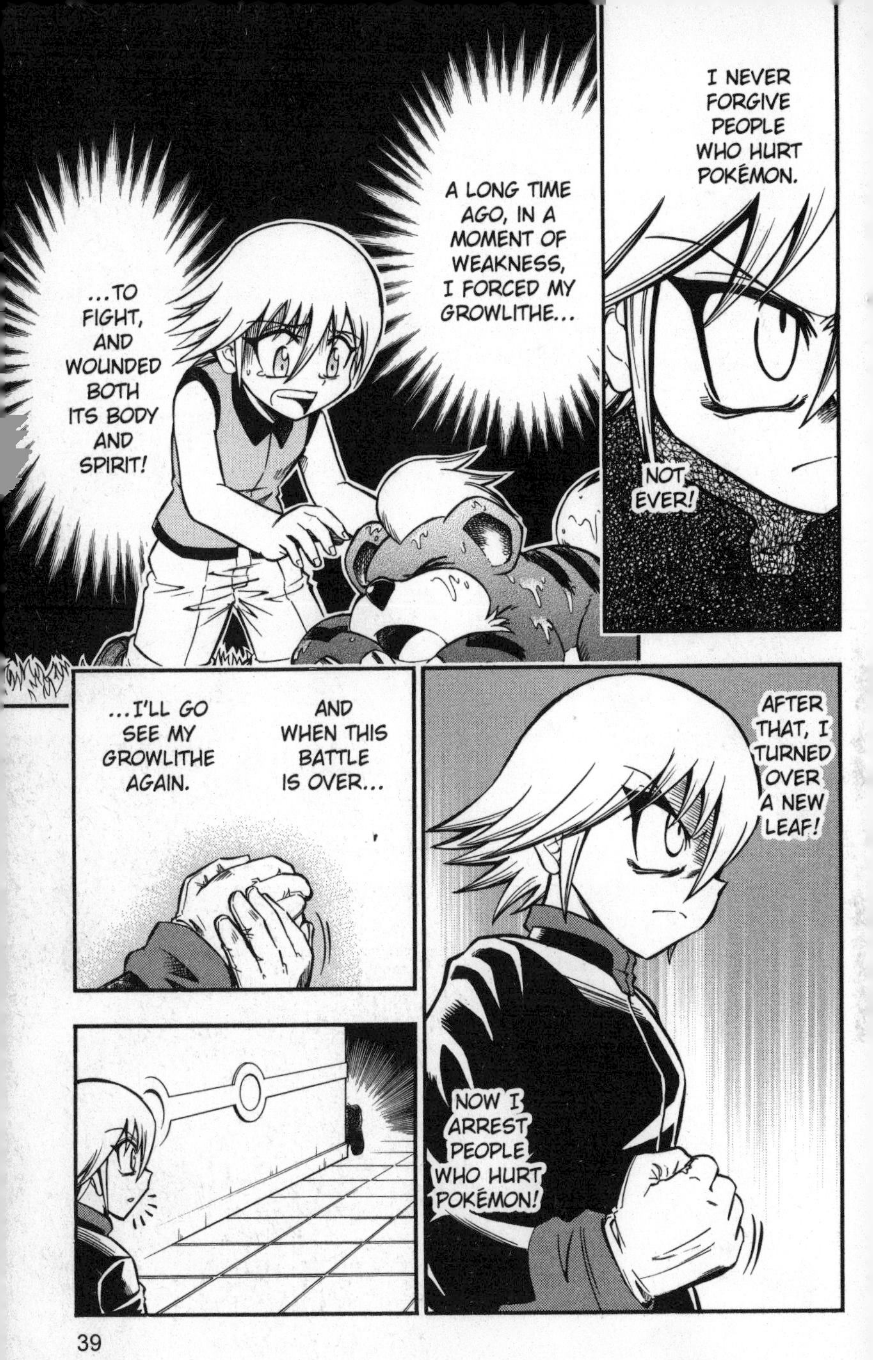
I NEVER FORGIVE PEOPLE WHO HURT POKÉMON.
NOT EVER!
A LONG TIME AGO, IN A MOMENT OF WEAKNESS, I FORCED MY GROWLITHE...
...TO FIGHT, AND WOUNDED BOTH ITS BODY AND SPIRIT!
AFTER THAT, I TURNED OVER A NEW LEAF!
NOW I ARREST PEOPLE WHO HURT POKÉMON!
AND WHEN THIS BATTLE IS OVER...
...I'LL GO SEE MY GROWLITHE AGAIN.

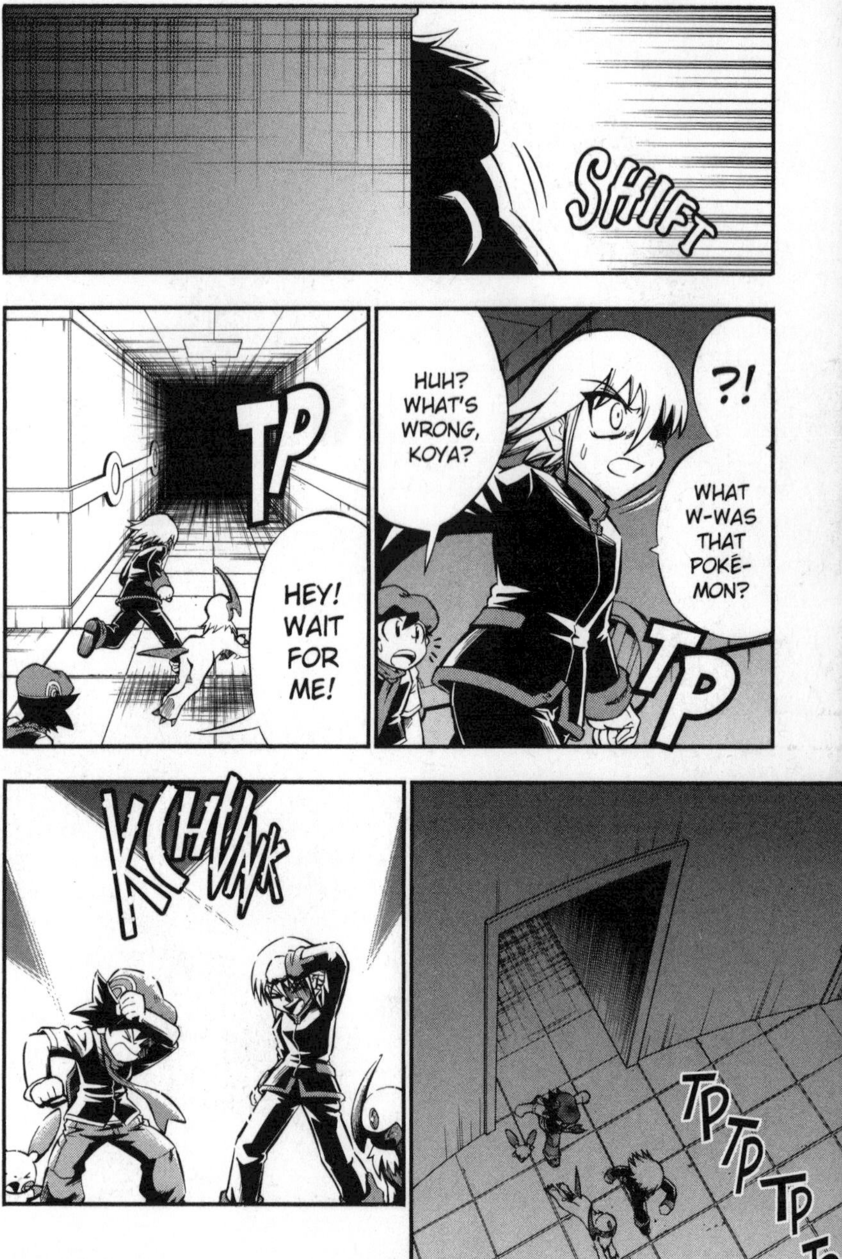
SHIFT
?!
WHAT W-WAS THAT POKÉMON?
HUH? WHAT'S WRONG, KOYA?
TP
TP
HEY! WAIT FOR ME!
TPTPTPTPTP
KCHUNK

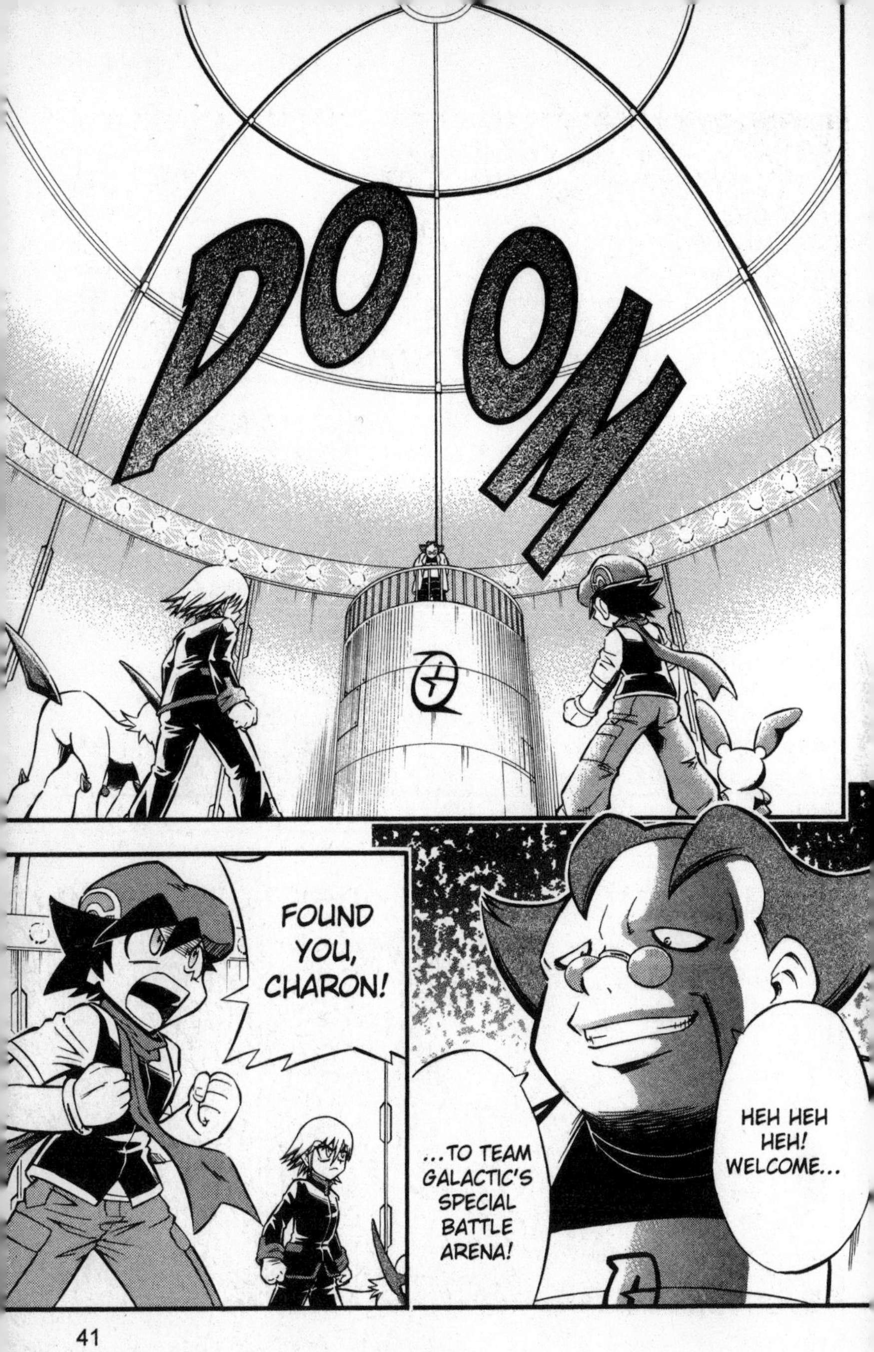
DOOM
HEH HEH HEH! WELCOME...
...TO TEAM GALACTIC'S SPECIAL BATTLE ARENA!
FOUND YOU, CHARON!

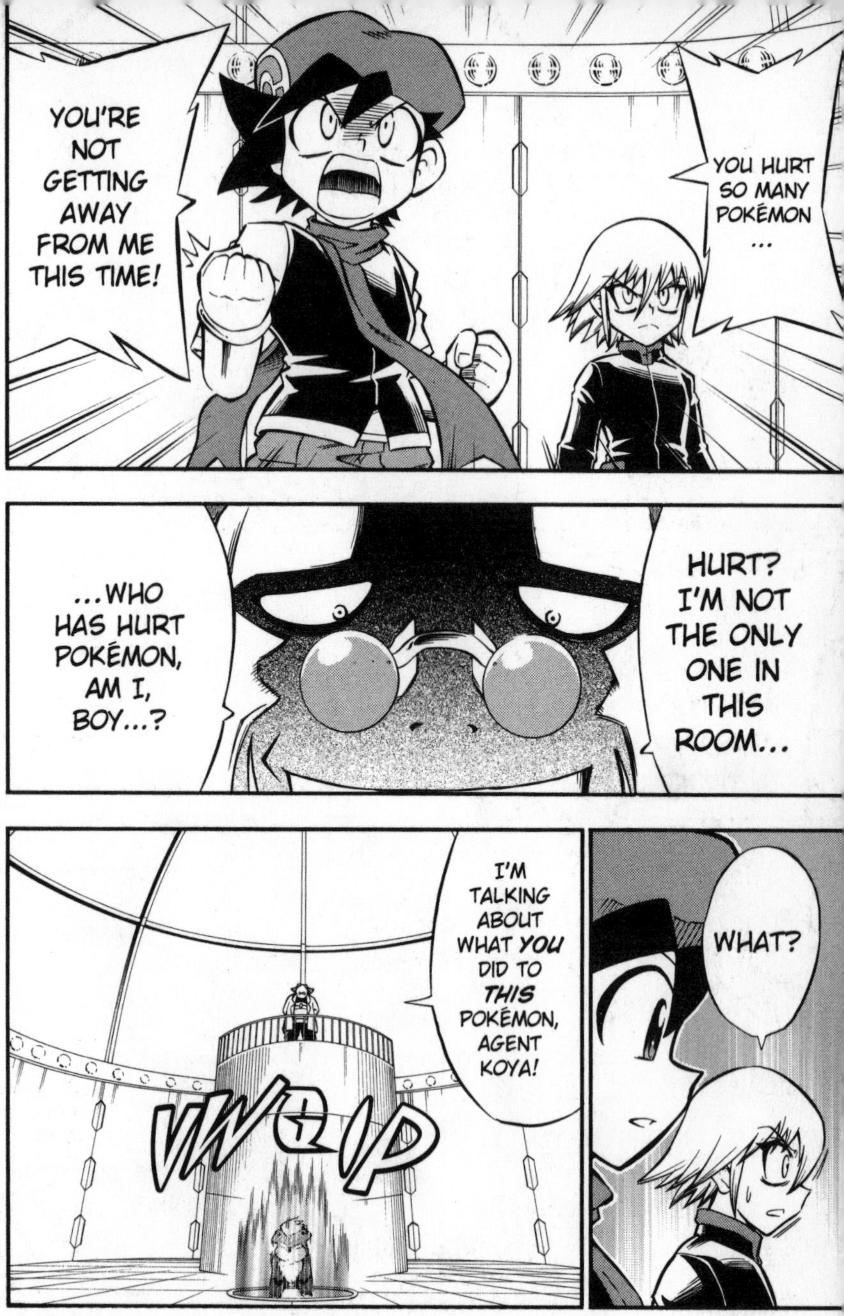
YOU HURT SO MANY POKÉMON ...
YOU'RE NOT GETTING AWAY FROM ME THIS TIME!
HURT? I'M NOT THE ONLY ONE IN THIS ROOM...
...WHO HAS HURT POKÉMON, AM I, BOY...?
WHAT?
I'M TALKING ABOUT WHAT *YOU* DID TO *THIS* POKÉMON, AGENT KOYA!
VWOIP

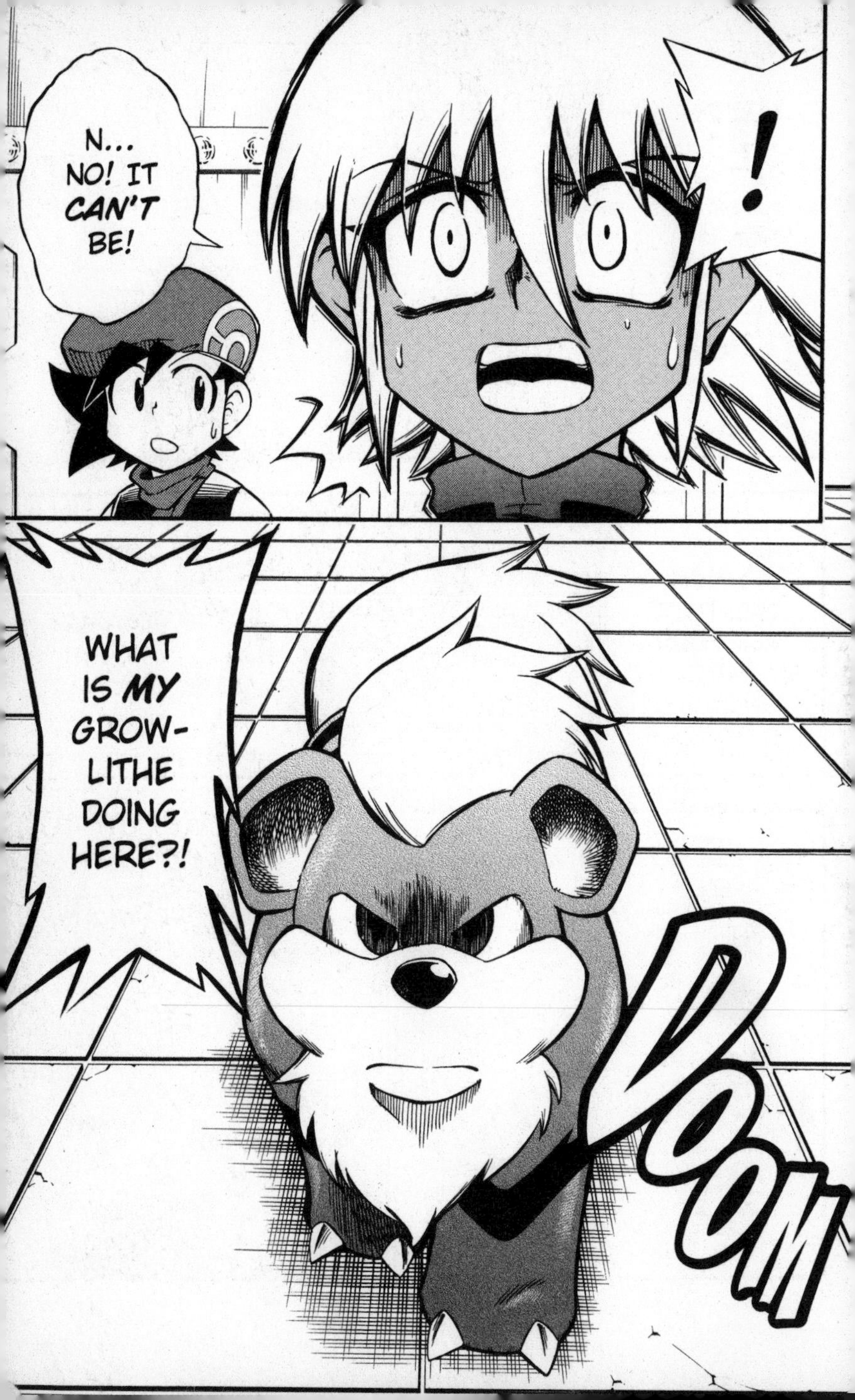
!
N... NO! IT *CAN'T* BE!
WHAT IS *MY* GROWLITHE DOING HERE?!
VOOM

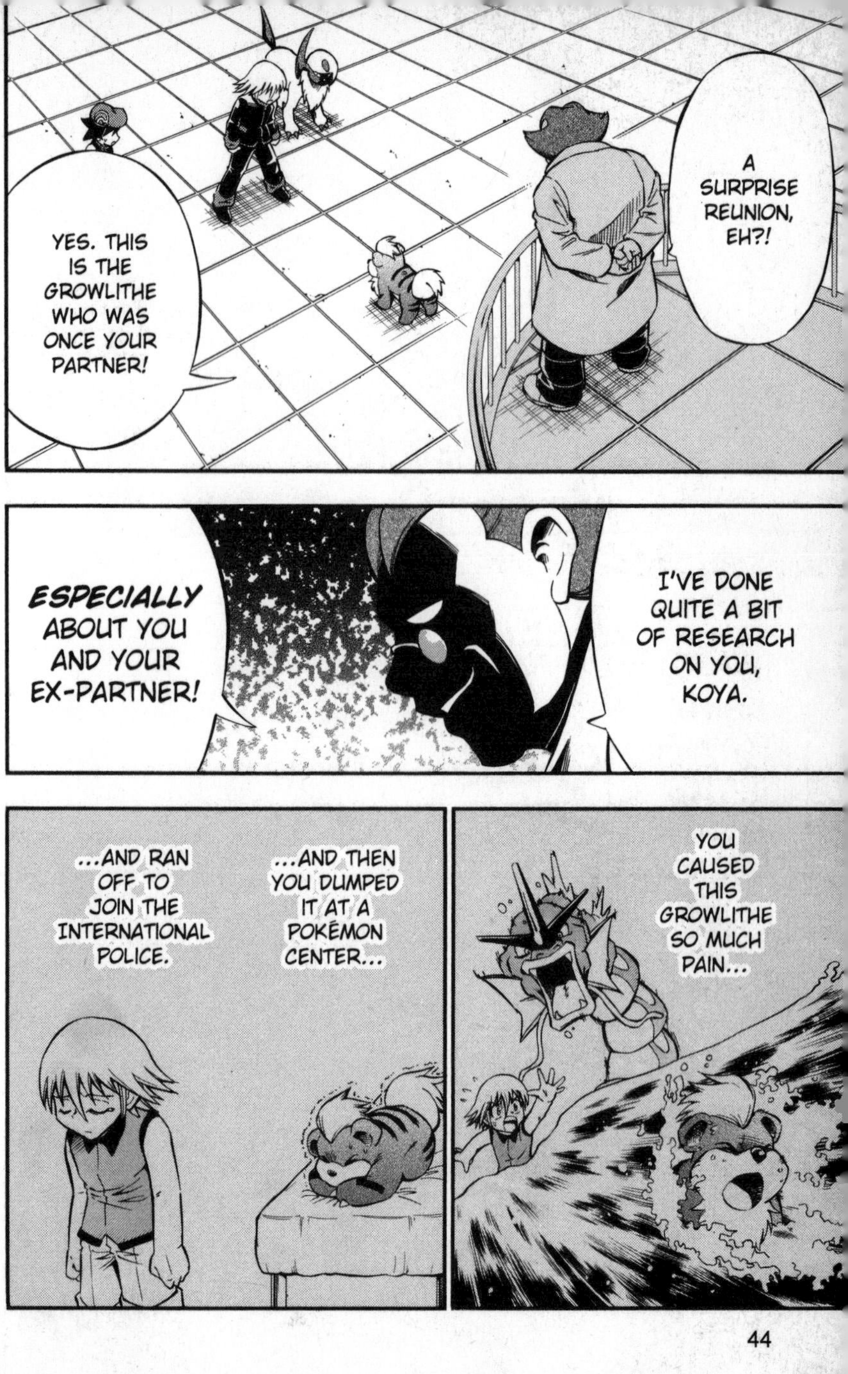
A SURPRISE REUNION, EH?!
YES. THIS IS THE GROWLITHE WHO WAS ONCE YOUR PARTNER!
I'VE DONE QUITE A BIT OF RESEARCH ON YOU, KOYA.
ESPECIALLY ABOUT YOU AND YOUR EX-PARTNER!
YOU CAUSED THIS GROWLITHE SO MUCH PAIN...
...AND THEN YOU DUMPED IT AT A POKÉMON CENTER...
...AND RAN OFF TO JOIN THE INTERNATIONAL POLICE.

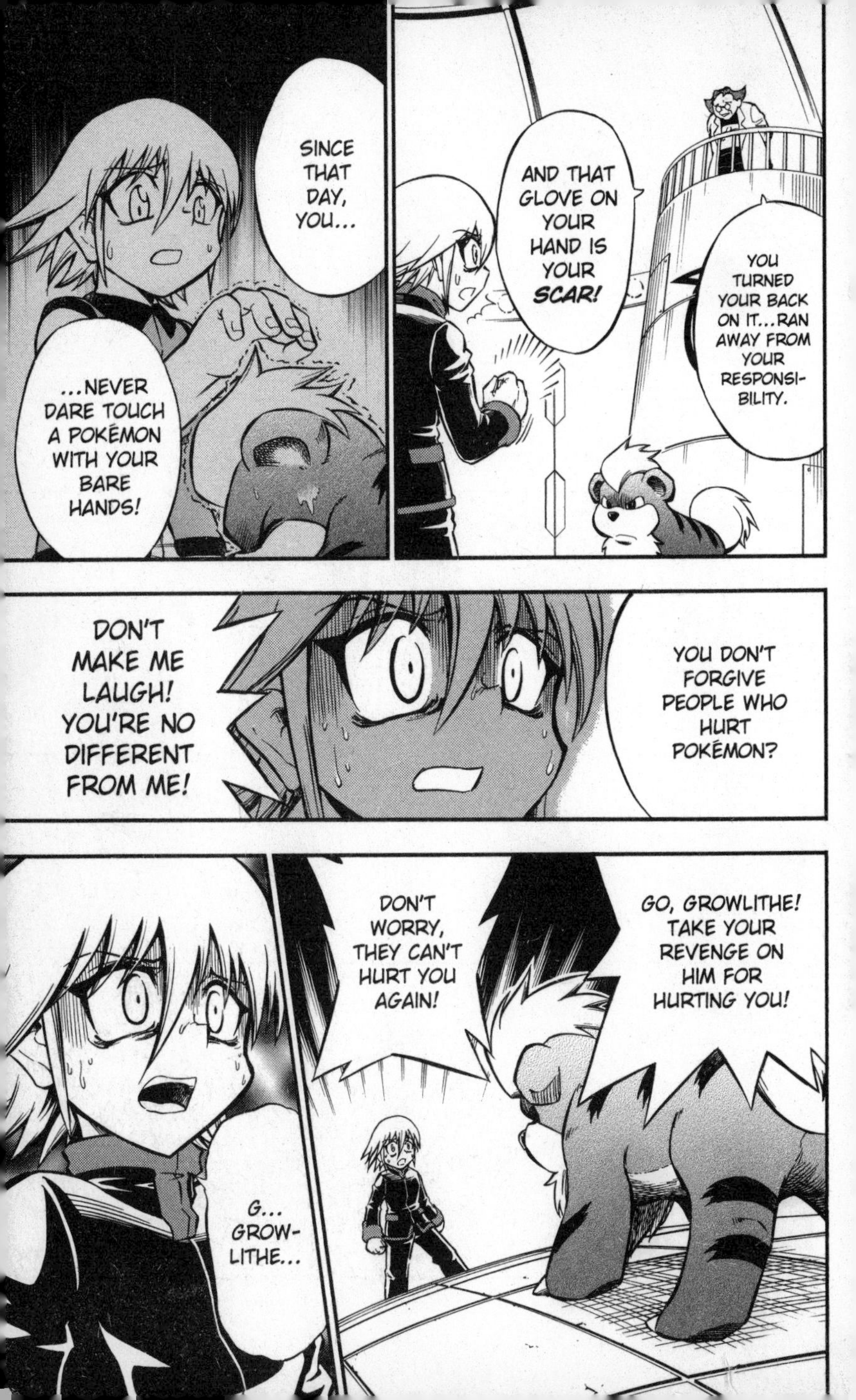
YOU TURNED YOUR BACK ON IT...RAN AWAY FROM YOUR RESPONSI-BILITY.
AND THAT GLOVE ON YOUR HAND IS YOUR ***SCAR!***
SINCE THAT DAY, YOU...
...NEVER DARE TOUCH A POKÉMON WITH YOUR BARE HANDS!
YOU DON'T FORGIVE PEOPLE WHO HURT POKÉMON?
DON'T MAKE ME LAUGH! YOU'RE NO DIFFERENT FROM ME!
GO, GROWLITHE! TAKE YOUR REVENGE ON HIM FOR HURTING YOU!
DON'T WORRY, THEY CAN'T HURT YOU AGAIN!
G... GROW-LITHE...

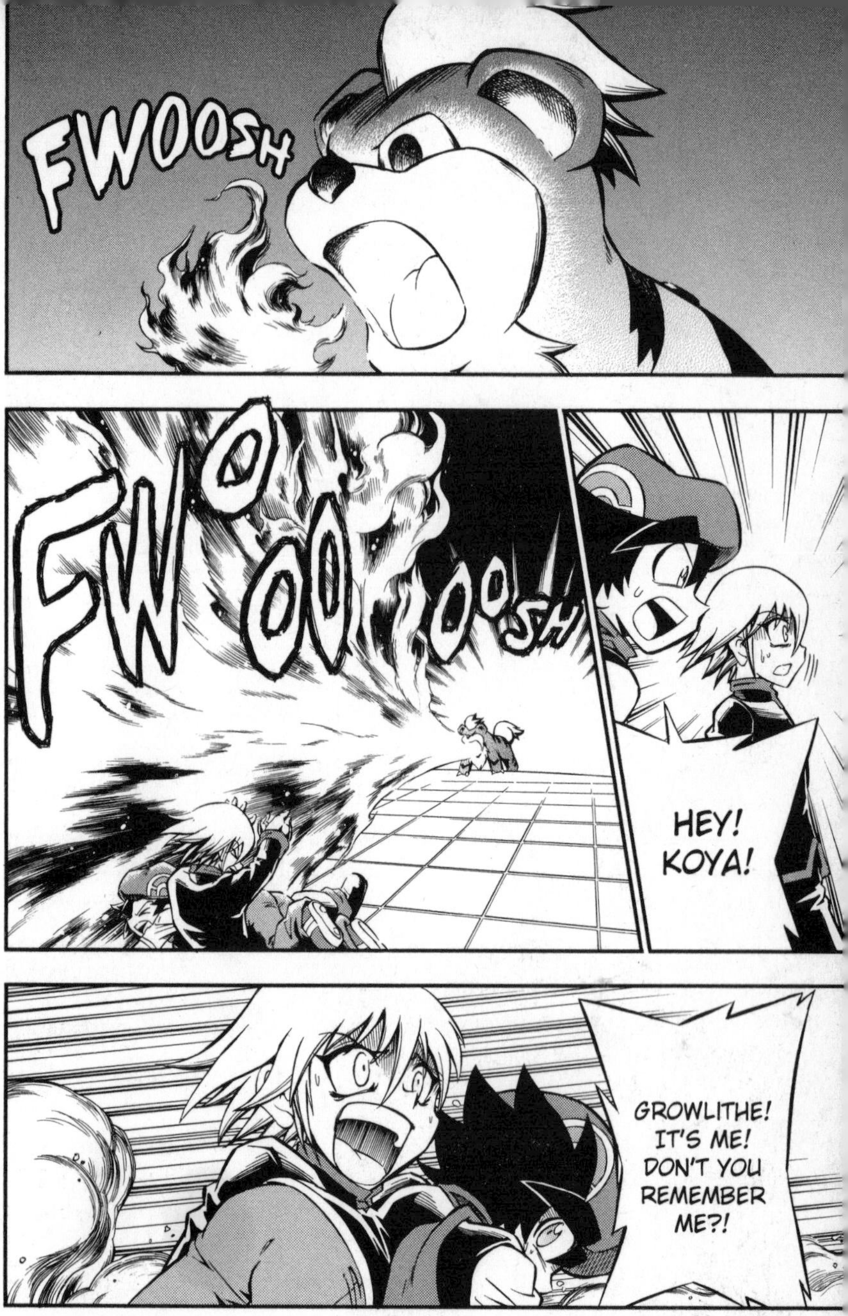
FWOOSH
FWOOOOOOOSH
HEY! KOYA!
GROWLITHE! IT'S ME! DON'T YOU REMEMBER ME?!

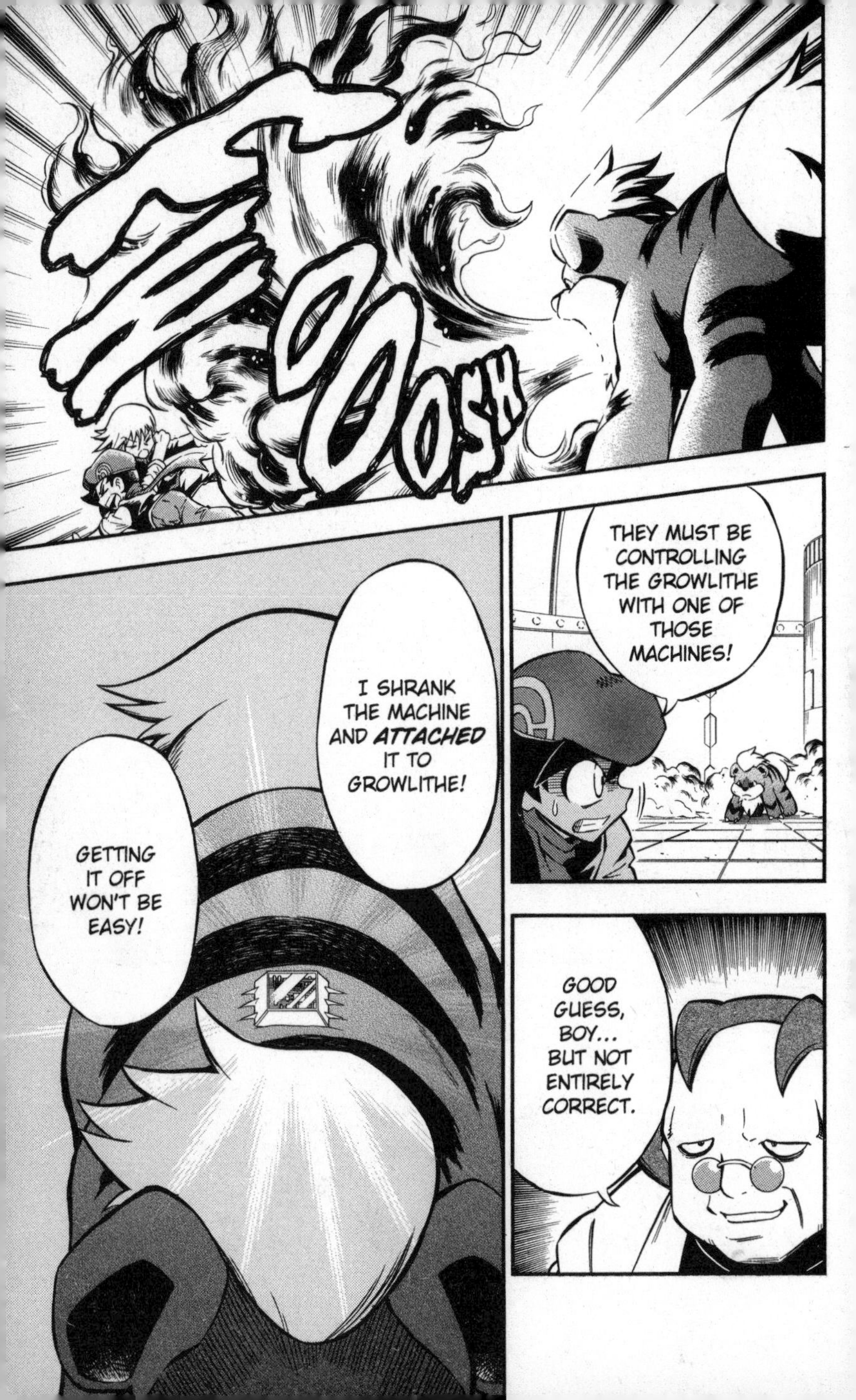
WHOOSH
THEY MUST BE CONTROLLING THE GROWLITHE WITH ONE OF THOSE MACHINES!
GOOD GUESS, BOY... BUT NOT ENTIRELY CORRECT.
I SHRANK THE MACHINE AND ***ATTACHED*** IT TO GROWLITHE!
GETTING IT OFF WON'T BE EASY!

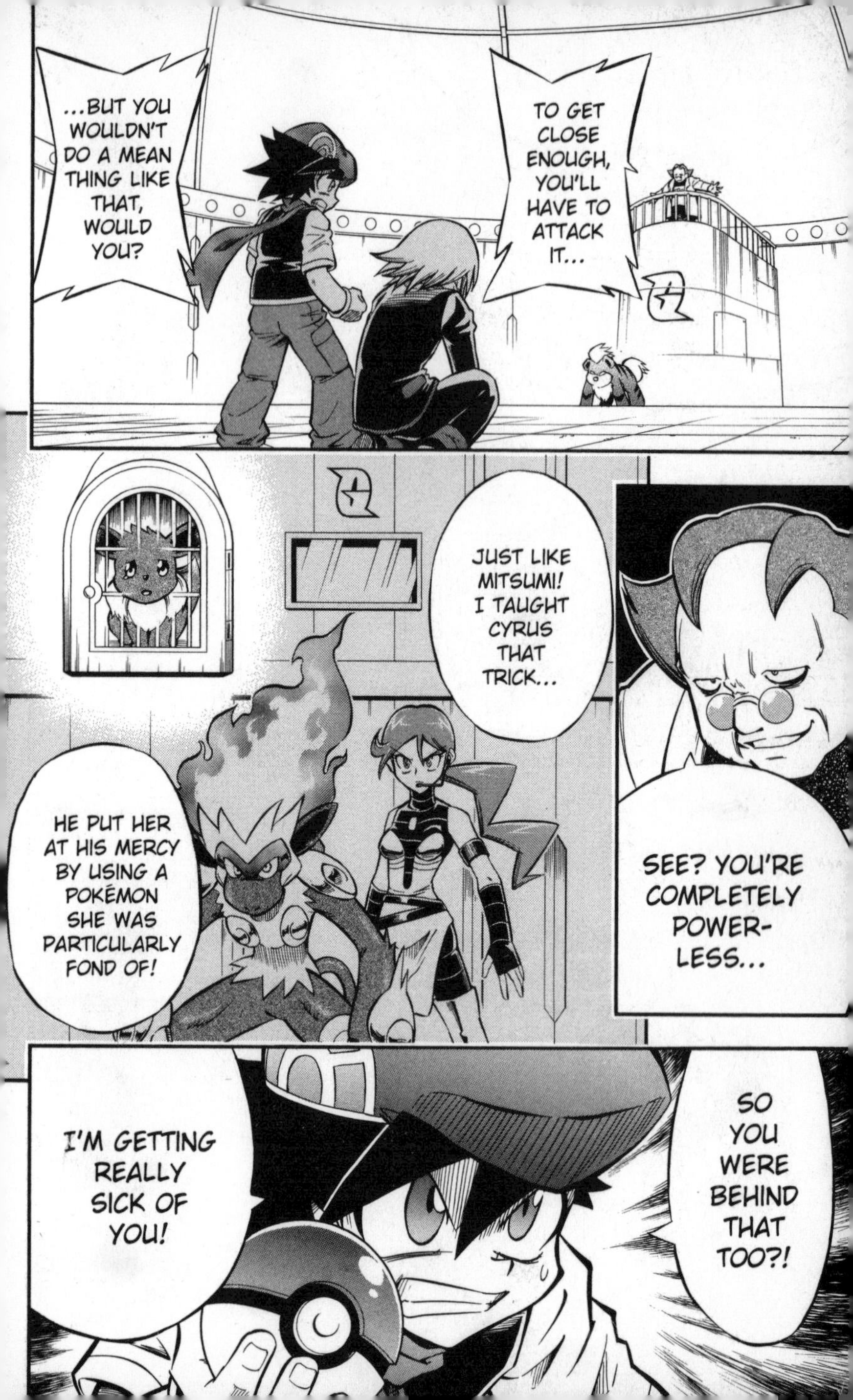
TO GET CLOSE ENOUGH, YOU'LL HAVE TO ATTACK IT...
...BUT YOU WOULDN'T DO A MEAN THING LIKE THAT, WOULD YOU?
SEE? YOU'RE COMPLETELY POWER-LESS...
JUST LIKE MITSUMI! I TAUGHT CYRUS THAT TRICK...
HE PUT HER AT HIS MERCY BY USING A POKÉMON SHE WAS PARTICULARLY FOND OF!
SO YOU WERE BEHIND THAT TOO?!
I'M GETTING REALLY SICK OF YOU!

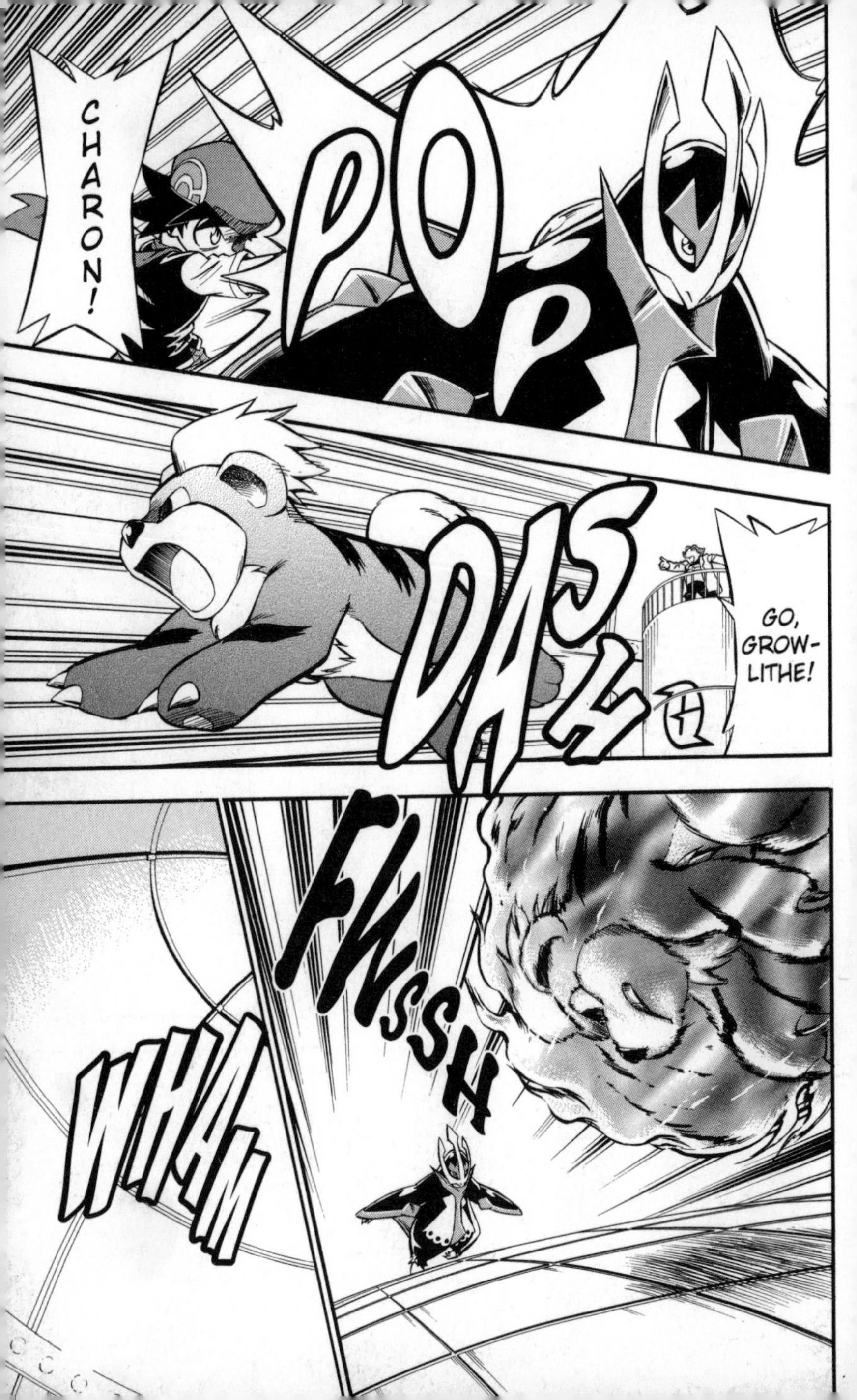
POP
CHARON!
GO, GROWLITHE!
DASH
FWSSH
WHAM

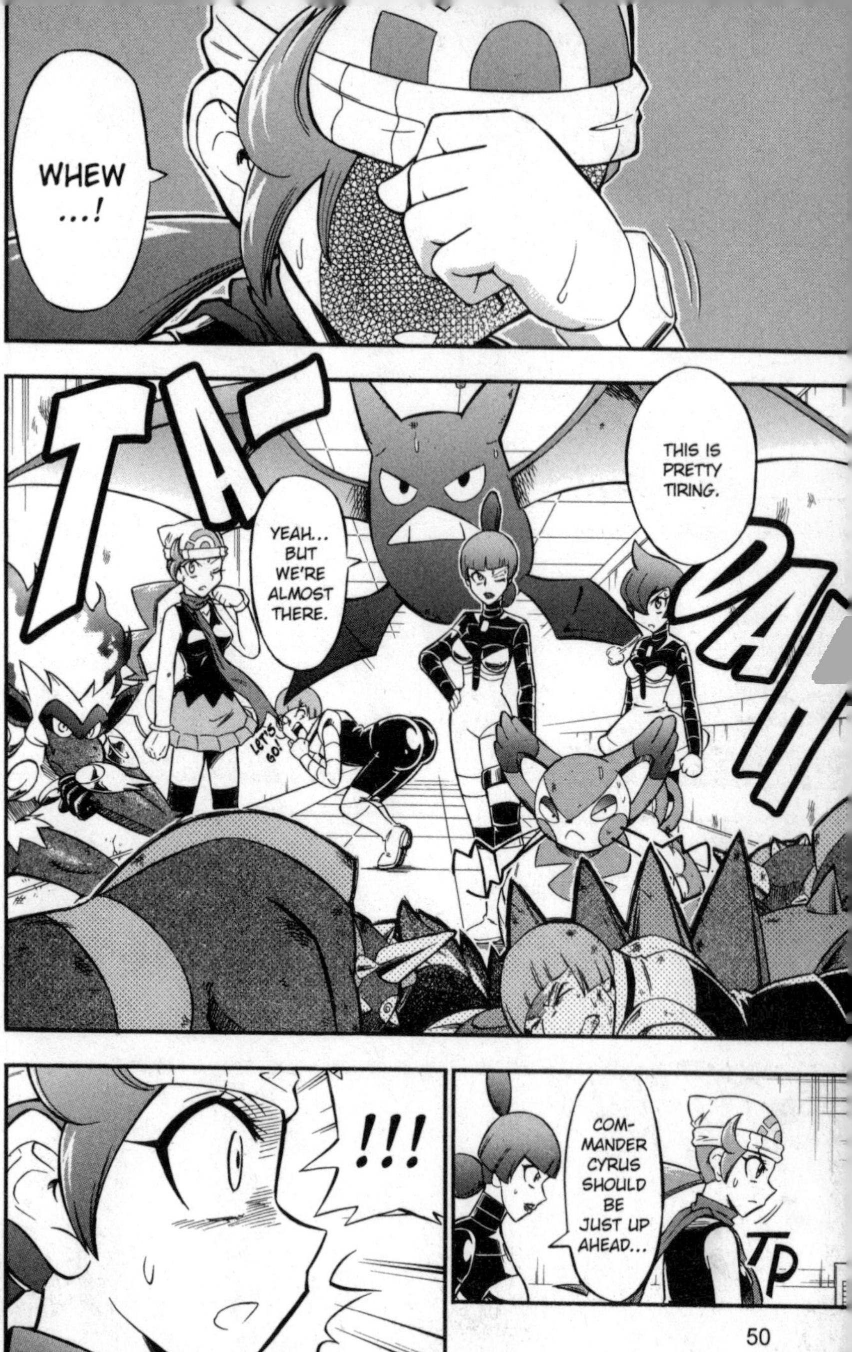
WHEW ...!
TA–
THIS IS PRETTY TIRING.
DAH
YEAH... BUT WE'RE ALMOST THERE.
LET'S GO!
COM-MANDER CYRUS SHOULD BE JUST UP AHEAD...
TP
!!!

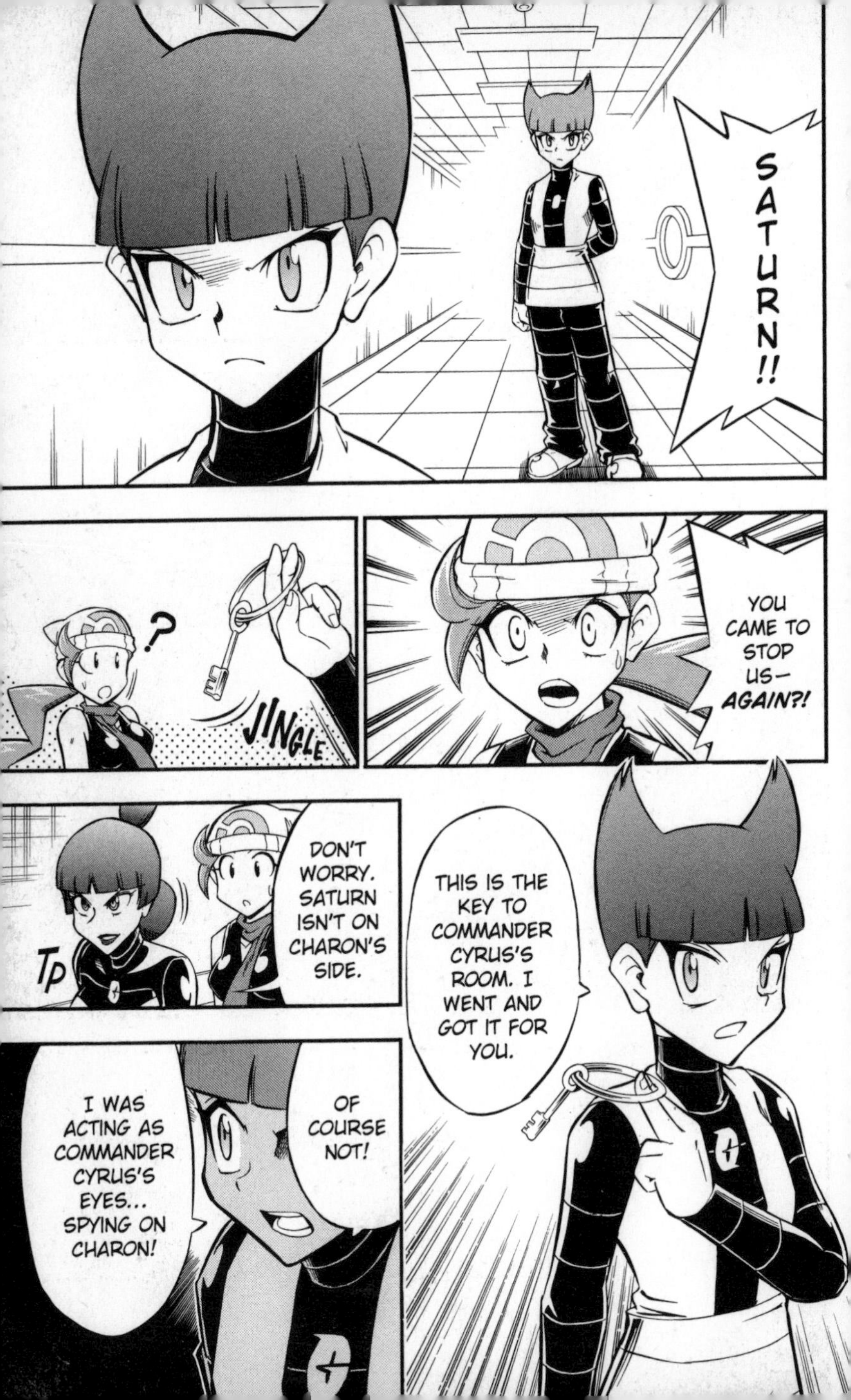
SATURN!!
YOU CAME TO STOP US— AGAIN?!
?
JINGLE
THIS IS THE KEY TO COMMANDER CYRUS'S ROOM. I WENT AND GOT IT FOR YOU.
DON'T WORRY. SATURN ISN'T ON CHARON'S SIDE.
TP
OF COURSE NOT!
I WAS ACTING AS COMMANDER CYRUS'S EYES... SPYING ON CHARON!

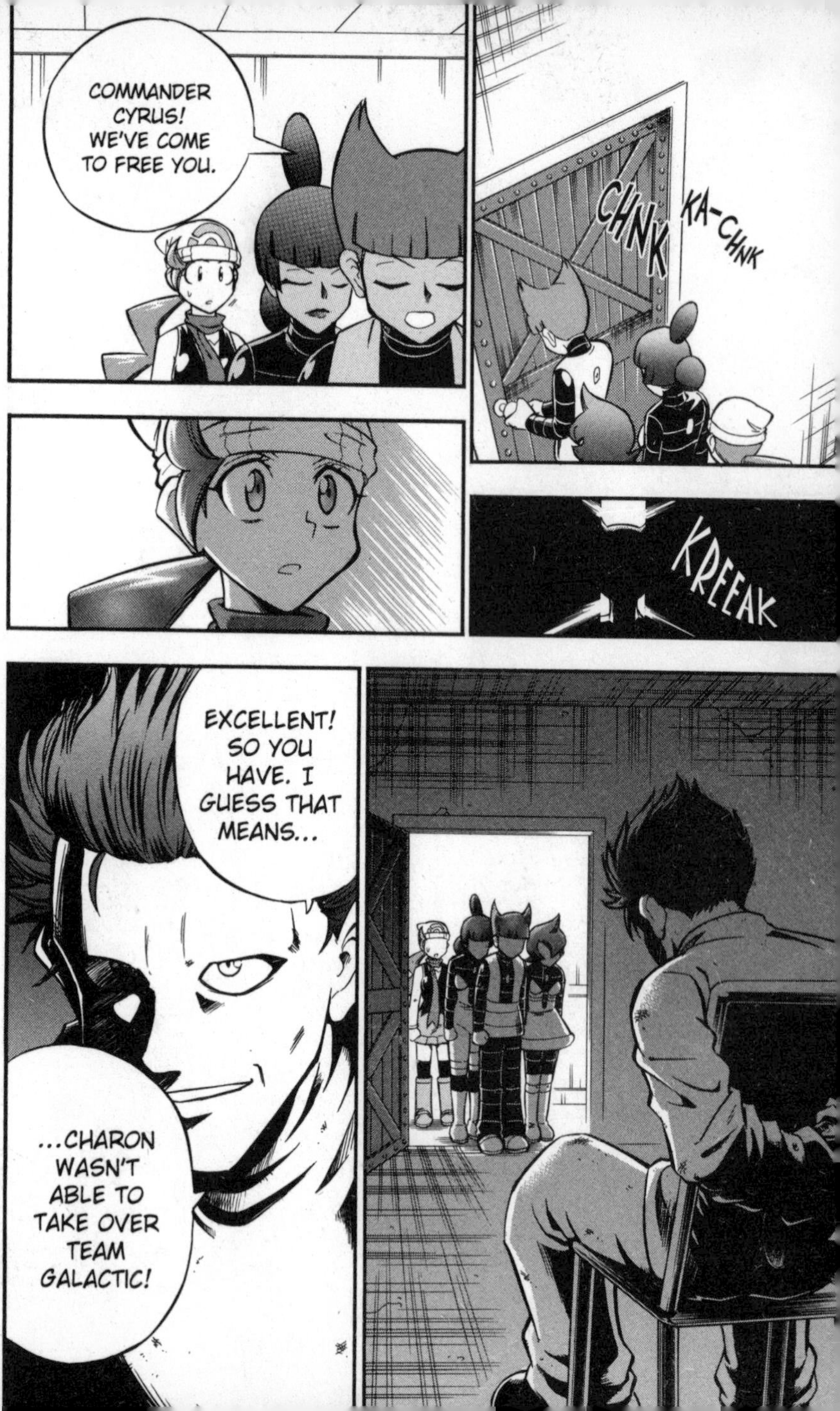
CHNK
KA-CHNK
COMMANDER CYRUS! WE'VE COME TO FREE YOU.
KREEAK
EXCELLENT! SO YOU HAVE. I GUESS THAT MEANS...
...CHARON WASN'T ABLE TO TAKE OVER TEAM GALACTIC!

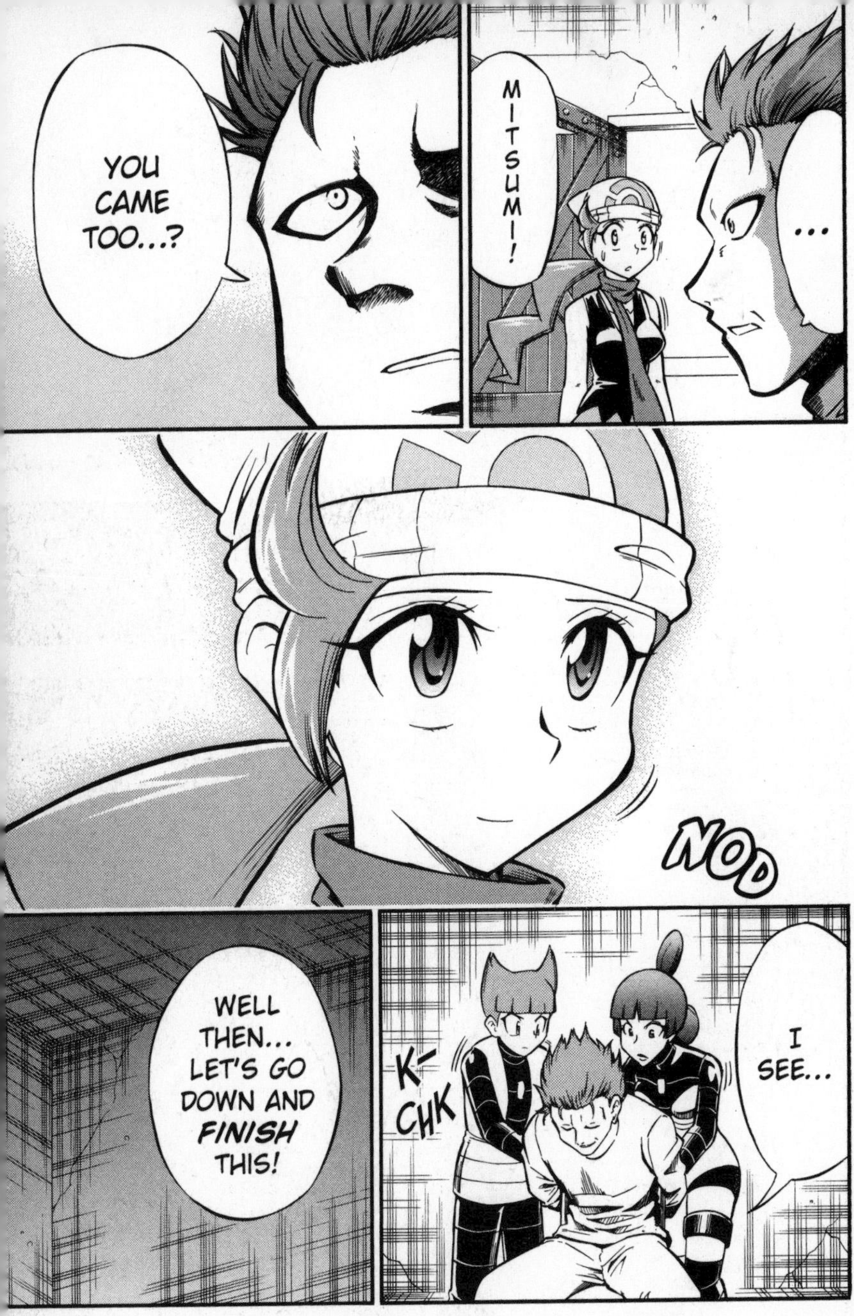
MITSUMI!
...
YOU CAME TOO...?
NOD
I SEE...
K-CHK
WELL THEN... LET'S GO DOWN AND FINISH THIS!

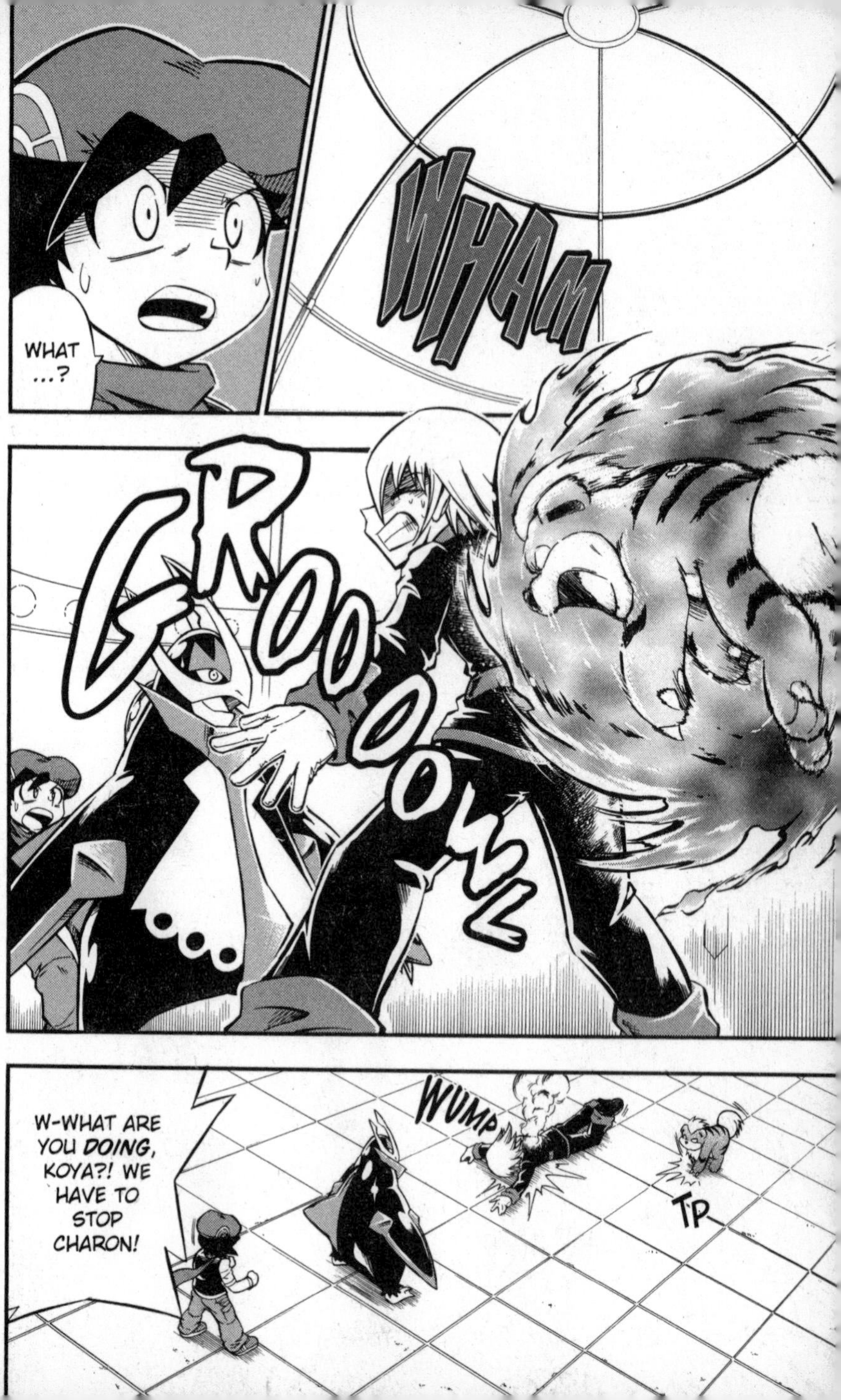
WHAM
WHAT ...?
GROOOOOWL
...
WUMP
TP
W-WHAT ARE YOU *DOING*, KOYA?! WE HAVE TO STOP CHARON!

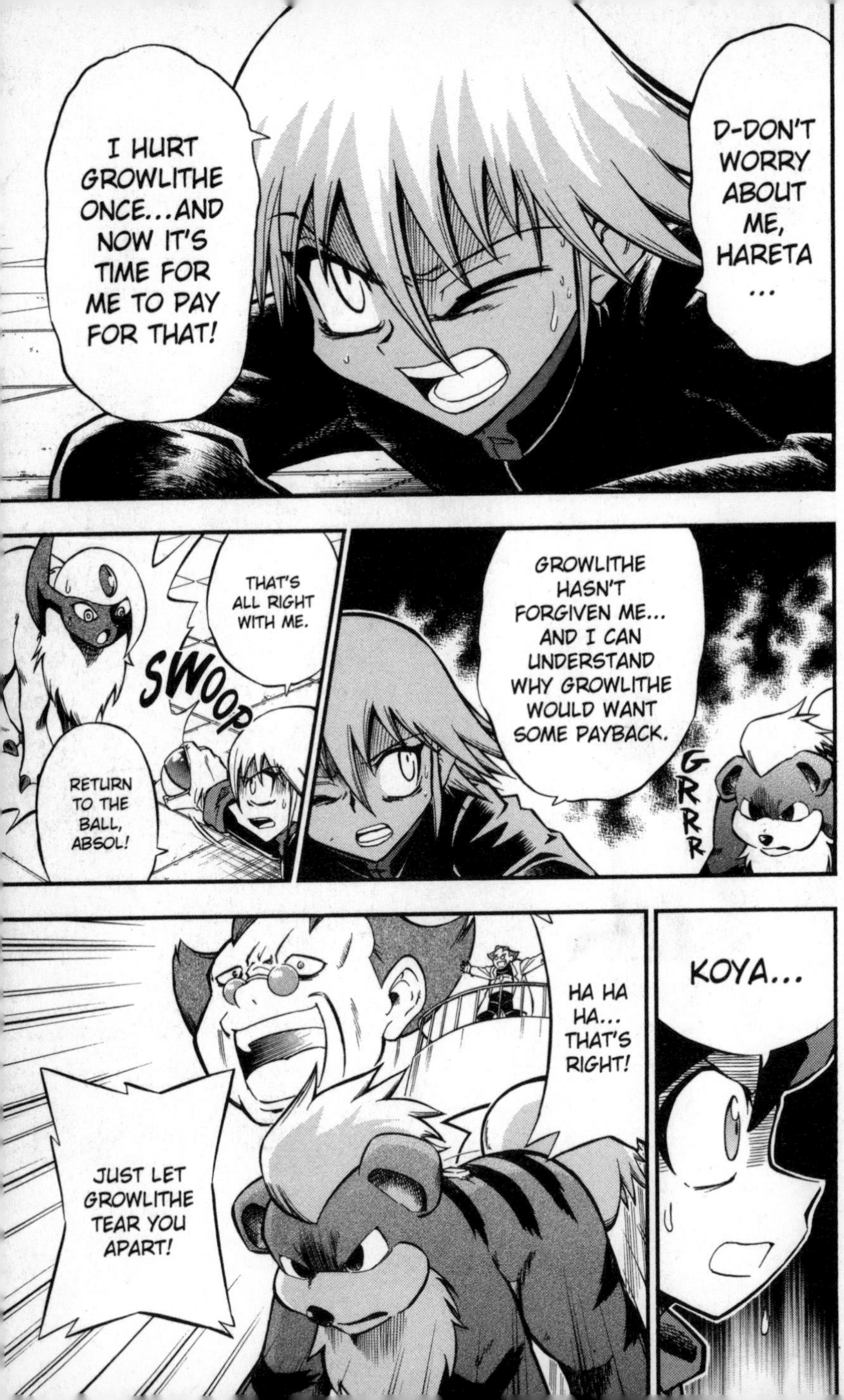
D-DON'T WORRY ABOUT ME, HARETA...
I HURT GROWLITHE ONCE...AND NOW IT'S TIME FOR ME TO PAY FOR THAT!
GROWLITHE HASN'T FORGIVEN ME... AND I CAN UNDERSTAND WHY GROWLITHE WOULD WANT SOME PAYBACK.
GRRR
THAT'S ALL RIGHT WITH ME.
SWOOP
RETURN TO THE BALL, ABSOL!
KOYA...
HA HA HA... THAT'S RIGHT!
JUST LET GROWLITHE TEAR YOU APART!

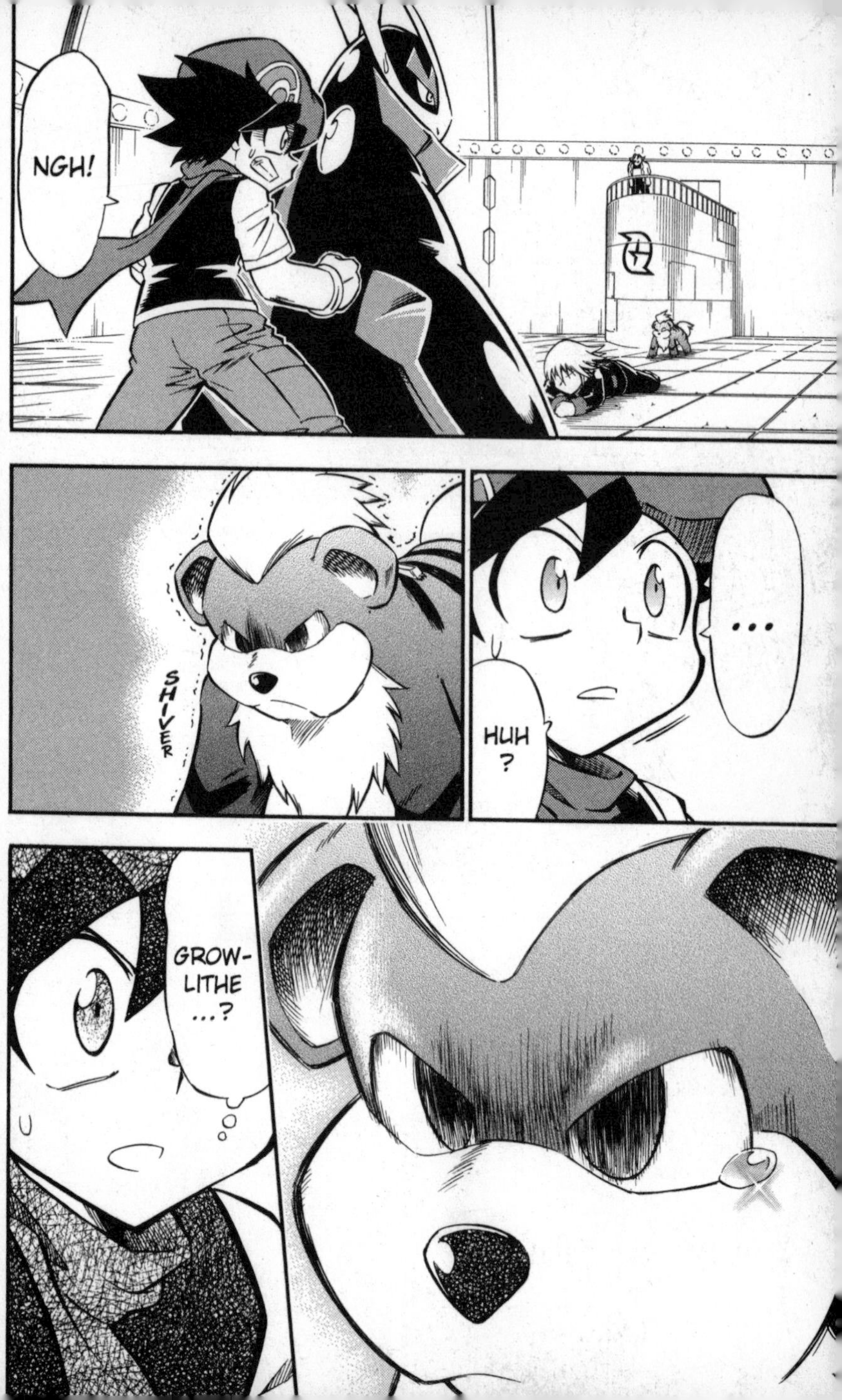
NGH!
...
HUH?
SHIVER
GROW-LITHE...?

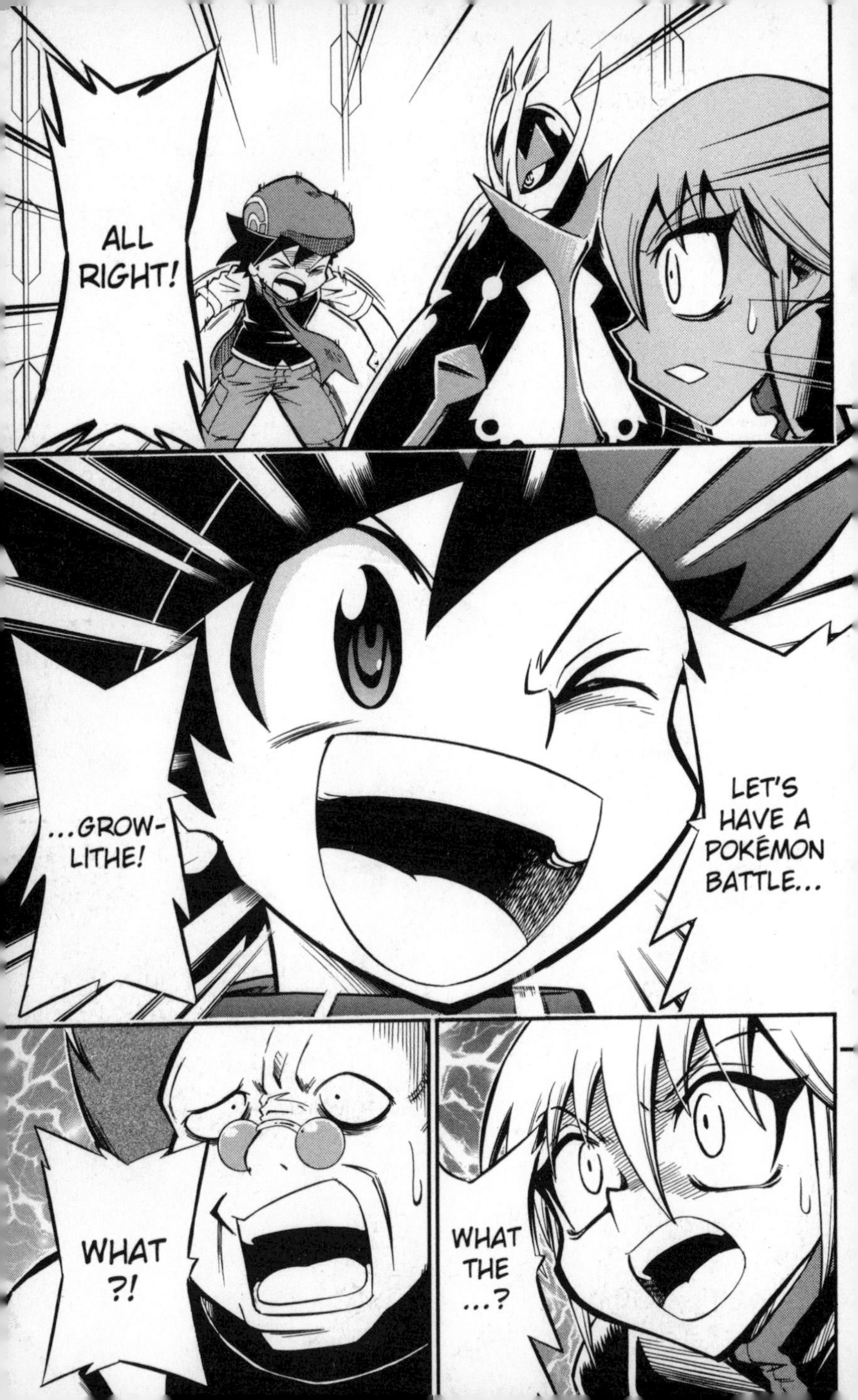
ALL RIGHT!
LET'S HAVE A POKÉMON BATTLE...
...GROW-LITHE!
WHAT THE ...?
WHAT ?!

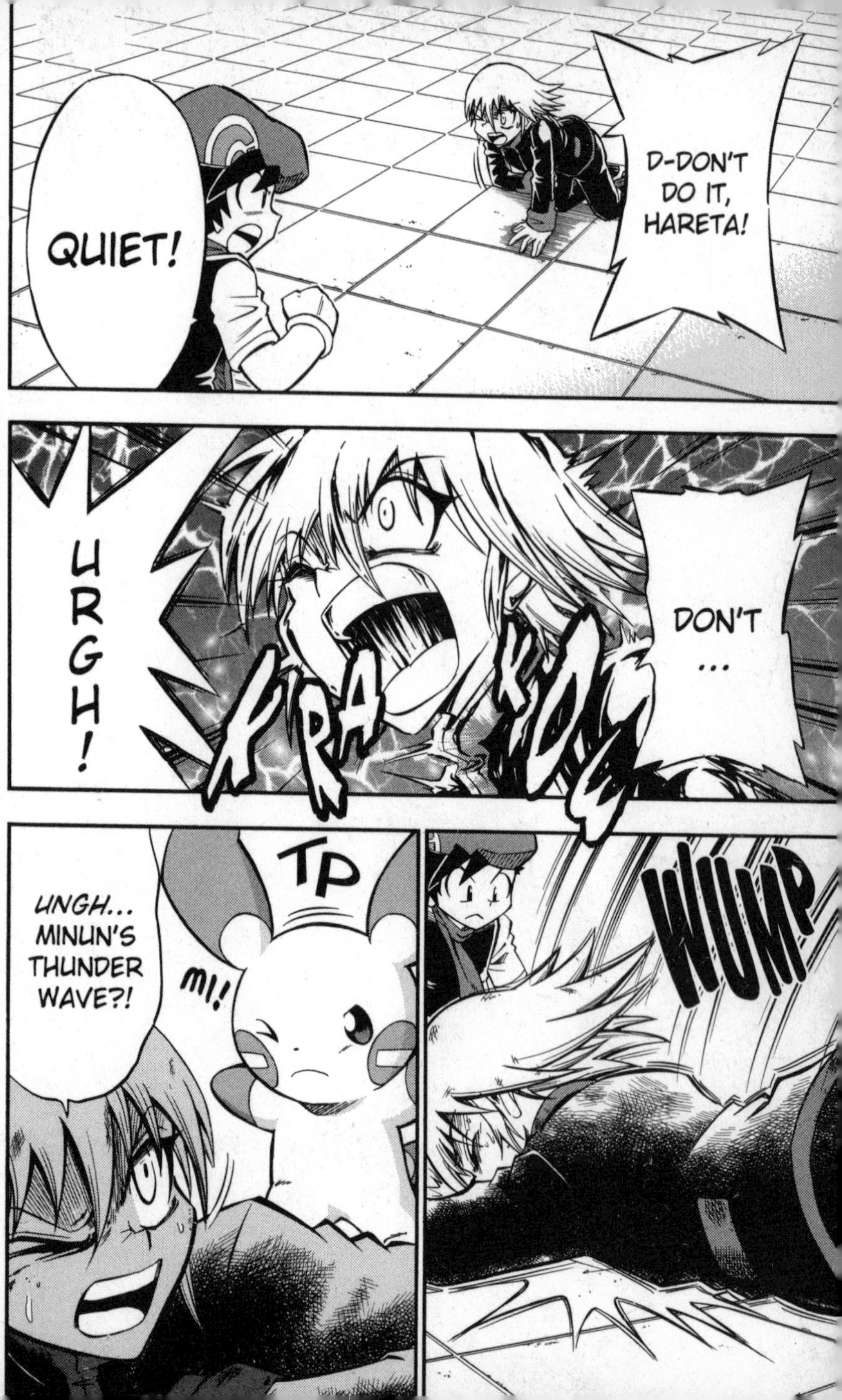
D-DON'T DO IT, HARETA!
QUIET!
DON'T ...
URGH!
WUMP
TP
MI!
UNGH... MINUN'S THUNDER WAVE?!

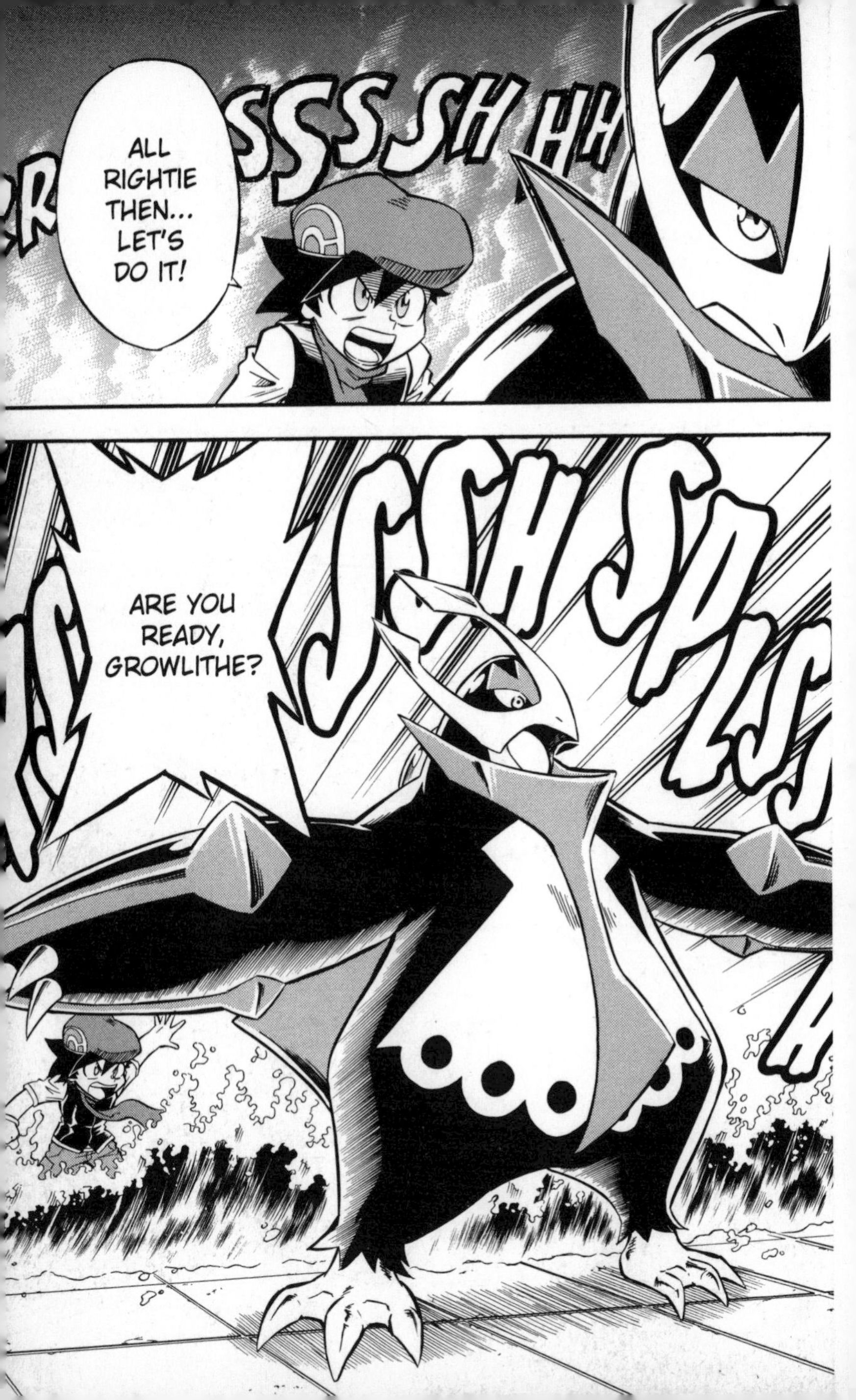
ALL RIGHTIE THEN... LET'S DO IT!
ARE YOU READY, GROWLITHE?

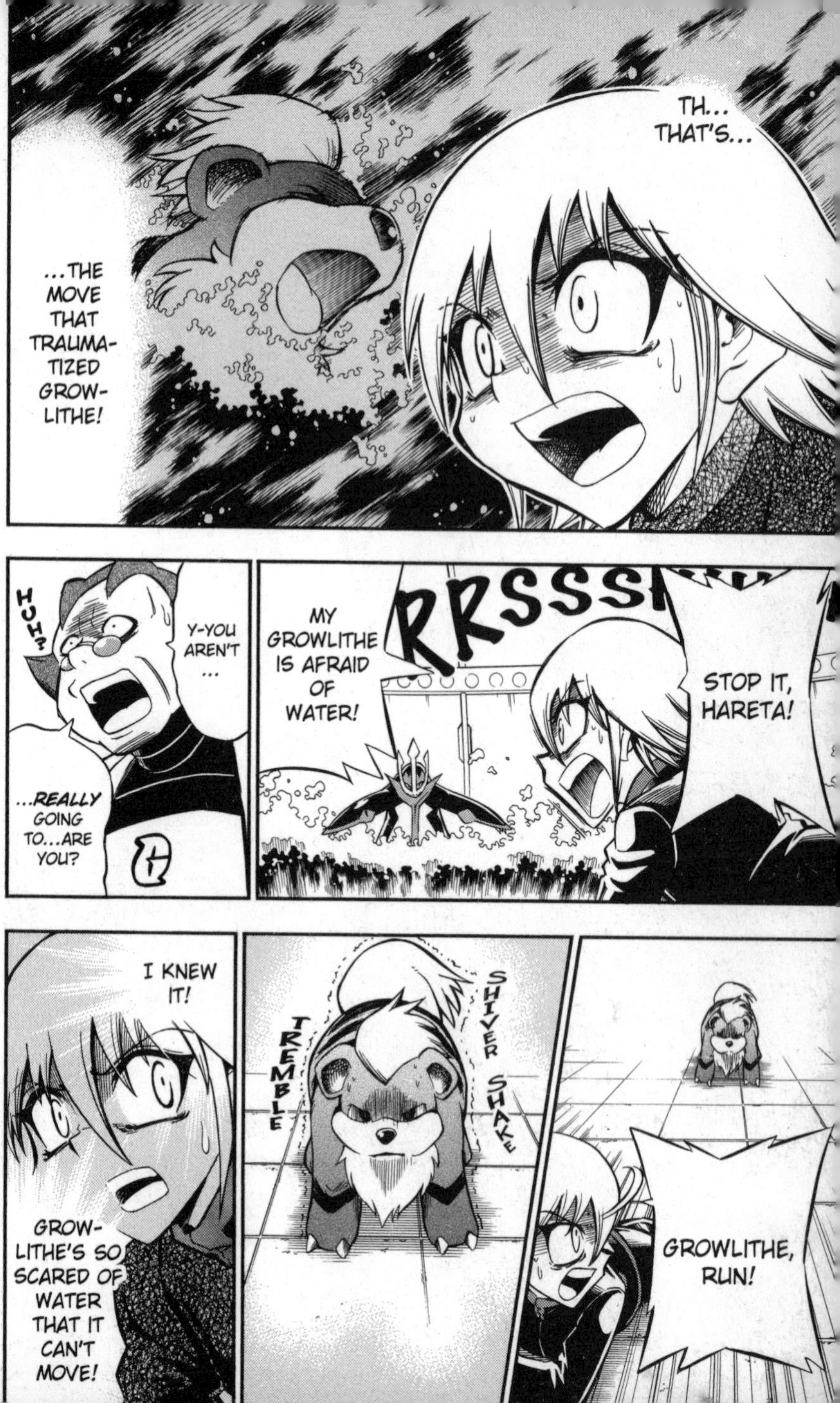
TH... THAT'S...
...THE MOVE THAT TRAUMATIZED GROWLITHE!
RRSSS
STOP IT, HARETA!
MY GROWLITHE IS AFRAID OF WATER!
HUH?
Y-YOU AREN'T ...
...REALLY GOING TO...ARE YOU?
GROWLITHE, RUN!
SHIVER SHAKE
TREMBLE
I KNEW IT!
GROWLITHE'S SO SCARED OF WATER THAT IT CAN'T MOVE!

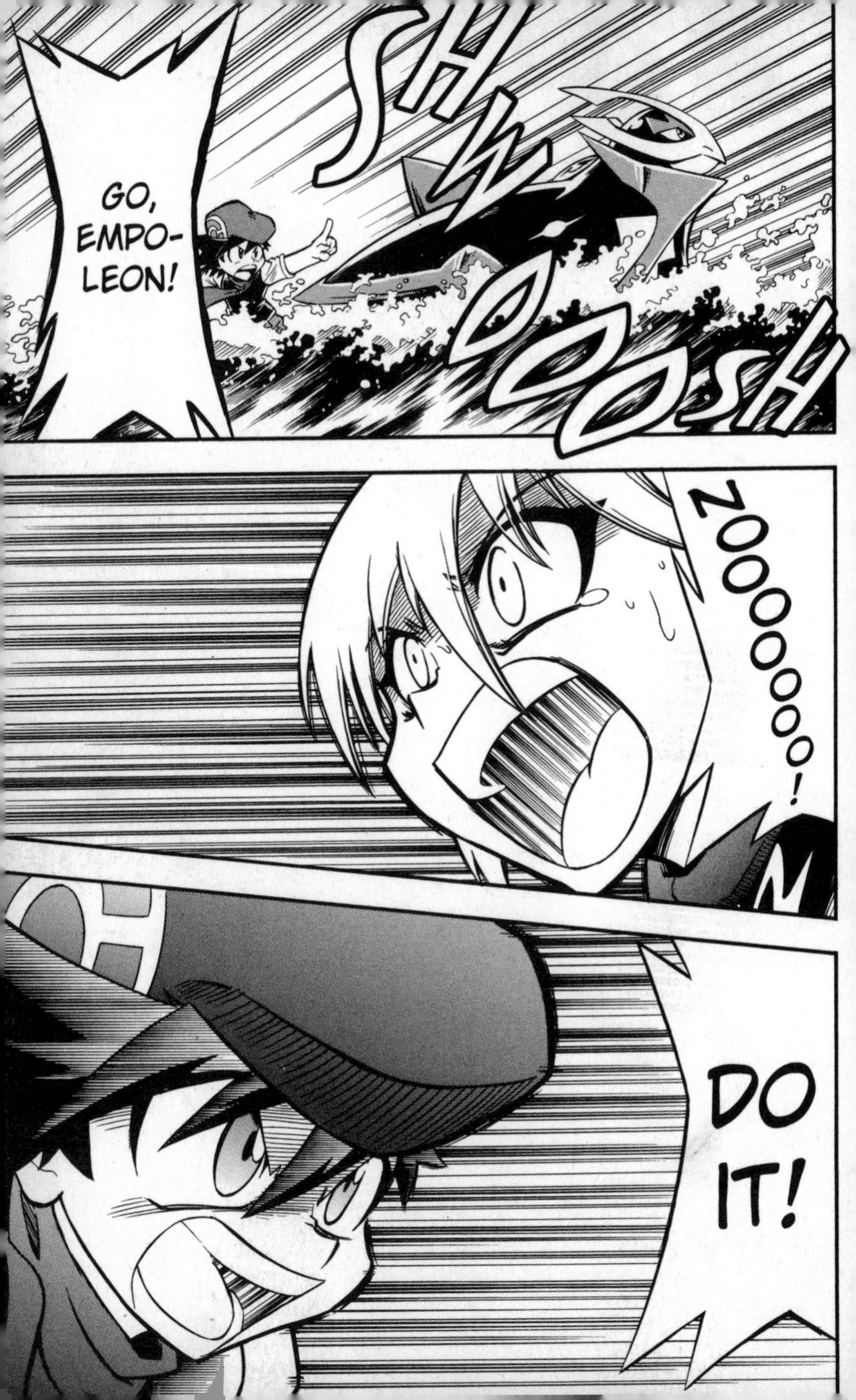
SHWOOOSH
GO, EMPO-LEON!
ZOOOOOOO!
DO IT!

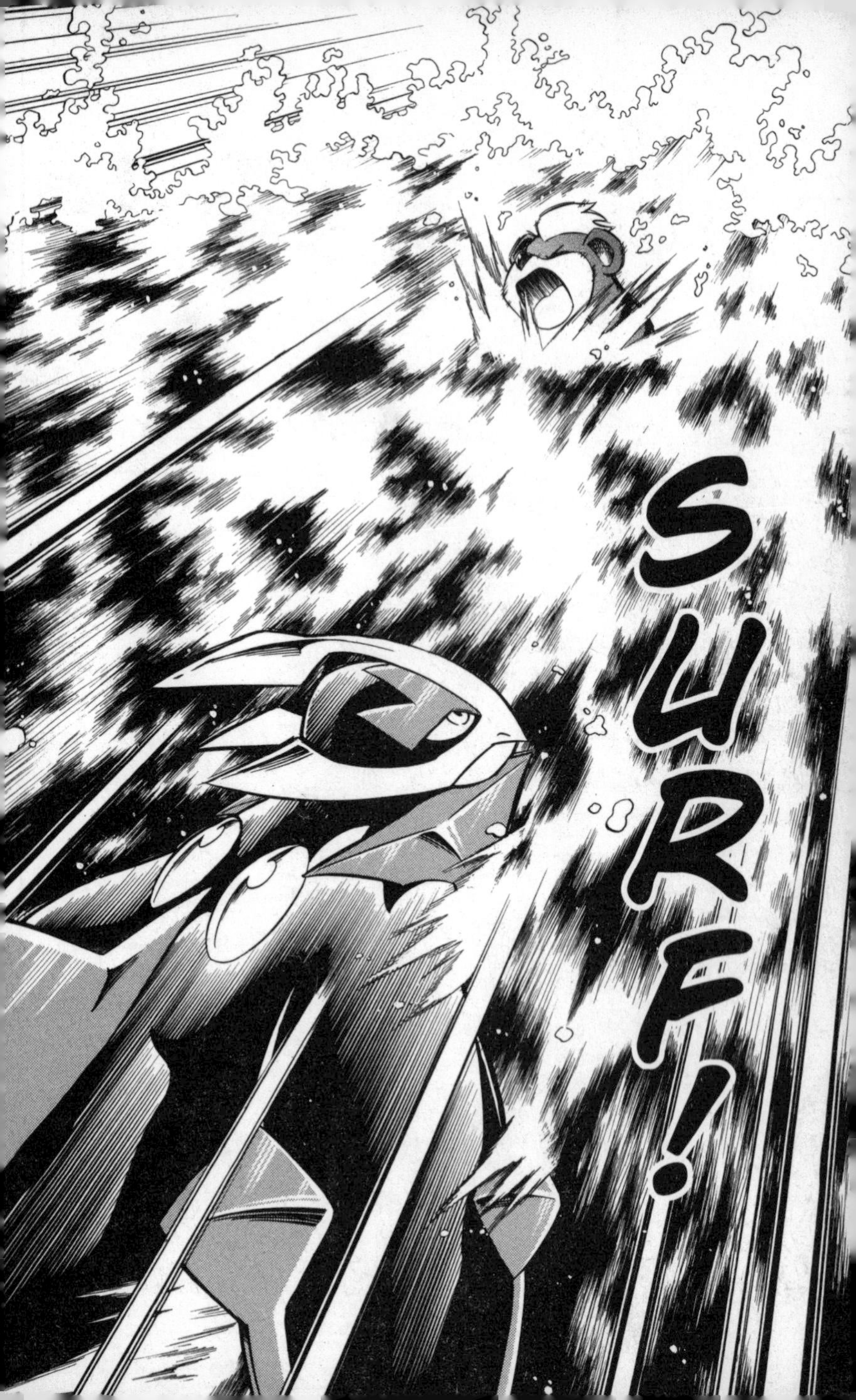
SURF!!

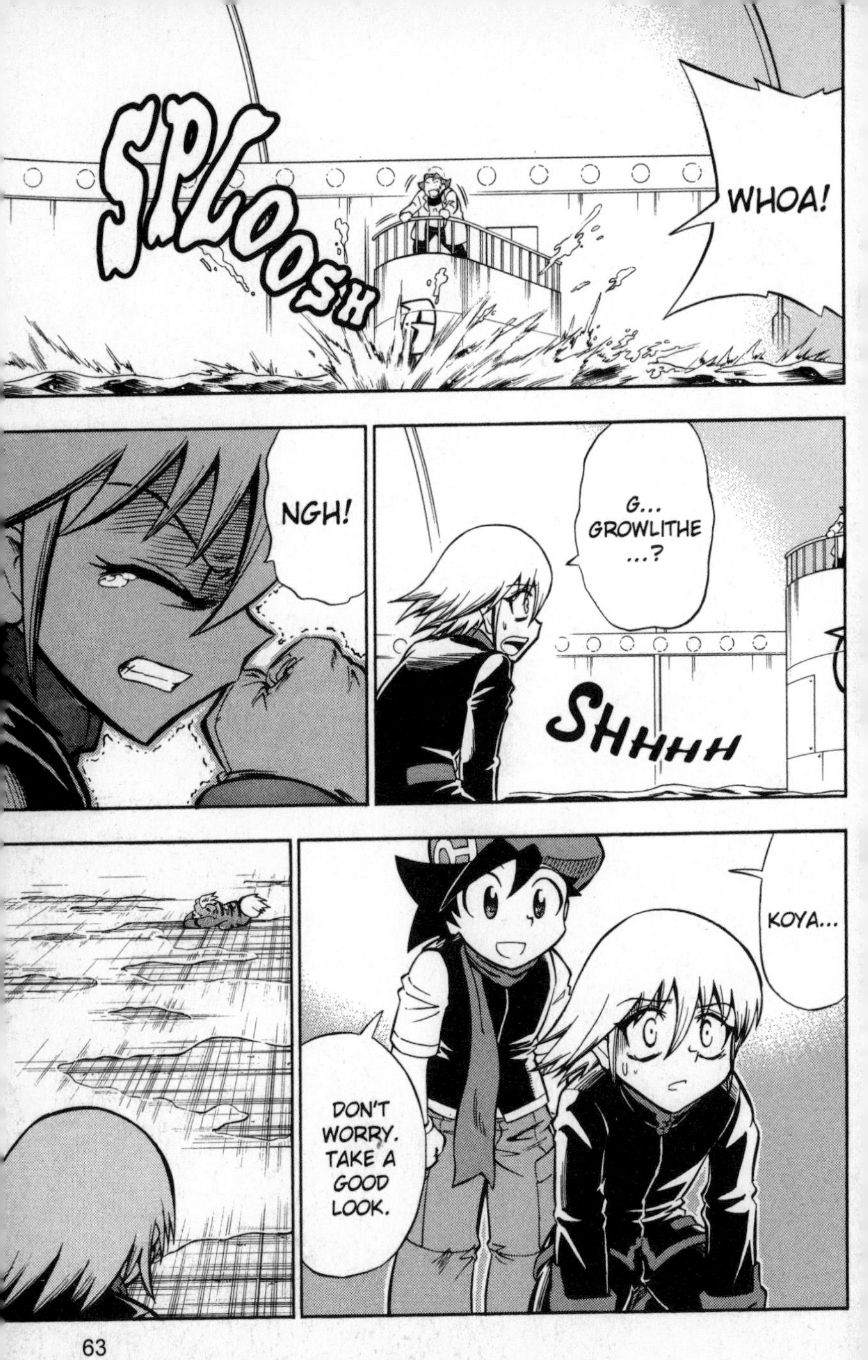
WHOA!
SPLOOSH
G... GROWLITHE ...?
SHHHH
NGH!
KOYA...
DON'T WORRY. TAKE A GOOD LOOK.

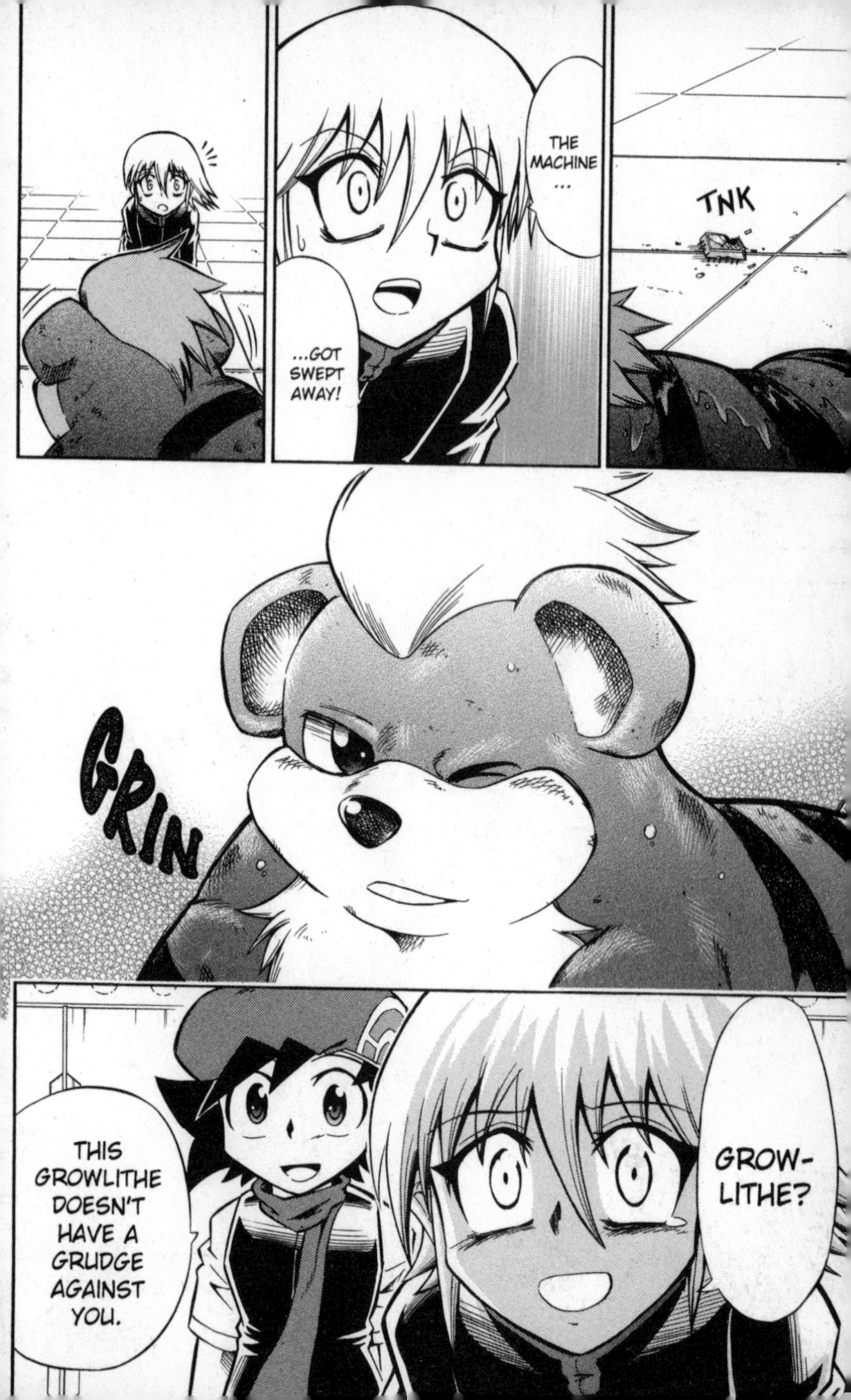
TNK
THE MACHINE ...
...GOT SWEPT AWAY!
GRIN
GROW-LITHE?
THIS GROWLITHE DOESN'T HAVE A GRUDGE AGAINST YOU.

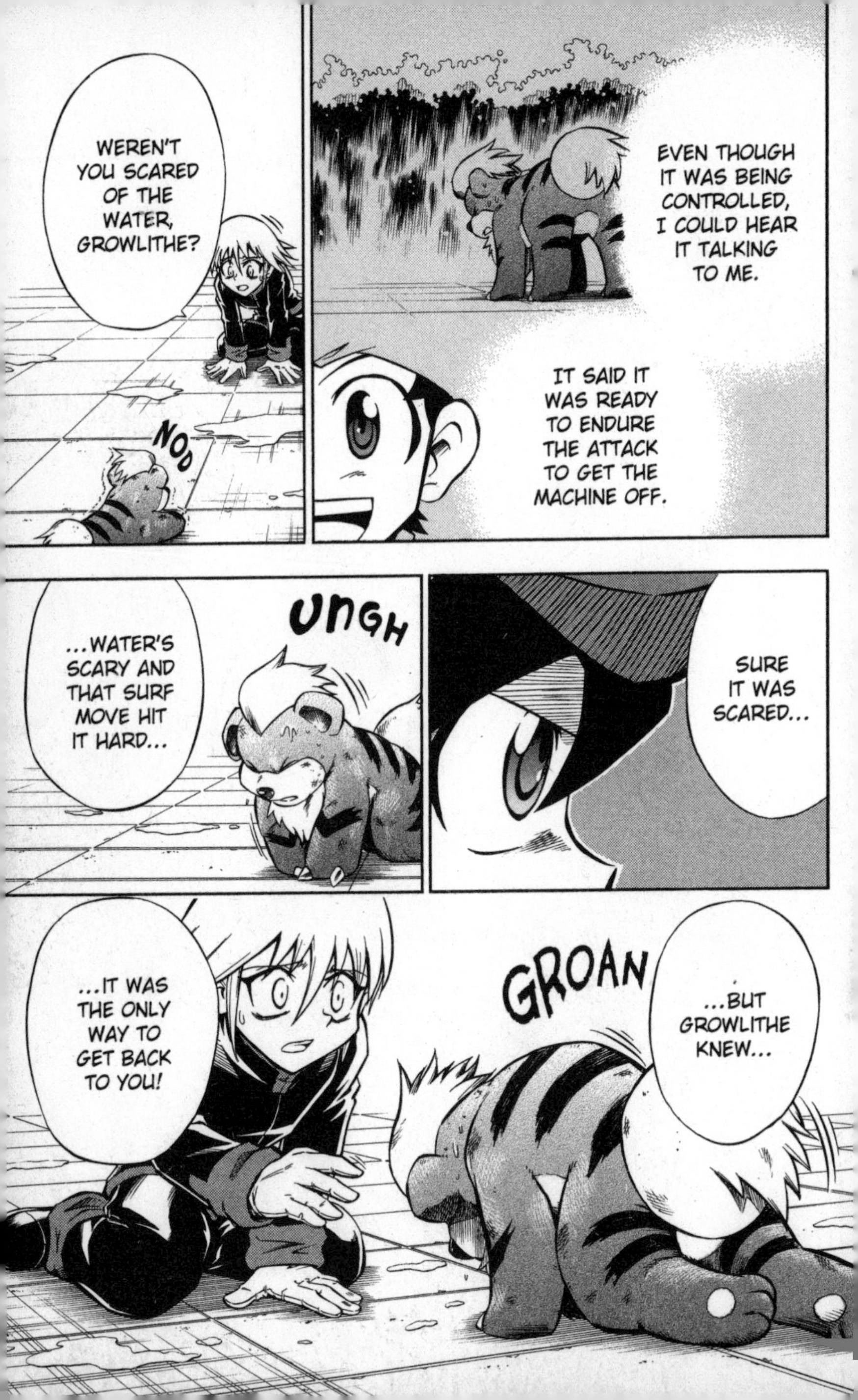
EVEN THOUGH IT WAS BEING CONTROLLED, I COULD HEAR IT TALKING TO ME.
IT SAID IT WAS READY TO ENDURE THE ATTACK TO GET THE MACHINE OFF.
WEREN'T YOU SCARED OF THE WATER, GROWLITHE?
NOD
SURE IT WAS SCARED...
UNGH
...WATER'S SCARY AND THAT SURF MOVE HIT IT HARD...
...BUT GROWLITHE KNEW...
GROAN
...IT WAS THE ONLY WAY TO GET BACK TO YOU!

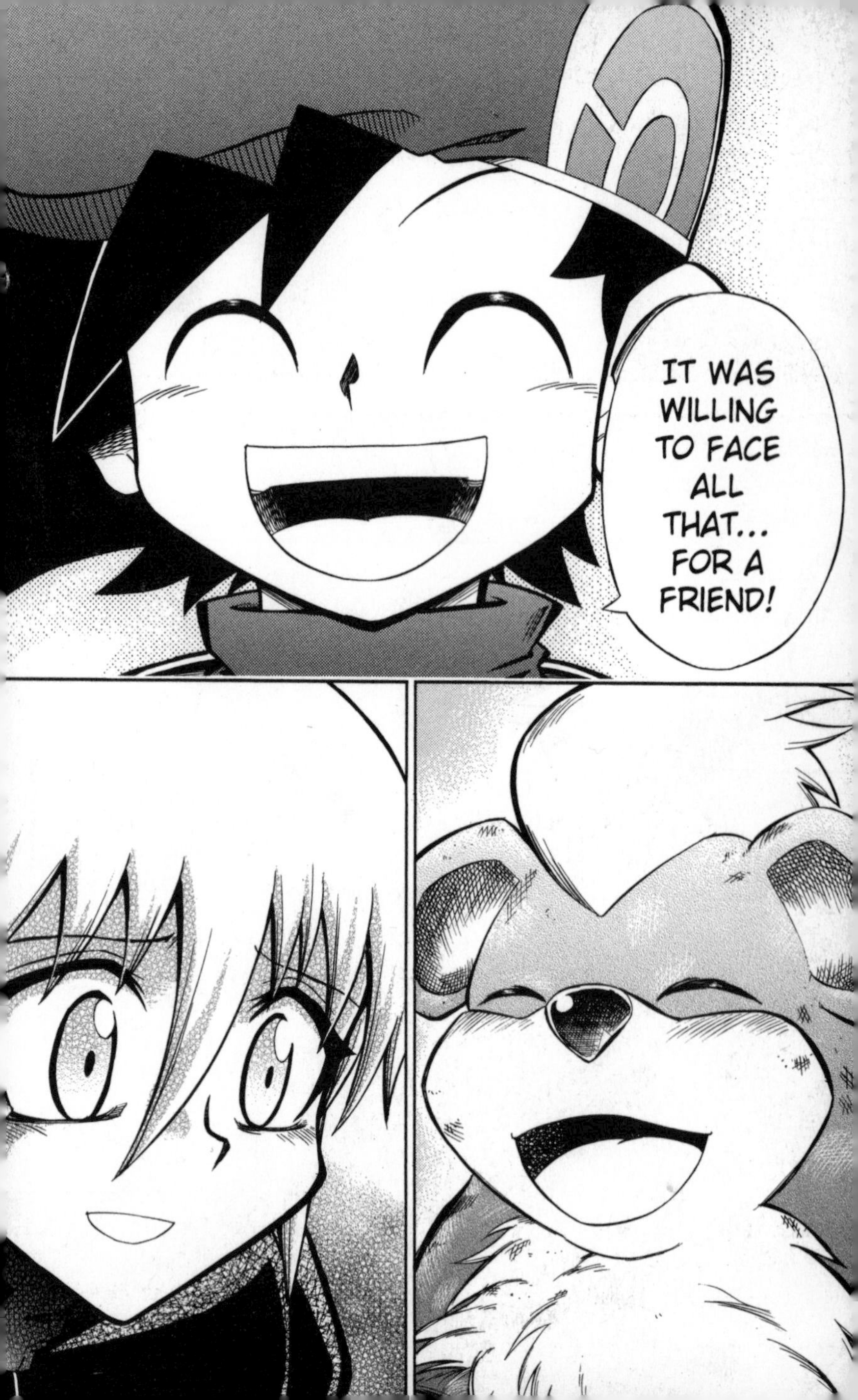
IT WAS WILLING TO FACE ALL THAT... FOR A FRIEND!

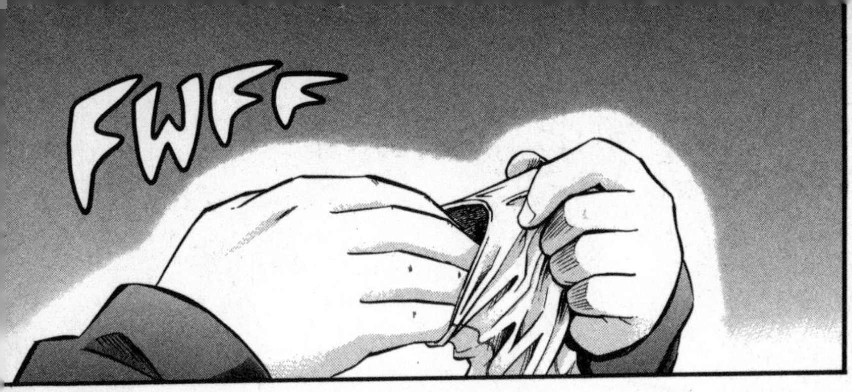
FWFF
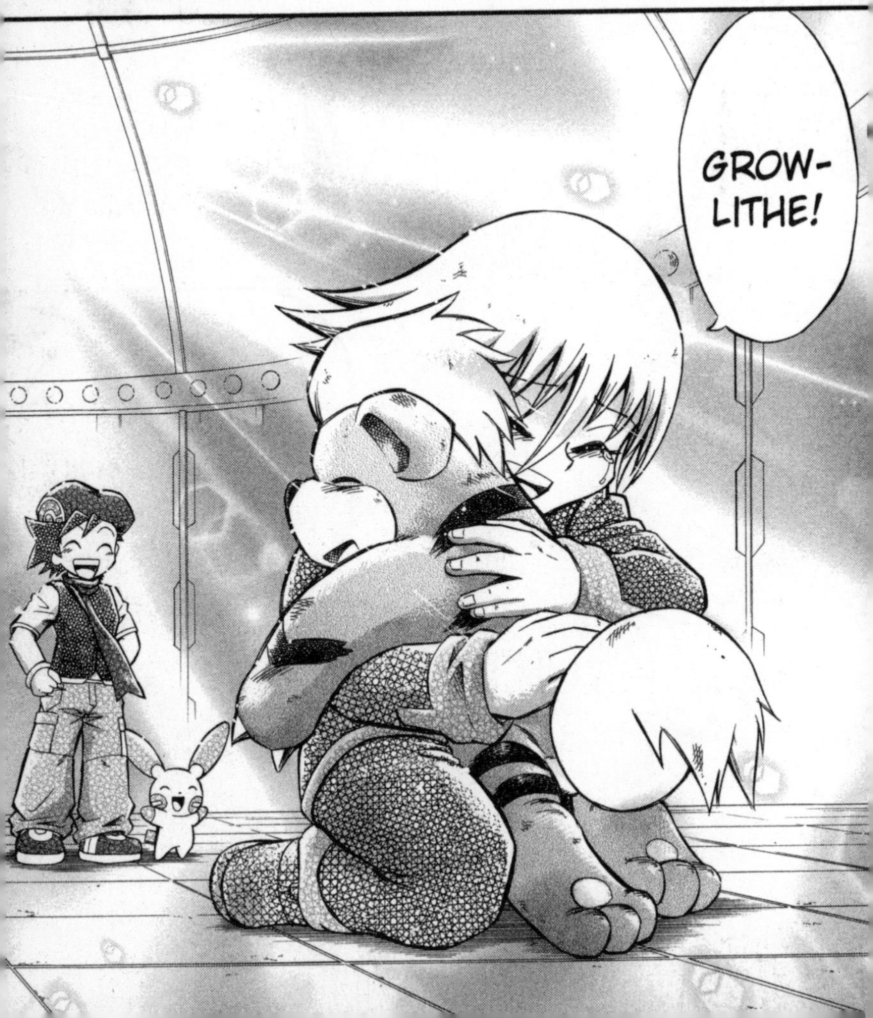
GROW-
LITHE!

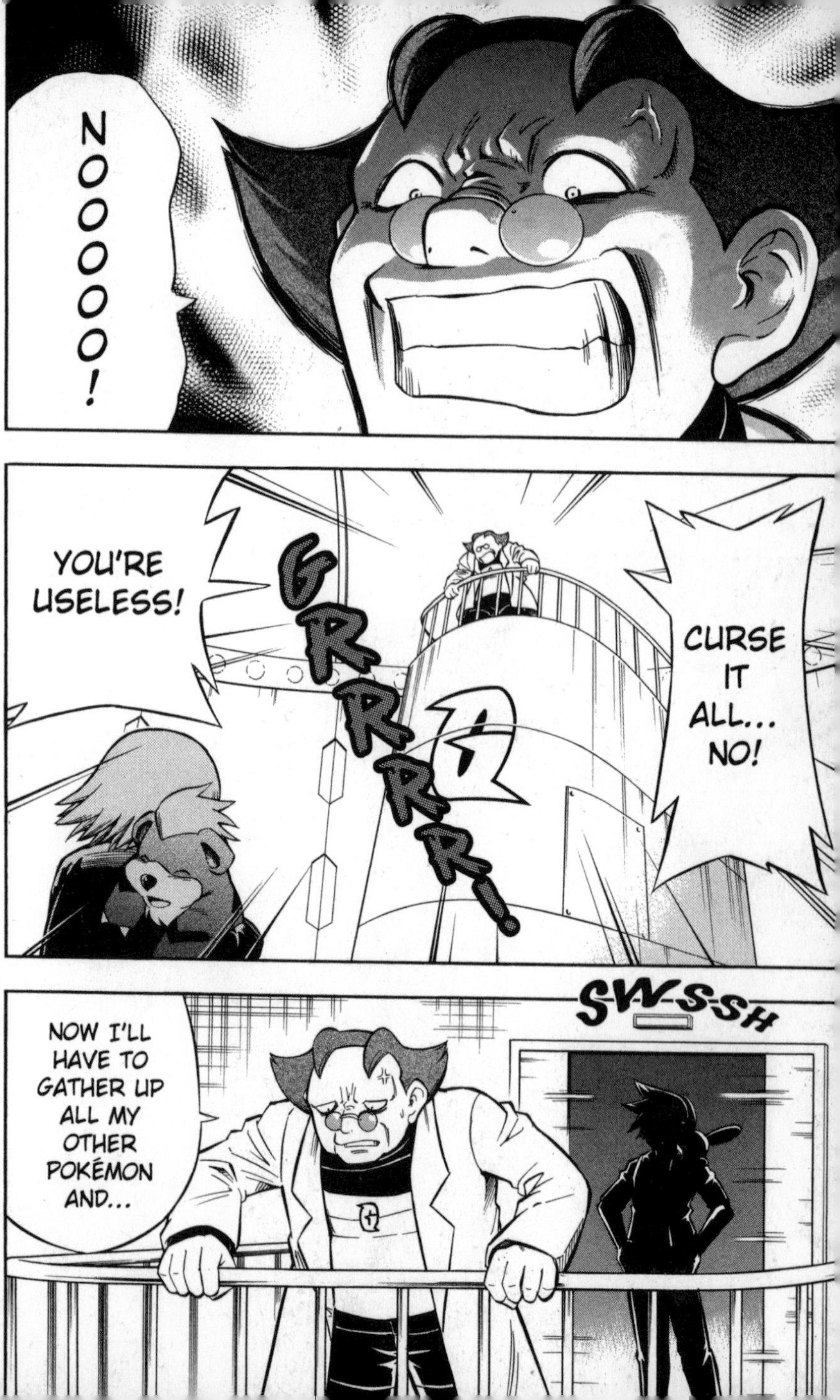
NOOOOOO!
CURSE IT ALL... NO!
GRRRRR!
YOU'RE USELESS!
SW-S-SH
NOW I'LL HAVE TO GATHER UP ALL MY OTHER POKÉMON AND...

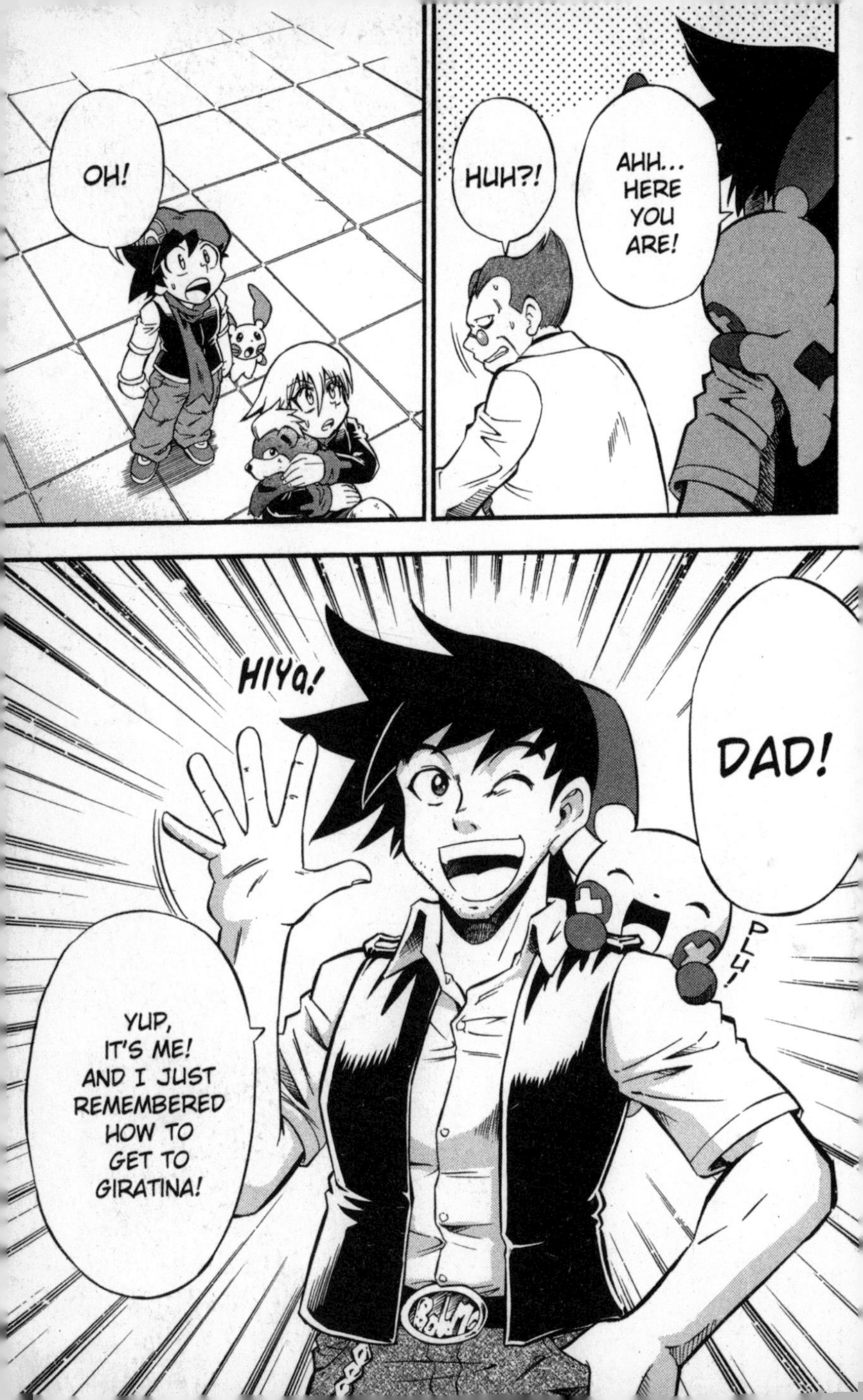
AHH... HERE YOU ARE!
HUH?!
OH!
DAD!
HIYA!
PLU!
YUP, IT'S ME! AND I JUST REMEMBERED HOW TO GET TO GIRATINA!

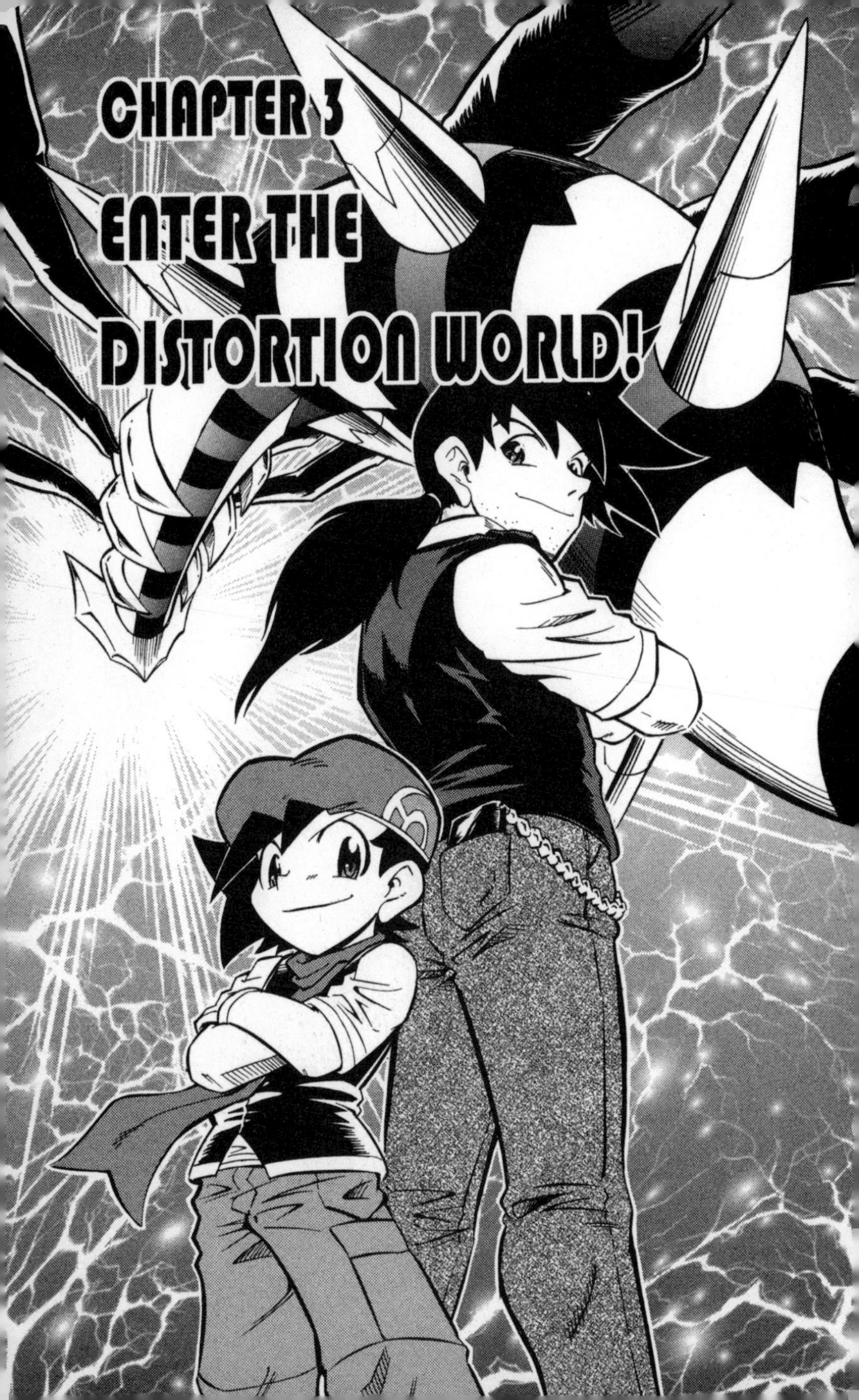
CHAPTER 3
ENTER THE
DISTORTION WORLD!

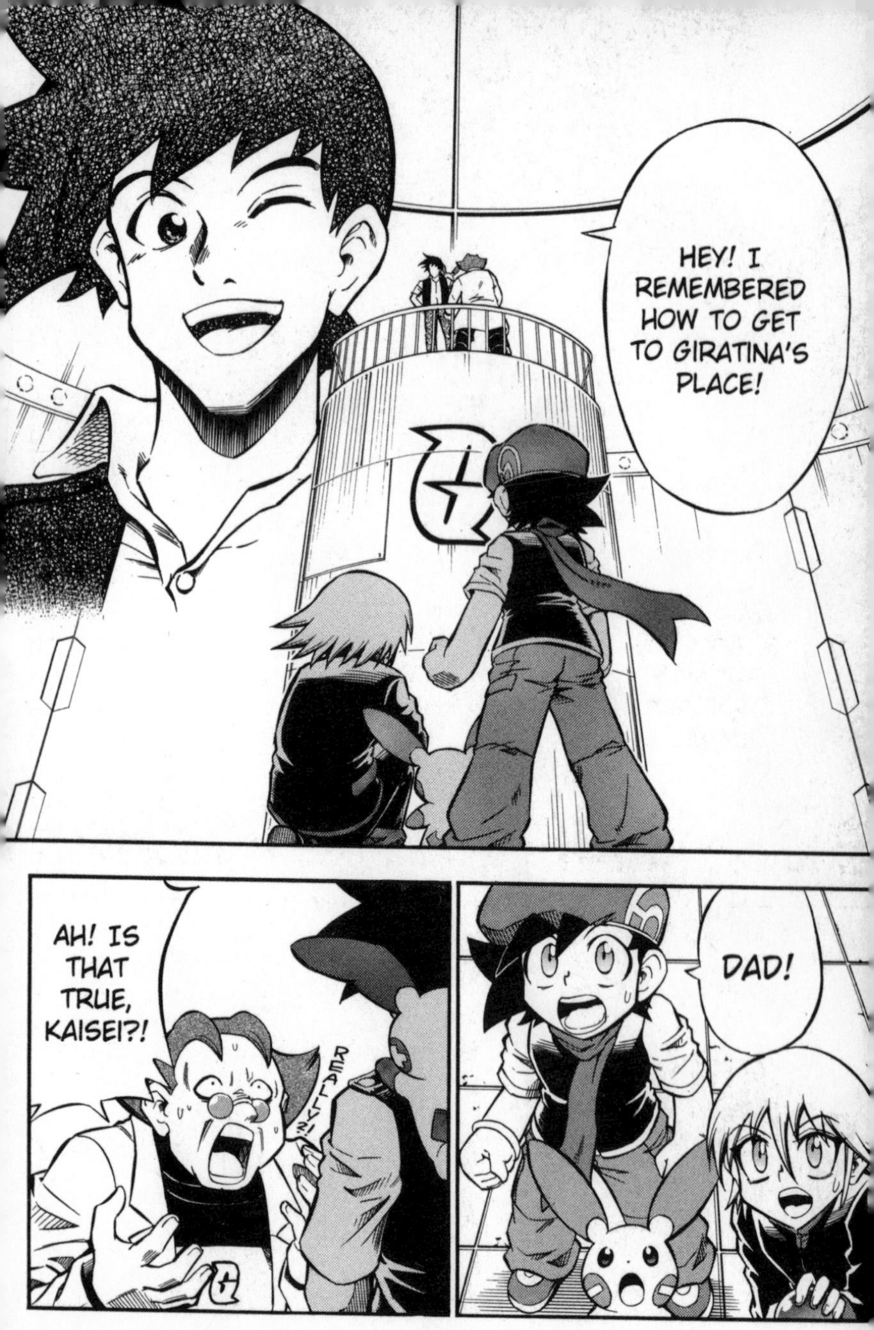
HEY! I REMEMBERED HOW TO GET TO GIRATINA'S PLACE!
DAD!
AH! IS THAT TRUE, KAISEI?!
REALLY?!

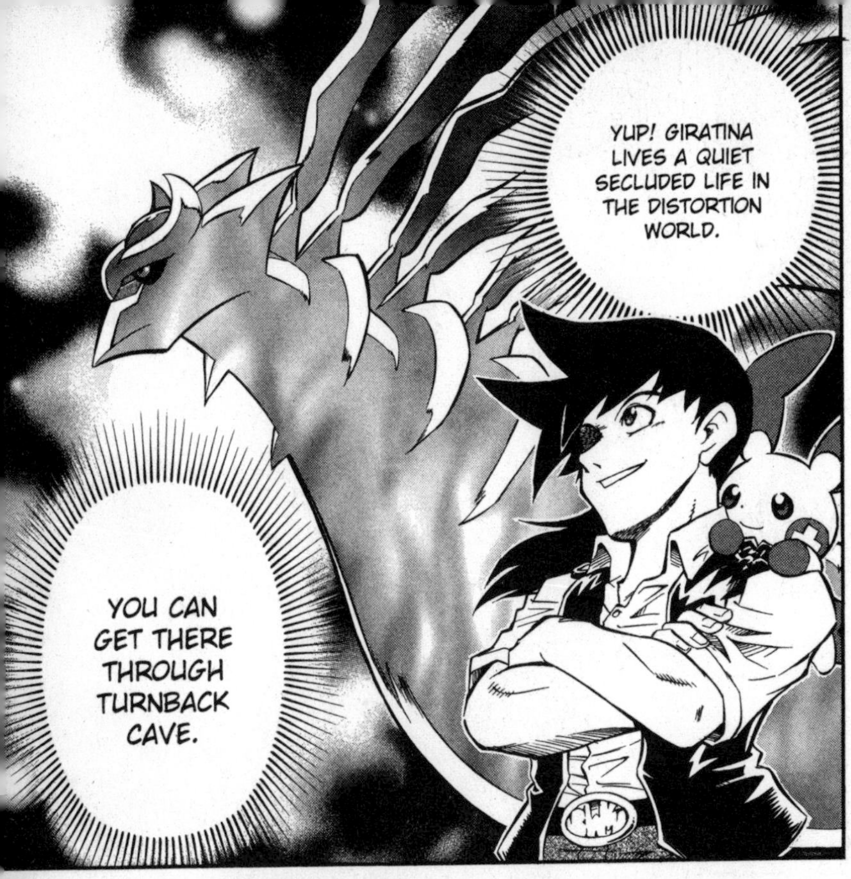
YUP! GIRATINA LIVES A QUIET SECLUDED LIFE IN THE DISTORTION WORLD.
YOU CAN GET THERE THROUGH TURNBACK CAVE.
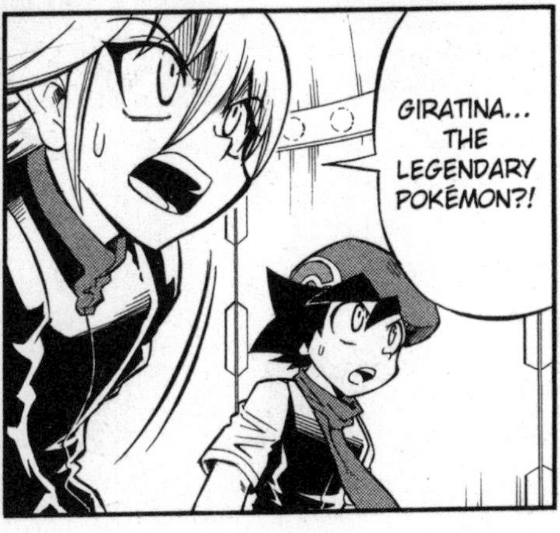
GIRATINA... THE LEGENDARY POKÉMON?!
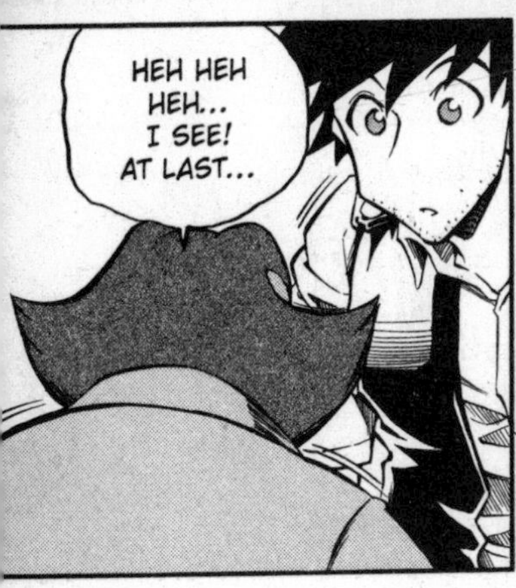
HEH HEH HEH... I SEE! AT LAST...

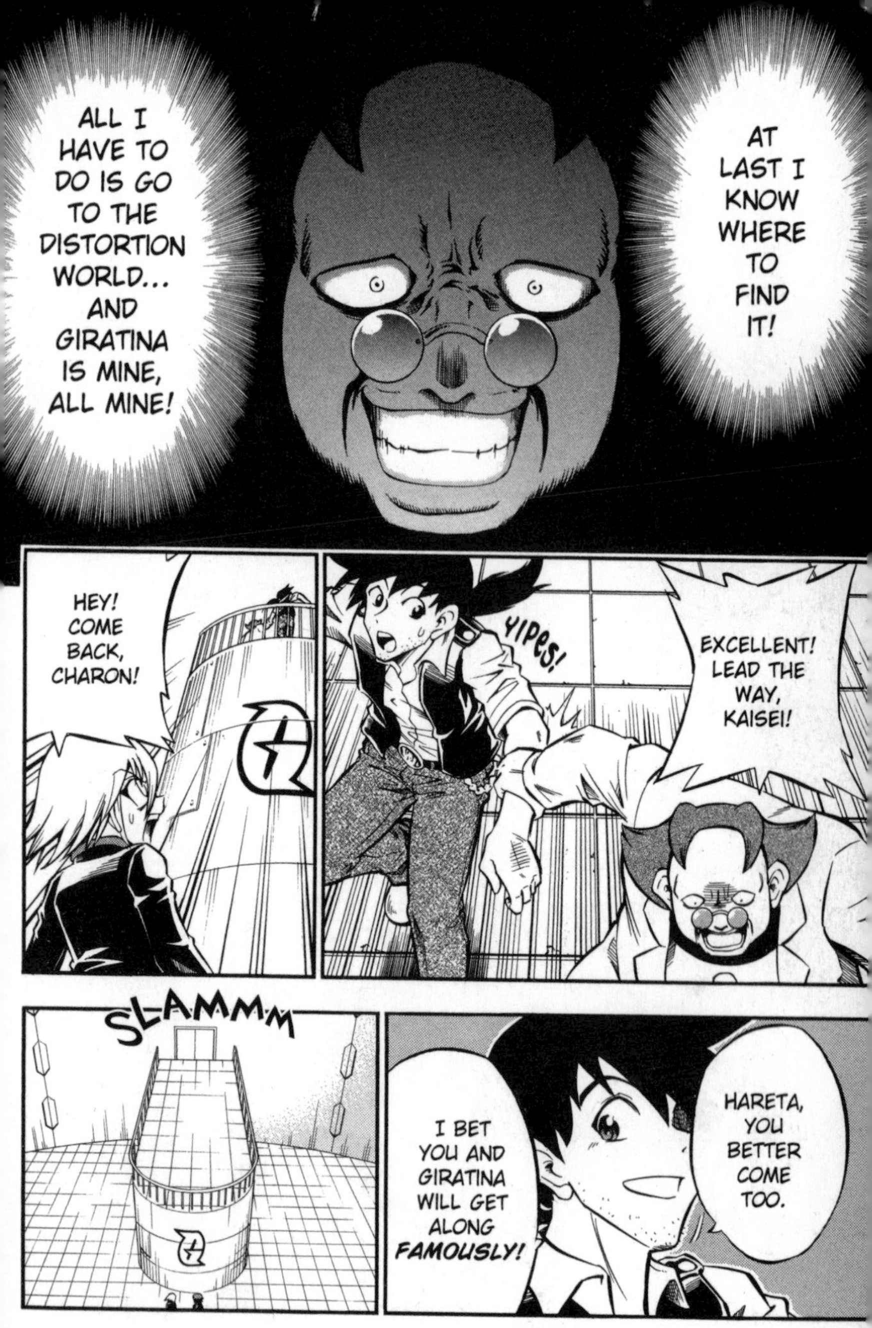
AT LAST I KNOW WHERE TO FIND IT!
ALL I HAVE TO DO IS GO TO THE DISTORTION WORLD... AND GIRATINA IS MINE, ALL MINE!
EXCELLENT! LEAD THE WAY, KAISEI!
YIPES!
HEY! COME BACK, CHARON!
HARETA, YOU BETTER COME TOO.
I BET YOU AND GIRATINA WILL GET ALONG FAMOUSLY!
SLAMMM

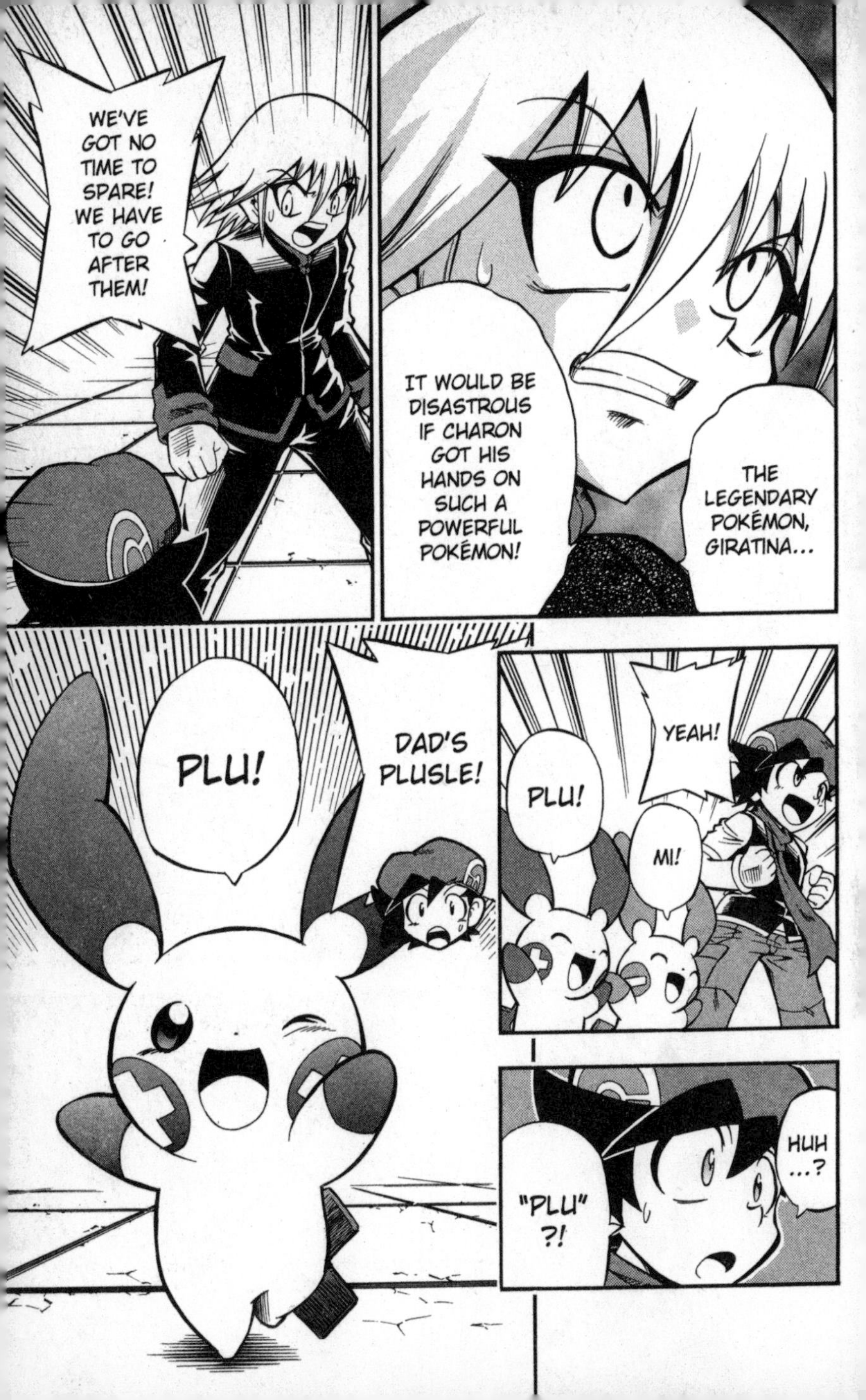
THE LEGENDARY POKÉMON, GIRATINA...
IT WOULD BE DISASTROUS IF CHARON GOT HIS HANDS ON SUCH A POWERFUL POKÉMON!
WE'VE GOT NO TIME TO SPARE! WE HAVE TO GO AFTER THEM!
YEAH!
PLU!
MI!
HUH...?
"PLU"?!
DAD'S PLUSLE!
PLU!

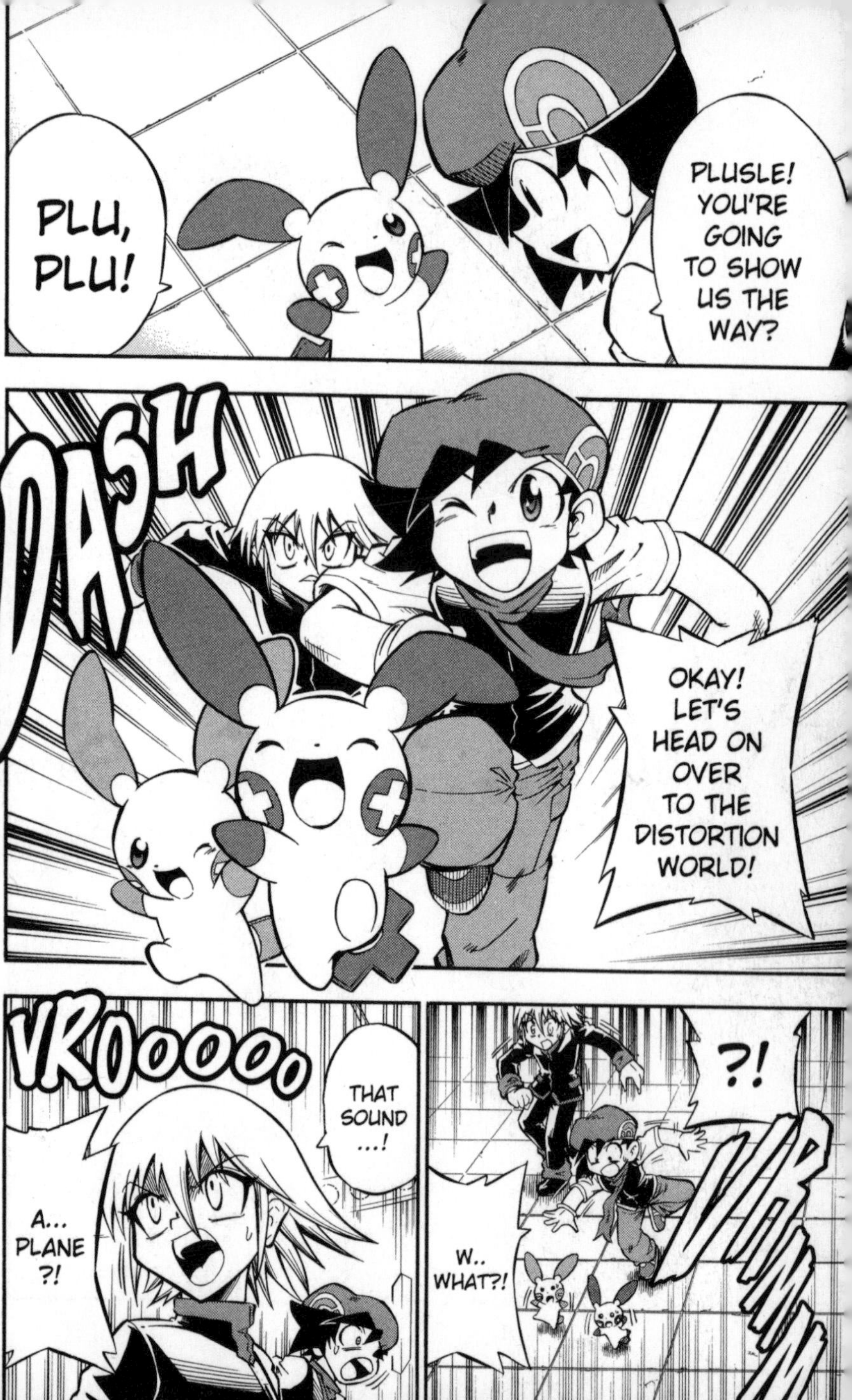
PLUSLE! YOU'RE GOING TO SHOW US THE WAY?
PLU, PLU!
DASH
OKAY! LET'S HEAD ON OVER TO THE DISTORTION WORLD!
?!
W.. WHAT?!
VROOOOO
THAT SOUND ...!
A... PLANE ?!

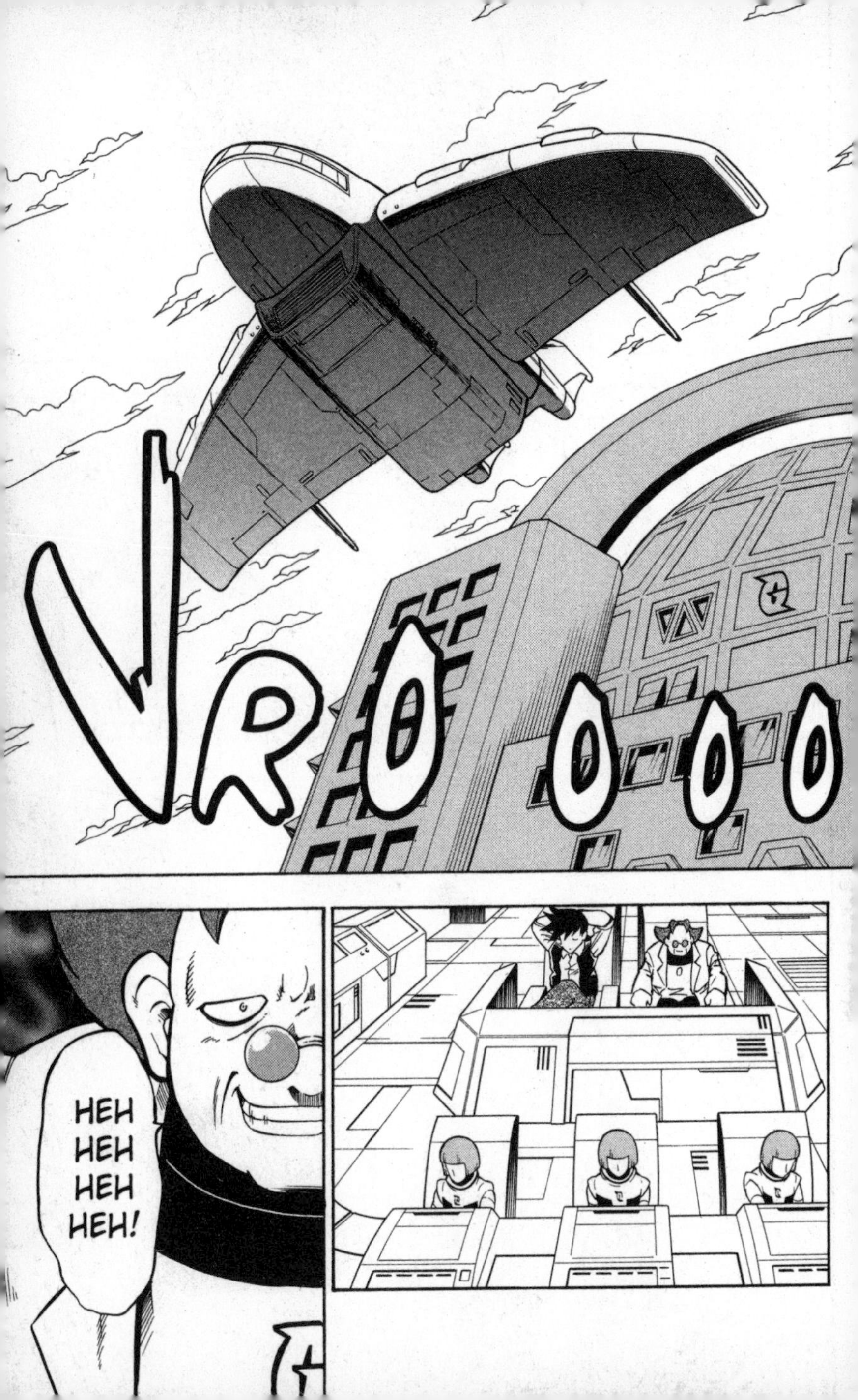
VROOOOO
HEH HEH HEH HEH!

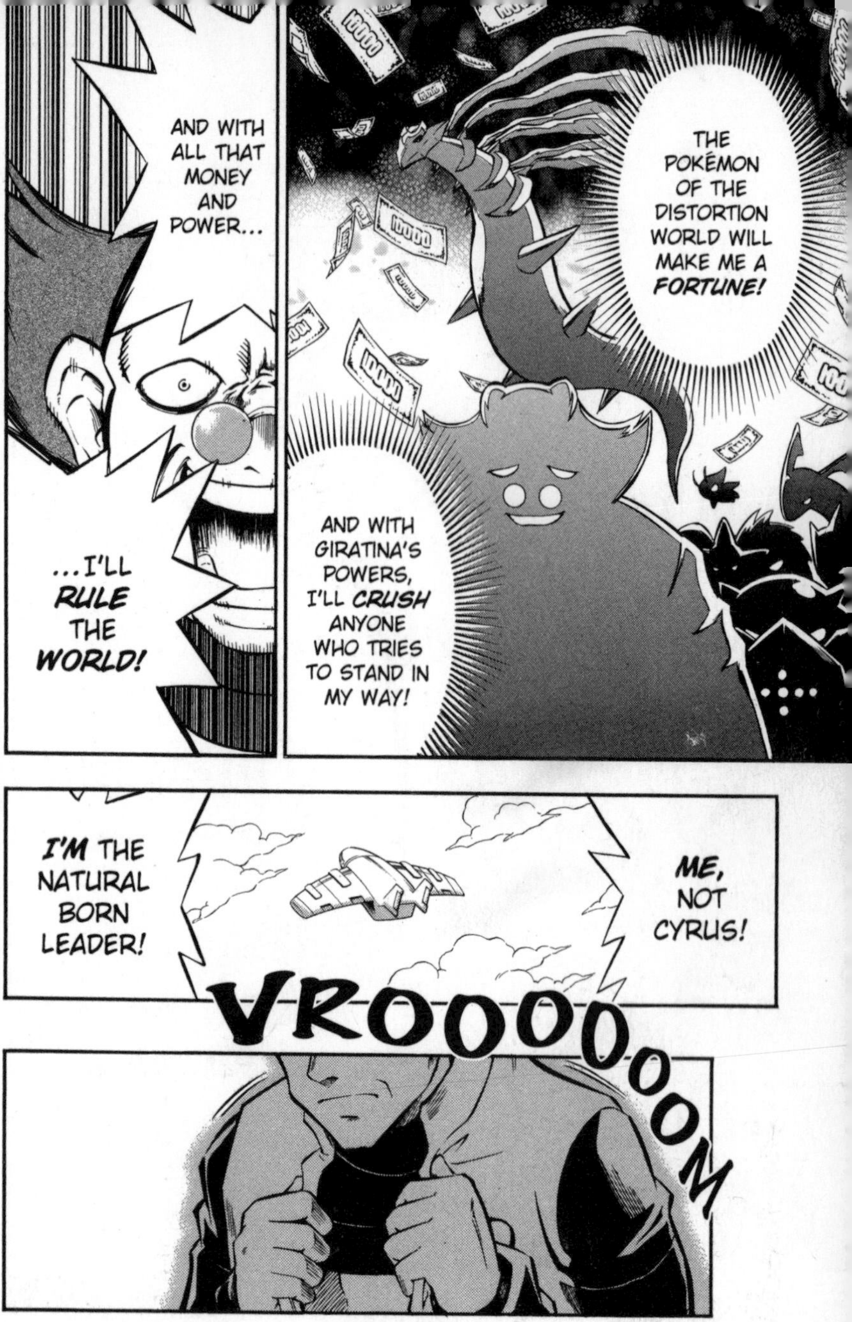
THE POKÉMON OF THE DISTORTION WORLD WILL MAKE ME A FORTUNE!
AND WITH GIRATINA'S POWERS, I'LL CRUSH ANYONE WHO TRIES TO STAND IN MY WAY!
AND WITH ALL THAT MONEY AND POWER...
...I'LL RULE THE WORLD!
I'M THE NATURAL BORN LEADER!
ME, NOT CYRUS!
VROOOOOOOM

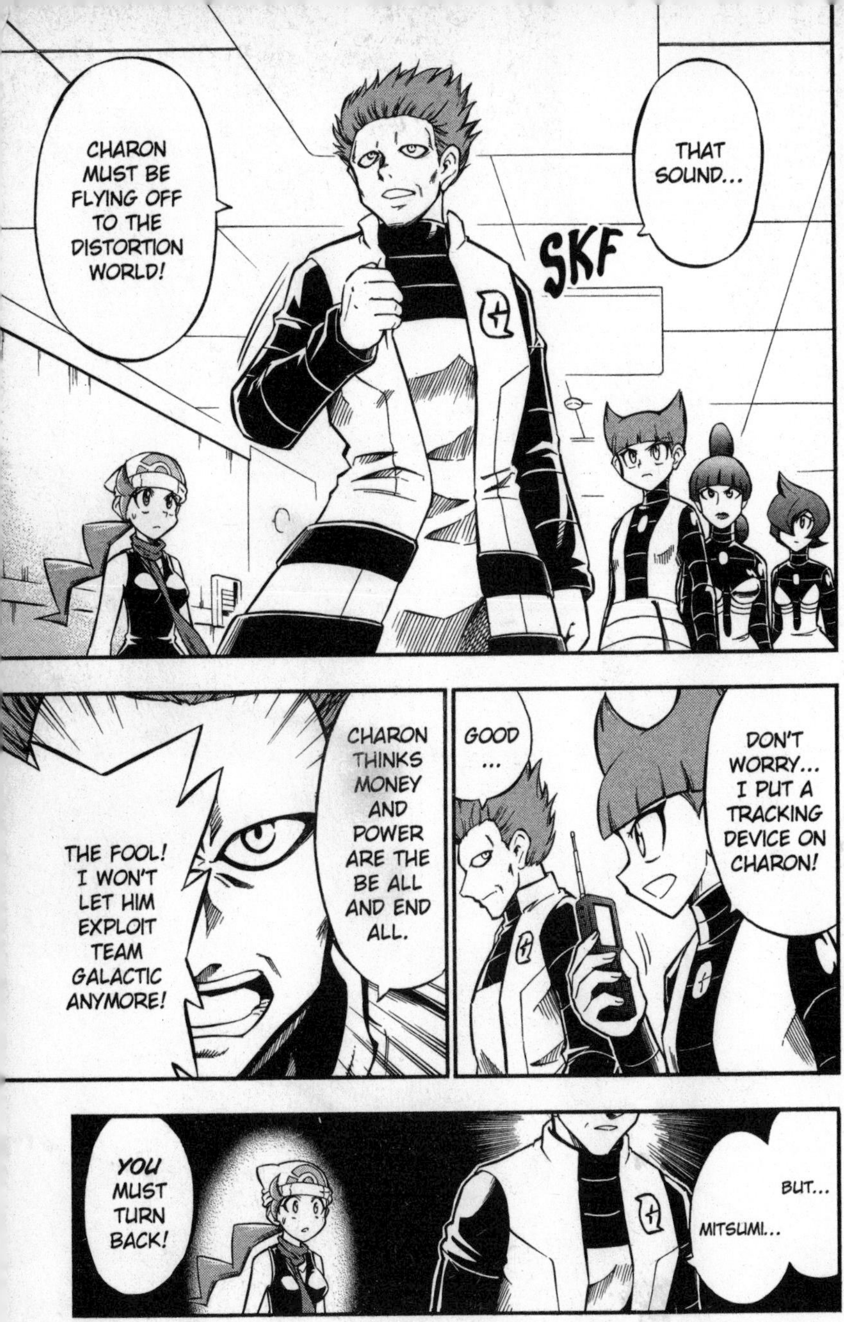
THAT SOUND...
SKF
CHARON MUST BE FLYING OFF TO THE DISTORTION WORLD!
DON'T WORRY... I PUT A TRACKING DEVICE ON CHARON!
GOOD...
CHARON THINKS MONEY AND POWER ARE THE BE ALL AND END ALL.
THE FOOL! I WON'T LET HIM EXPLOIT TEAM GALACTIC ANYMORE!
BUT... MITSUMI...
YOU MUST TURN BACK!

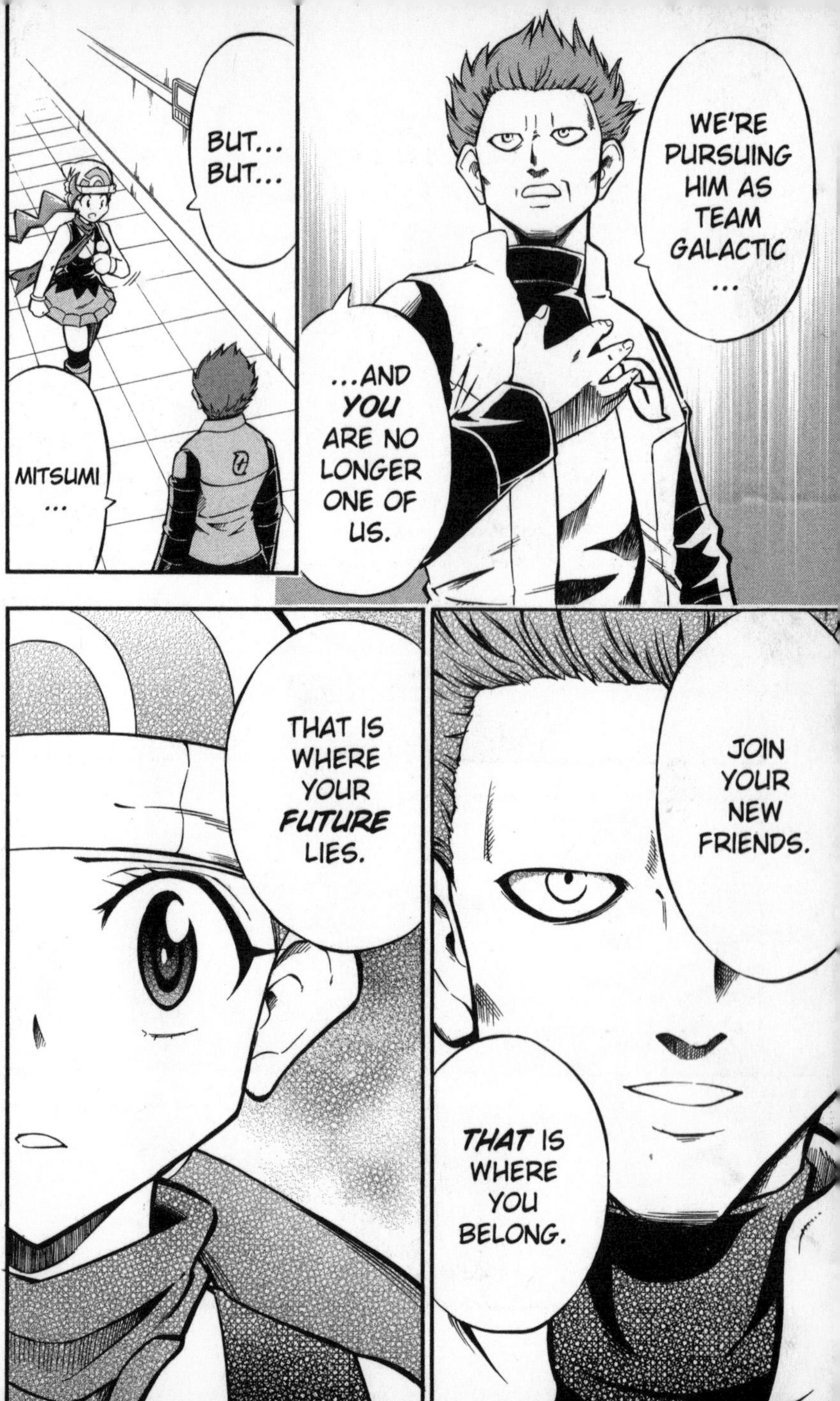
WE'RE PURSUING HIM AS TEAM GALACTIC...
...AND *YOU* ARE NO LONGER ONE OF US.
BUT... BUT...
MITSUMI...
JOIN YOUR NEW FRIENDS.
THAT IS WHERE YOU BELONG.
THAT IS WHERE YOUR *FUTURE* LIES.

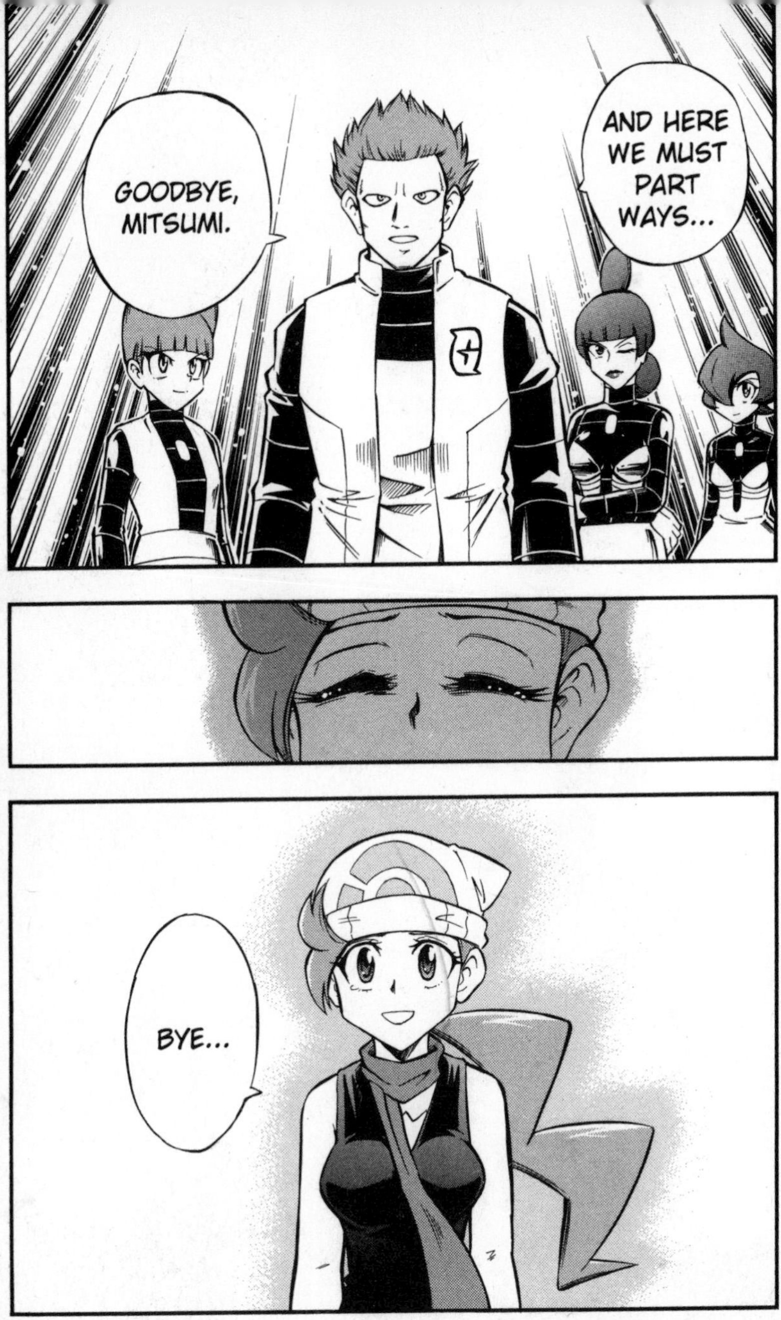
AND HERE WE MUST PART WAYS...
GOODBYE, MITSUMI.
BYE...

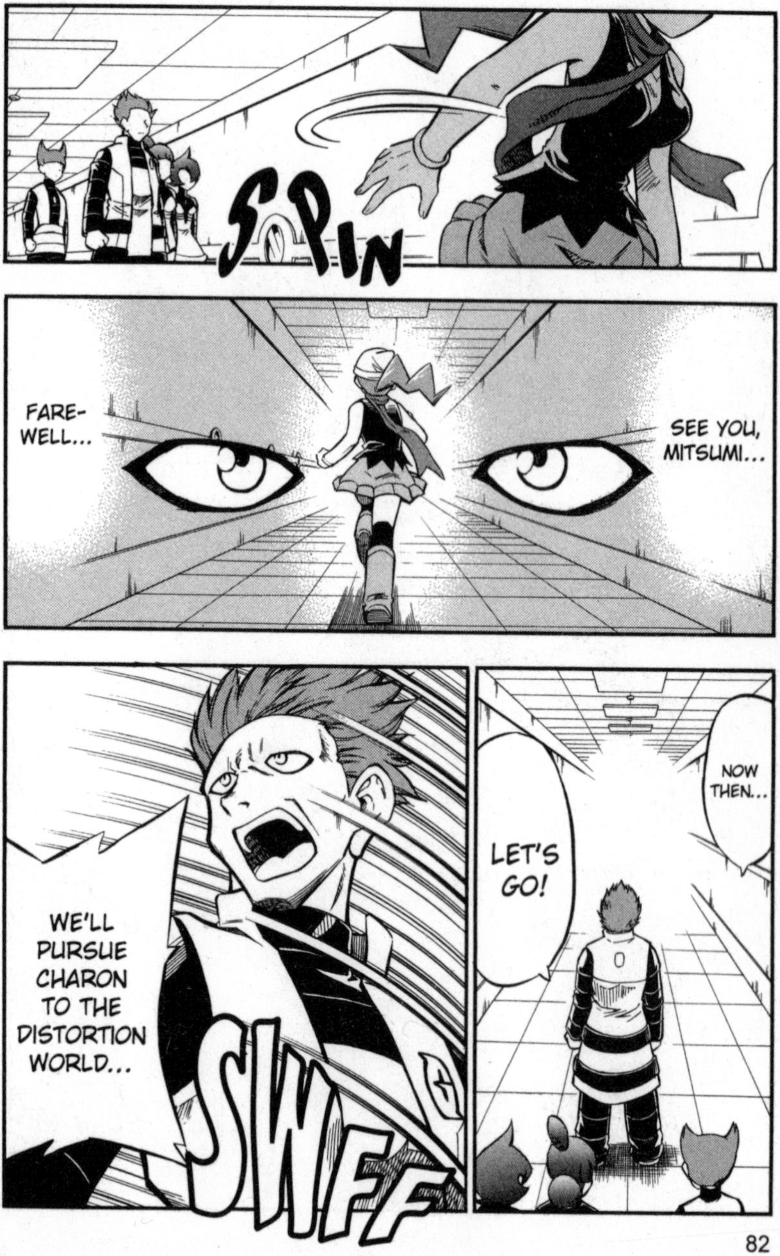
SPIN
SEE YOU, MITSUMI...
FARE-WELL...
NOW THEN...
LET'S GO!
WE'LL PURSUE CHARON TO THE DISTORTION WORLD...
SWFF

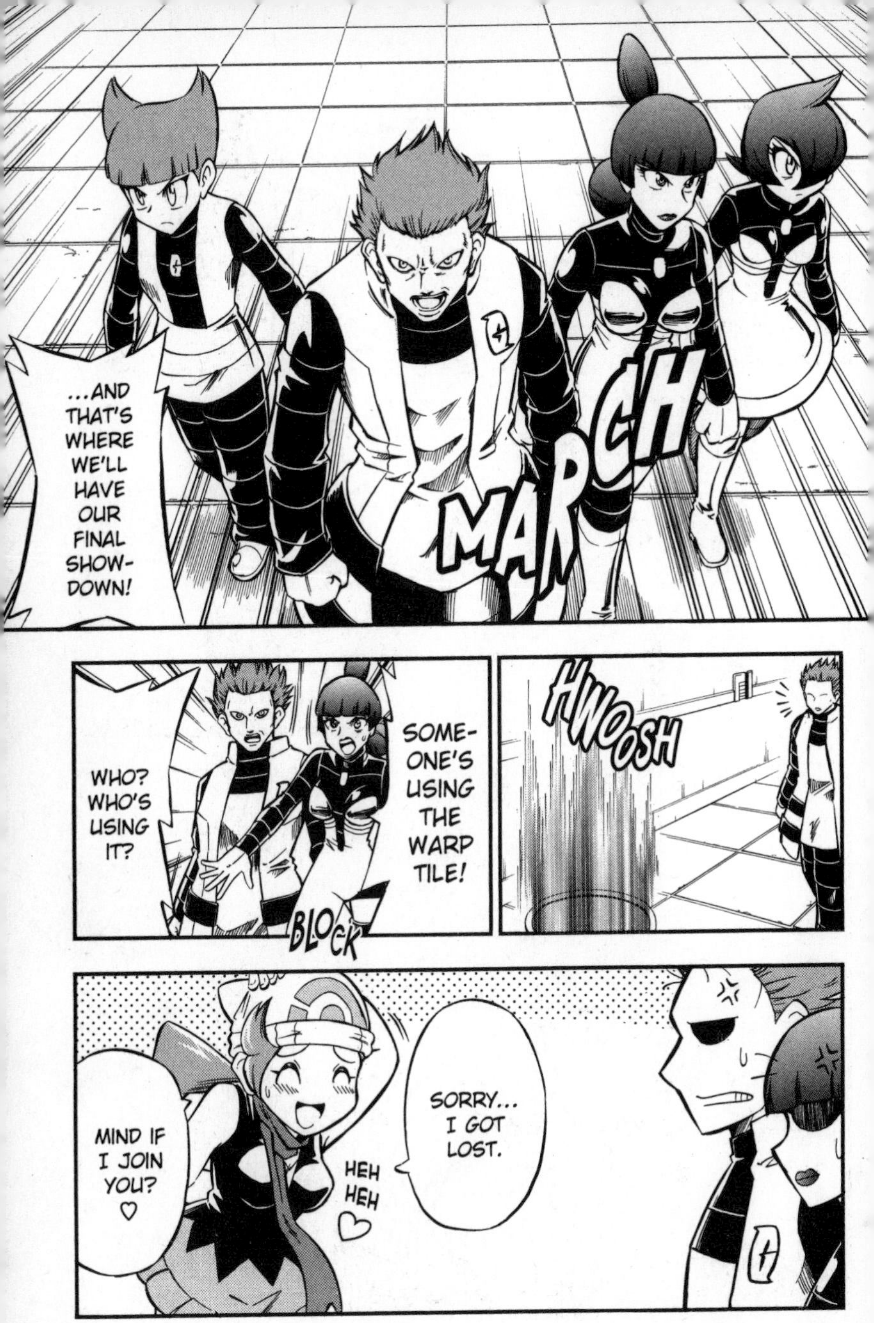
...AND THAT'S WHERE WE'LL HAVE OUR FINAL SHOW-DOWN!
MARCH
HWOOSH
SOME-ONE'S USING THE WARP TILE!
WHO? WHO'S USING IT?
BLOCK
SORRY... I GOT LOST.
HEH HEH ♡
MIND IF I JOIN YOU? ♡

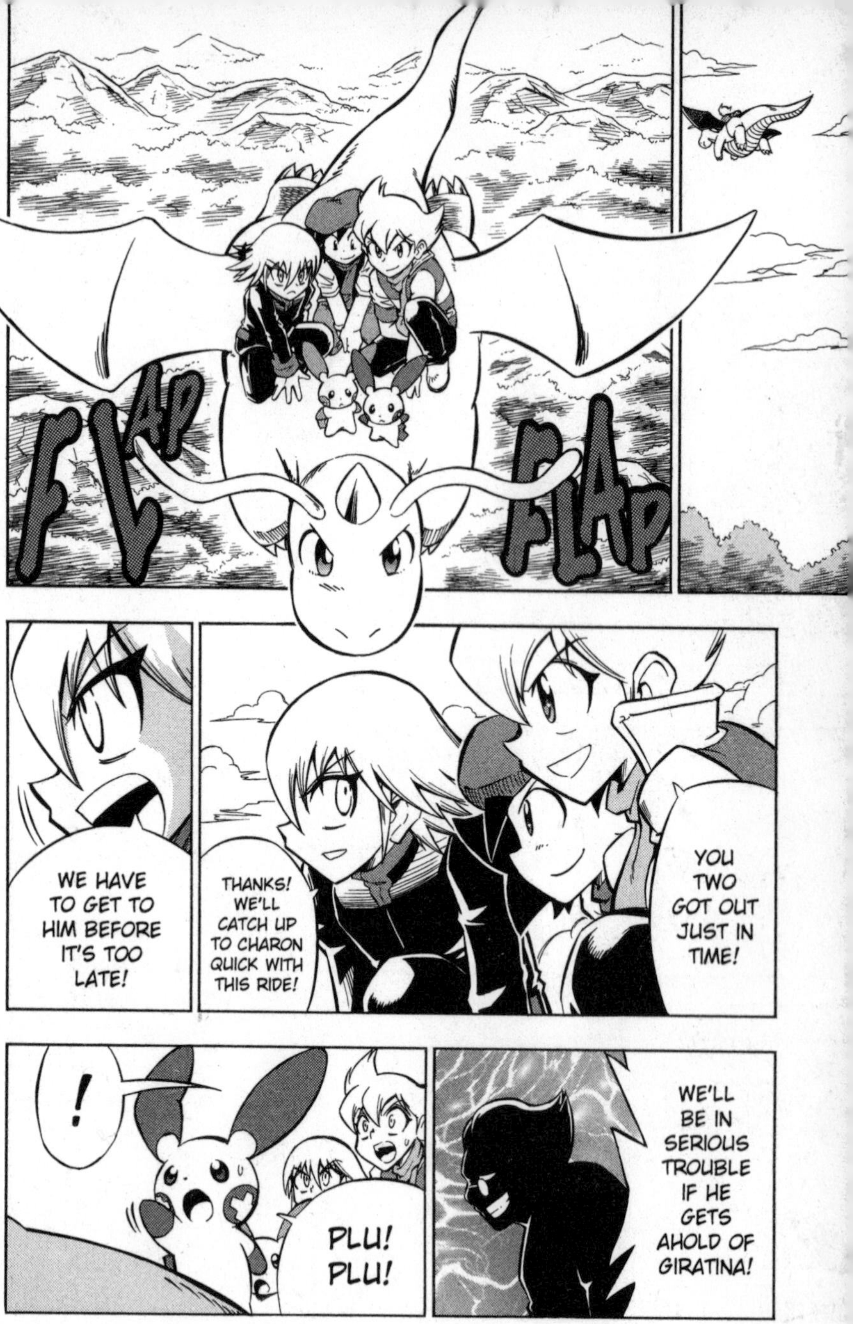
FLAP
FLAP
YOU TWO GOT OUT JUST IN TIME!
THANKS! WE'LL CATCH UP TO CHARON QUICK WITH THIS RIDE!
WE HAVE TO GET TO HIM BEFORE IT'S TOO LATE!
WE'LL BE IN SERIOUS TROUBLE IF HE GETS AHOLD OF GIRATINA!
!
PLU! PLU!

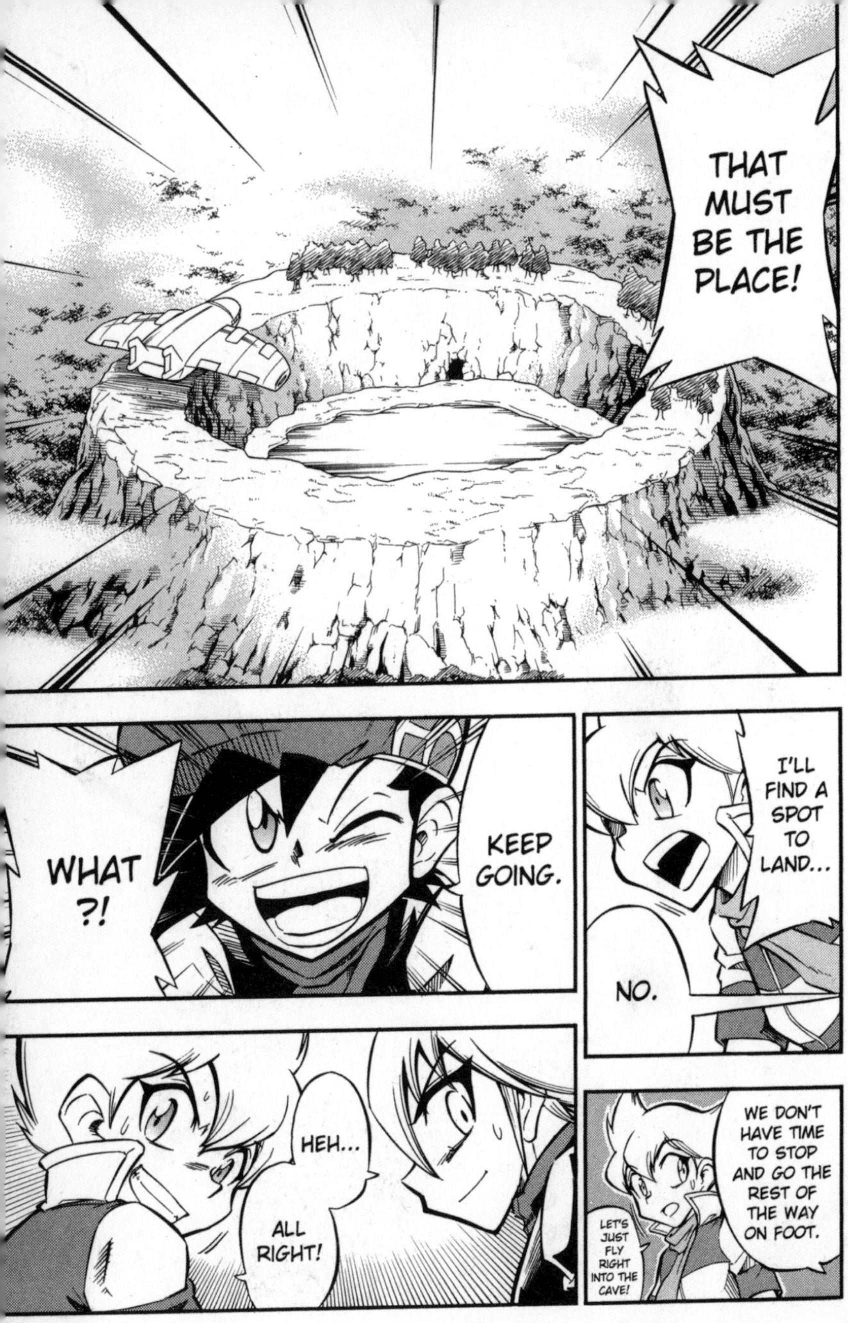
THAT MUST BE THE PLACE!
I'LL FIND A SPOT TO LAND...
NO.
KEEP GOING.
WHAT?!
WE DON'T HAVE TIME TO STOP AND GO THE REST OF THE WAY ON FOOT.
LET'S JUST FLY RIGHT INTO THE CAVE!
HEH...
ALL RIGHT!

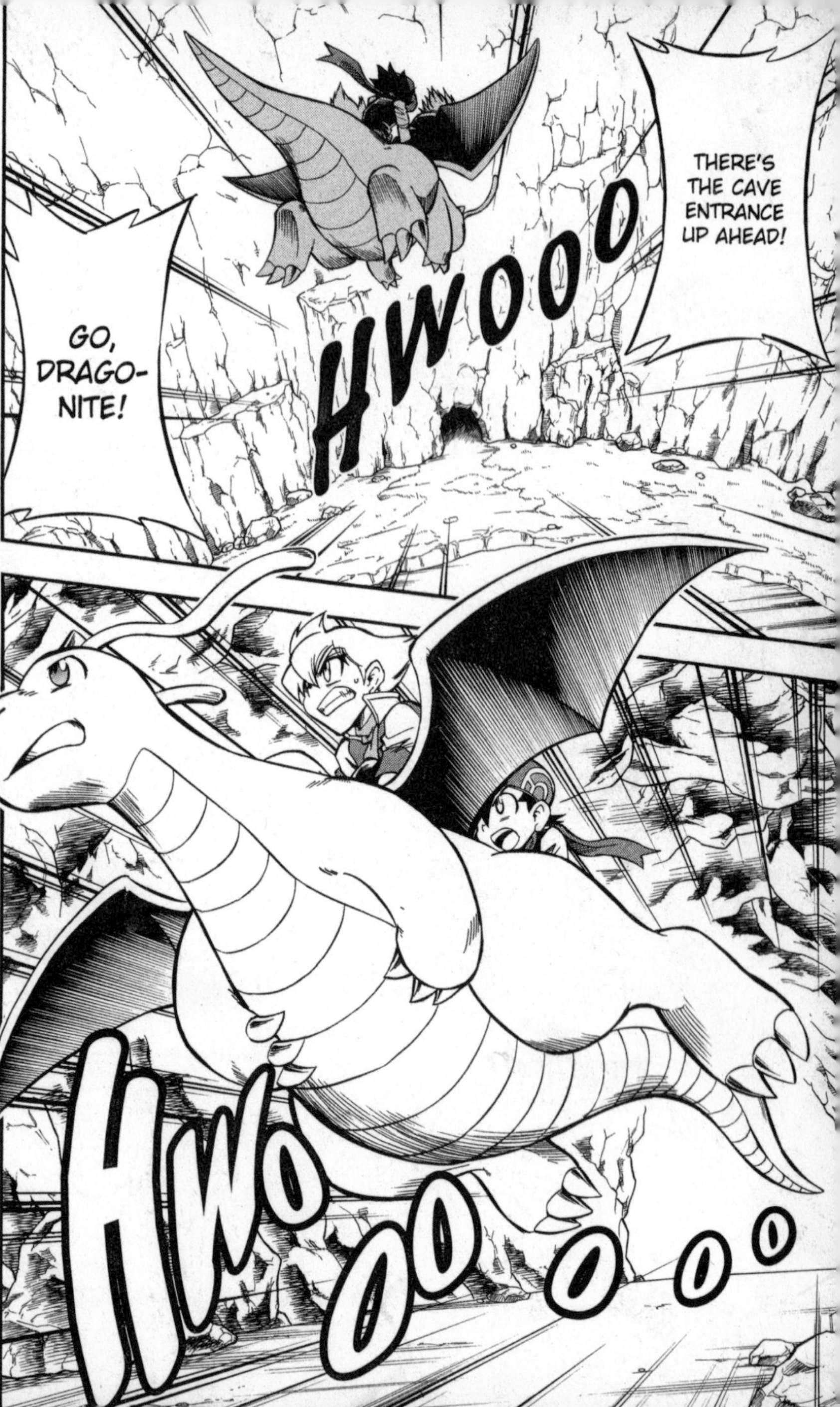
THERE'S THE CAVE ENTRANCE UP AHEAD!
HWOOO
GO, DRAGO-NITE!
HWOOOO...

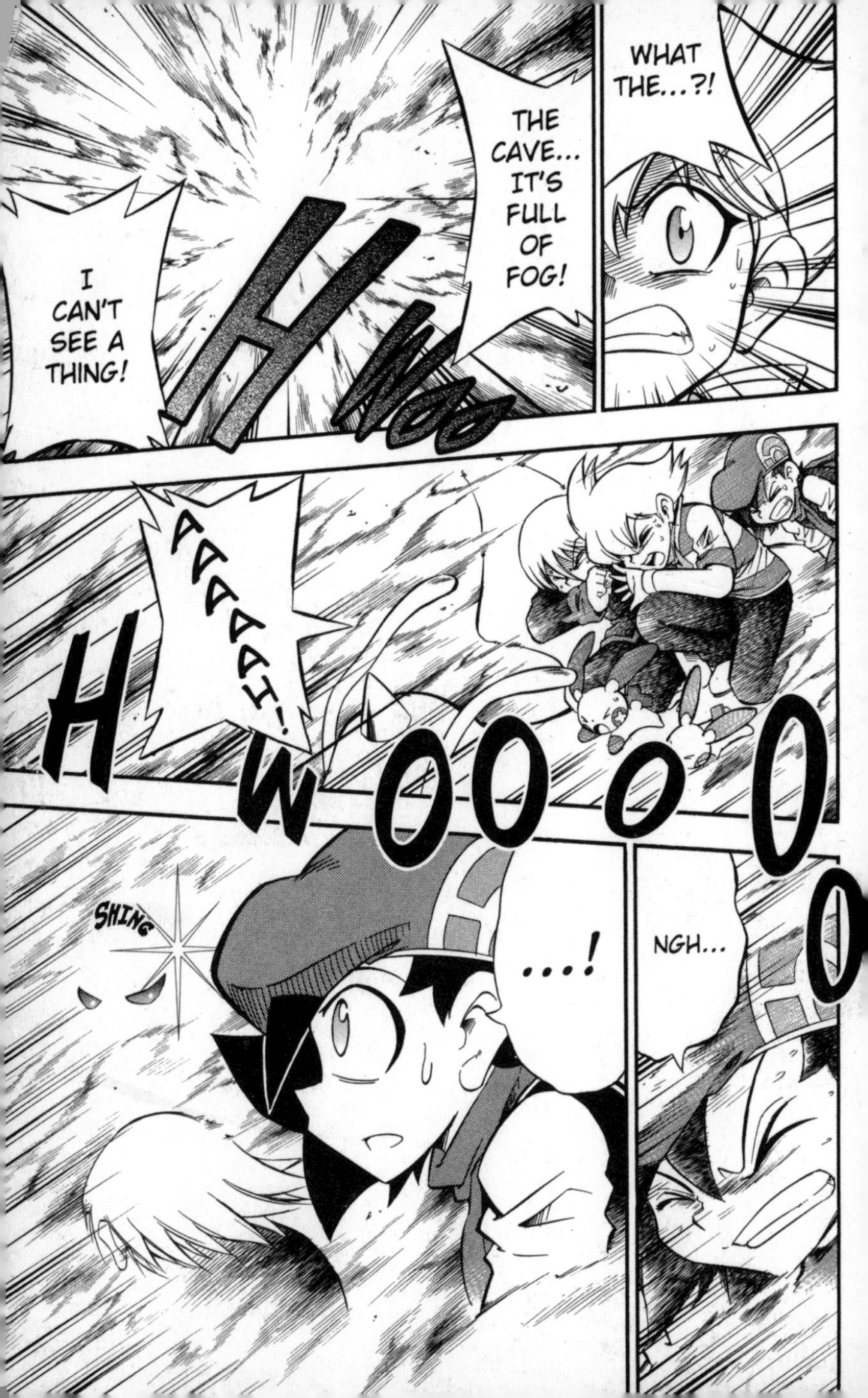
WHAT THE...?!
THE CAVE... IT'S FULL OF FOG!
I CAN'T SEE A THING!
HWOO
AAAAAAH!
HWOOOOO
NGH...
...!
SHING

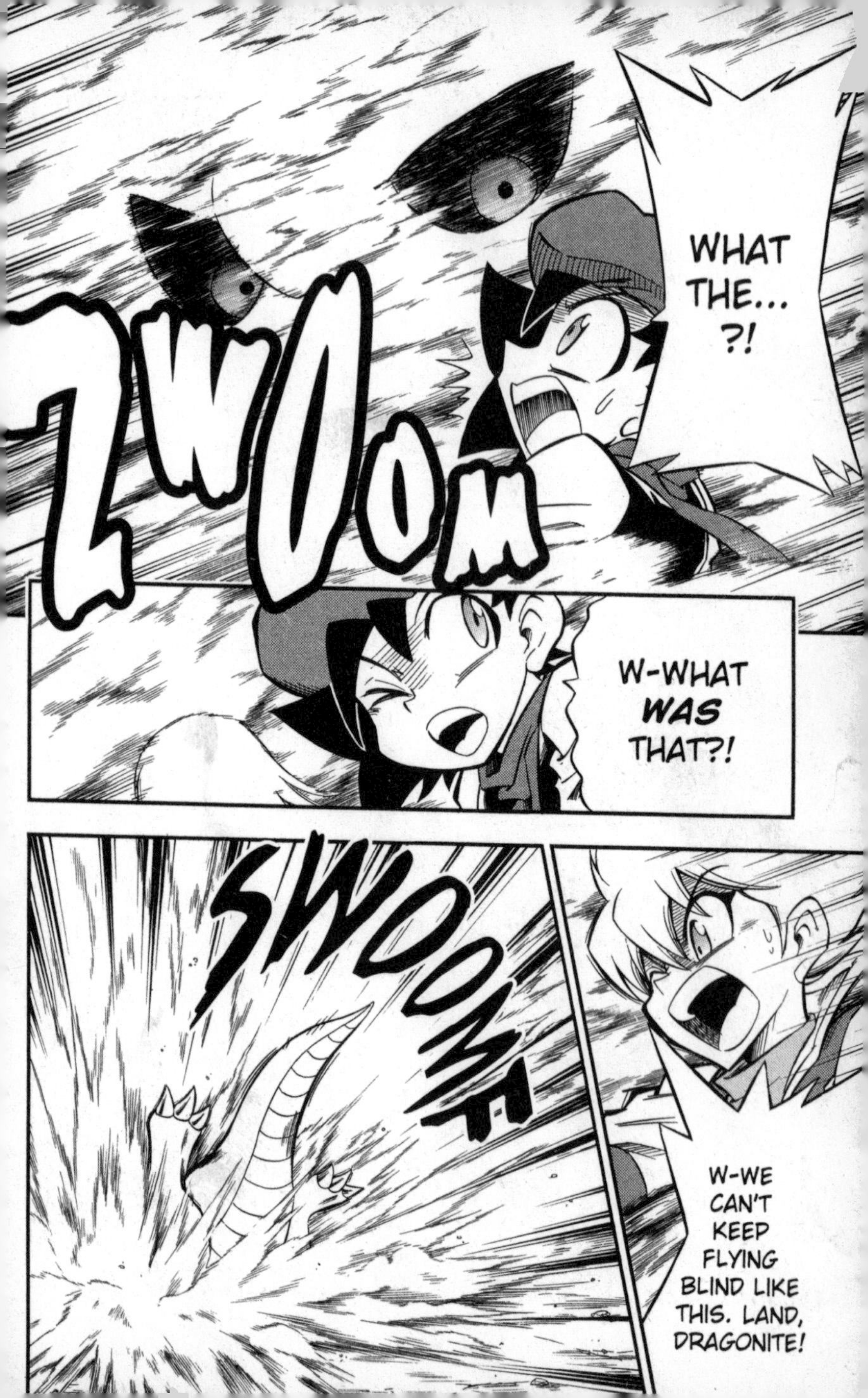
ZWOOM
WHAT THE... ?!
W-WHAT *WAS* THAT?!
W-WE CAN'T KEEP FLYING BLIND LIKE THIS. LAND, DRAGONITE!
SWOOMF

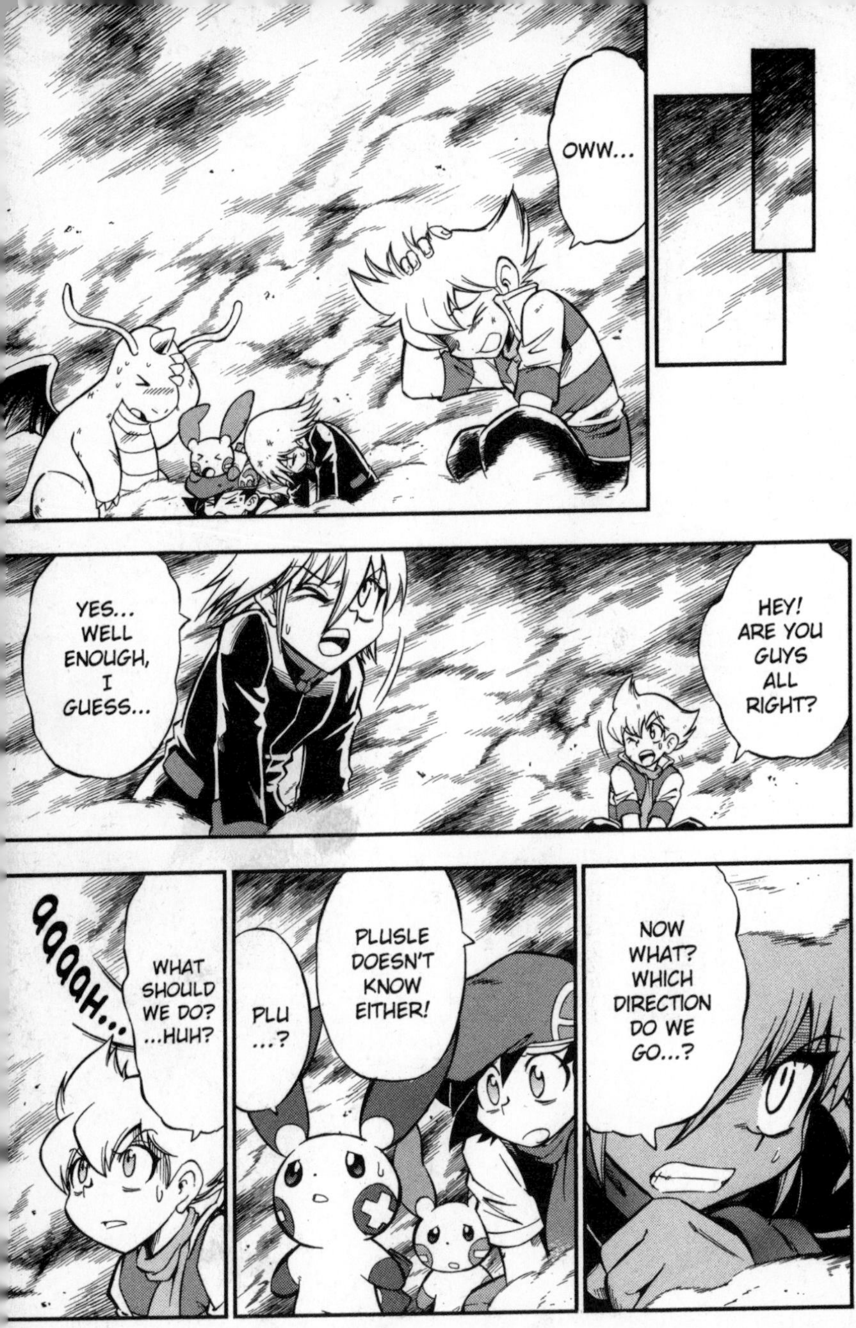
OWW...
HEY! ARE YOU GUYS ALL RIGHT?
YES... WELL ENOUGH, I GUESS...
NOW WHAT? WHICH DIRECTION DO WE GO...?
PLUSLE DOESN'T KNOW EITHER!
PLU ...?
WHAT SHOULD WE DO? ...HUH?
aaaah...

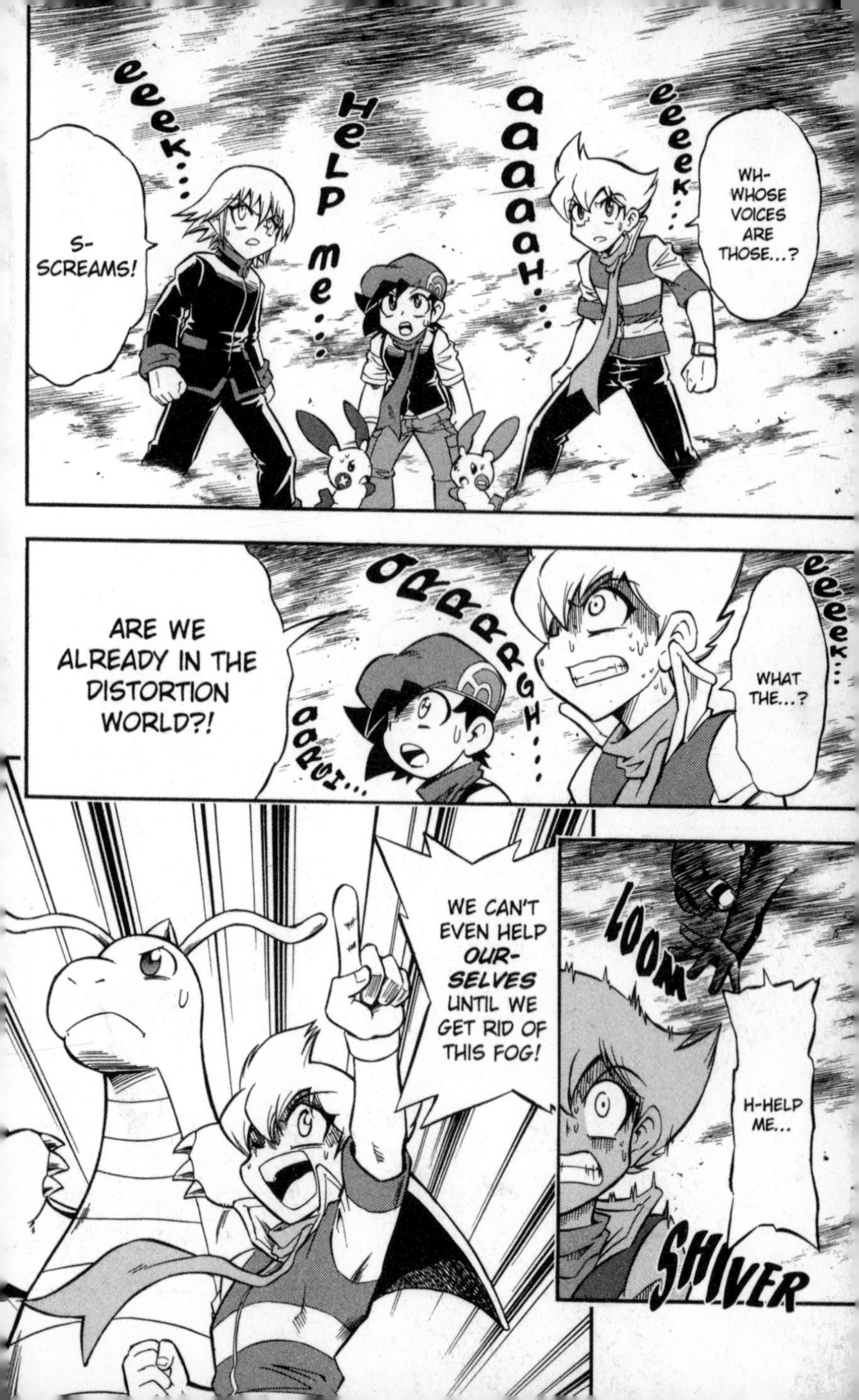
eeeek...
WH- WHOSE VOICES ARE THOSE...?
aaaaaaH...
HeLP me...
eeek...
S- SCREAMS!
eeeek...
WHAT THE...?
GRRRRRGH...
ARE WE ALREADY IN THE DISTORTION WORLD?!
LOOM
H-HELP ME...
SHIVER
WE CAN'T EVEN HELP OUR-SELVES UNTIL WE GET RID OF THIS FOG!

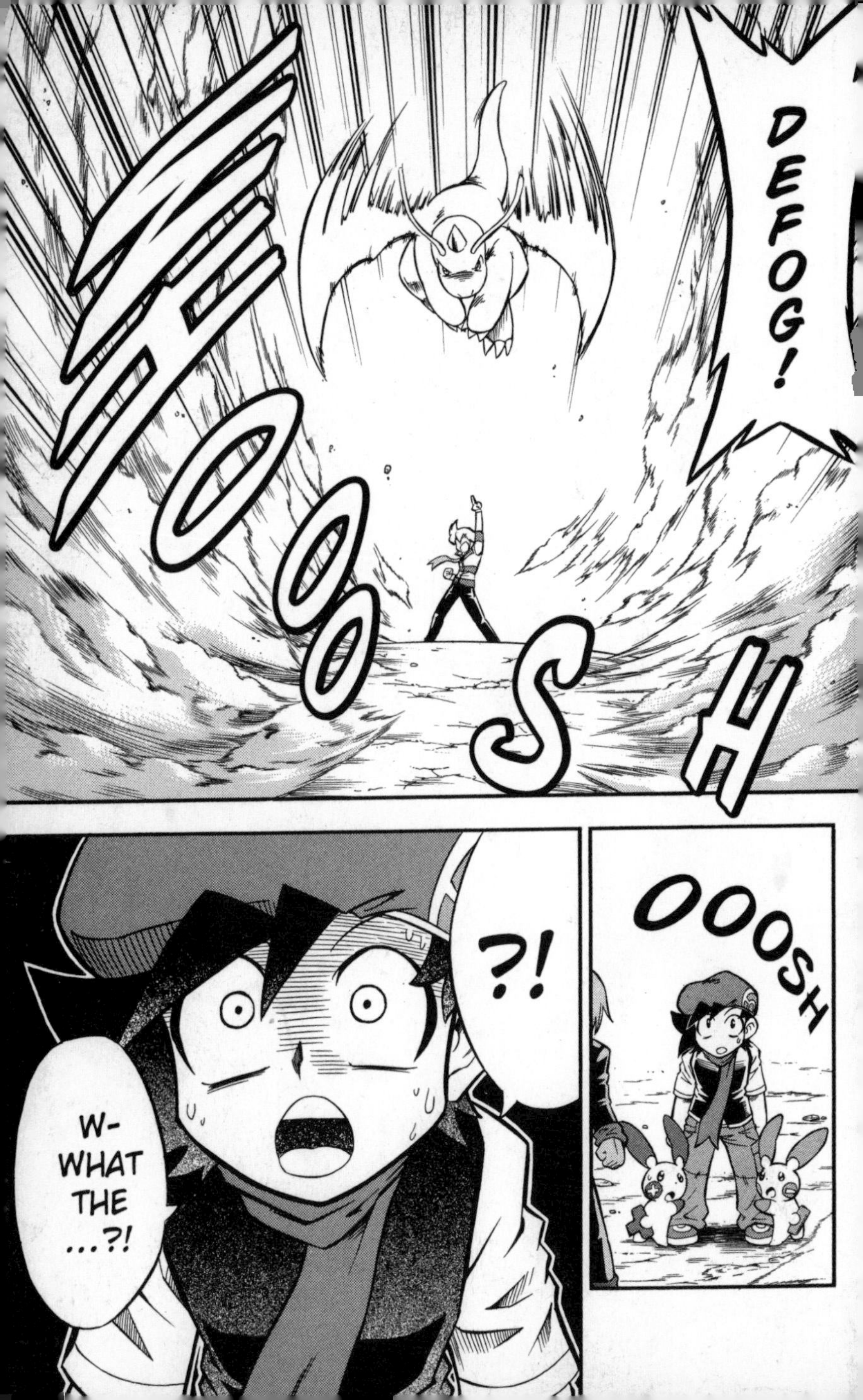
DEFOG!
WHOOOSH
OOOSH
?!
W- WHAT THE ...?!

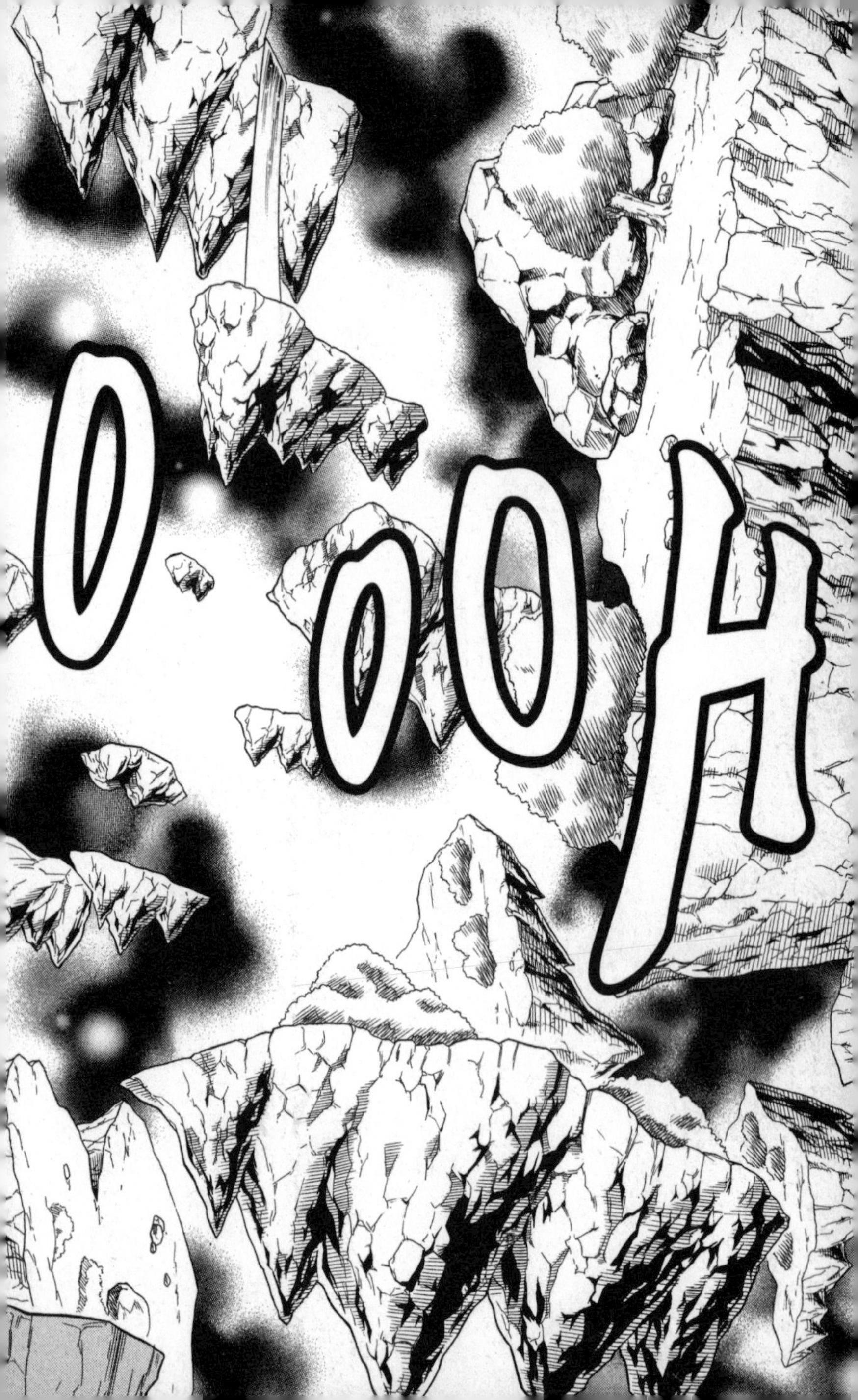
O OOH

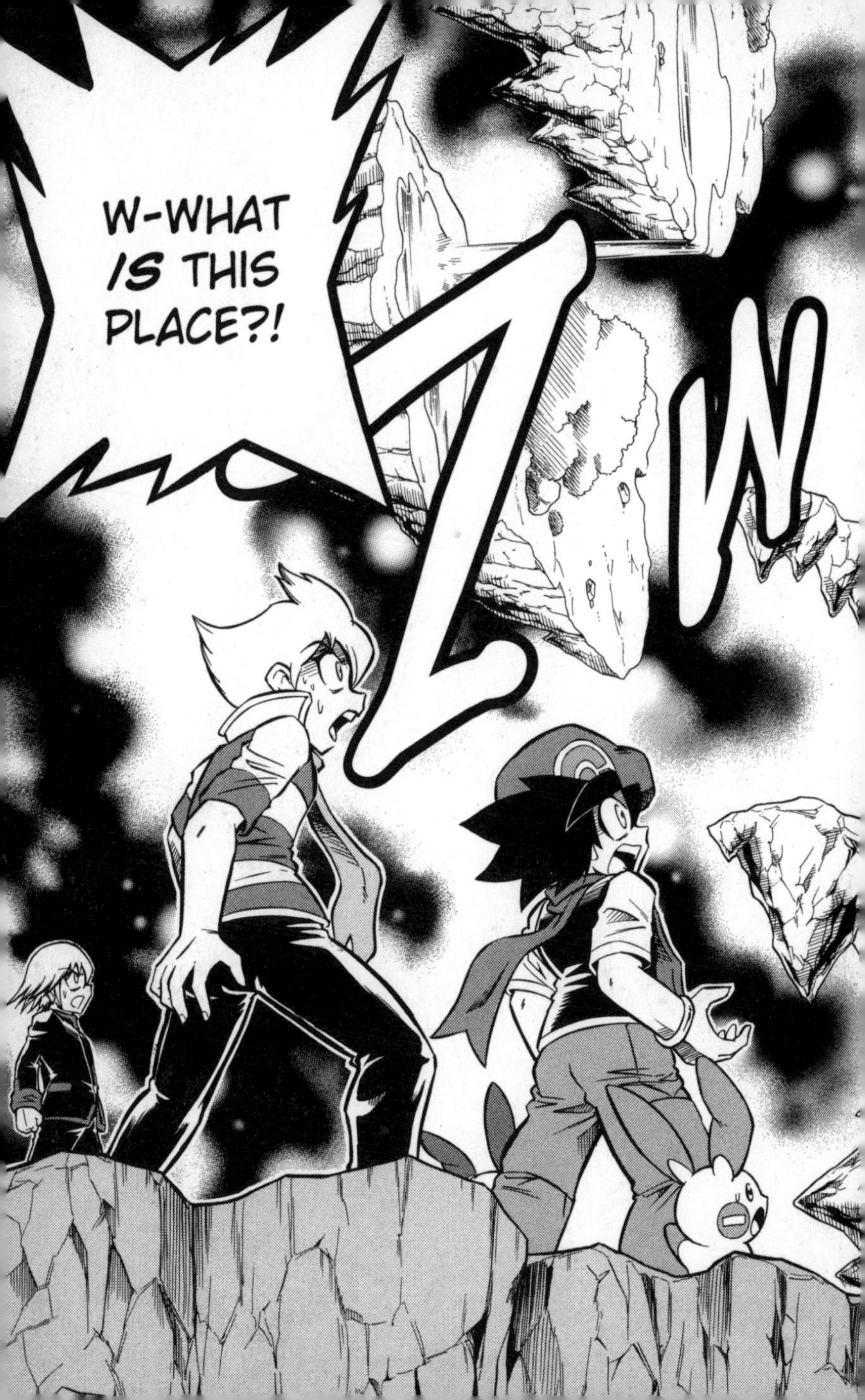
W-WHAT IS THIS PLACE?!
ZW

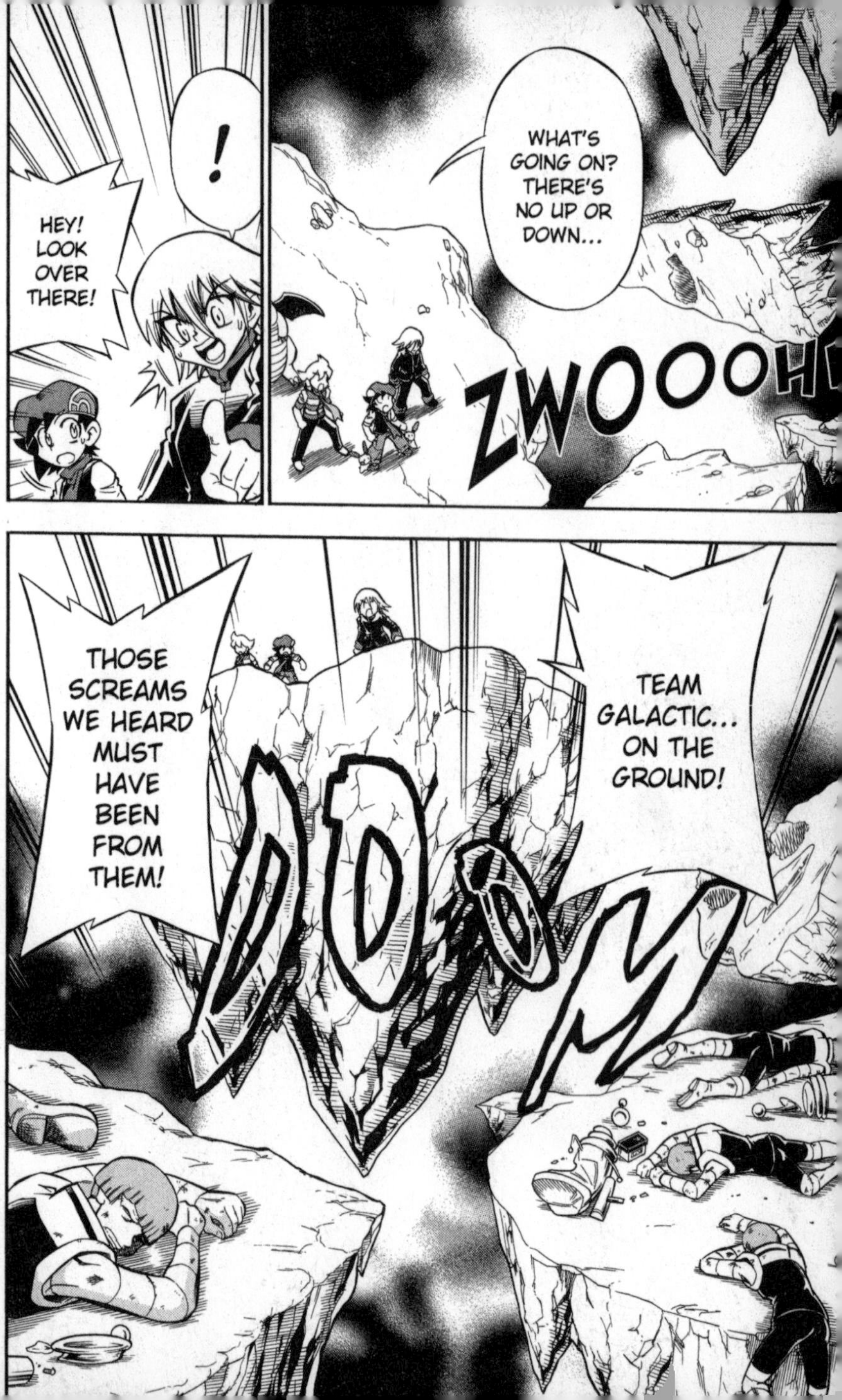
WHAT'S GOING ON? THERE'S NO UP OR DOWN...
ZWOOOOH
!
HEY! LOOK OVER THERE!
TEAM GALACTIC... ON THE GROUND!
THOSE SCREAMS WE HEARD MUST HAVE BEEN FROM THEM!
DOOM

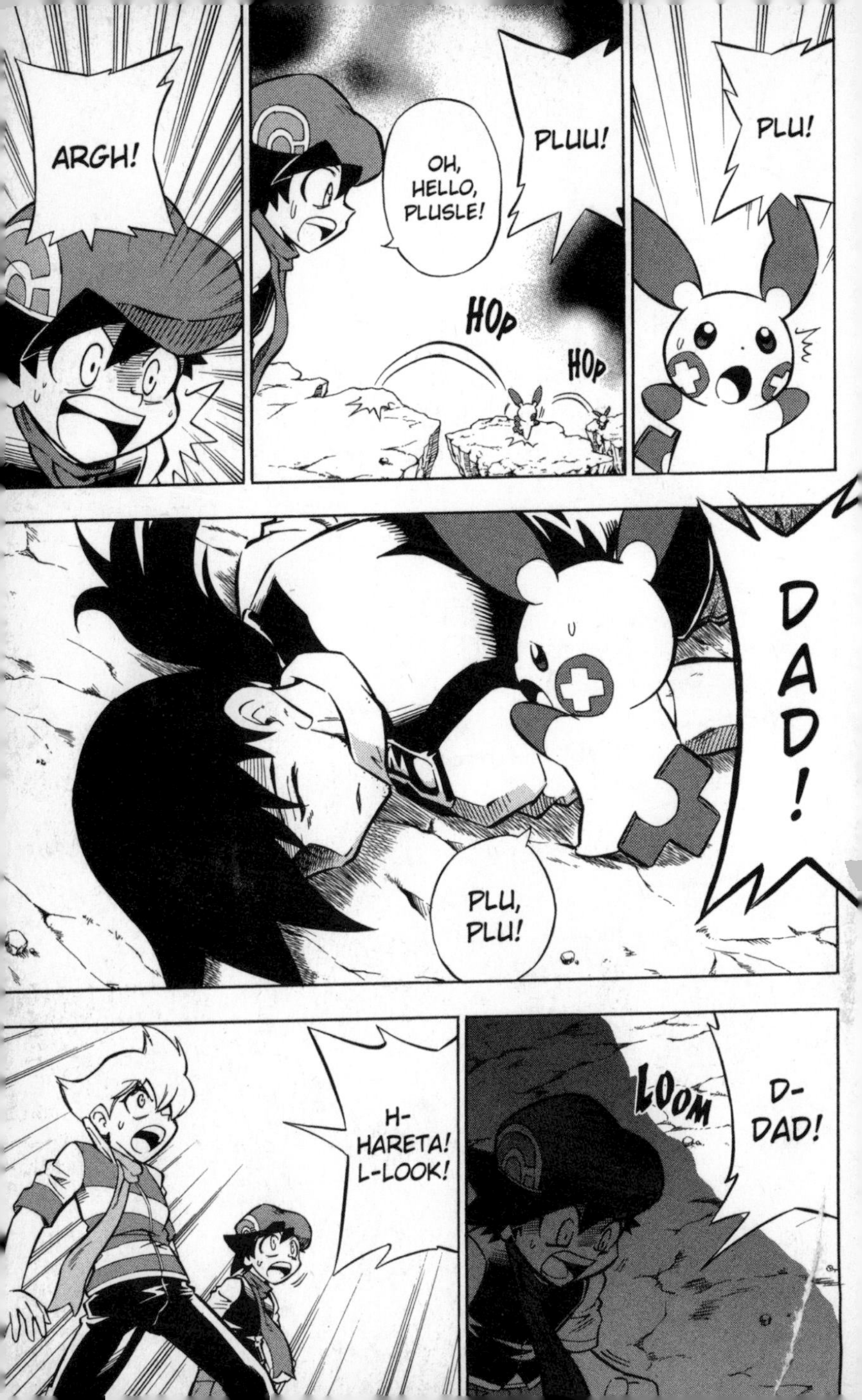
PLU!
PLUU!
OH, HELLO, PLUSLE!
HOP
HOP
ARGH!
DAD!
PLU, PLU!
D-DAD!
LOOM
H-HARETA! L-LOOK!

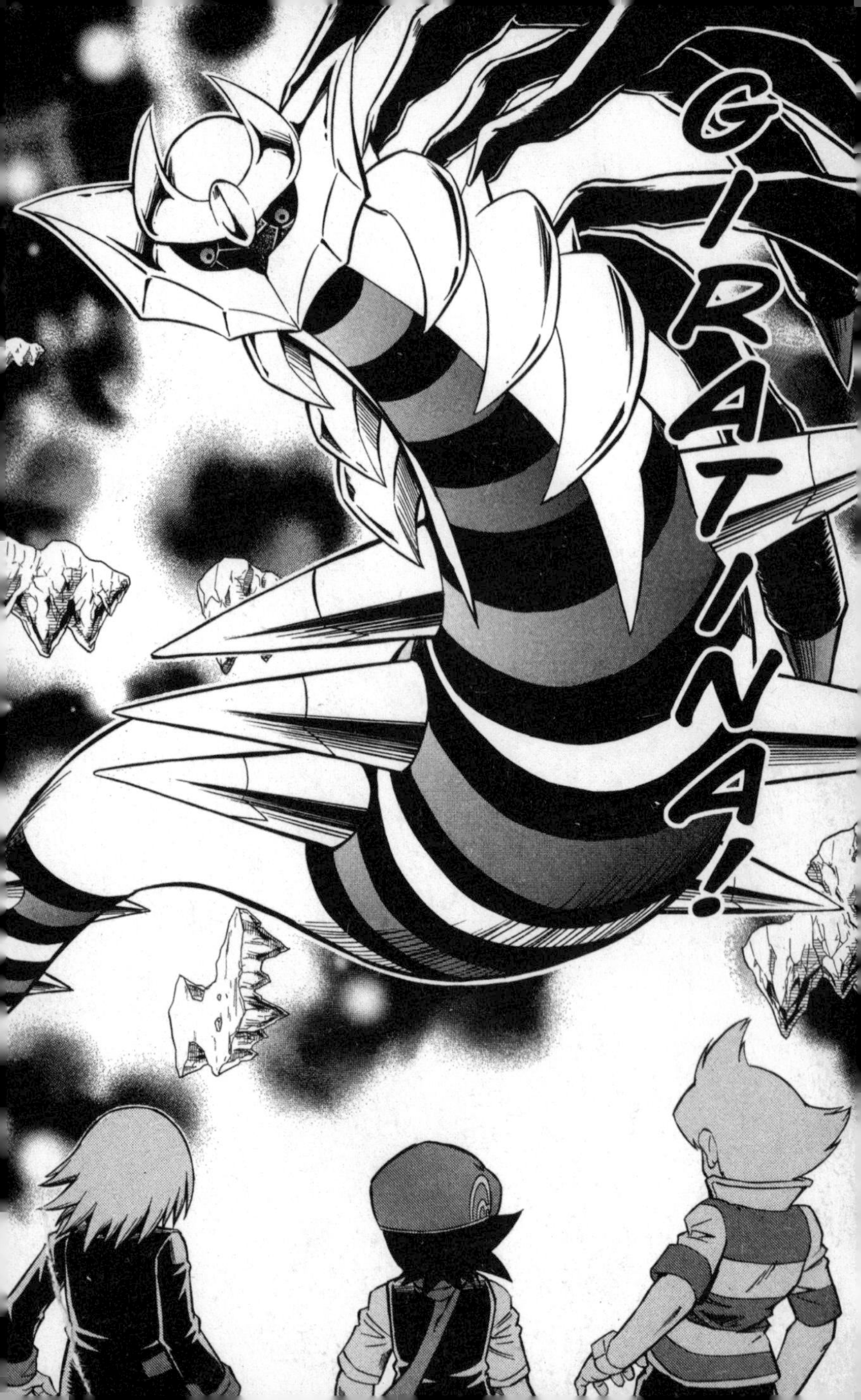
GIRATINA!

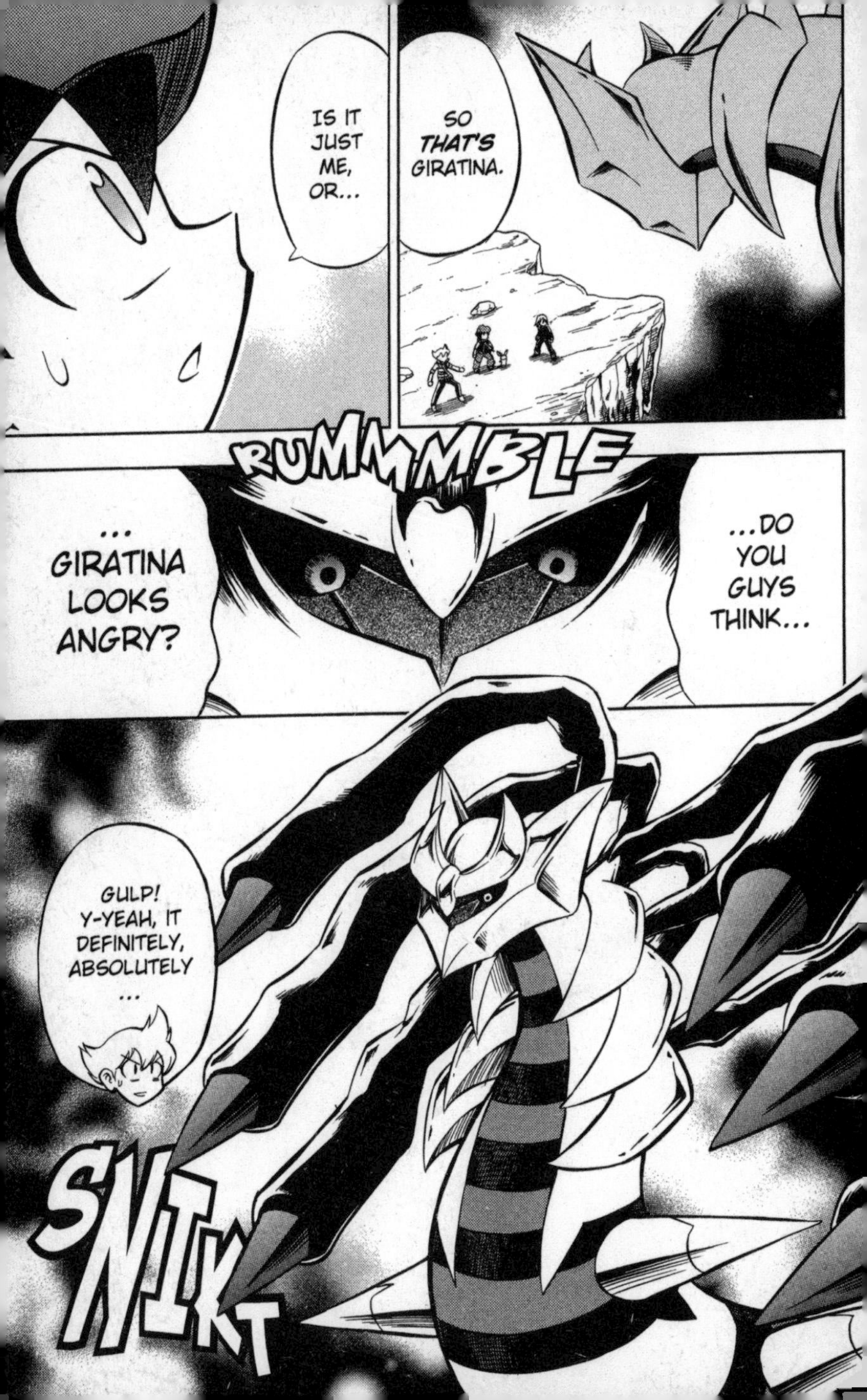
SO THAT'S GIRATINA.
IS IT JUST ME, OR...
RUMMMBLE
...DO YOU GUYS THINK...
... GIRATINA LOOKS ANGRY?
GULP! Y-YEAH, IT DEFINITELY, ABSOLUTELY ...
SNIKT

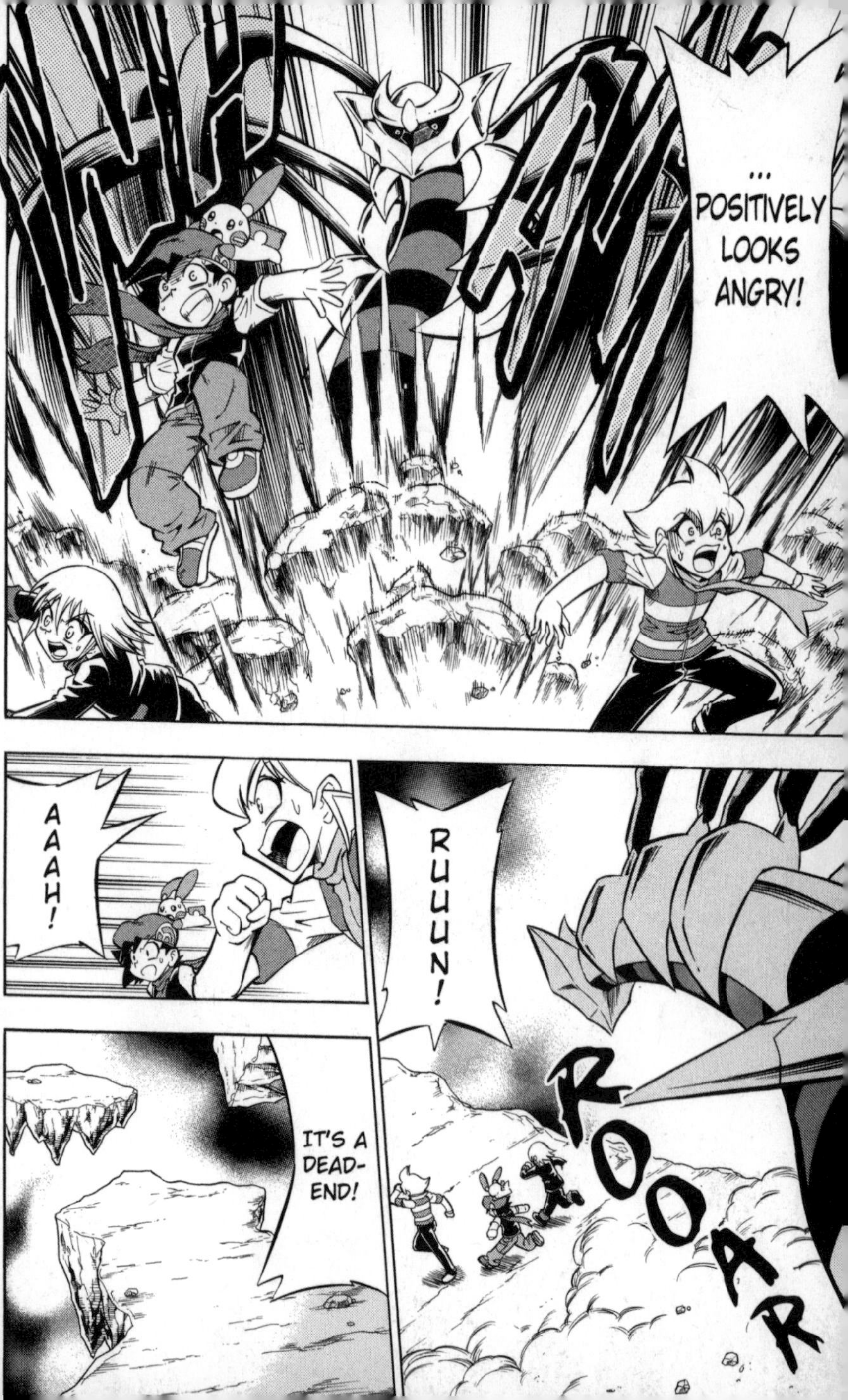
...POSITIVELY LOOKS ANGRY!
RUUUN!
ROOOAR
AAAH!
IT'S A DEAD-END!

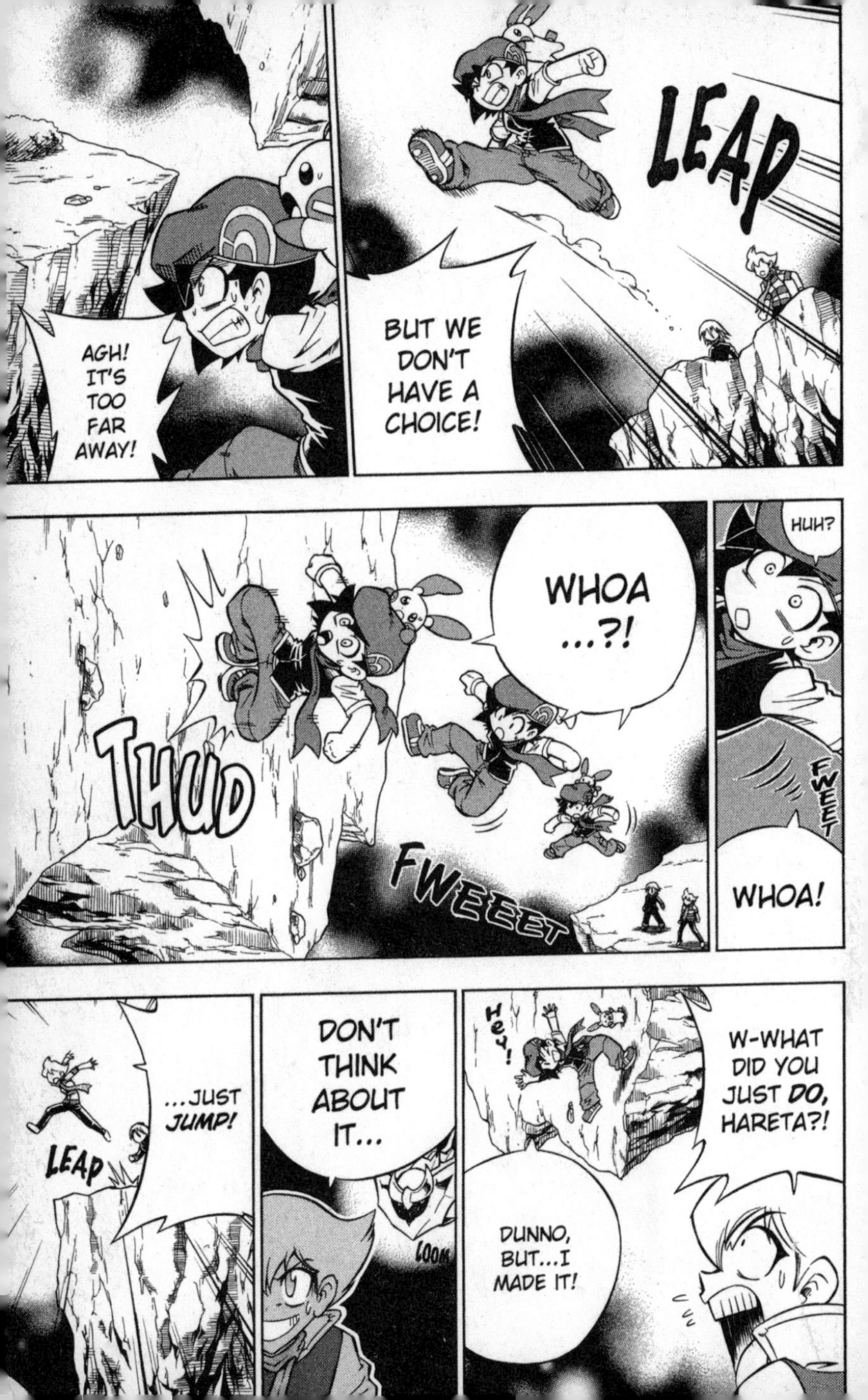
LEAP
BUT WE DON'T HAVE A CHOICE!
AGH! IT'S TOO FAR AWAY!
HUH?
FWEET
WHOA!
WHOA ...?!
THUD
FWEEEET
W-WHAT DID YOU JUST *DO*, HARETA?!
Hey!
DUNNO, BUT...I MADE IT!
DON'T THINK ABOUT IT...
LOOM
...JUST *JUMP!*
LEAP

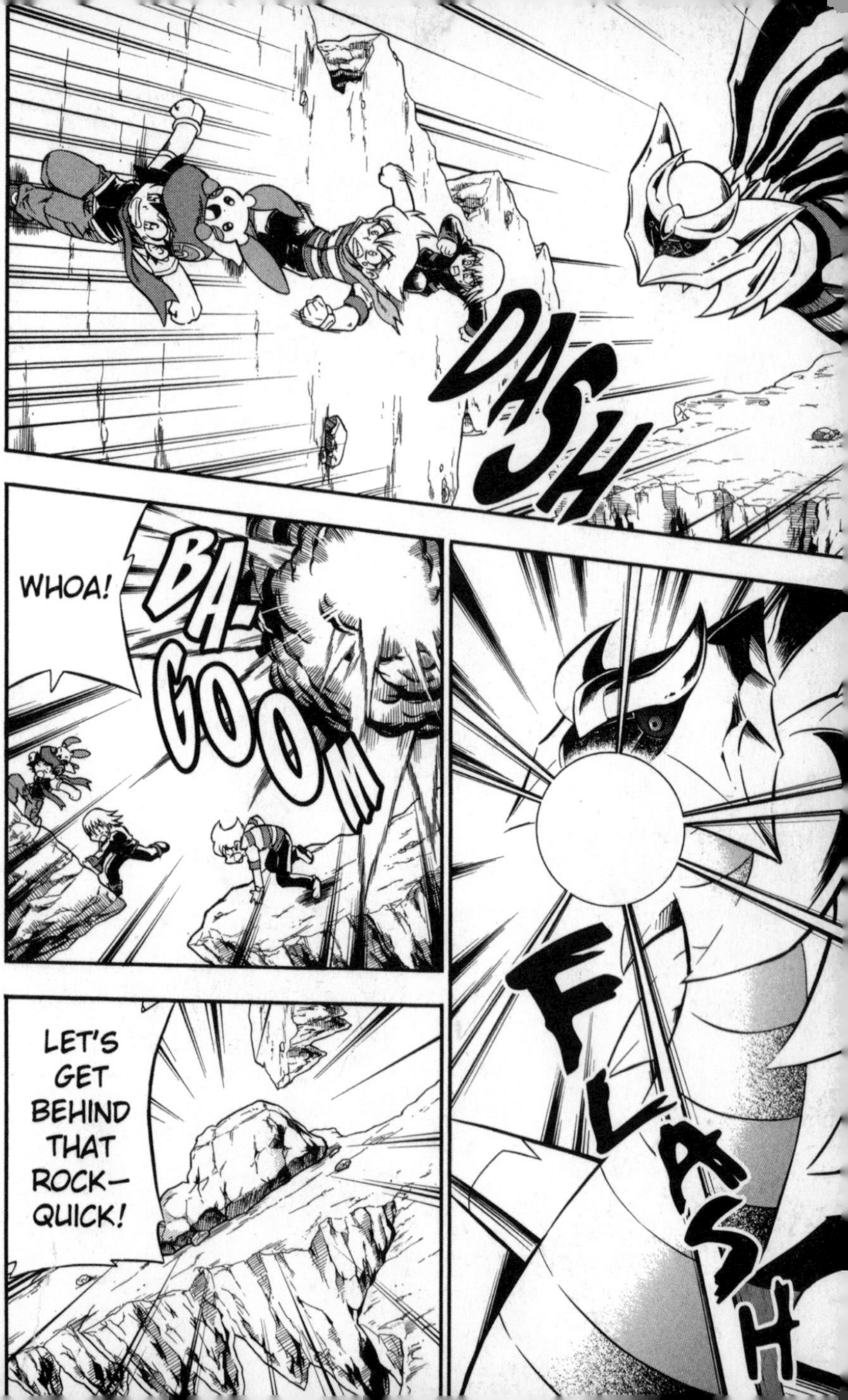
DASH
FLASH
BA-GOOOM
WHOA!
LET'S GET BEHIND THAT ROCK— QUICK!

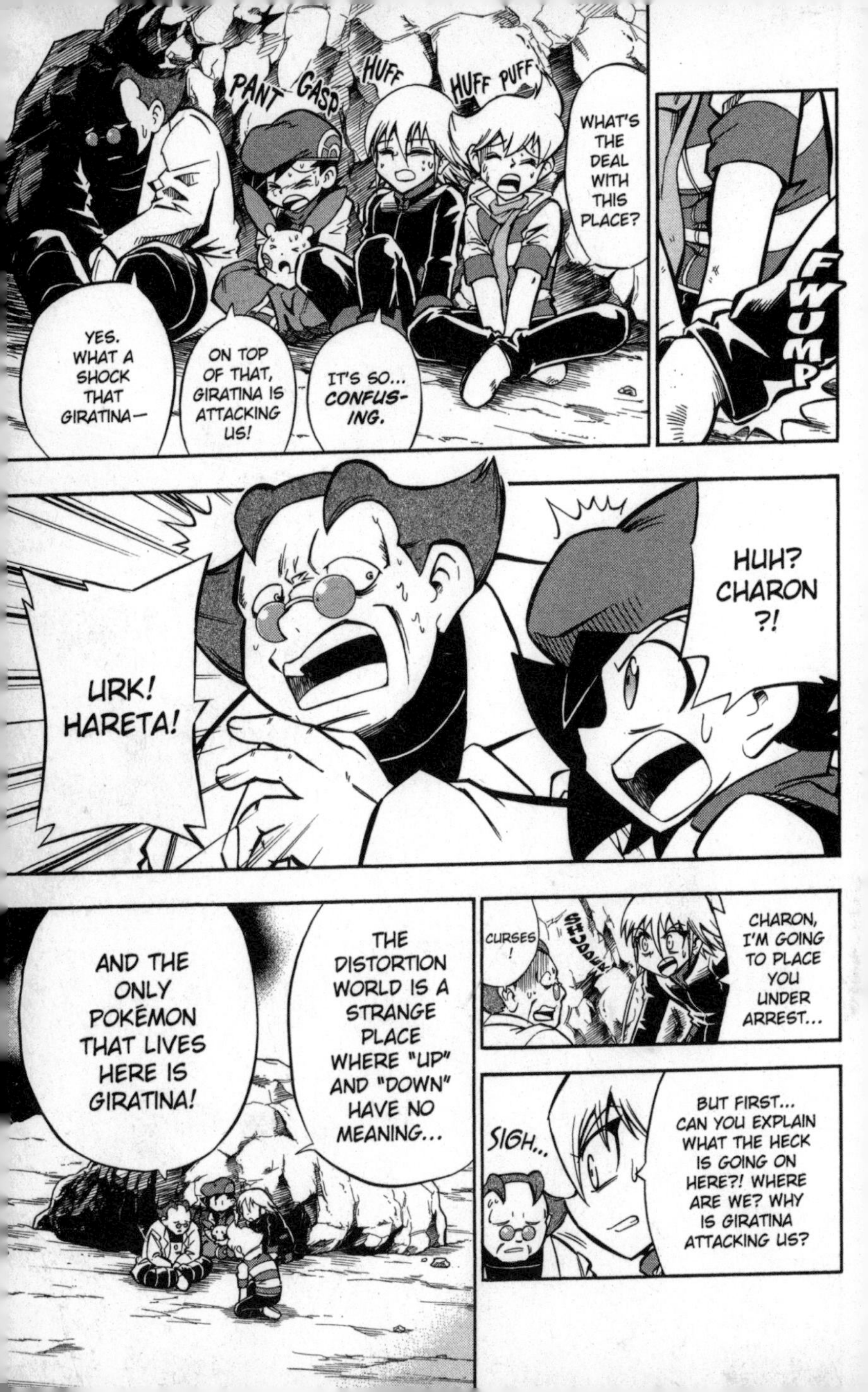
FWUMP
HUFF PUFF
HUFF
GASP
PANT
WHAT'S THE DEAL WITH THIS PLACE?
IT'S SO... CONFUSING.
ON TOP OF THAT, GIRATINA IS ATTACKING US!
YES. WHAT A SHOCK THAT GIRATINA—
HUH? CHARON?!
URK! HARETA!
CHARON, I'M GOING TO PLACE YOU UNDER ARREST...
SHUDDER
CURSES!
BUT FIRST... CAN YOU EXPLAIN WHAT THE HECK IS GOING ON HERE?! WHERE ARE WE? WHY IS GIRATINA ATTACKING US?
SIGH...
THE DISTORTION WORLD IS A STRANGE PLACE WHERE "UP" AND "DOWN" HAVE NO MEANING...
AND THE ONLY POKÉMON THAT LIVES HERE IS GIRATINA!

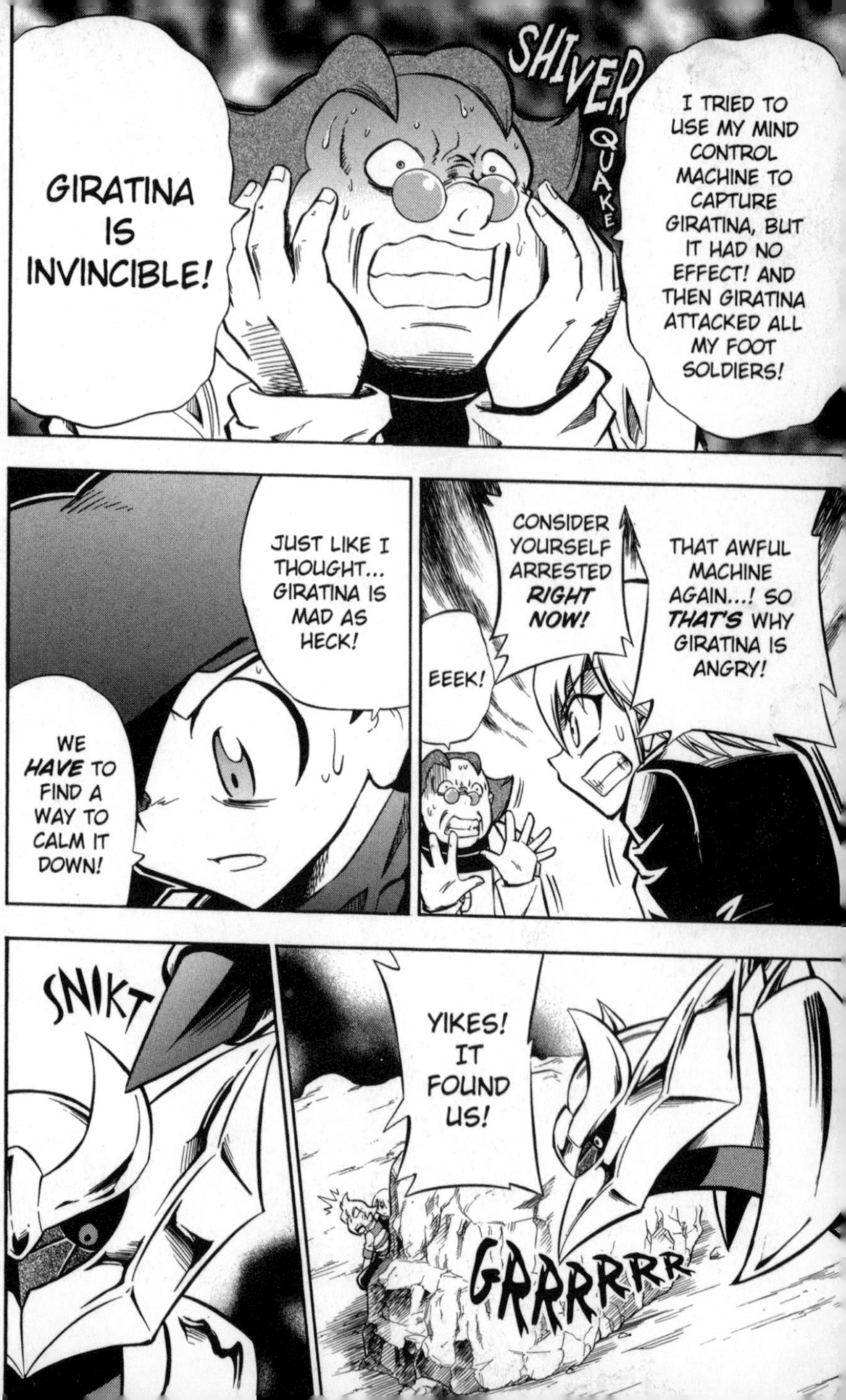
SHIVER
QUAKE
I TRIED TO USE MY MIND CONTROL MACHINE TO CAPTURE GIRATINA, BUT IT HAD NO EFFECT! AND THEN GIRATINA ATTACKED ALL MY FOOT SOLDIERS!
GIRATINA IS INVINCIBLE!
THAT AWFUL MACHINE AGAIN...! SO THAT'S WHY GIRATINA IS ANGRY!
CONSIDER YOURSELF ARRESTED RIGHT NOW!
EEEK!
JUST LIKE I THOUGHT... GIRATINA IS MAD AS HECK!
WE HAVE TO FIND A WAY TO CALM IT DOWN!
YIKES! IT FOUND US!
GRRRRRR
SNIKT

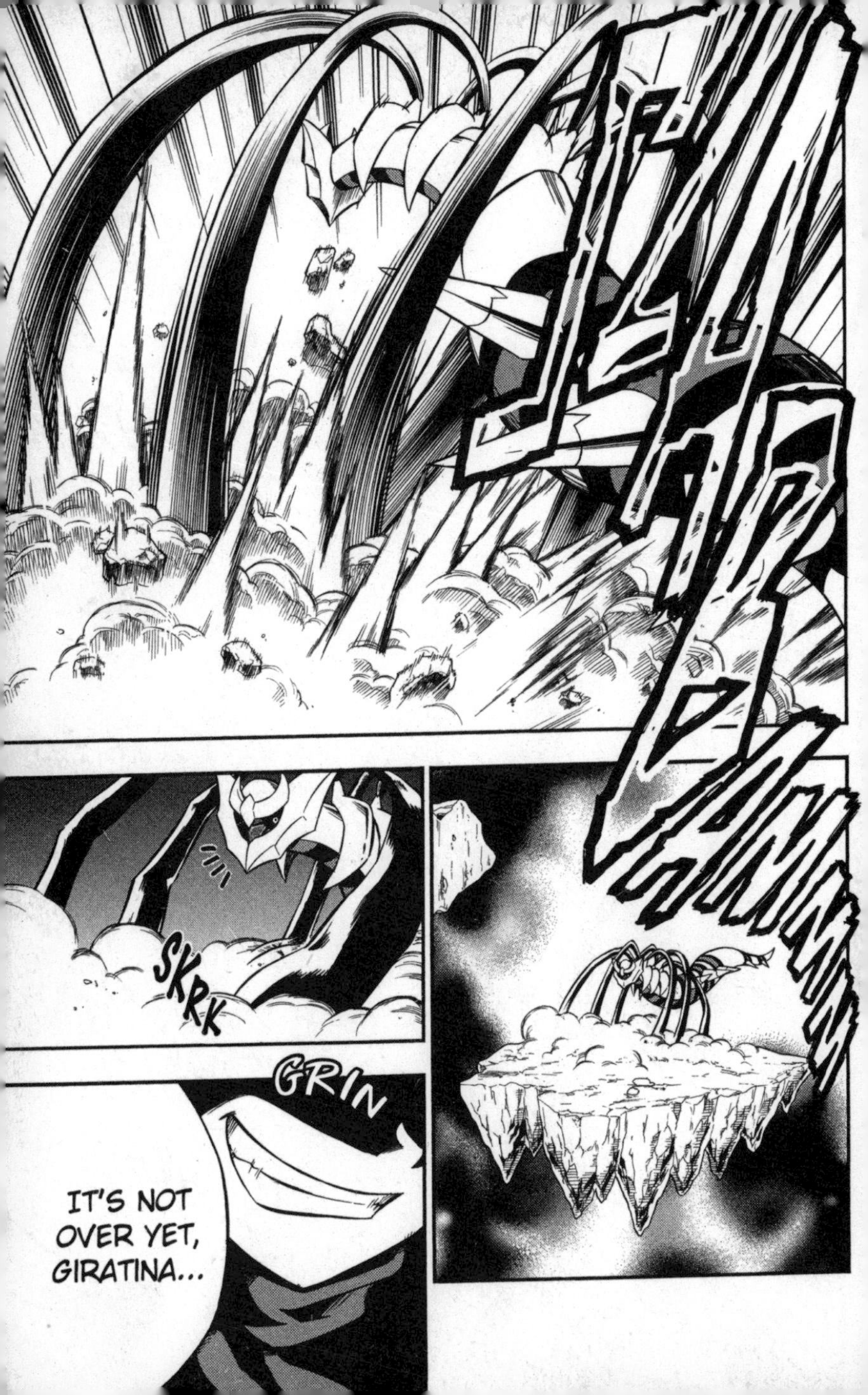
SKRK
GRIN
IT'S NOT OVER YET, GIRATINA...

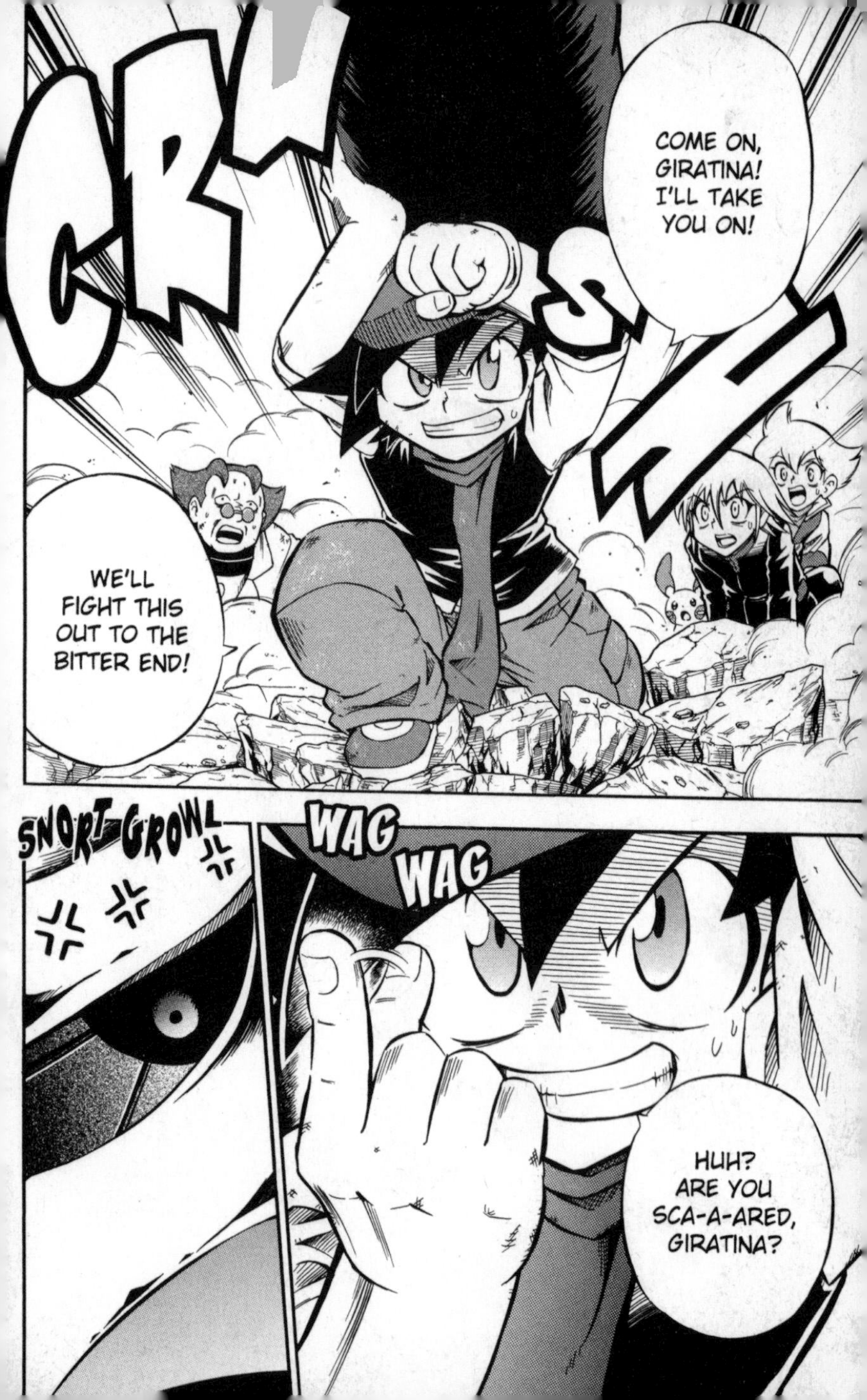
COME ON, GIRATINA! I'LL TAKE YOU ON!
WE'LL FIGHT THIS OUT TO THE BITTER END!
WAG WAG
HUH? ARE YOU SCA-A-ARED, GIRATINA?
SNORT GROWL

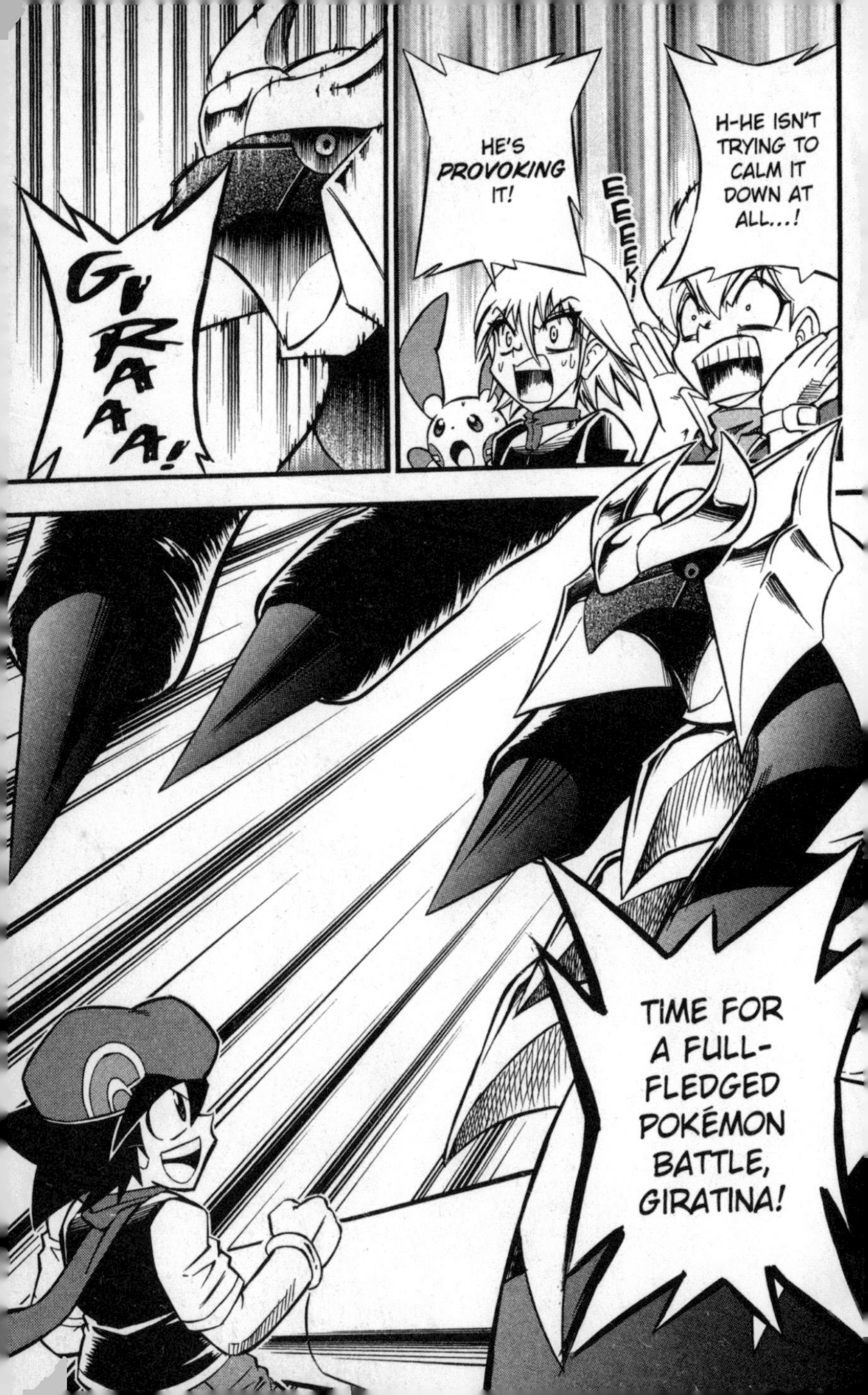
H-HE ISN'T TRYING TO CALM IT DOWN AT ALL...!
EEEEK!
HE'S PROVOKING IT!
GIRAAAA!
TIME FOR A FULL-FLEDGED POKÉMON BATTLE, GIRATINA!

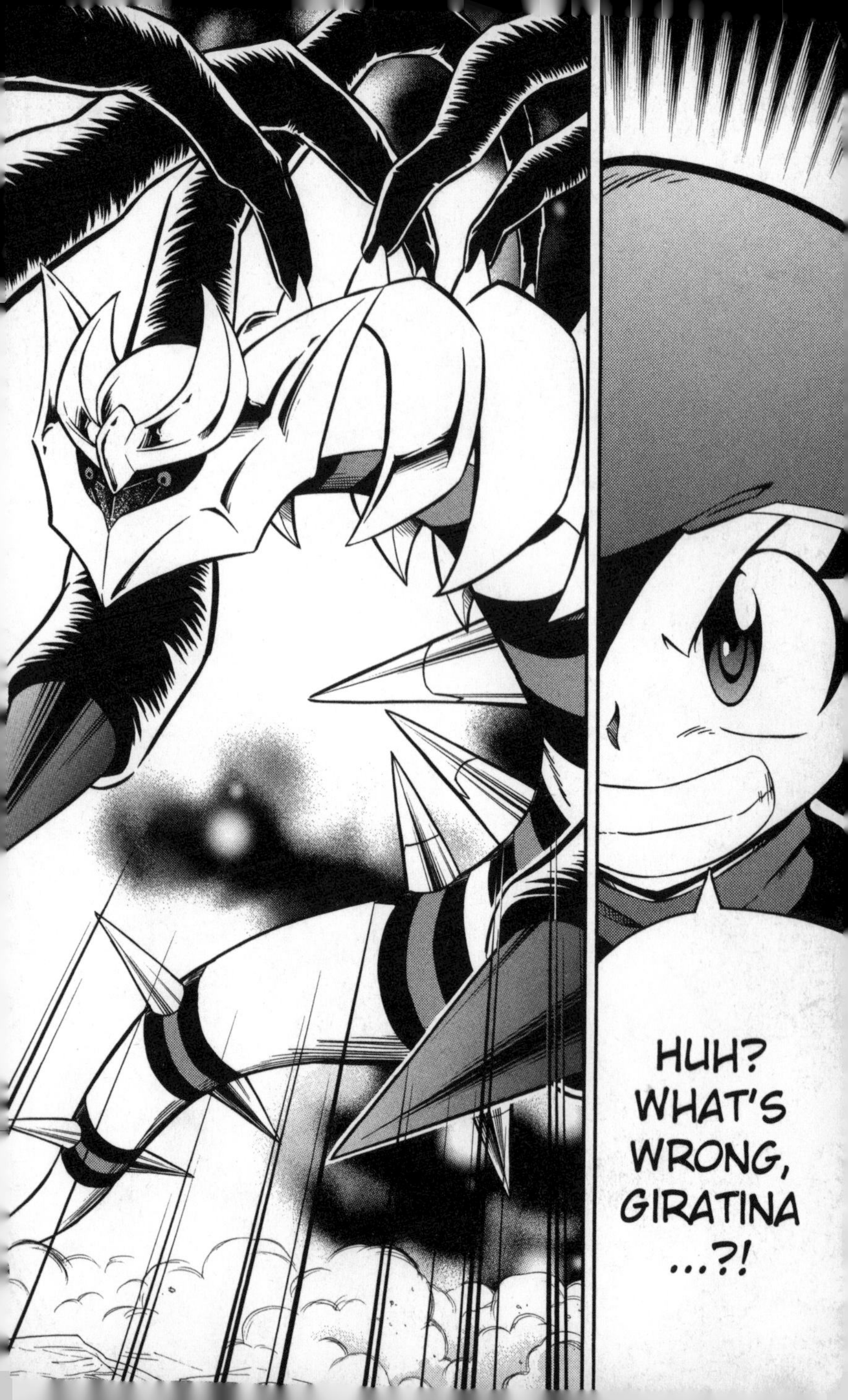
HUH? WHAT'S WRONG, GIRATINA ...?!

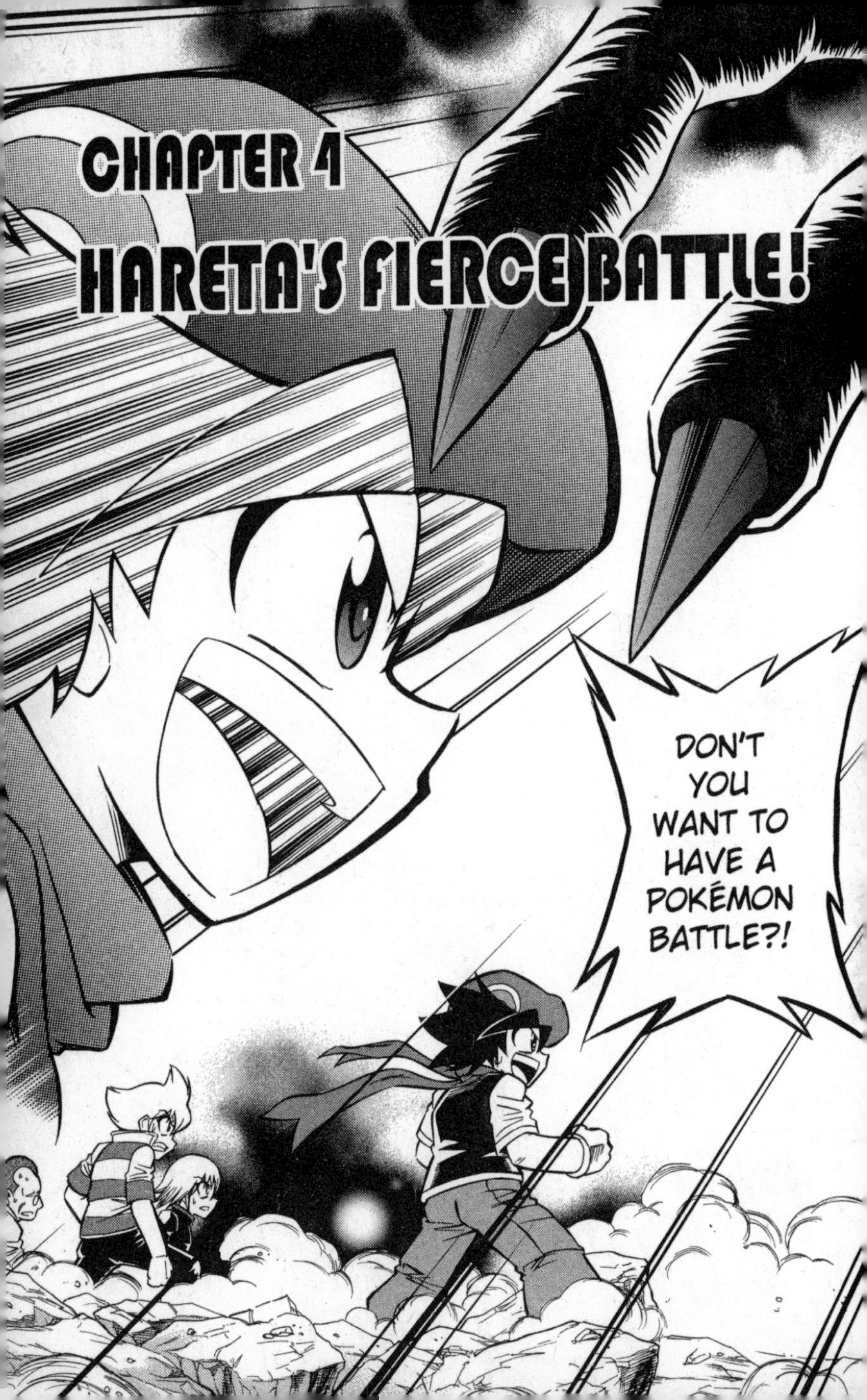
CHAPTER 4
HARETA'S FIERCE BATTLE!
DON'T YOU WANT TO HAVE A POKÉMON BATTLE?!

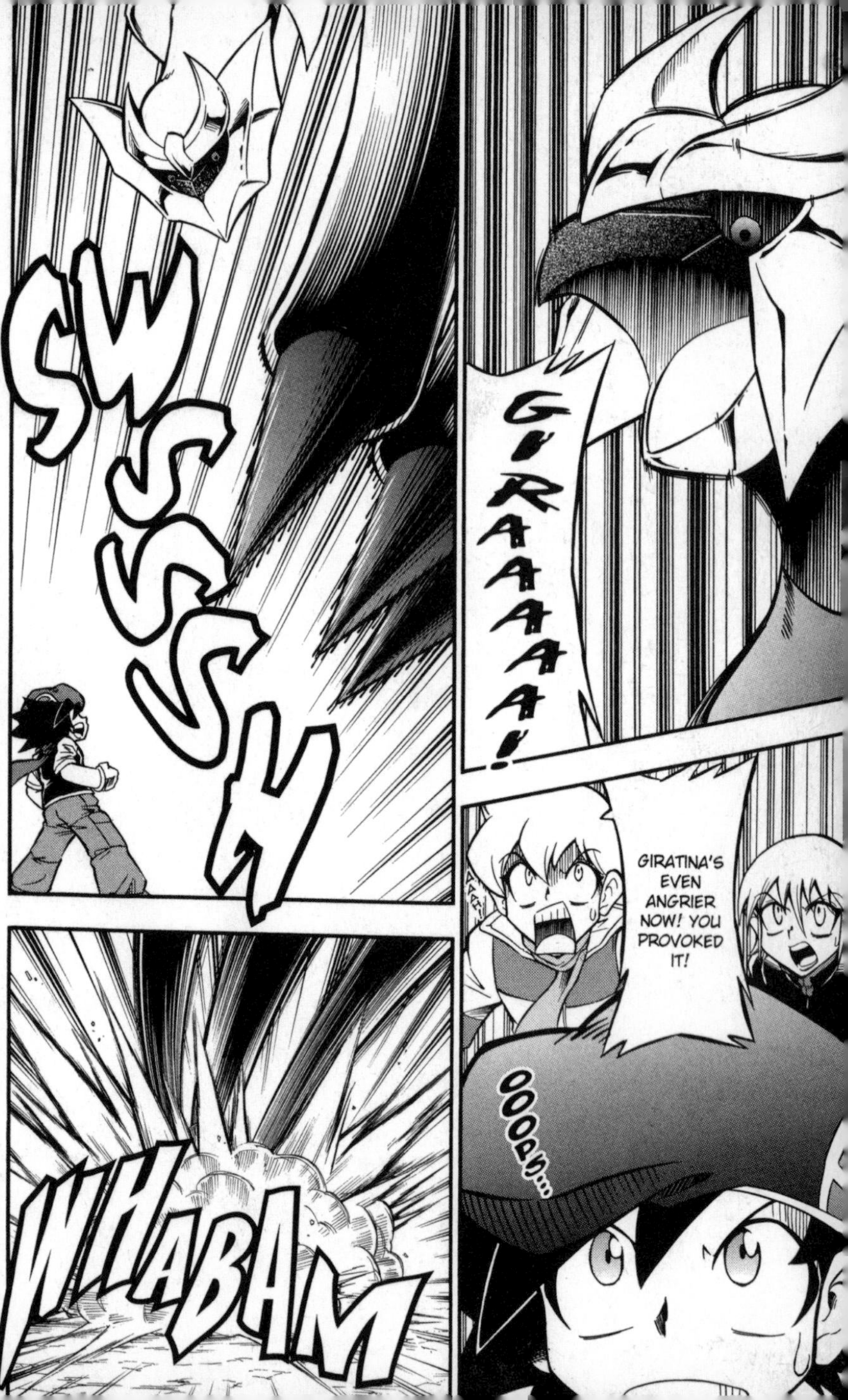
GIRAAAAAA!
SWSSSH
GIRATINA'S EVEN ANGRIER NOW! YOU PROVOKED IT!
OOOPS...
WHABAM

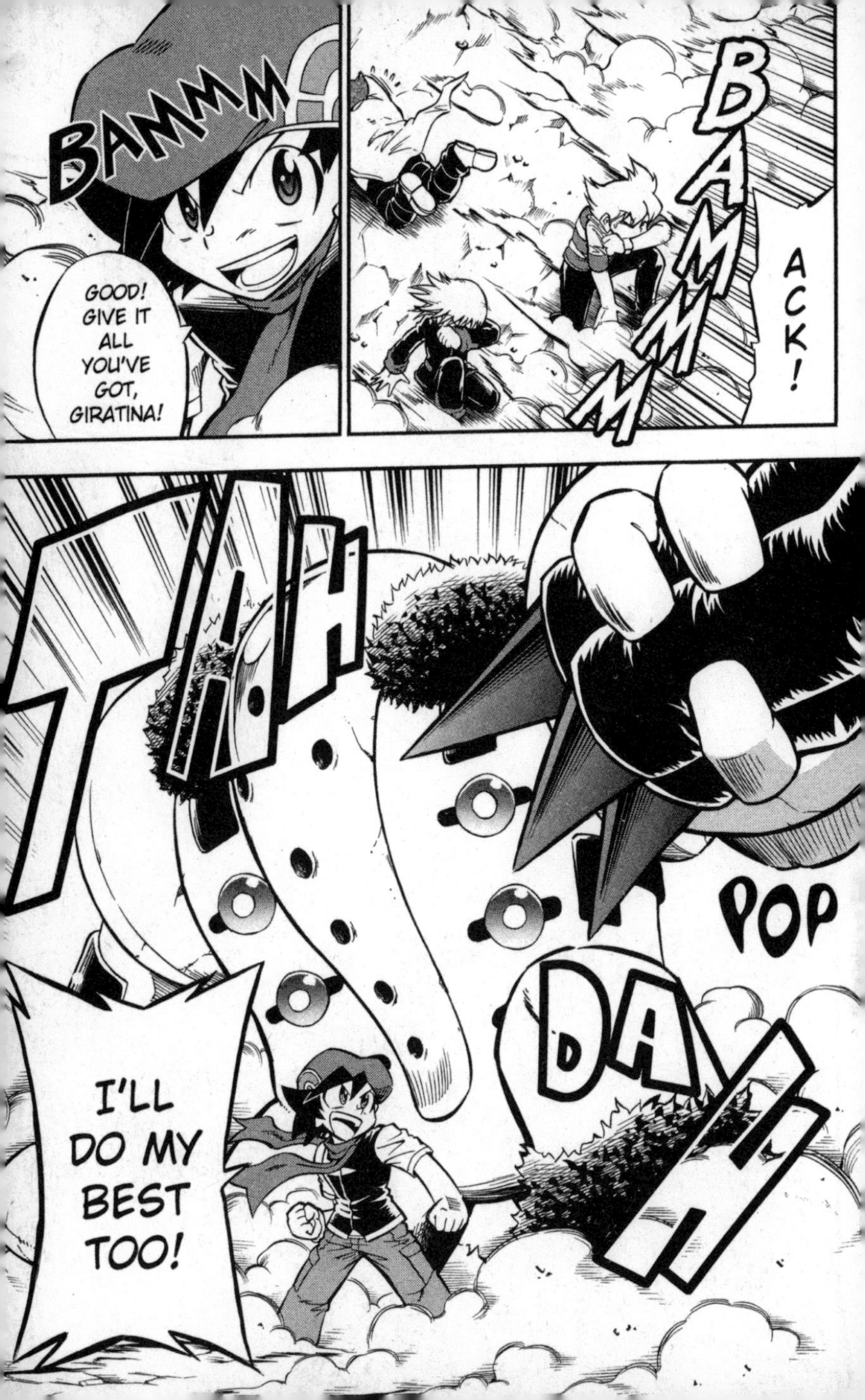
BAMMMM
ACK!
BAMMM
GOOD! GIVE IT ALL YOU'VE GOT, GIRATINA!
POP
I'LL DO MY BEST TOO!

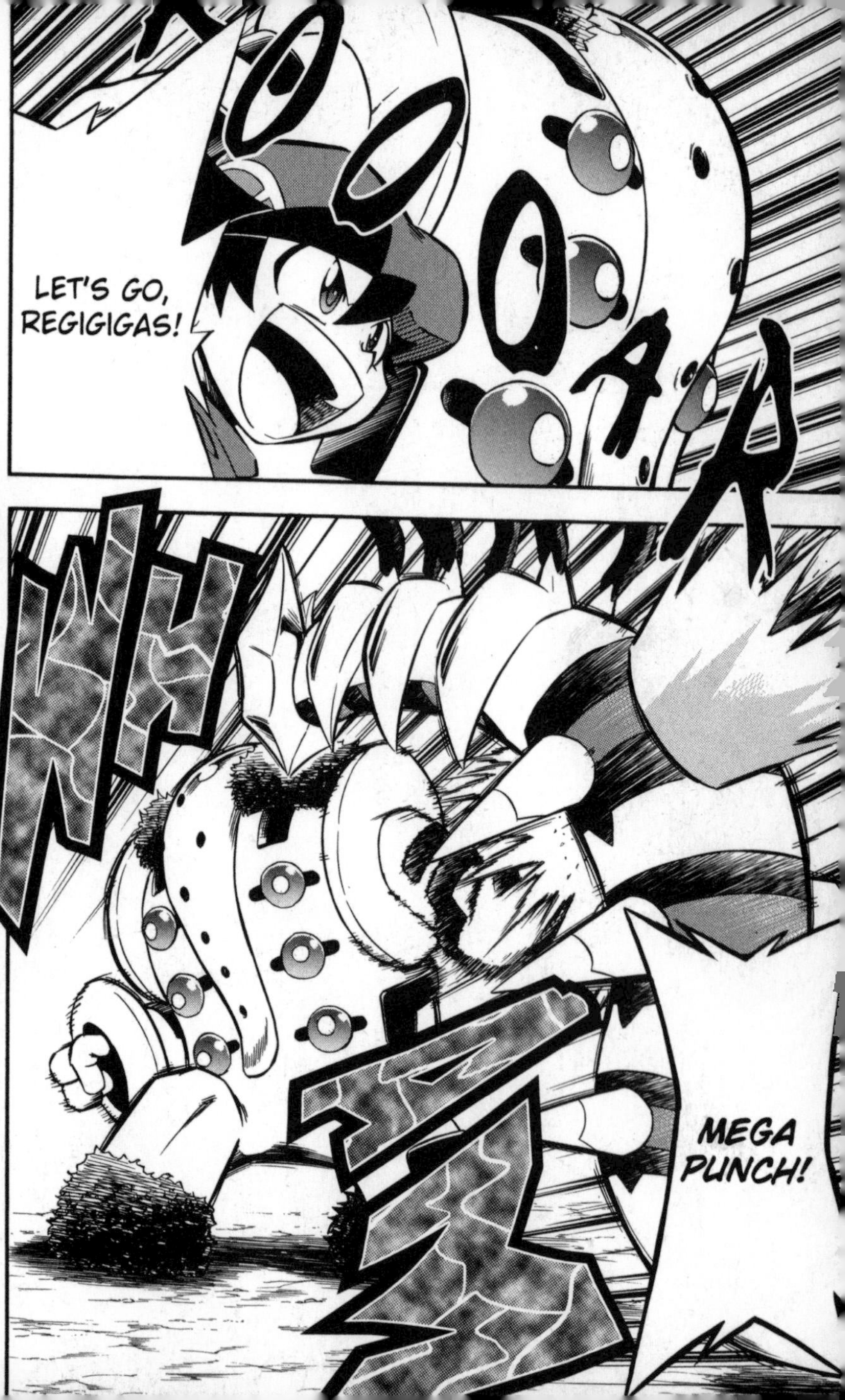
LET'S GO, REGIGIGAS!
MEGA PUNCH!

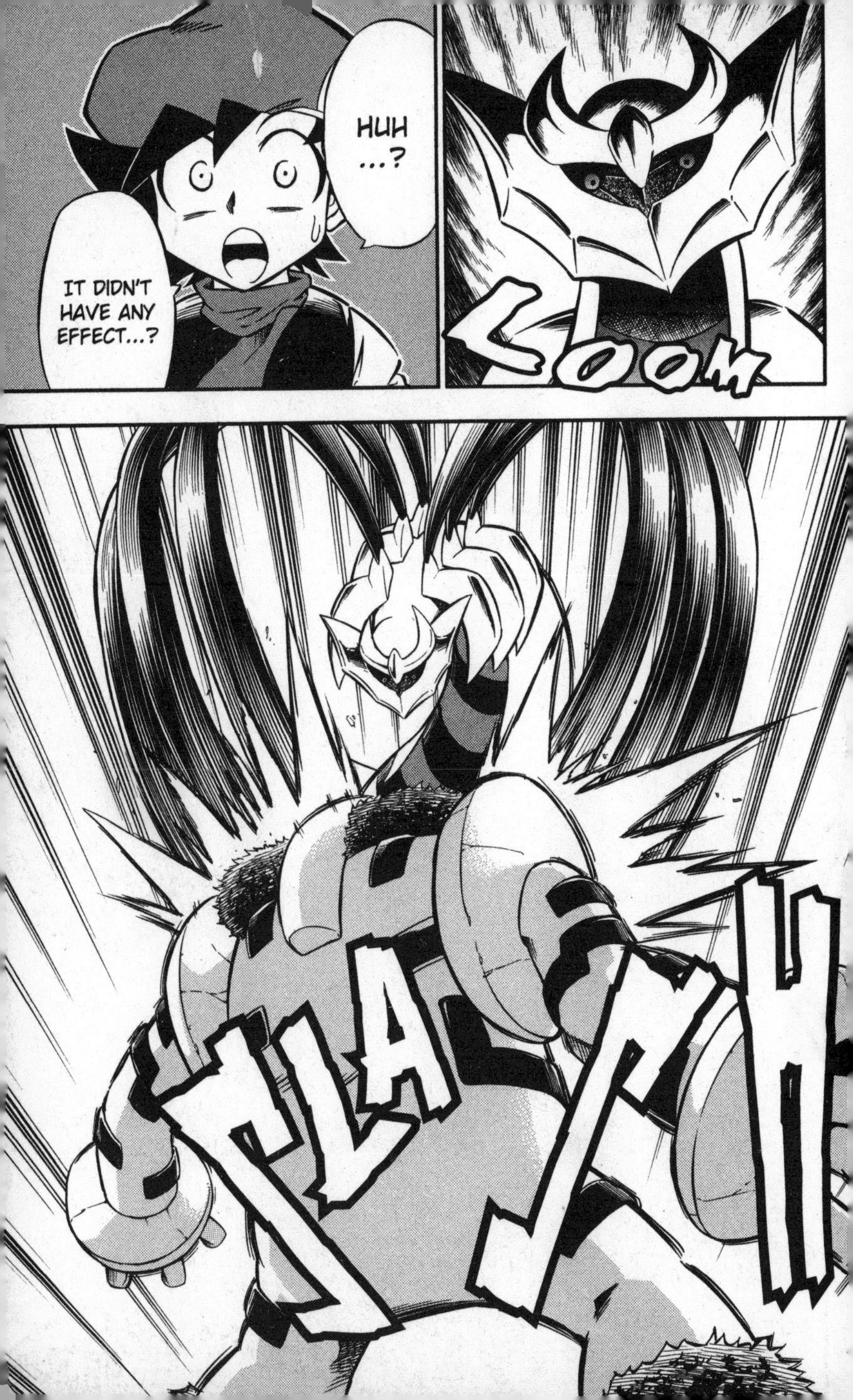
LOOM
HUH ...?
IT DIDN'T HAVE ANY EFFECT...?
THWACK

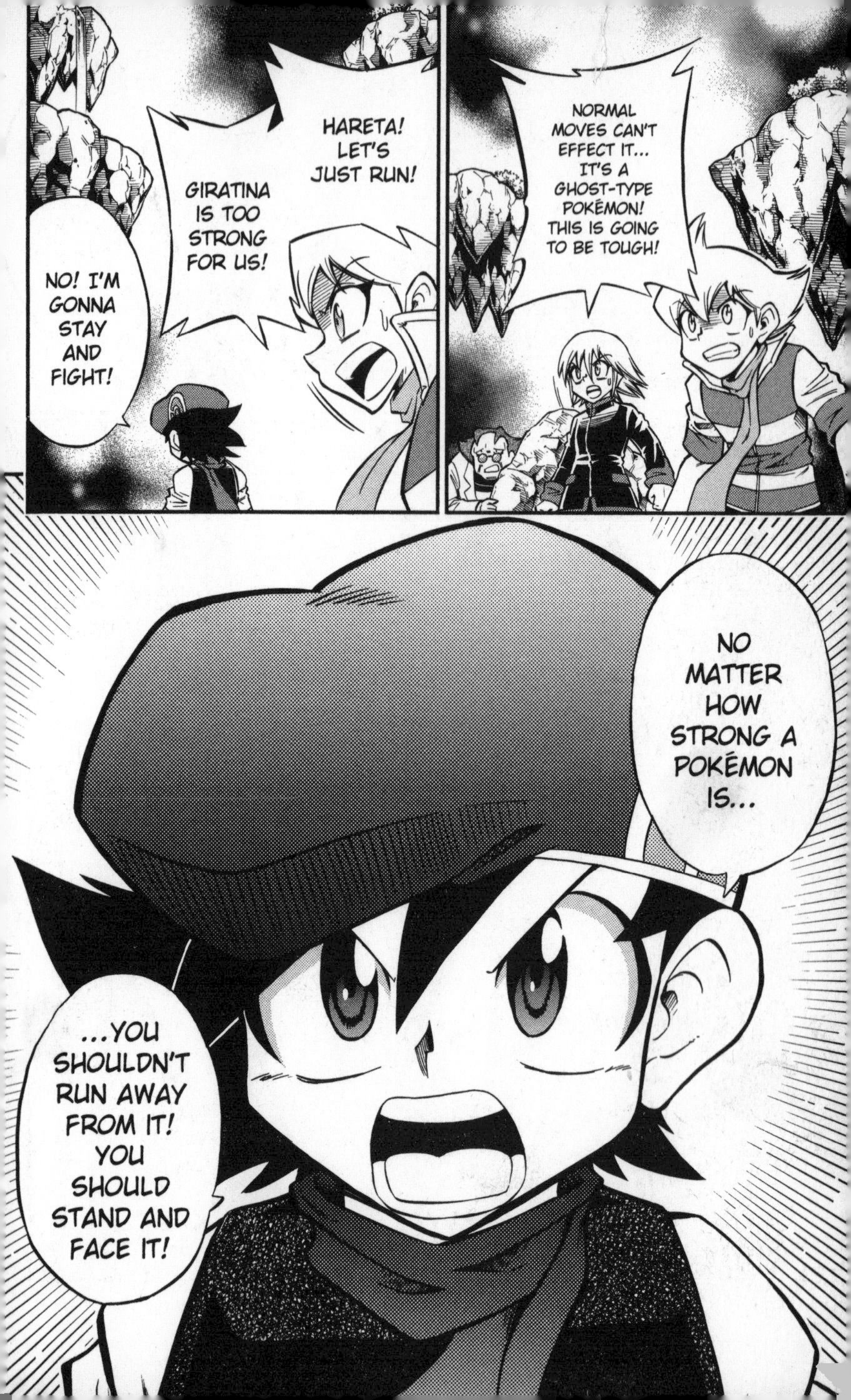
NORMAL MOVES CAN'T EFFECT IT... IT'S A GHOST-TYPE POKÉMON! THIS IS GOING TO BE TOUGH!
HARETA! LET'S JUST RUN!
GIRATINA IS TOO STRONG FOR US!
NO! I'M GONNA STAY AND FIGHT!
NO MATTER HOW STRONG A POKÉMON IS...
...YOU SHOULDN'T RUN AWAY FROM IT! YOU SHOULD STAND AND FACE IT!

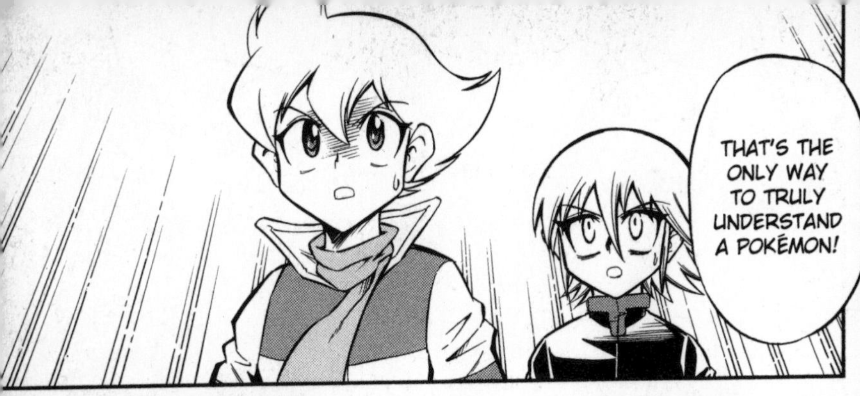
THAT'S THE ONLY WAY TO TRULY UNDERSTAND A POKÉMON!

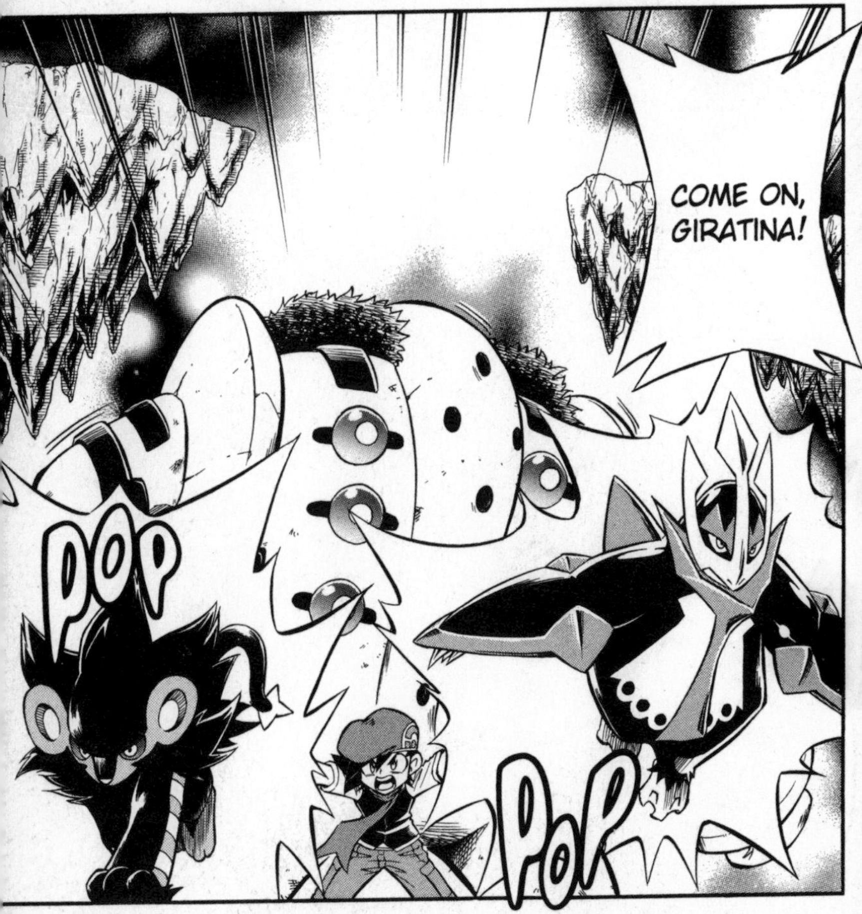
COME ON, GIRATINA!
POP
POP

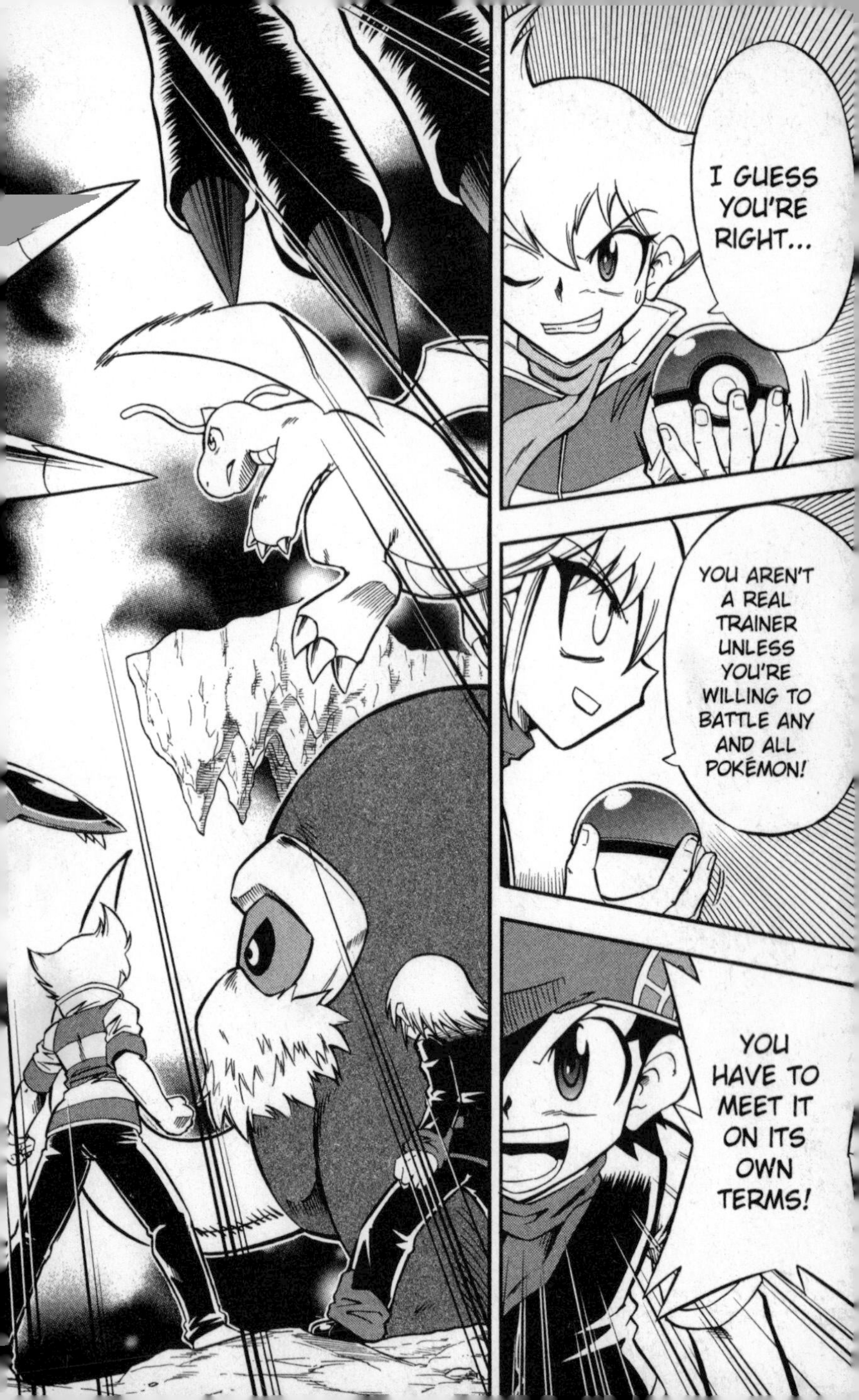
I GUESS YOU'RE RIGHT...
YOU AREN'T A REAL TRAINER UNLESS YOU'RE WILLING TO BATTLE ANY AND ALL POKÉMON!
YOU HAVE TO MEET IT ON ITS OWN TERMS!

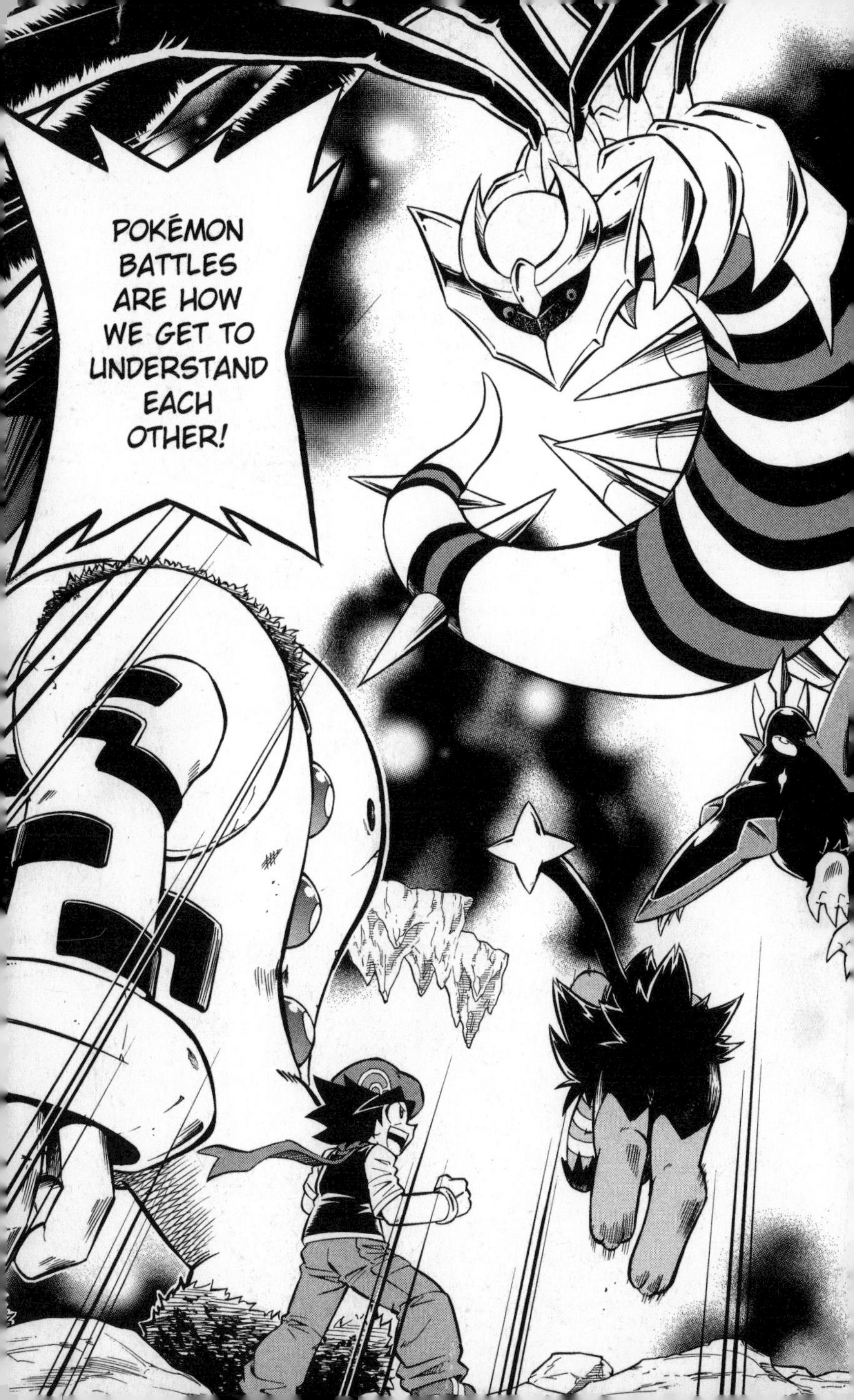
POKÉMON BATTLES ARE HOW WE GET TO UNDERSTAND EACH OTHER!

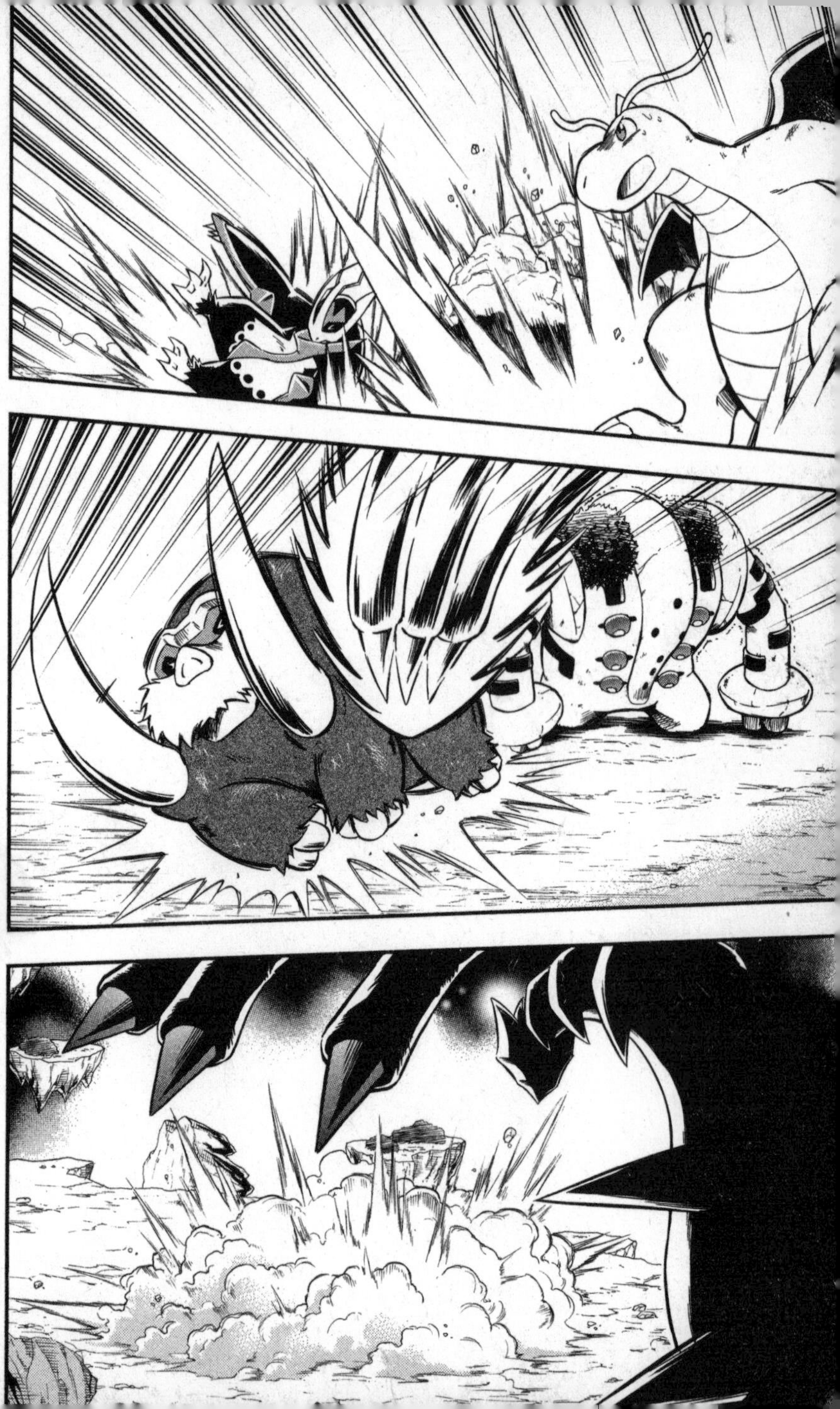

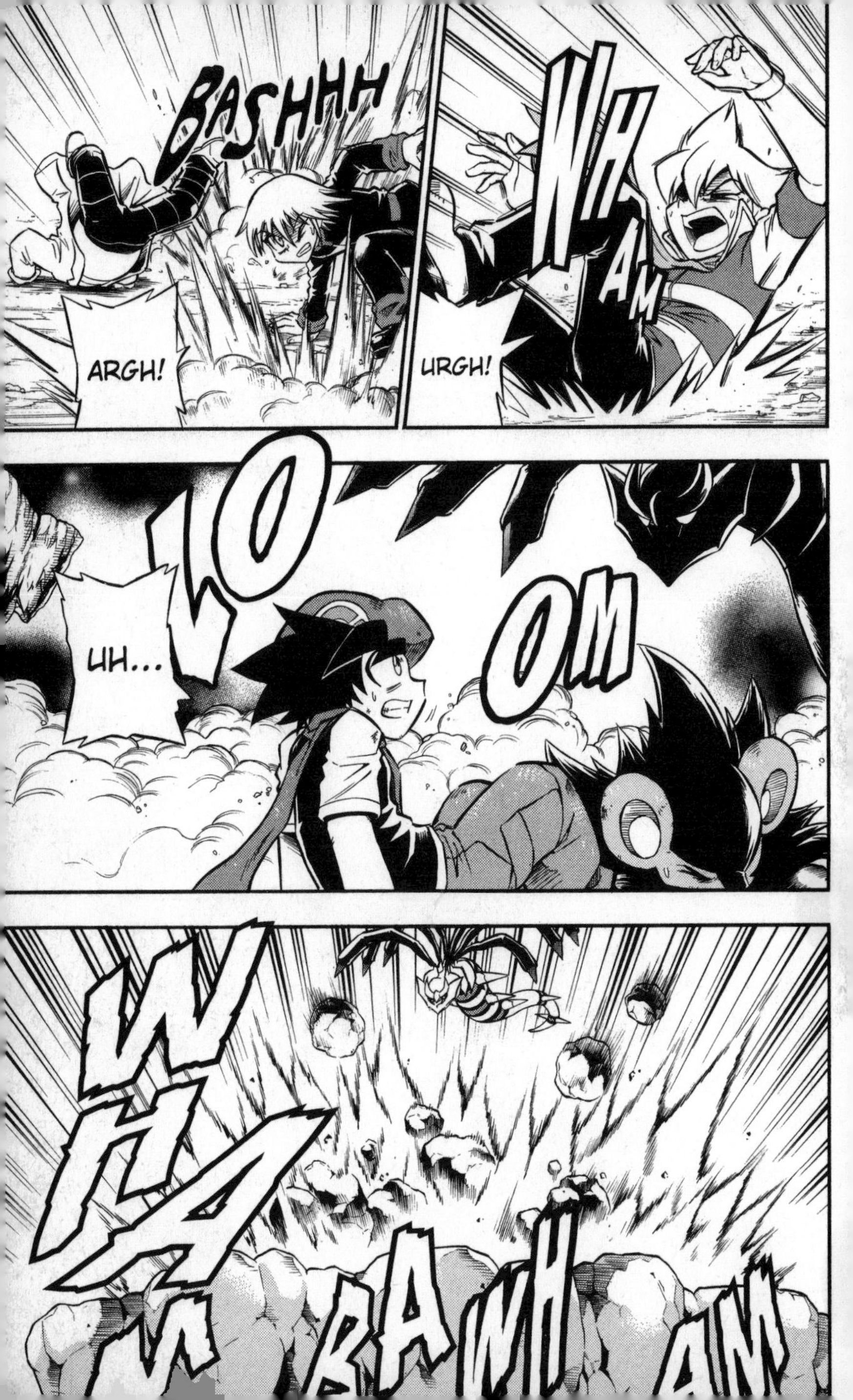
WHAM
URGH!
BASHHH
ARGH!
VOOM
UH...

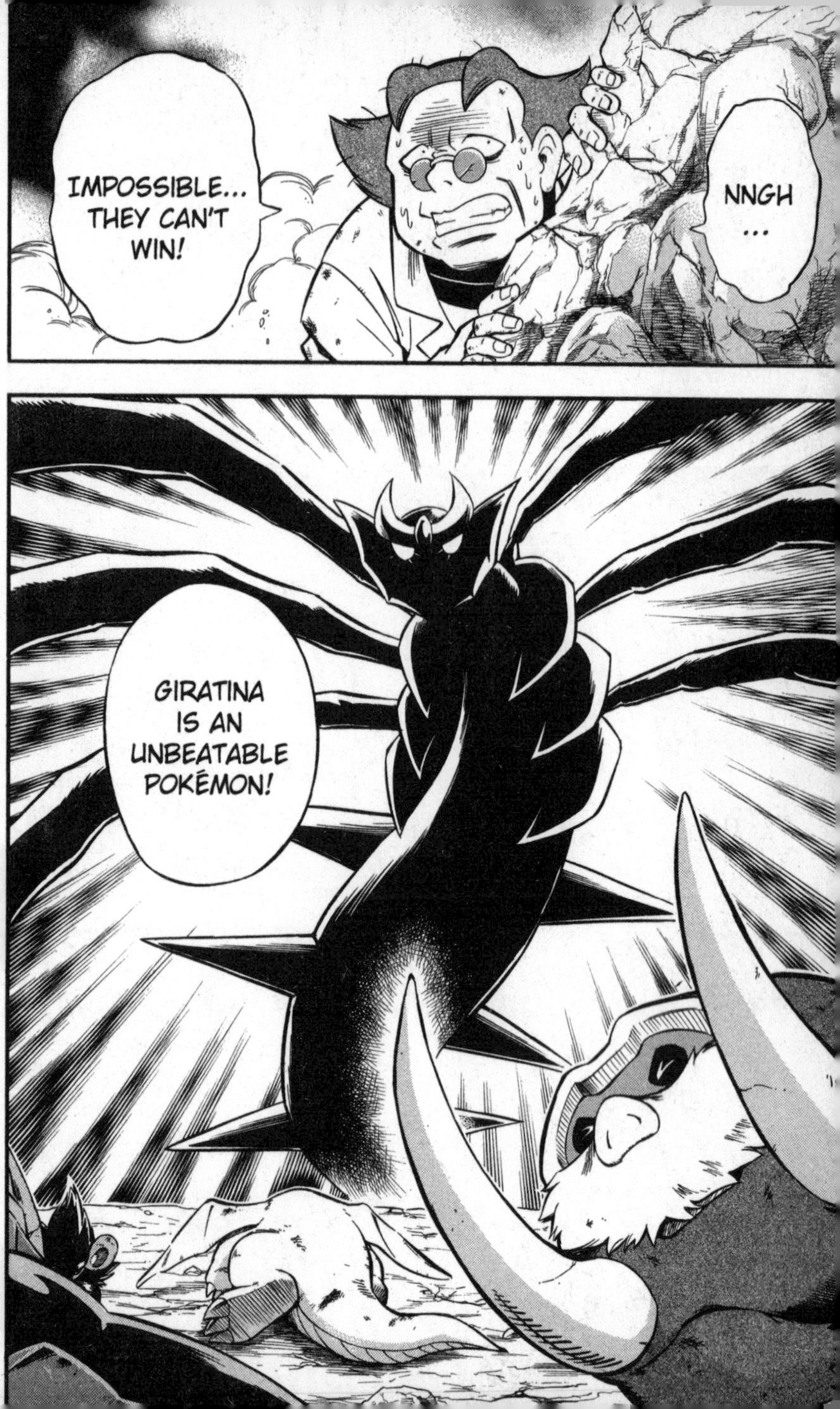
NNGH ...
IMPOSSIBLE... THEY CAN'T WIN!
GIRATINA IS AN UNBEATABLE POKÉMON!

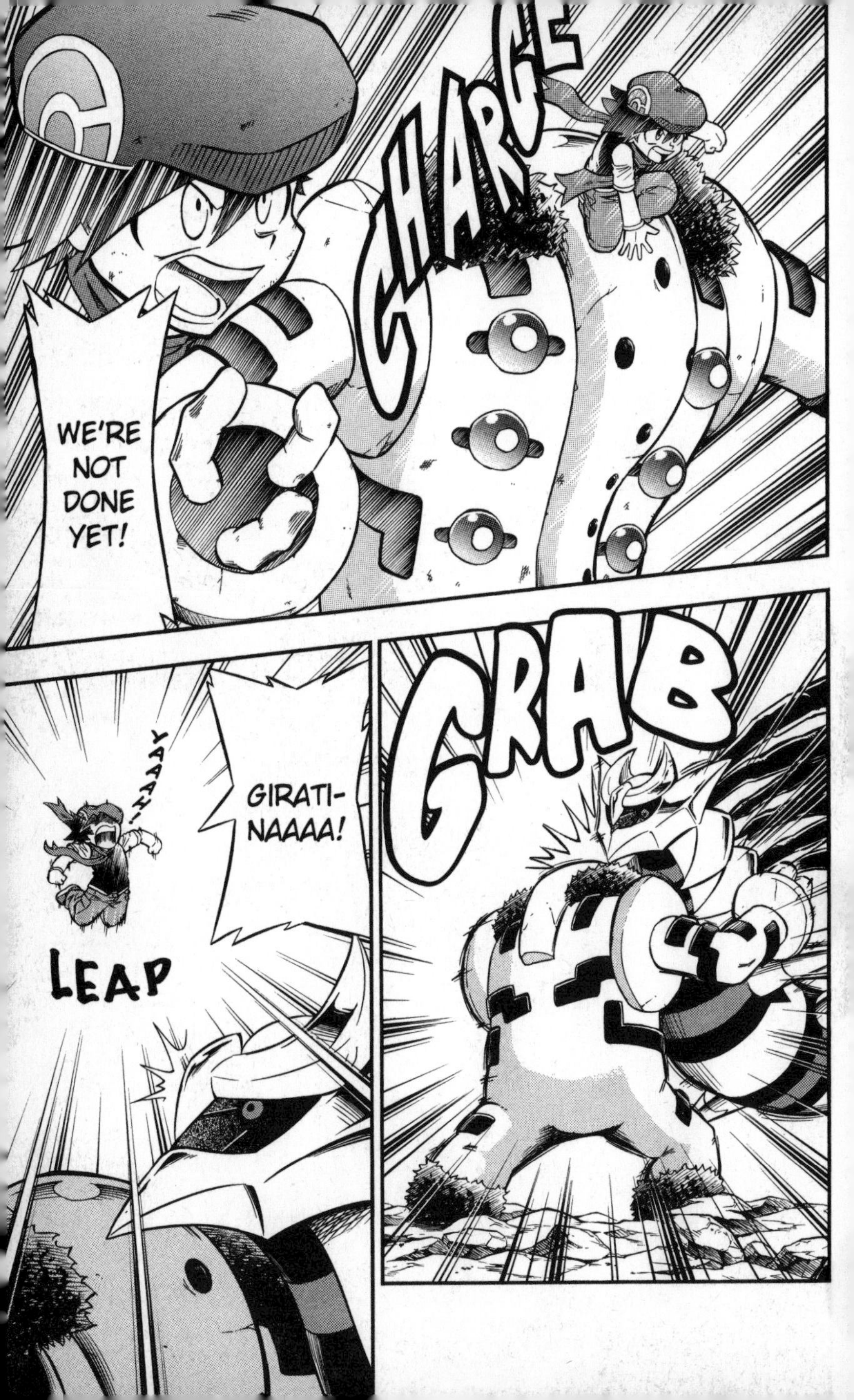
CHARGE
WE'RE NOT DONE YET!
GRAB
GIRATI-NAAAA!
YAAAAH!
LEAP

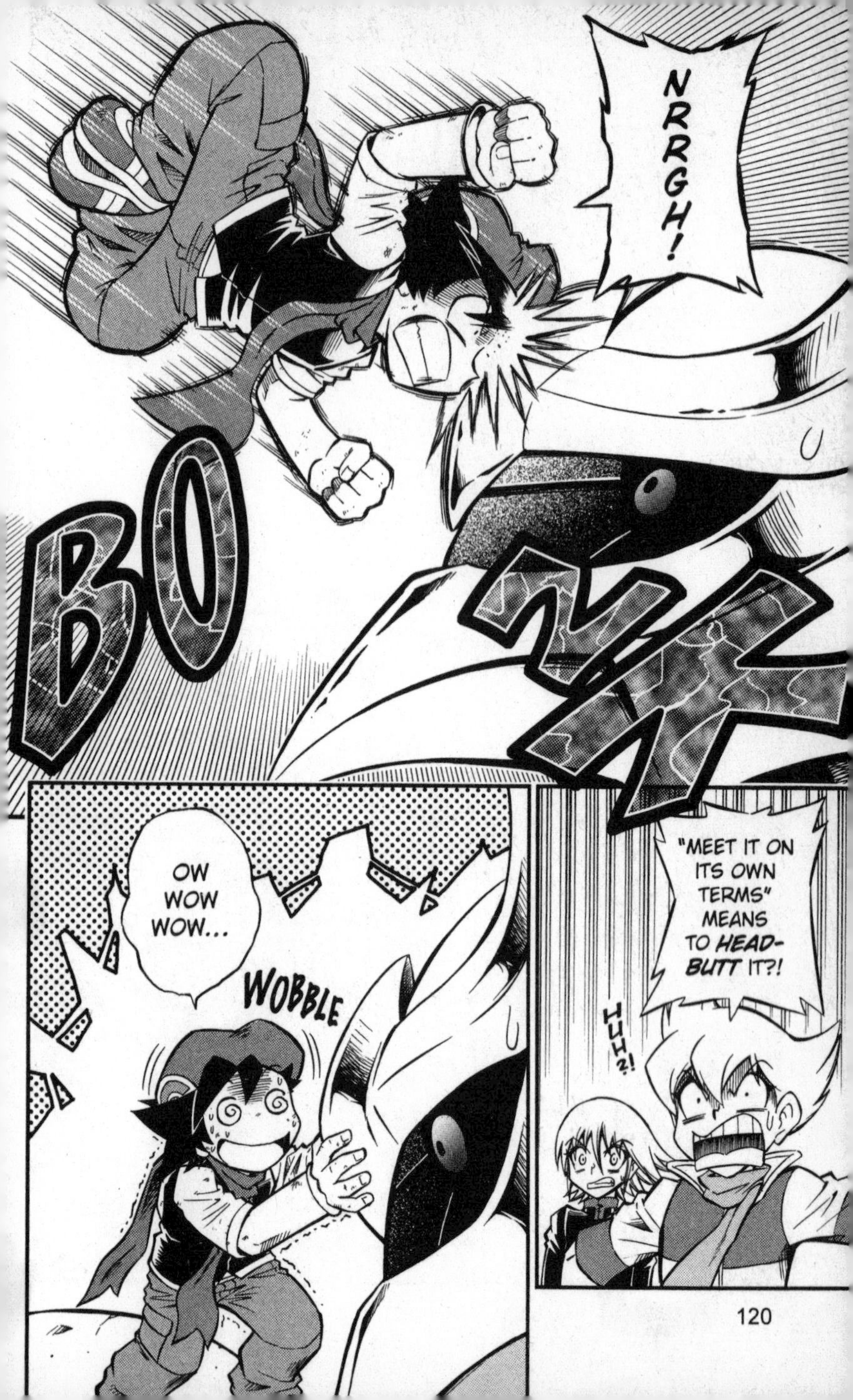
NRRGH!
BONK
"MEET IT ON ITS OWN TERMS" MEANS TO HEAD-BUTT IT?!
HUH?!
OW WOW WOW...
WOBBLE

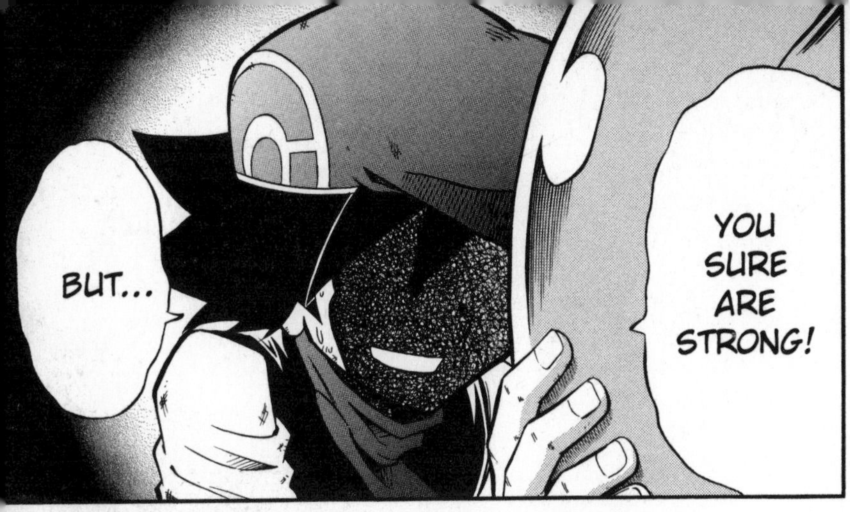
YOU SURE ARE STRONG!
BUT...

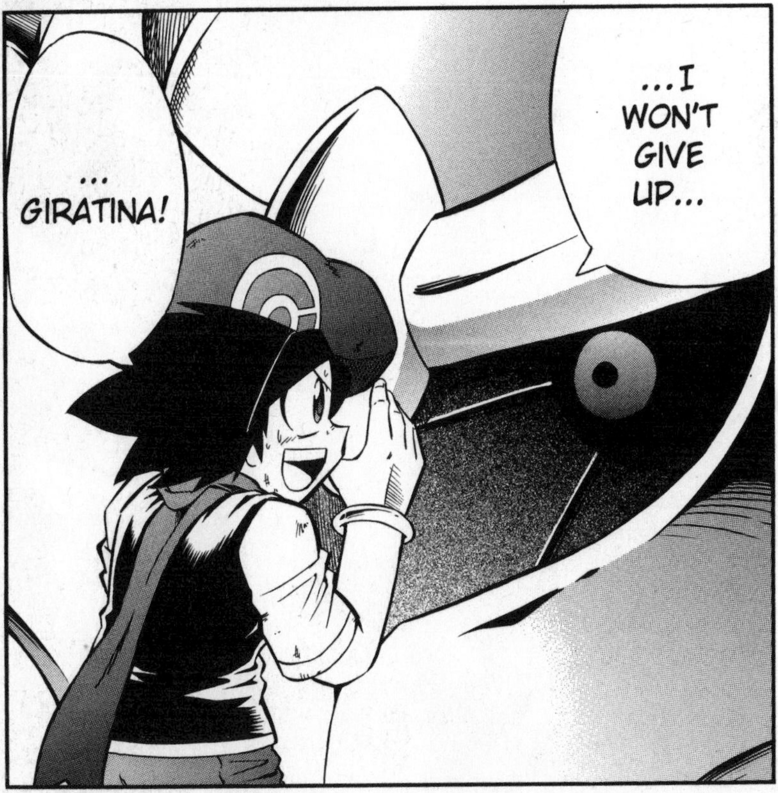
...I WON'T GIVE UP...
... GIRATINA!

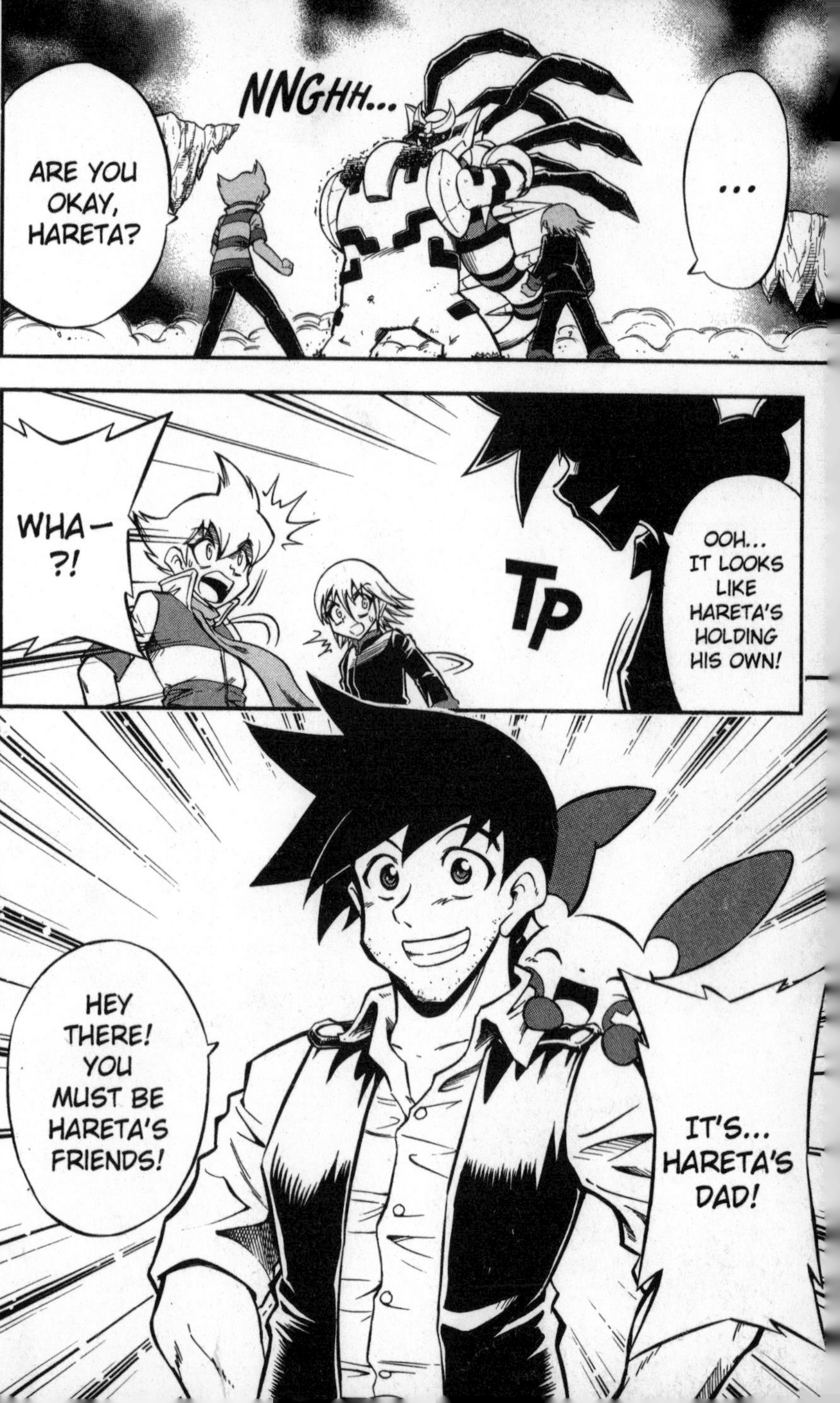
...
NNGHH...
ARE YOU OKAY, HARETA?
OOH... IT LOOKS LIKE HARETA'S HOLDING HIS OWN!
TP
WHA—?!
HEY THERE! YOU MUST BE HARETA'S FRIENDS!
IT'S... HARETA'S DAD!

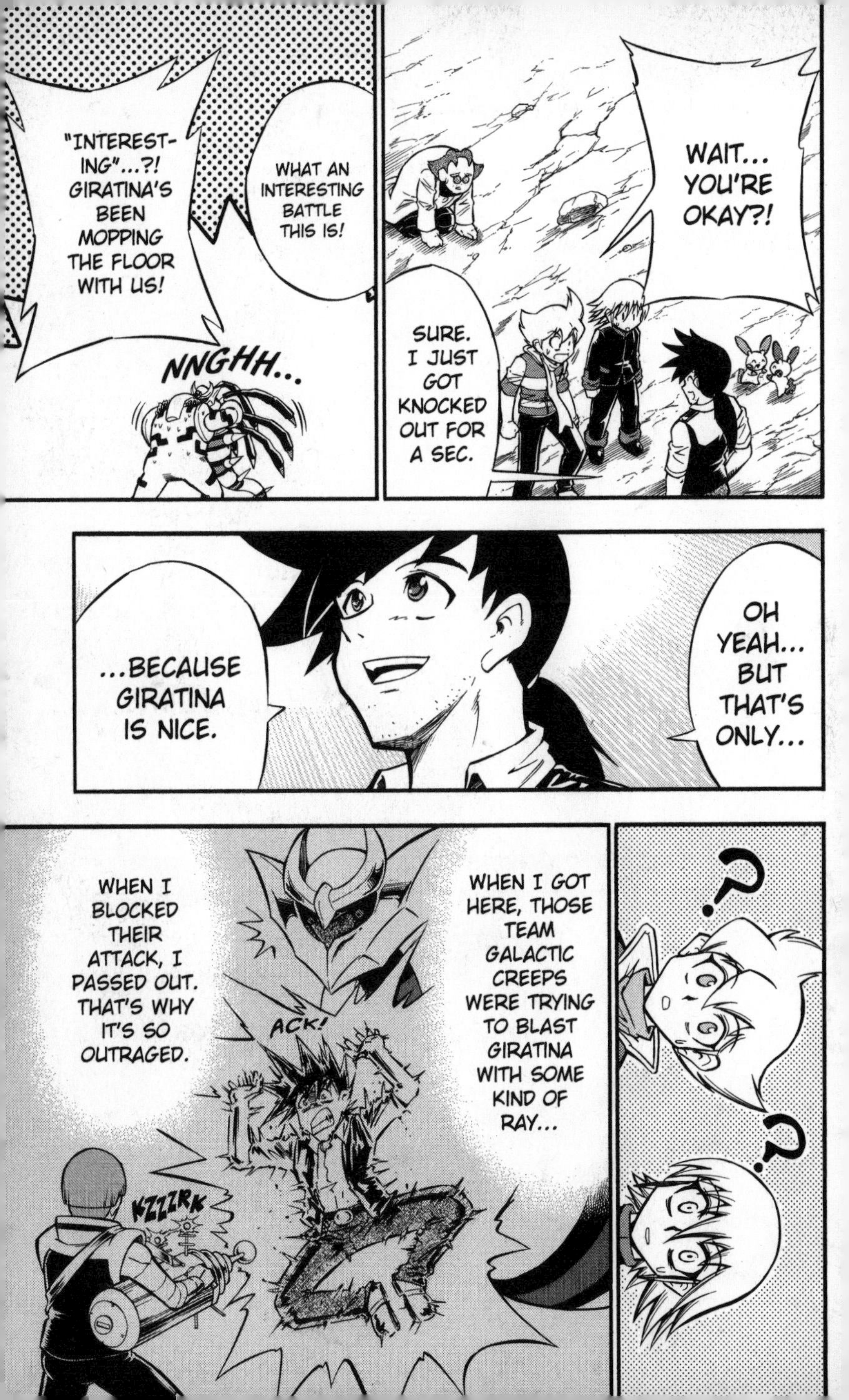
WAIT... YOU'RE OKAY?!
SURE. I JUST GOT KNOCKED OUT FOR A SEC.
WHAT AN INTERESTING BATTLE THIS IS!
"INTERESTING"...?! GIRATINA'S BEEN MOPPING THE FLOOR WITH US!
NNGHH...
OH YEAH... BUT THAT'S ONLY...
...BECAUSE GIRATINA IS NICE.
?
?
WHEN I GOT HERE, THOSE TEAM GALACTIC CREEPS WERE TRYING TO BLAST GIRATINA WITH SOME KIND OF RAY...
WHEN I BLOCKED THEIR ATTACK, I PASSED OUT. THAT'S WHY IT'S SO OUTRAGED.
ACK!
KZZZRK

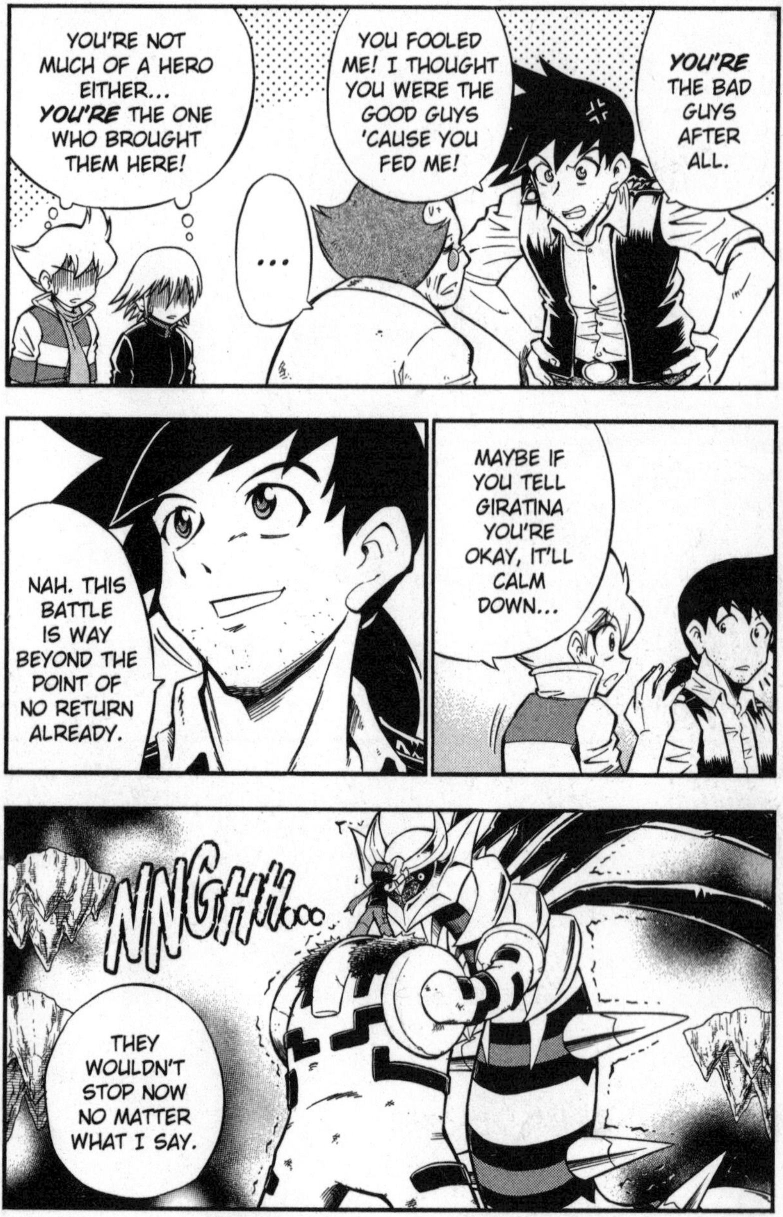
YOU'RE THE BAD GUYS AFTER ALL.
YOU FOOLED ME! I THOUGHT YOU WERE THE GOOD GUYS 'CAUSE YOU FED ME!
...
YOU'RE NOT MUCH OF A HERO EITHER... YOU'RE THE ONE WHO BROUGHT THEM HERE!
MAYBE IF YOU TELL GIRATINA YOU'RE OKAY, IT'LL CALM DOWN...
NAH. THIS BATTLE IS WAY BEYOND THE POINT OF NO RETURN ALREADY.
NNGHH...
THEY WOULDN'T STOP NOW NO MATTER WHAT I SAY.

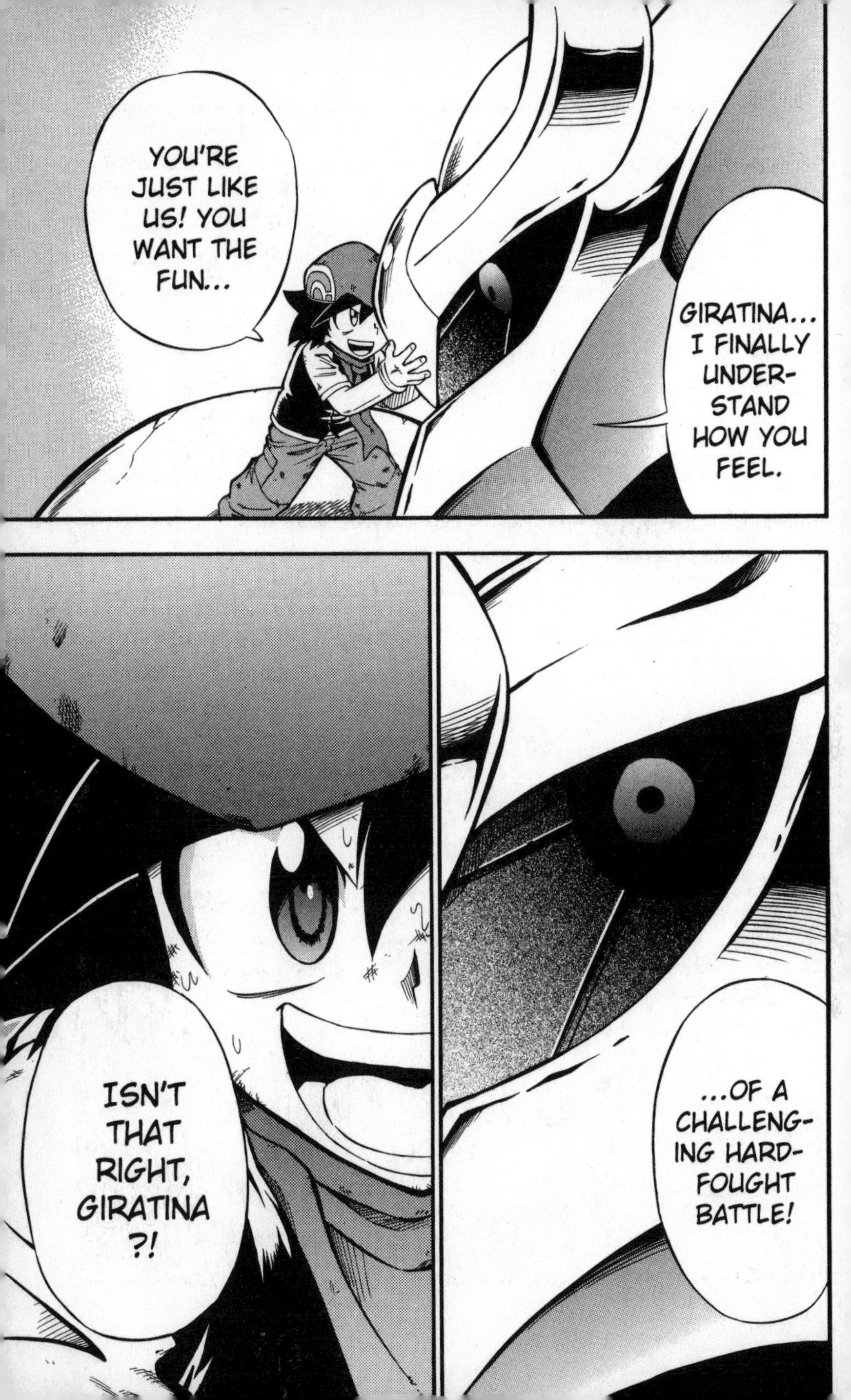
GIRATINA... I FINALLY UNDERSTAND HOW YOU FEEL.
YOU'RE JUST LIKE US! YOU WANT THE FUN...
...OF A CHALLENGING HARD-FOUGHT BATTLE!
ISN'T THAT RIGHT, GIRATINA?!

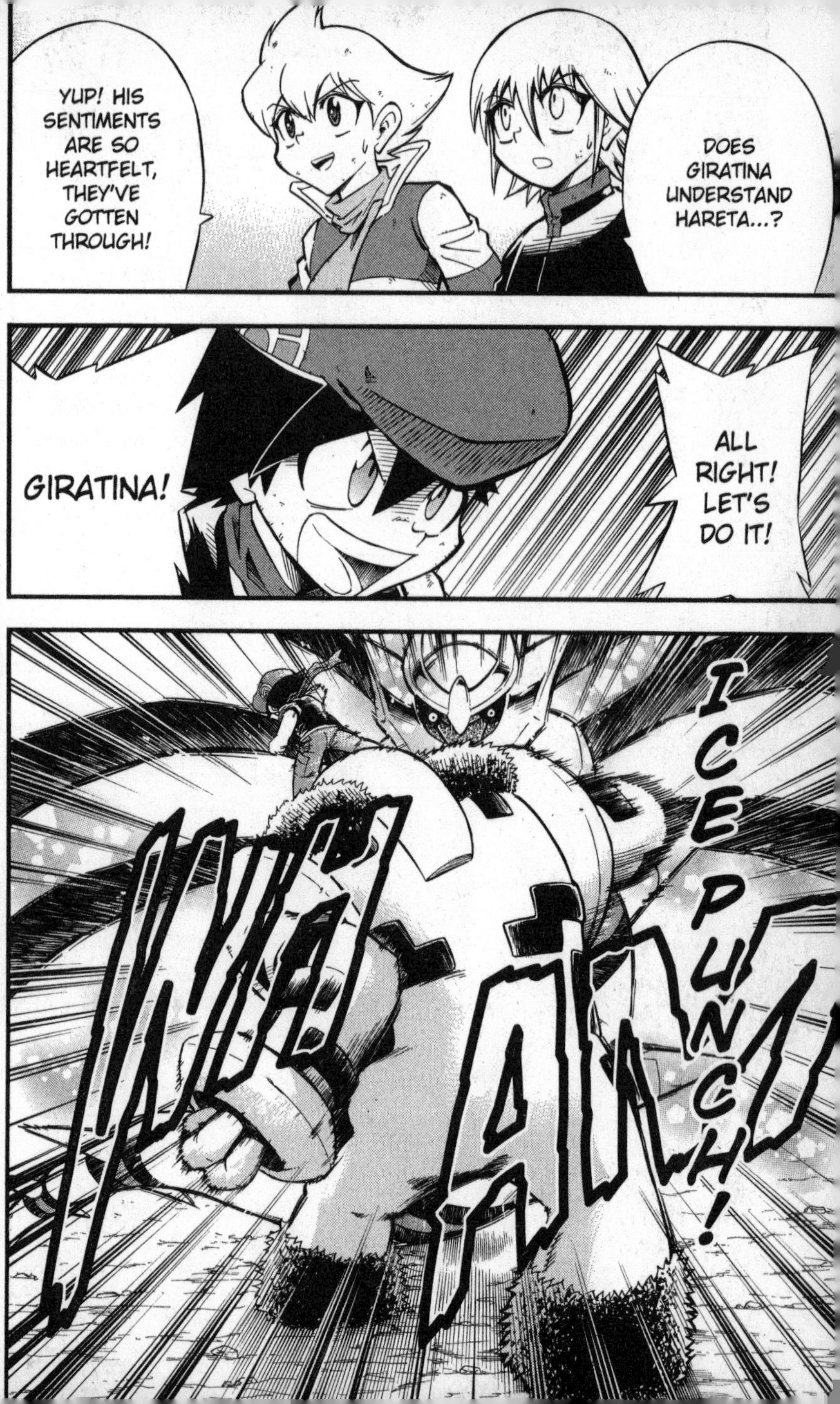
DOES GIRATINA UNDERSTAND HARETA...?
YUP! HIS SENTIMENTS ARE SO HEARTFELT, THEY'VE GOTTEN THROUGH!
ALL RIGHT! LET'S DO IT!
GIRATINA!
ICE PUNCH!

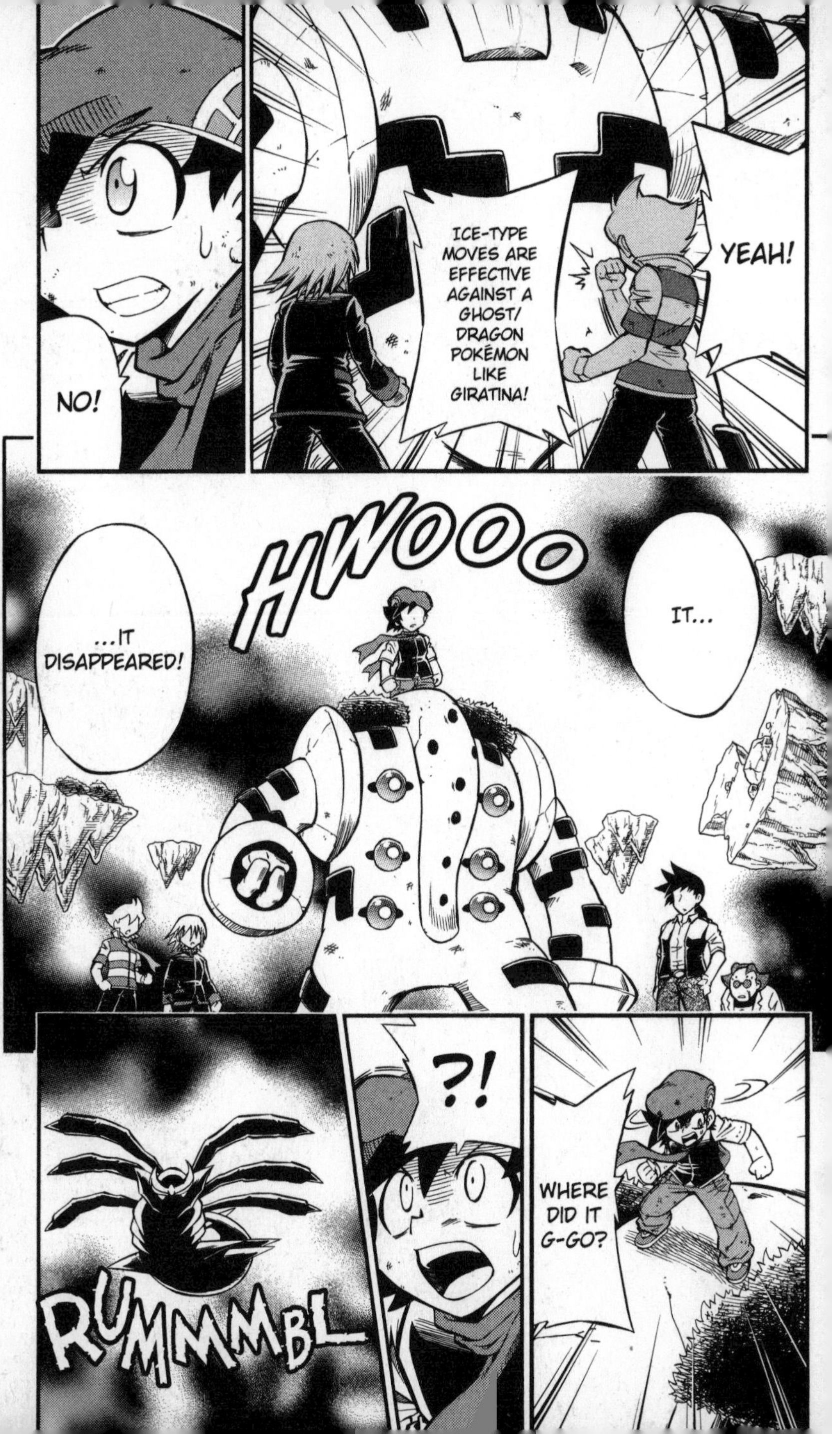
ICE-TYPE MOVES ARE EFFECTIVE AGAINST A GHOST/ DRAGON POKÉMON LIKE GIRATINA!
YEAH!
NO!
HWOOO
IT...
...IT DISAPPEARED!
WHERE DID IT G-GO?
?!
RUMMMBL

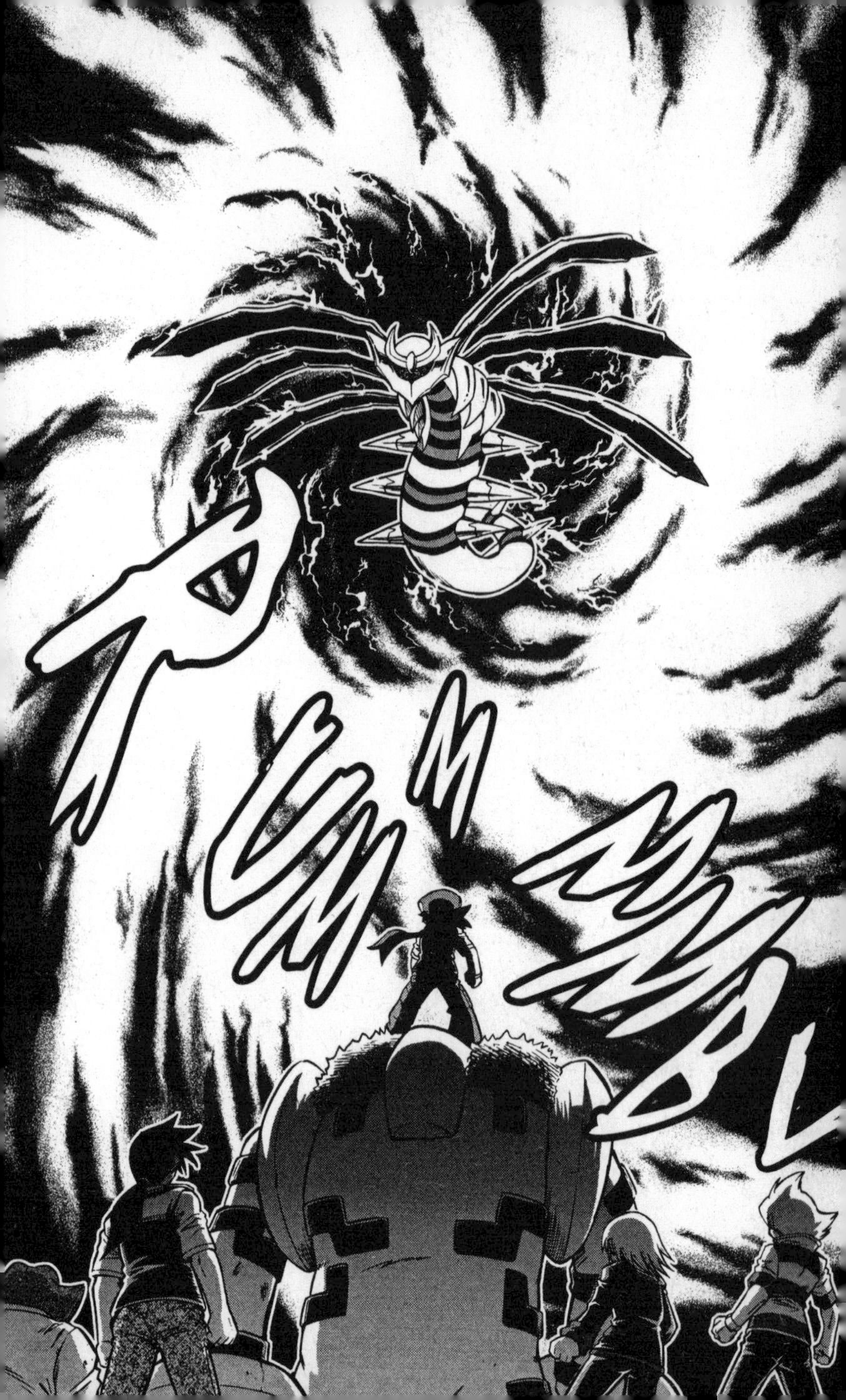
RUMMMBL

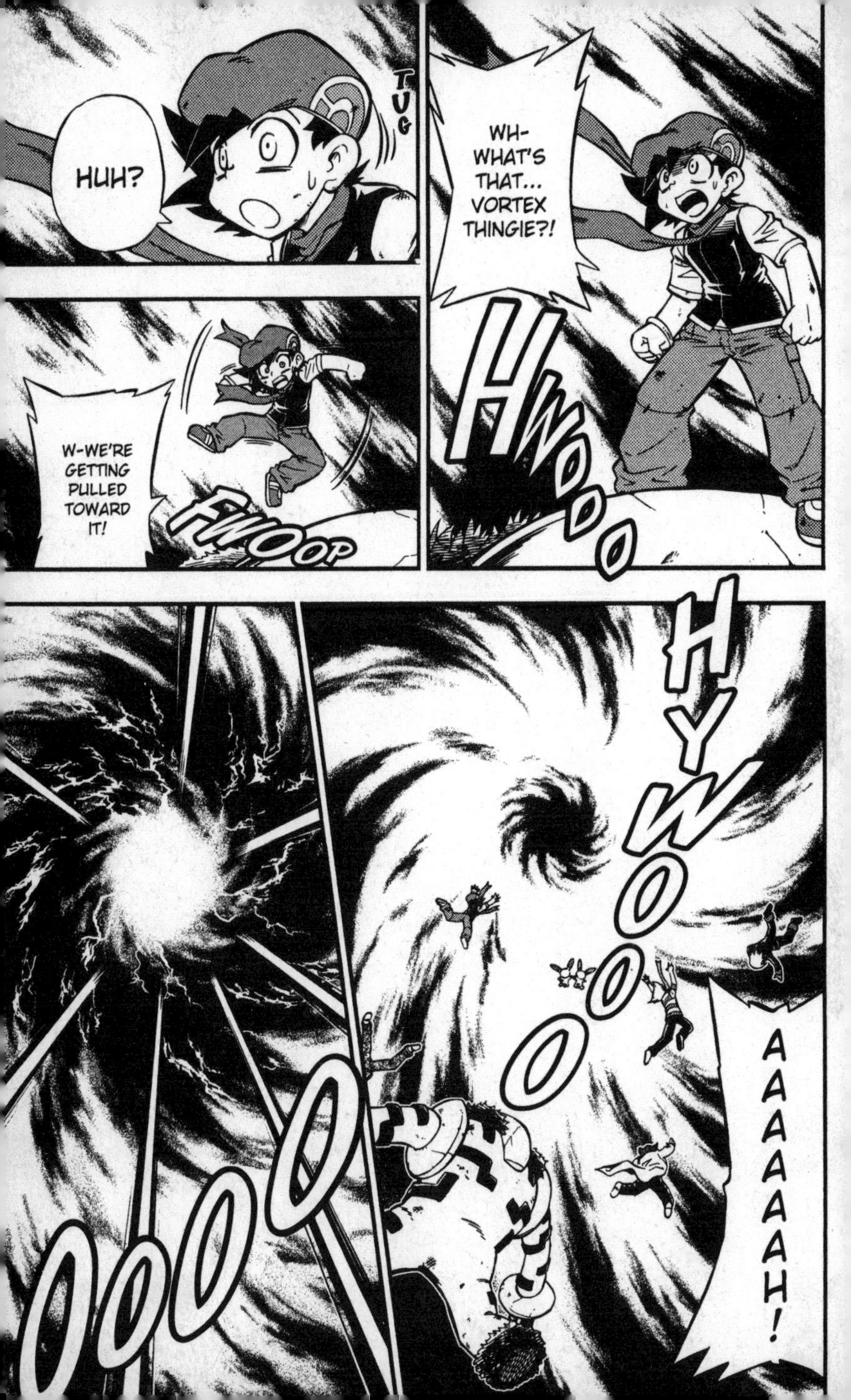
WH-WHAT'S THAT... VORTEX THINGIE?!
HWOOOO
TUG
HUH?
W-WE'RE GETTING PULLED TOWARD IT!
FWOOOP
HYWOOOOOOOOOOOO
AAAAAAAH!

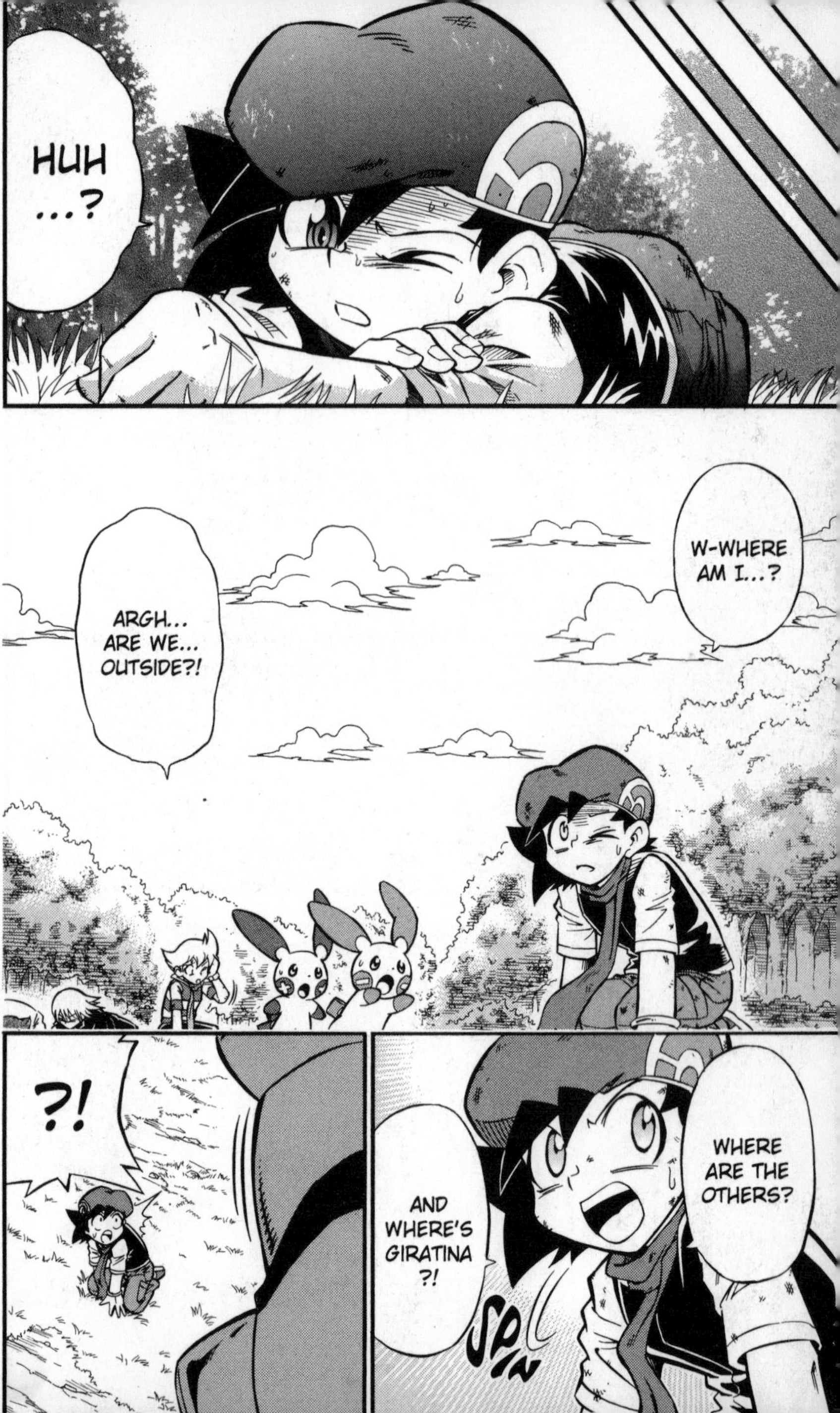
HUH ...?
W-WHERE AM I...?
ARGH... ARE WE... OUTSIDE?!
WHERE ARE THE OTHERS?
AND WHERE'S GIRATINA ?!
SPIN
?!

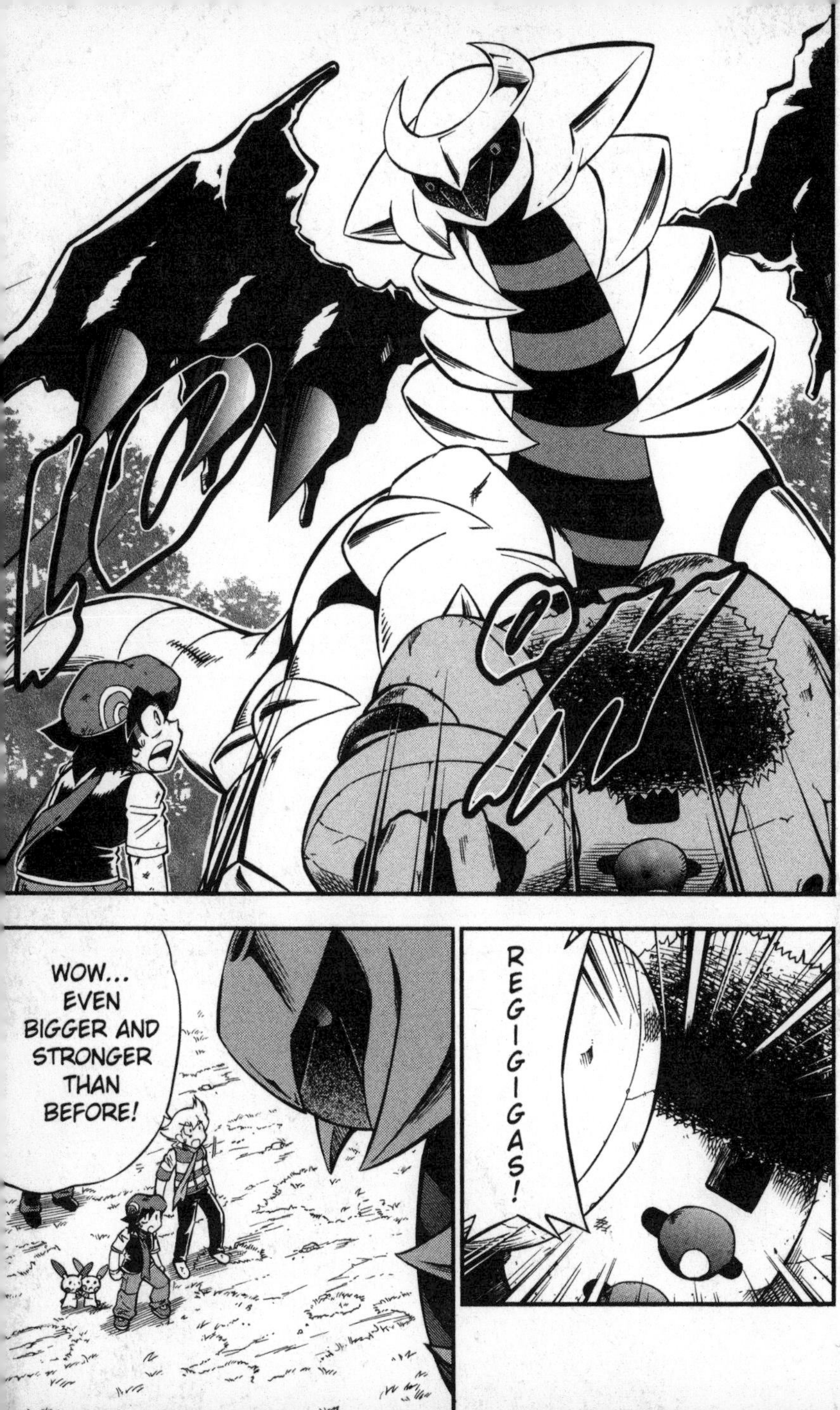
REGIGIGAS!
WOW... EVEN BIGGER AND STRONGER THAN BEFORE!

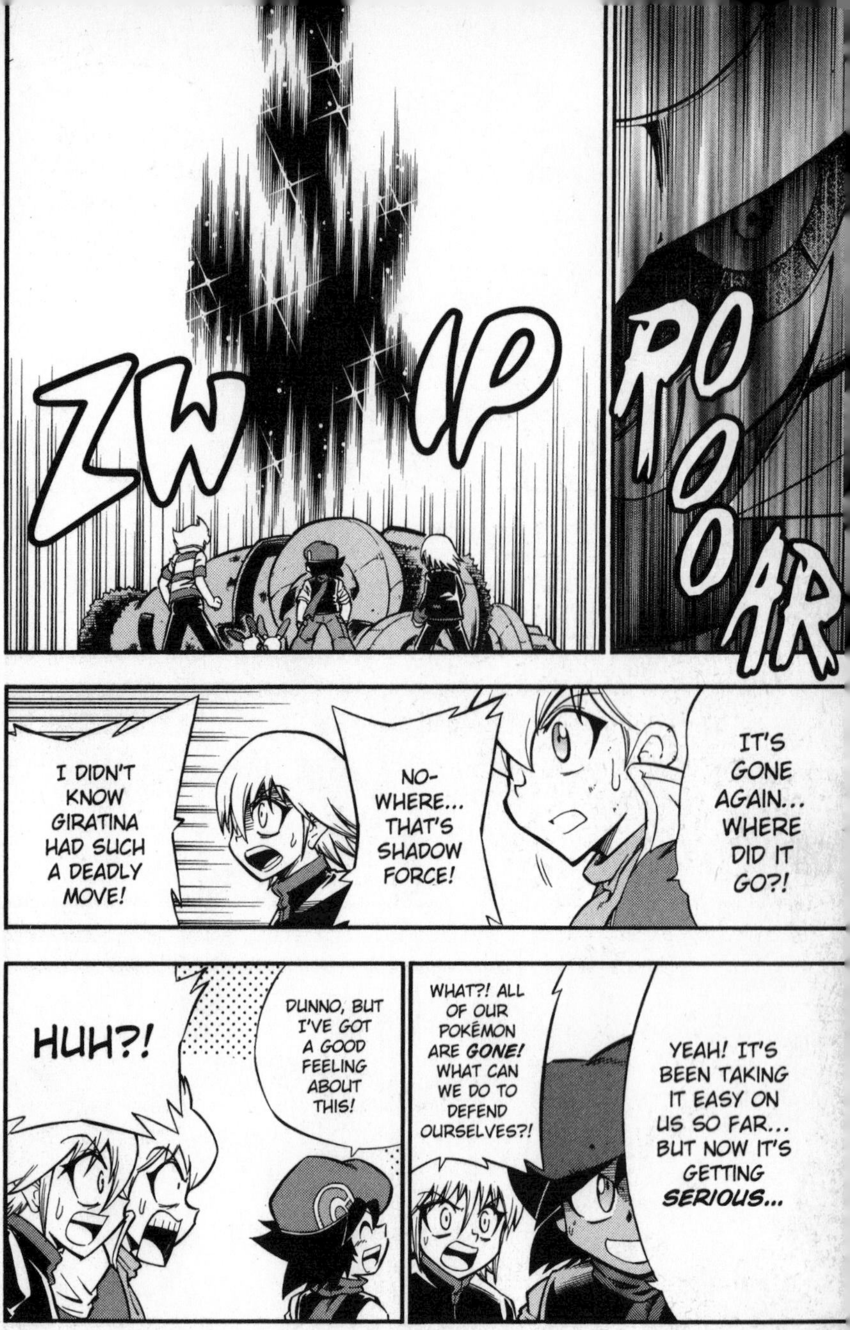
ROOOAR
ZWIP
IT'S GONE AGAIN... WHERE DID IT GO?!
NO-WHERE... THAT'S SHADOW FORCE!
I DIDN'T KNOW GIRATINA HAD SUCH A DEADLY MOVE!
YEAH! IT'S BEEN TAKING IT EASY ON US SO FAR... BUT NOW IT'S GETTING **SERIOUS...**
WHAT?! ALL OF OUR POKÉMON ARE **GONE!** WHAT CAN WE DO TO DEFEND OURSELVES?!
DUNNO, BUT I'VE GOT A GOOD FEELING ABOUT THIS!
HUH?!

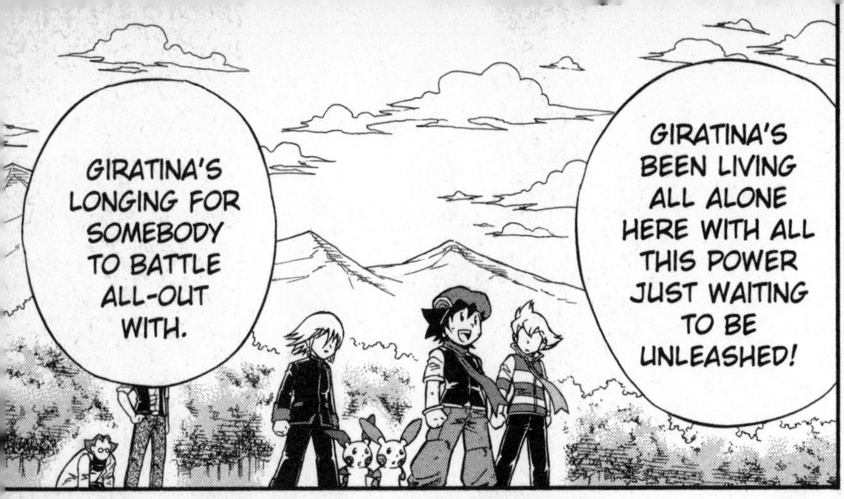
GIRATINA'S BEEN LIVING ALL ALONE HERE WITH ALL THIS POWER JUST WAITING TO BE UNLEASHED!
GIRATINA'S LONGING FOR SOMEBODY TO BATTLE ALL-OUT WITH.
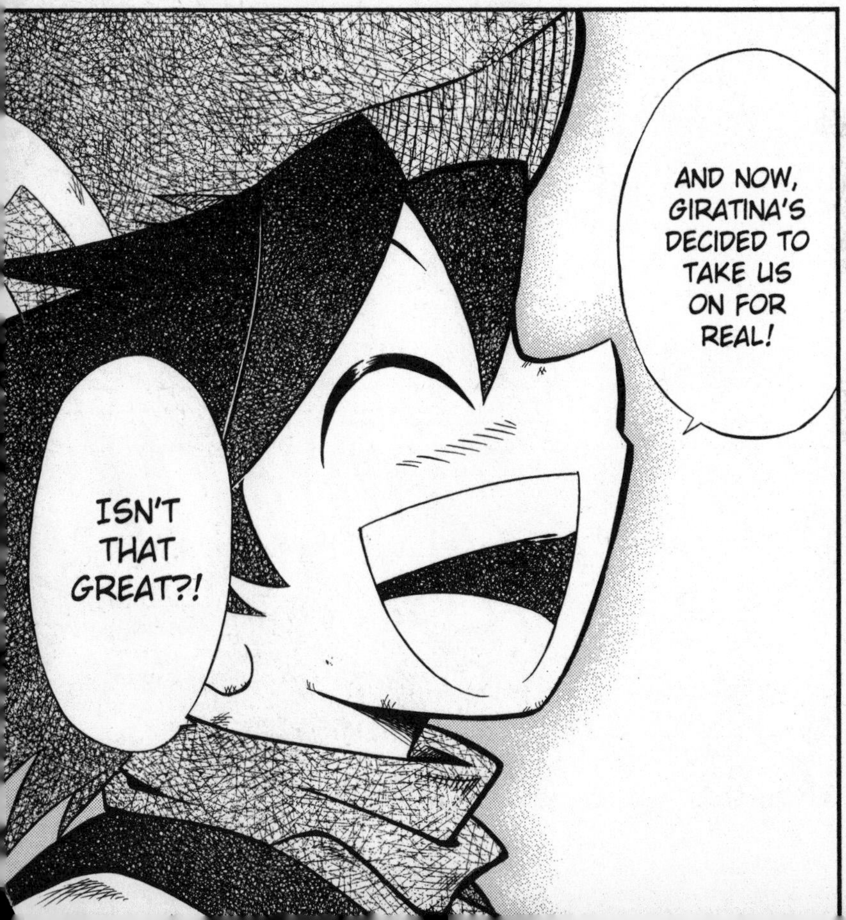
AND NOW, GIRATINA'S DECIDED TO TAKE US ON FOR REAL!
ISN'T THAT GREAT?!

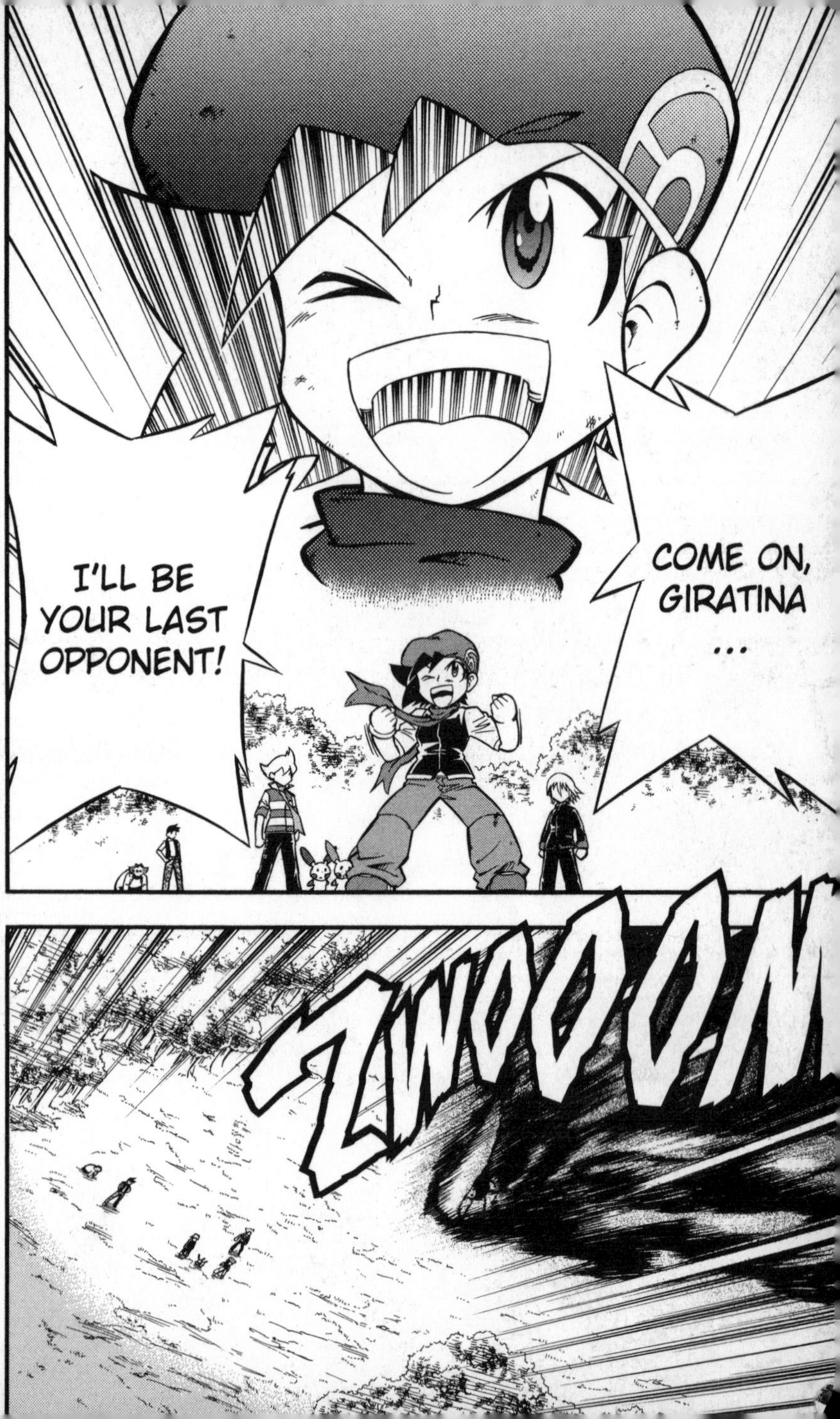
COME ON, GIRATINA ...
I'LL BE YOUR LAST OPPONENT!
ZWOOOM

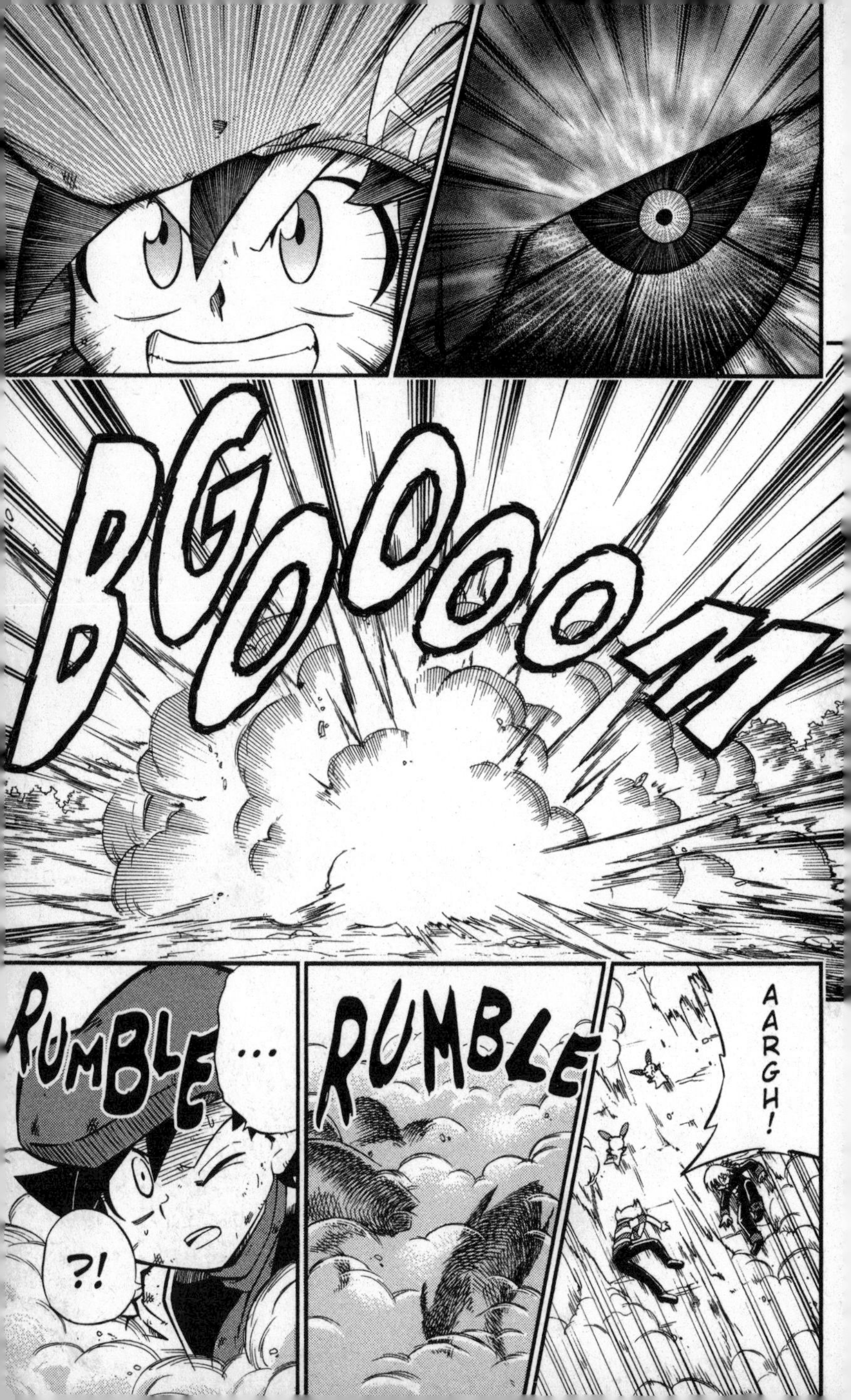
BOOOOOM
AARGH!
RUMBLE
RUMBLE...
?!

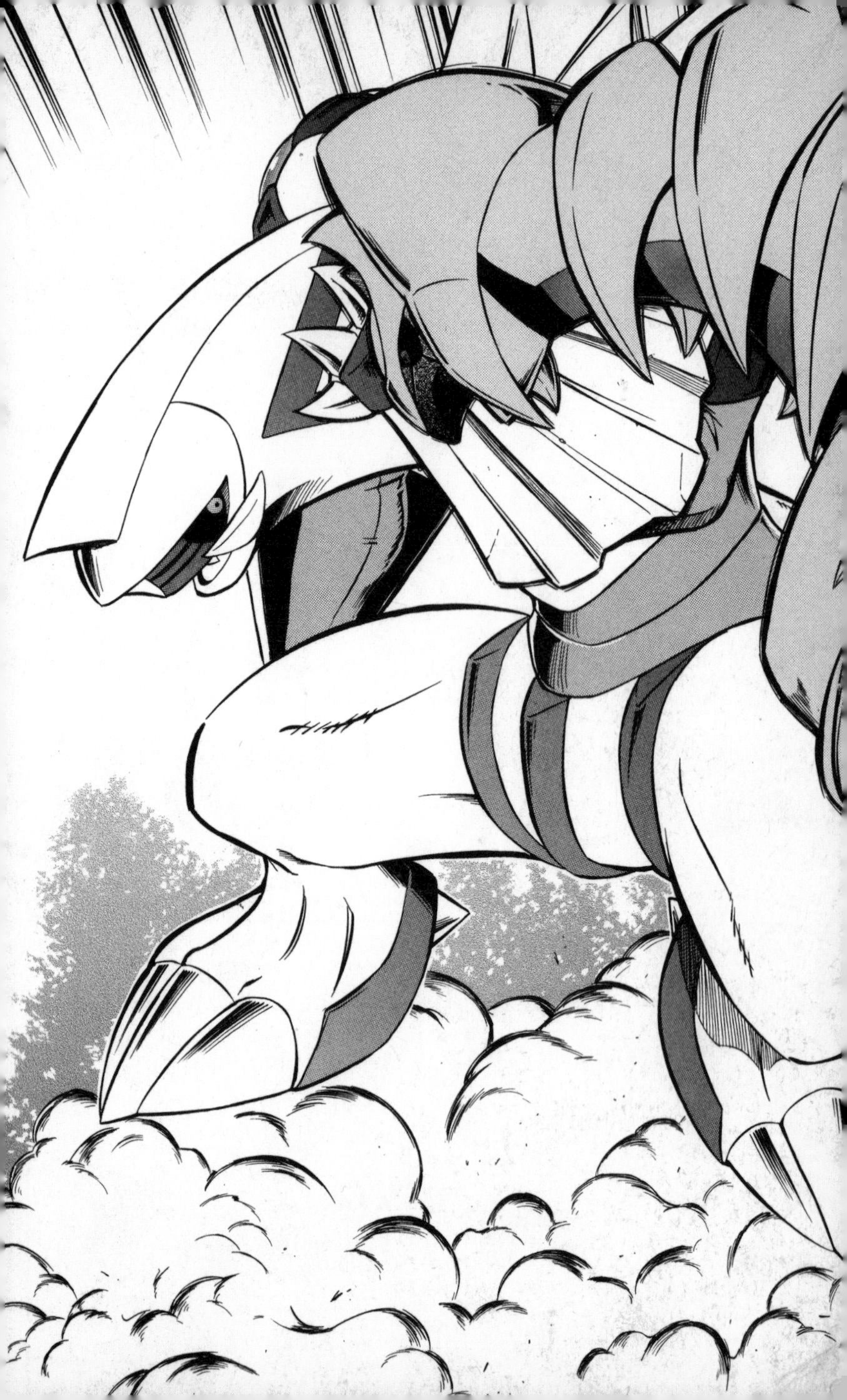

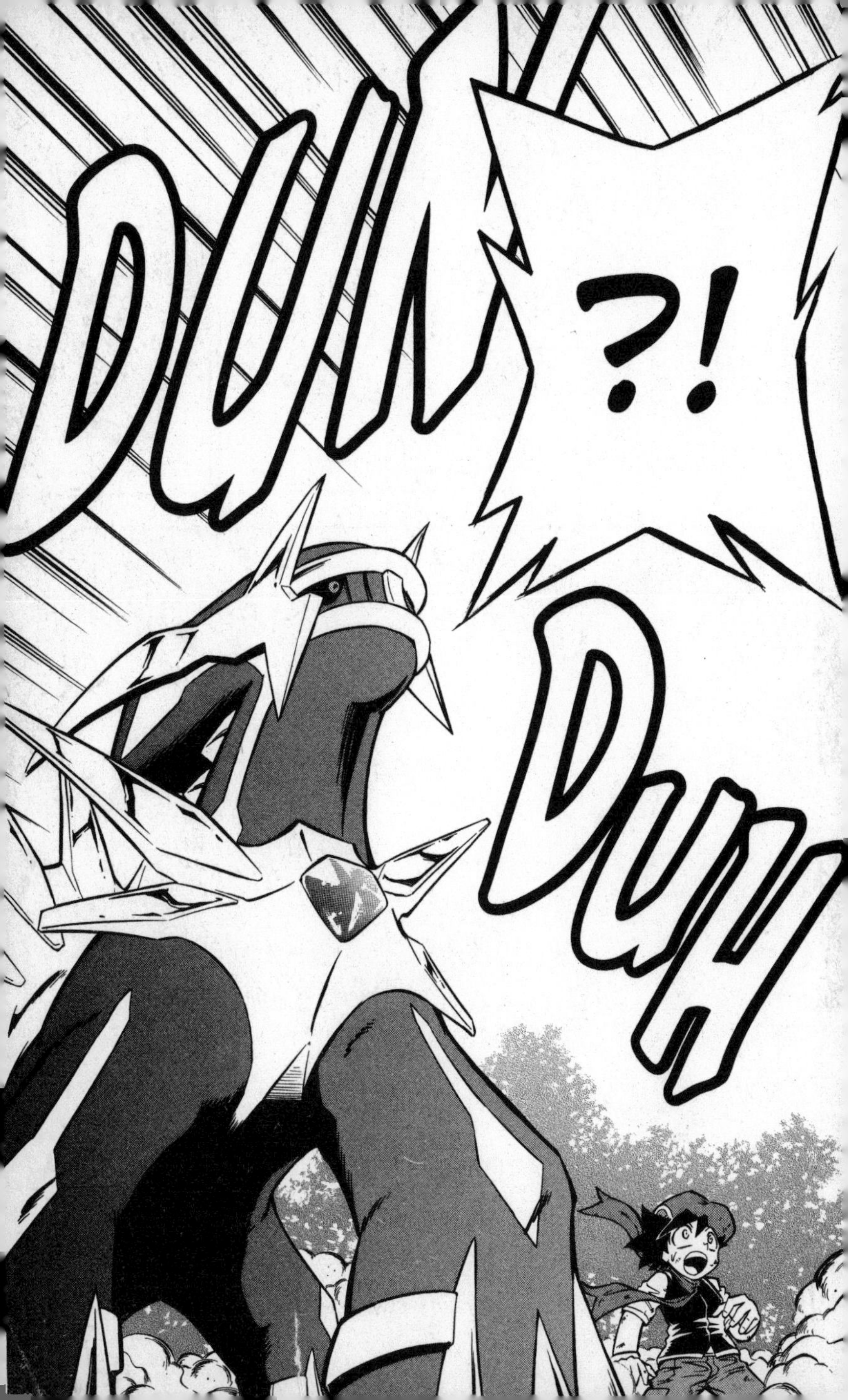

?!
DUN
DUN

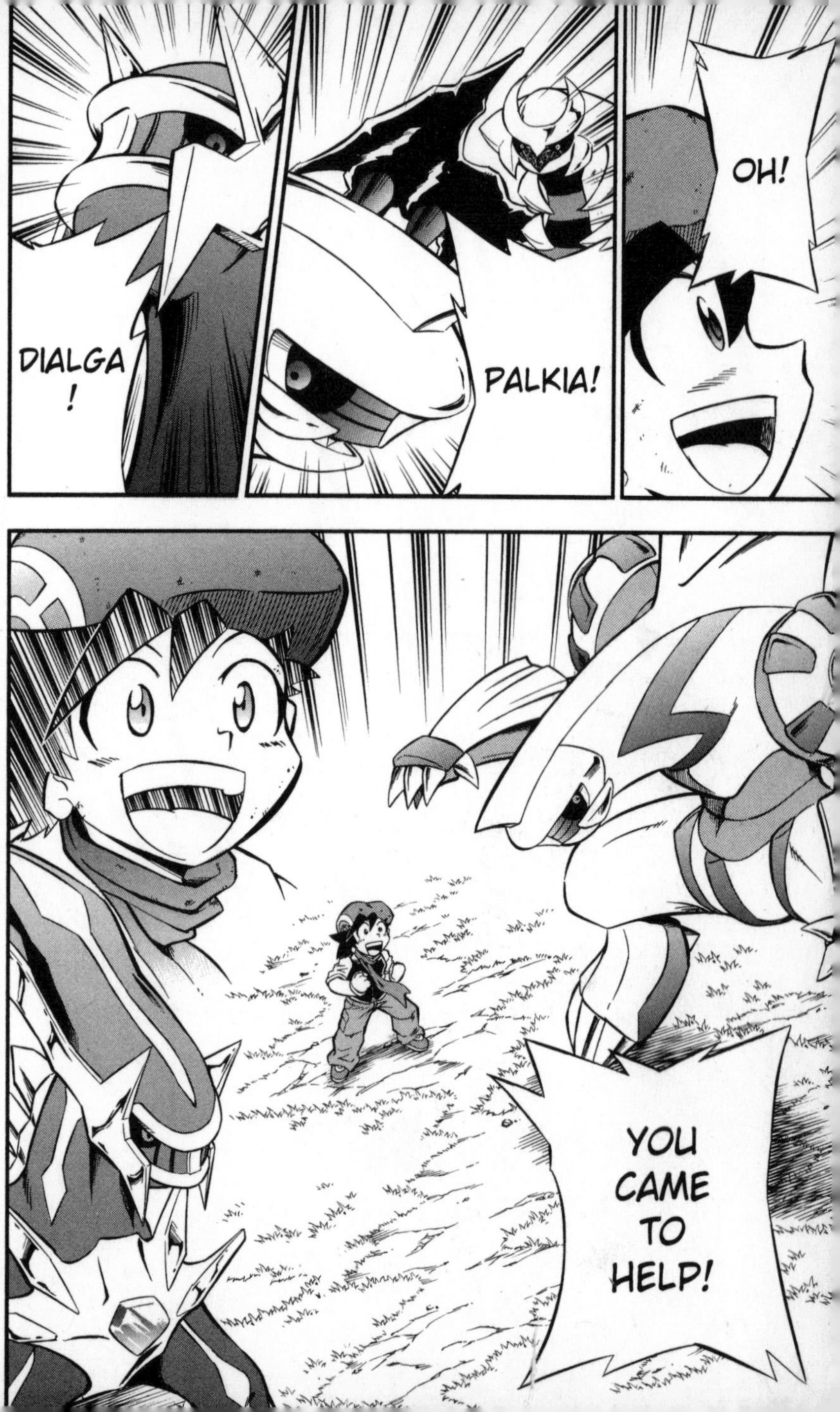
OH!
PALKIA!
DIALGA !
YOU CAME TO HELP!

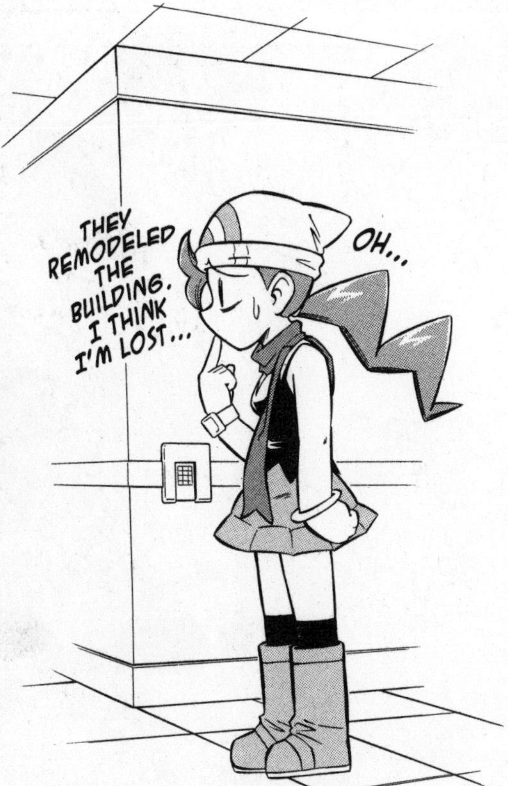
OH...
THEY REMODELED THE BUILDING. I THINK I'M LOST...

FINAL CHAPTER
GATHERING OF THE LEGENDARY POKÉMON!

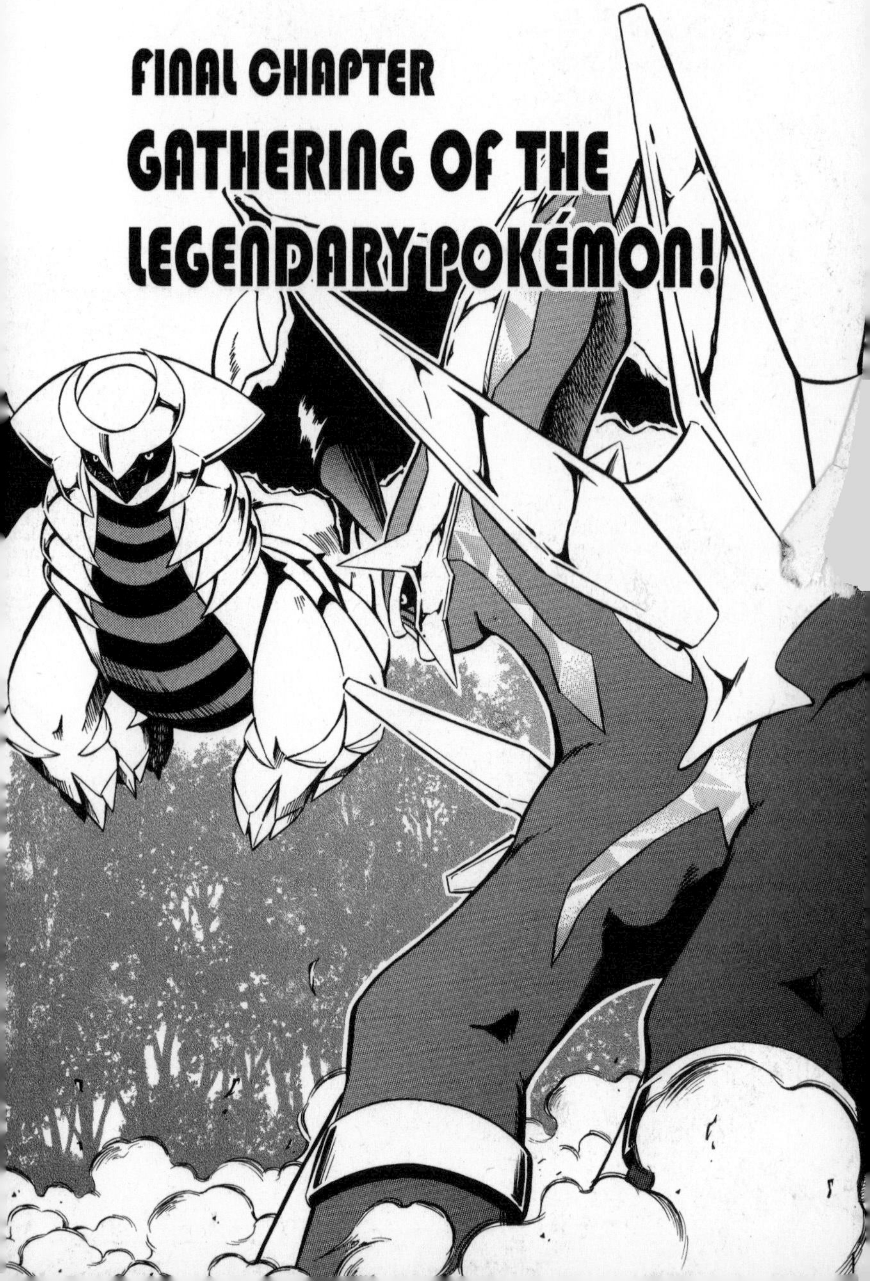

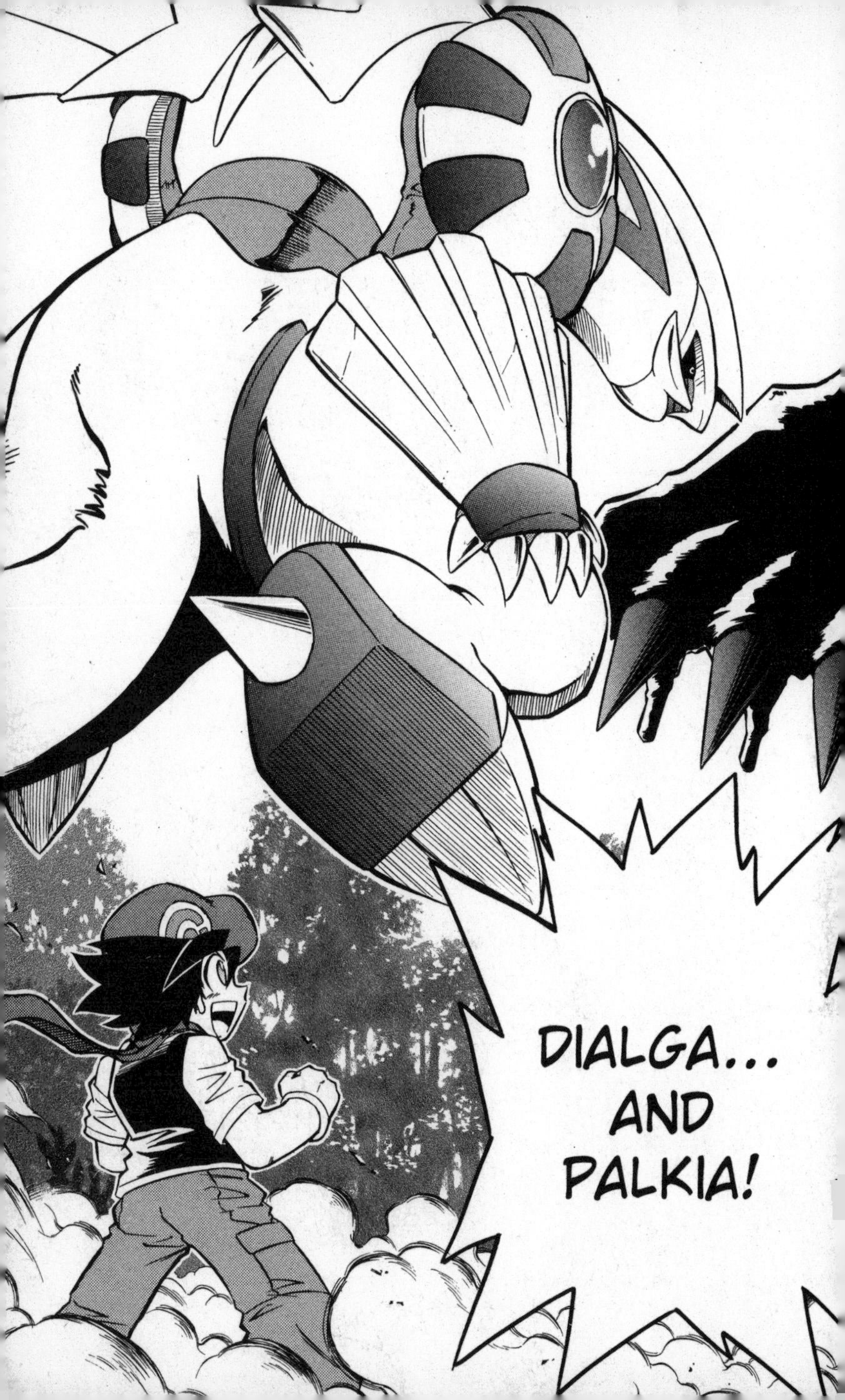
DIALGA... AND PALKIA!

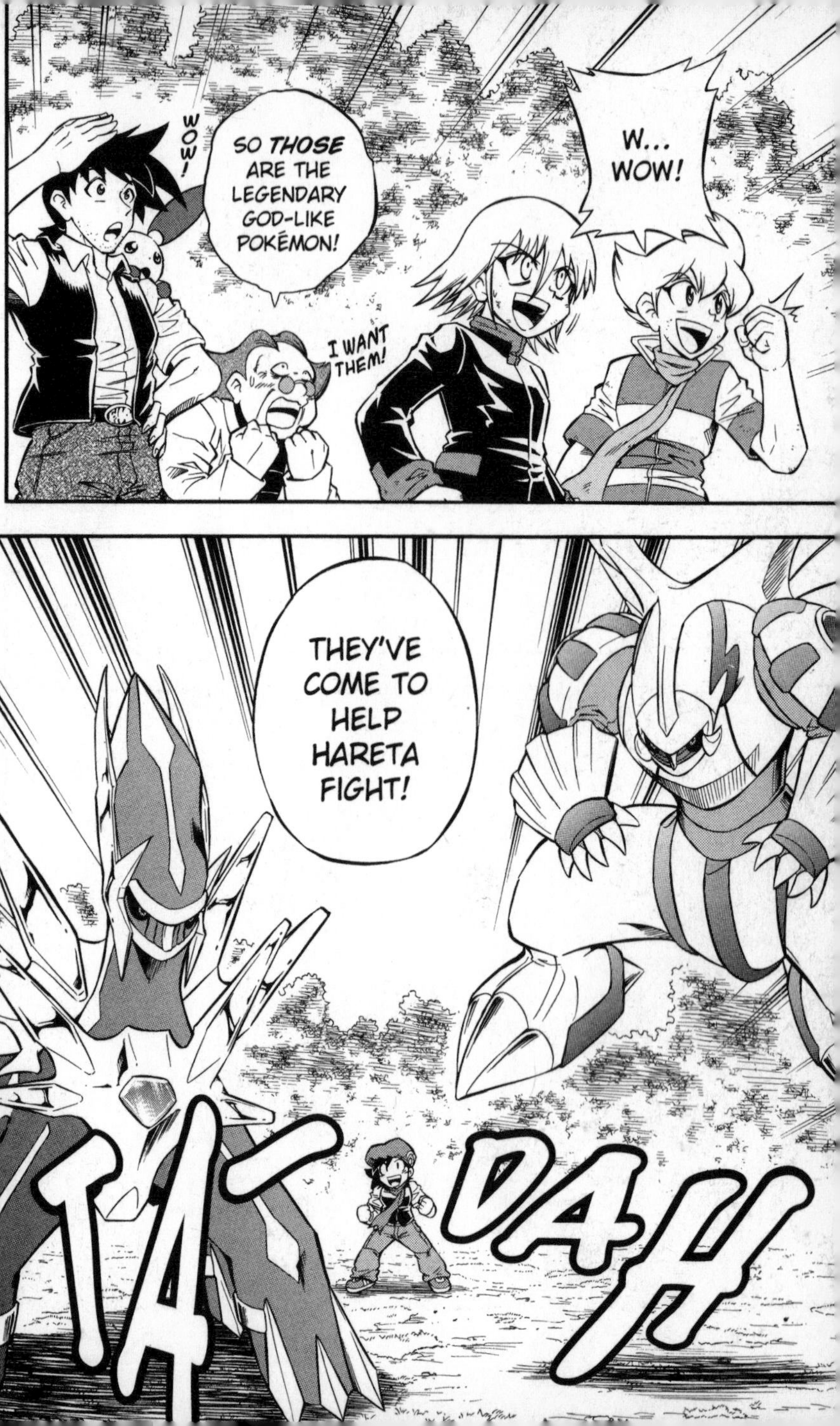
W... WOW!
SO THOSE ARE THE LEGENDARY GOD-LIKE POKéMON!
WOW!
I WANT THEM!
THEY'VE COME TO HELP HARETA FIGHT!
TA-DAH

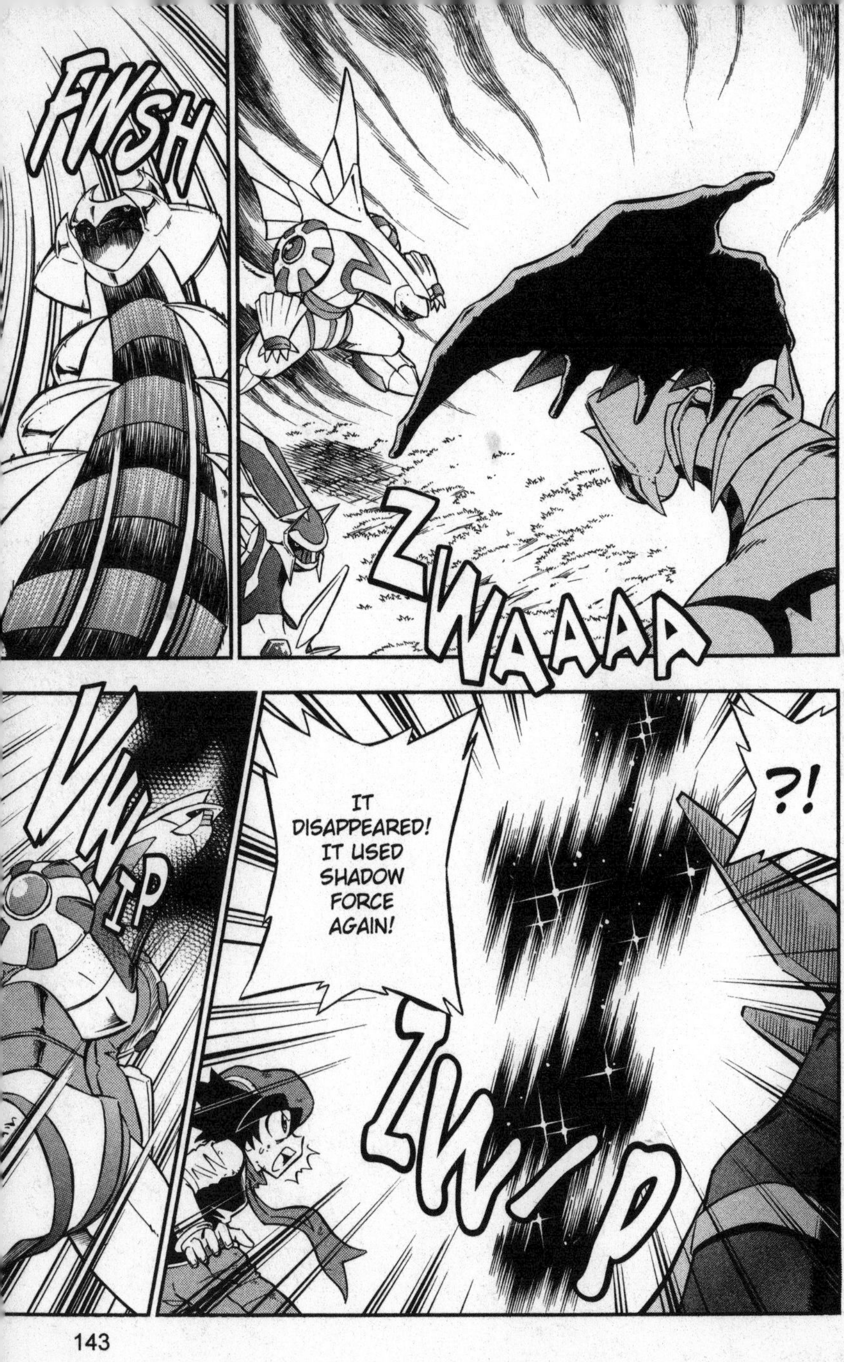
ZWAAAA
FWSH
?!
IT DISAPPEARED! IT USED SHADOW FORCE AGAIN!
ZWIP
VWIP

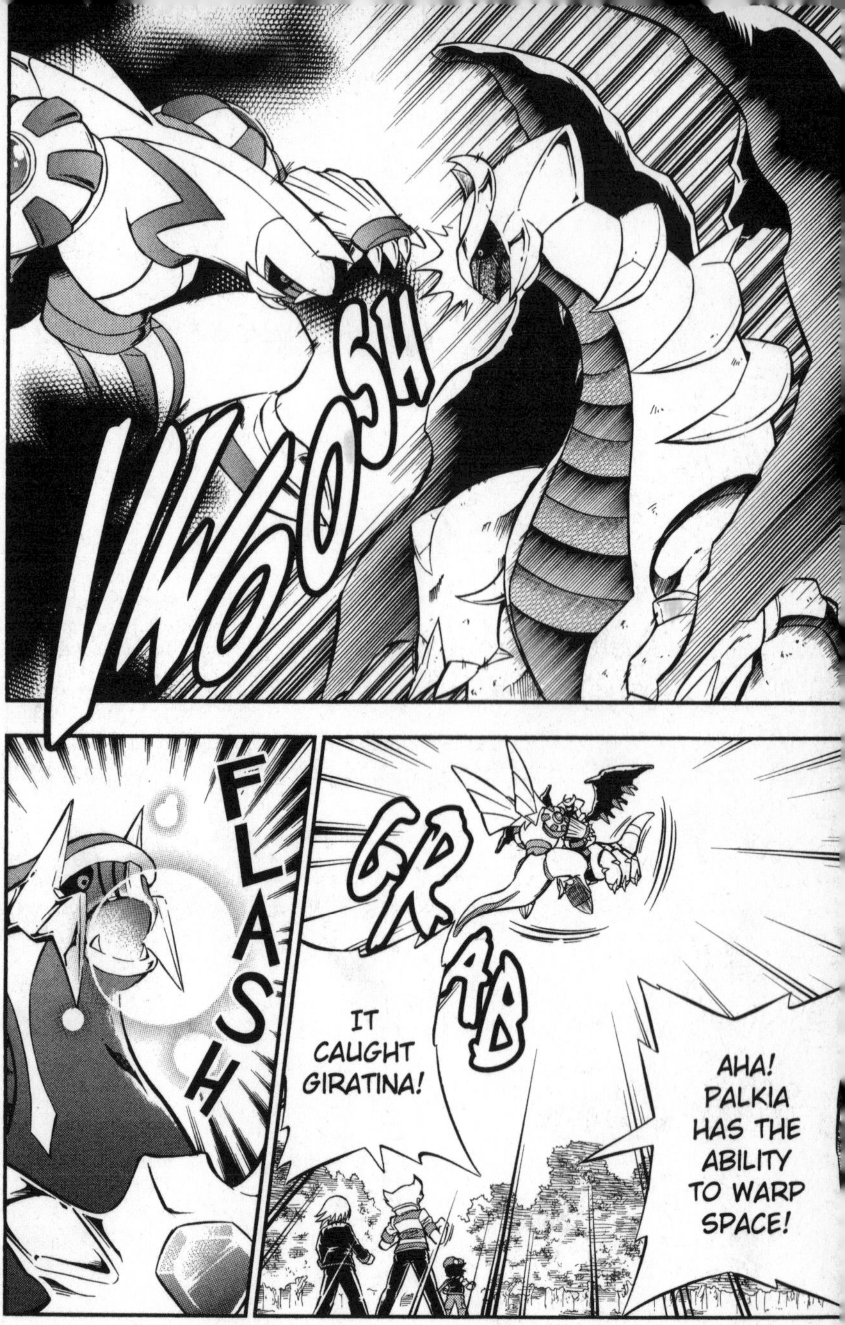
WHOOSH
GRAB
IT CAUGHT GIRATINA!
AHA! PALKIA HAS THE ABILITY TO WARP SPACE!
FLASH

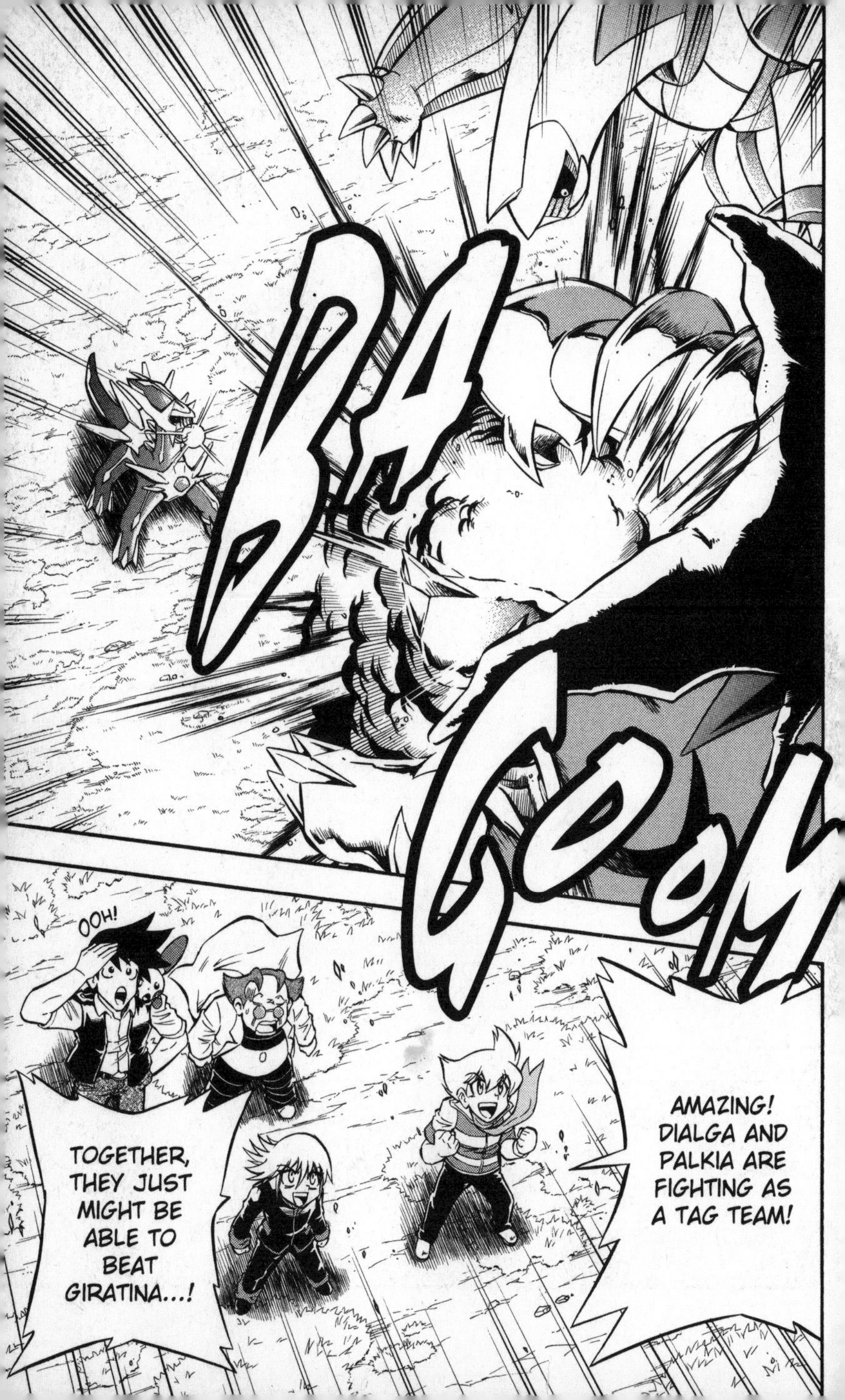
BA
GOOM
AMAZING! DIALGA AND PALKIA ARE FIGHTING AS A TAG TEAM!
OOH!
TOGETHER, THEY JUST MIGHT BE ABLE TO BEAT GIRATINA...!

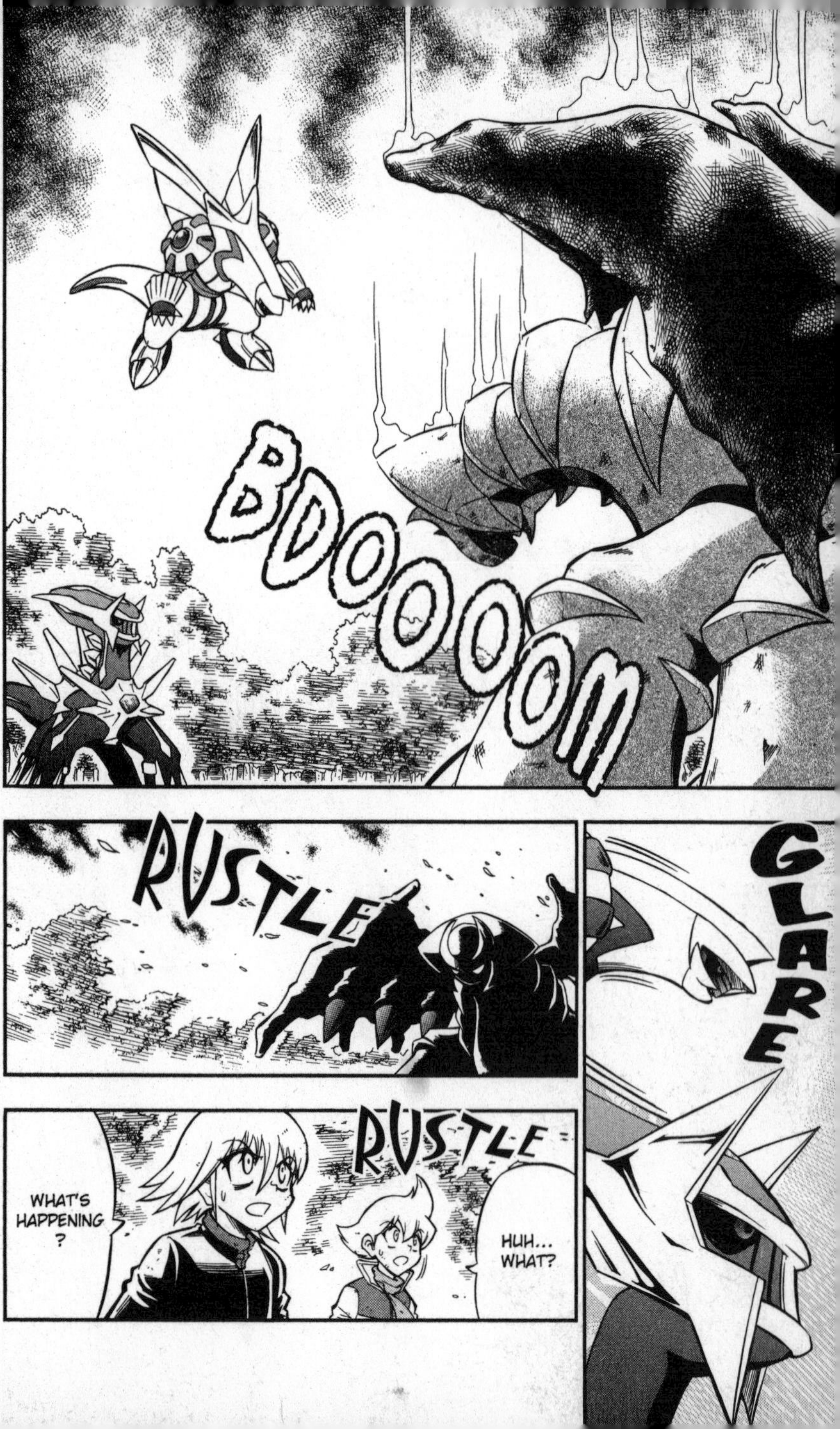
BDOOOOOM
GLARE
RUSTLE
RUSTLE
HUH... WHAT?
WHAT'S HAPPENING ?

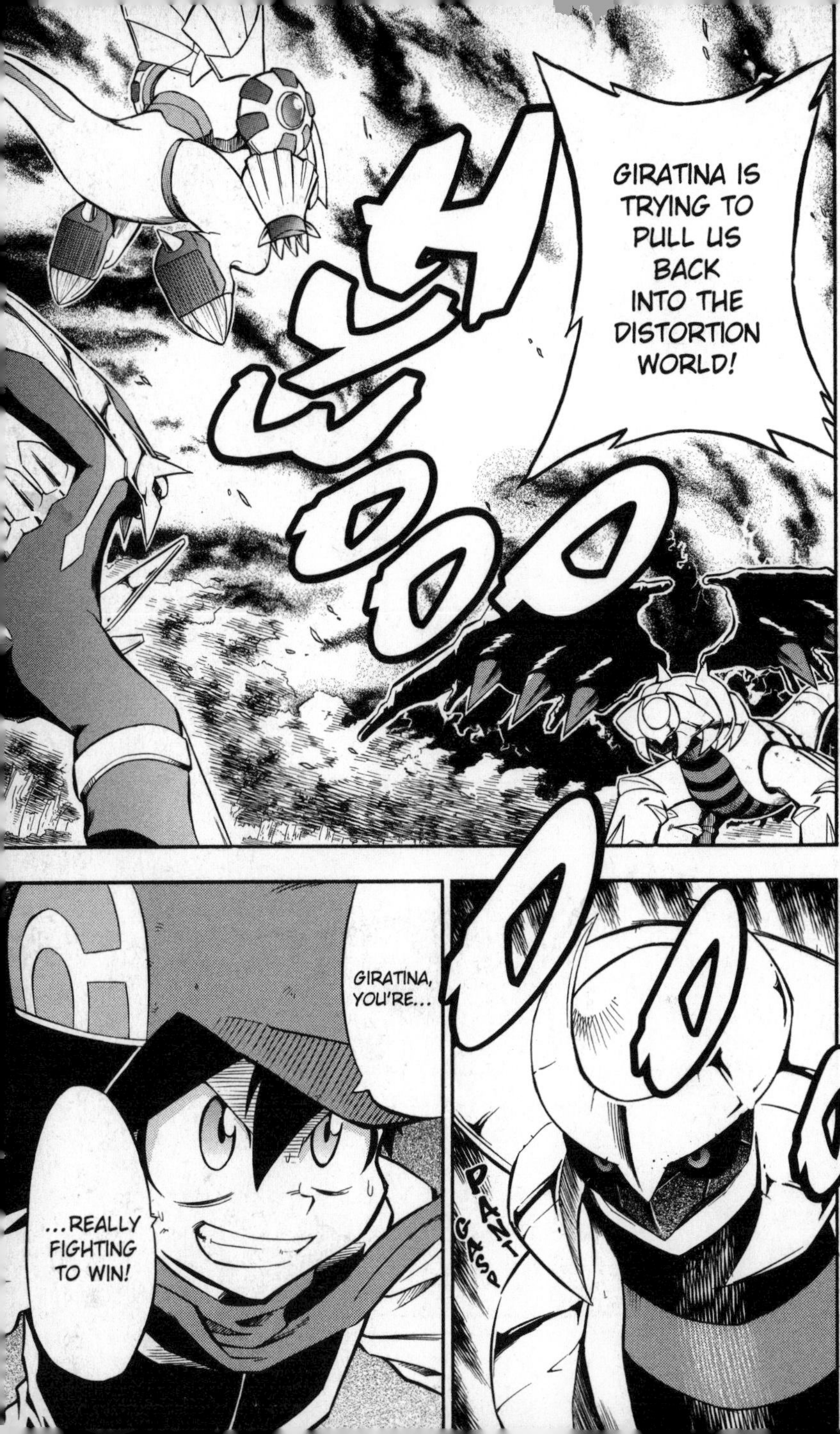
GIRATINA IS TRYING TO PULL US BACK INTO THE DISTORTION WORLD!
PANT GASP
GIRATINA, YOU'RE...
...REALLY FIGHTING TO WIN!

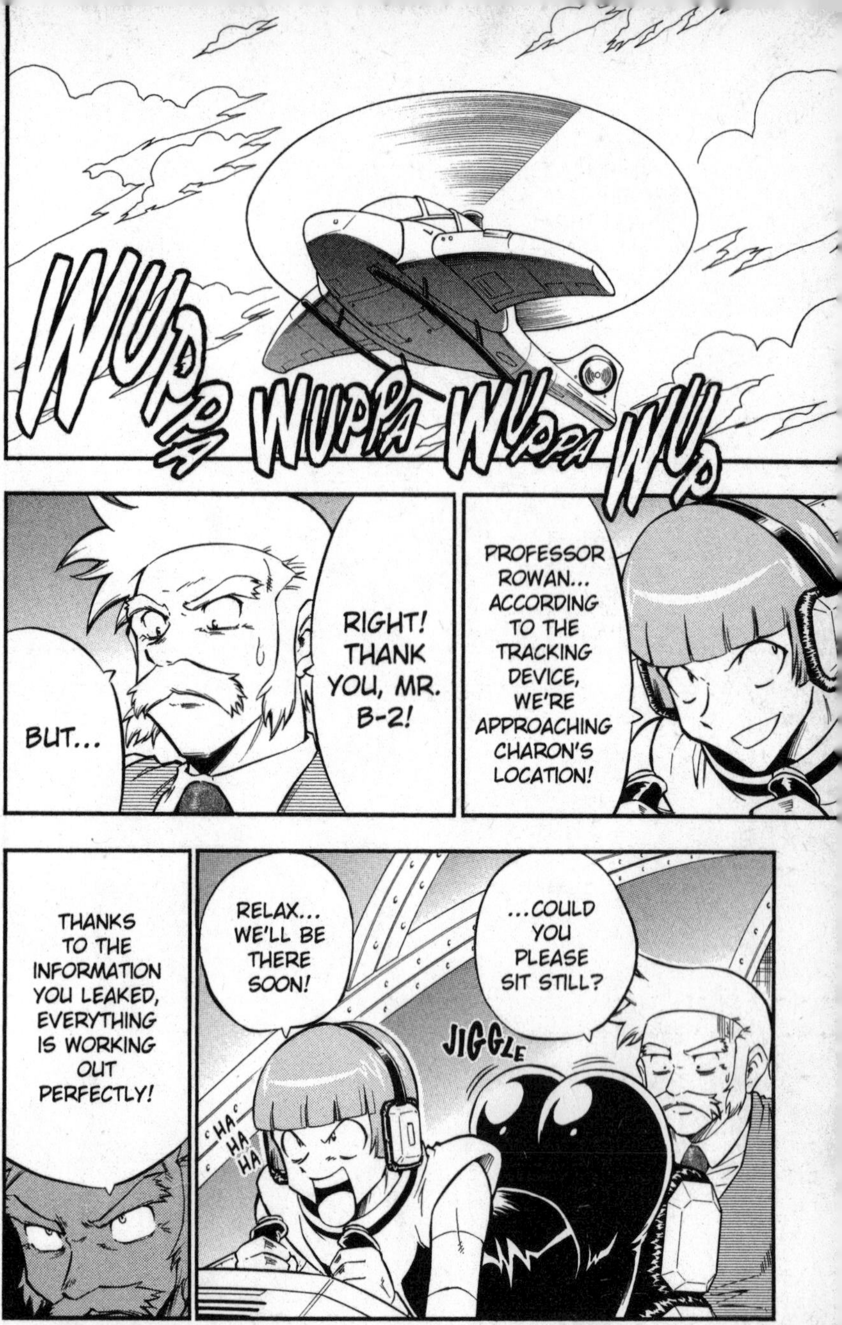
WUPPA WUPPA WUPPA WUP
PROFESSOR ROWAN... ACCORDING TO THE TRACKING DEVICE, WE'RE APPROACHING CHARON'S LOCATION!
RIGHT! THANK YOU, MR. B-2!
BUT...
...COULD YOU PLEASE SIT STILL?
JIGGLE
RELAX... WE'LL BE THERE SOON!
HA HA HA
THANKS TO THE INFORMATION YOU LEAKED, EVERYTHING IS WORKING OUT PERFECTLY!

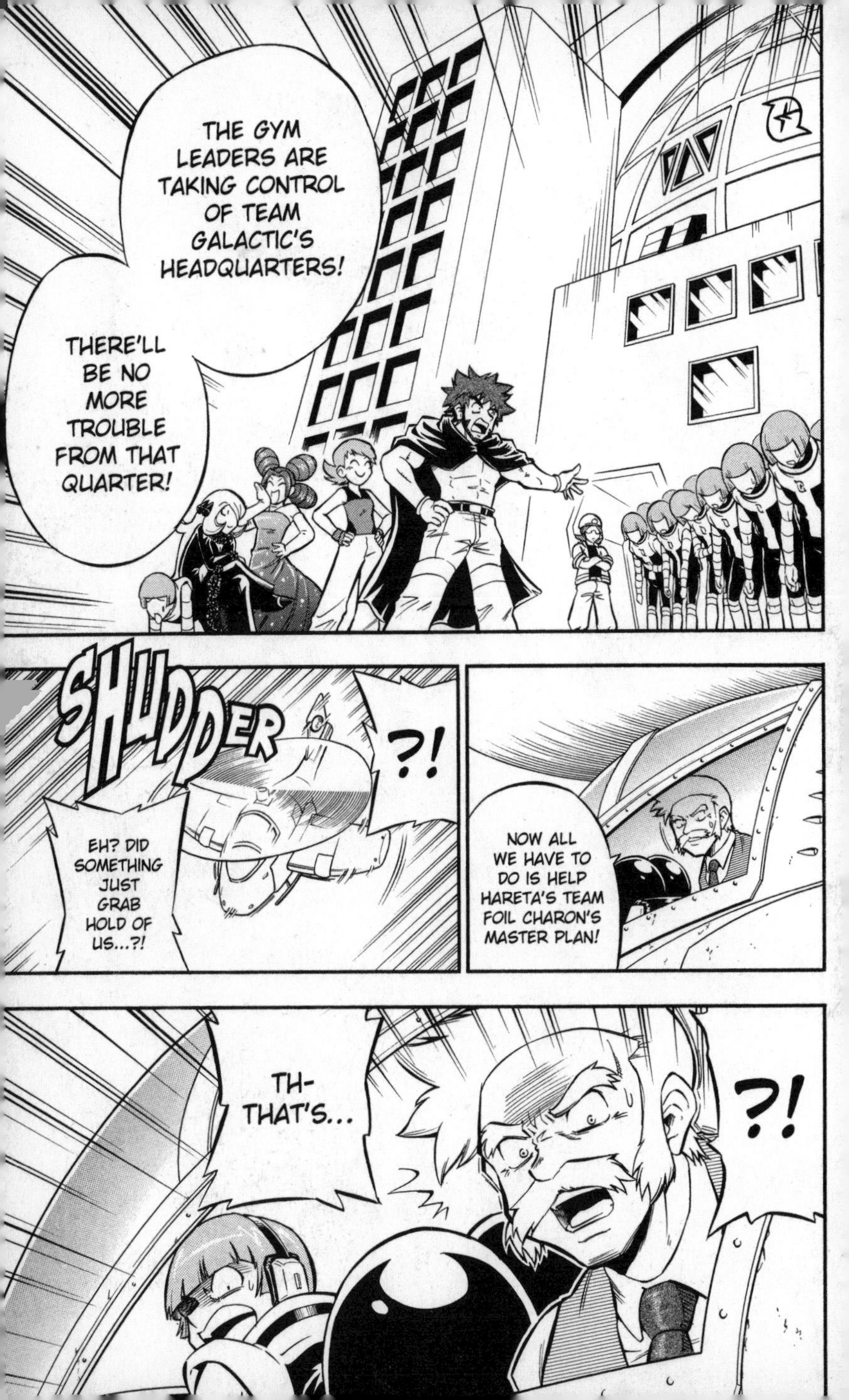
THE GYM LEADERS ARE TAKING CONTROL OF TEAM GALACTIC'S HEADQUARTERS!
THERE'LL BE NO MORE TROUBLE FROM THAT QUARTER!
NOW ALL WE HAVE TO DO IS HELP HARETA'S TEAM FOIL CHARON'S MASTER PLAN!
?!
SHUDDER
EH? DID SOMETHING JUST GRAB HOLD OF US...?!
?!
TH-THAT'S...

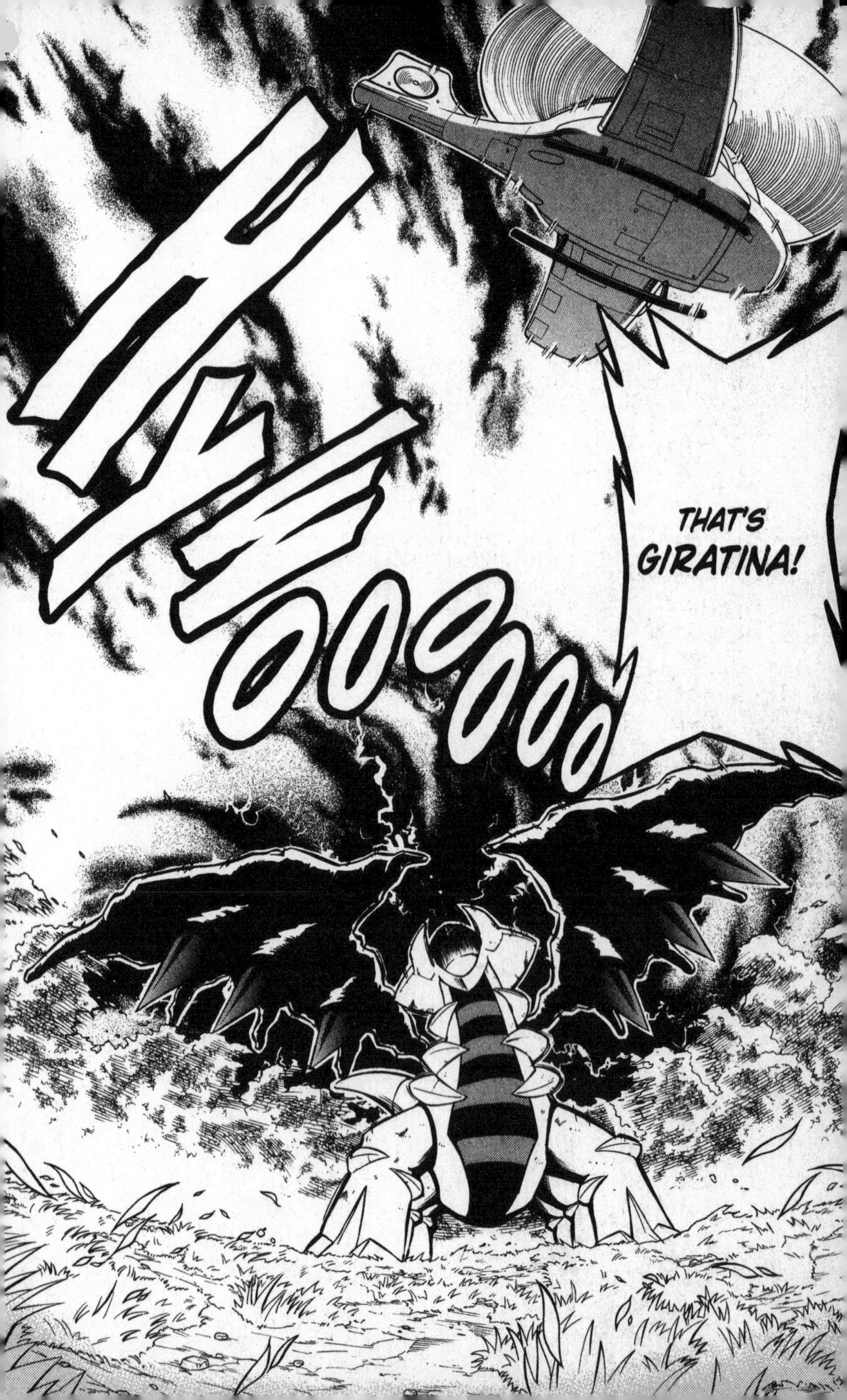
THAT'S GIRATINA!

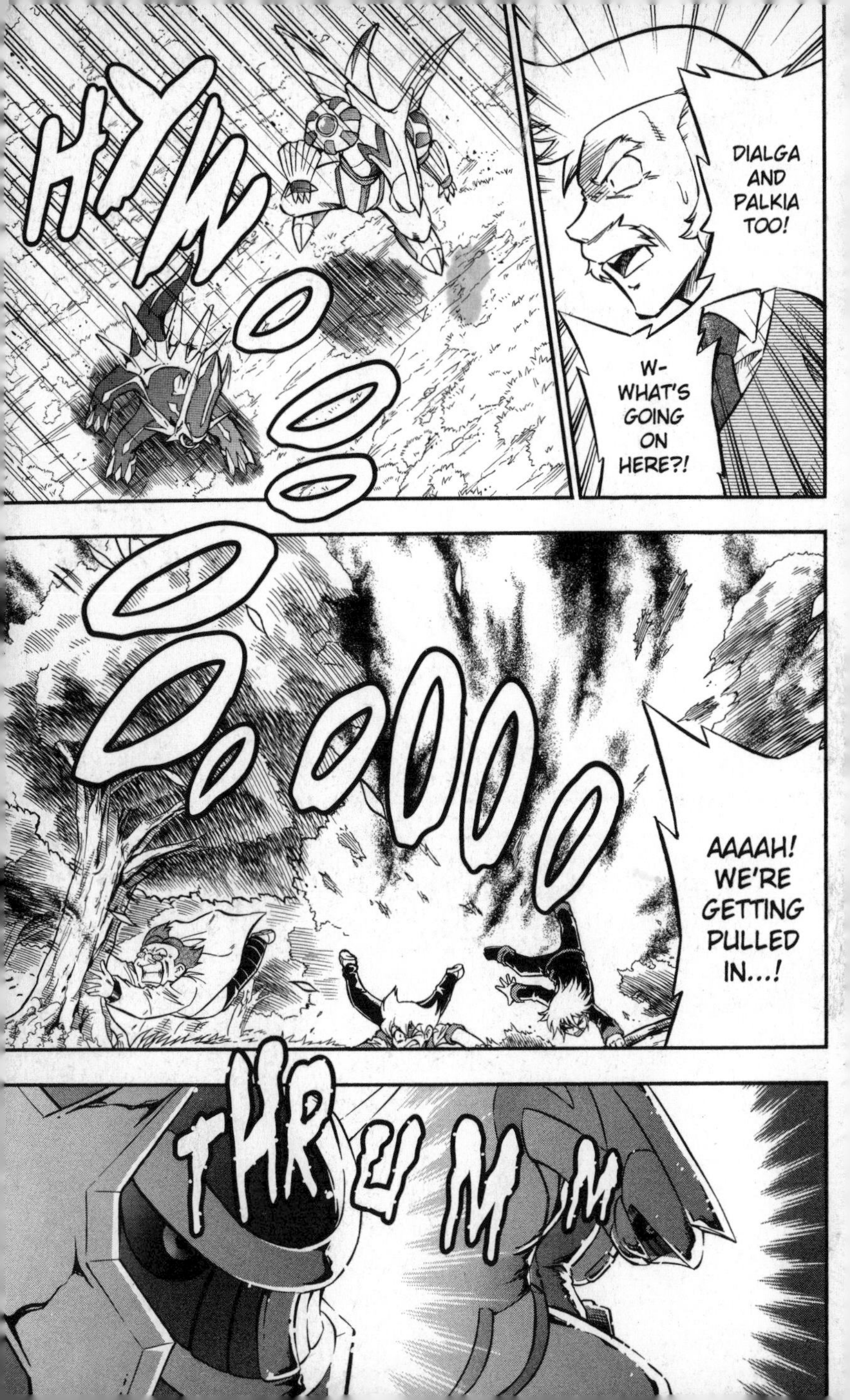
DIALGA AND PALKIA TOO!
W- WHAT'S GOING ON HERE?!
HYWOOOOOO
AAAAH! WE'RE GETTING PULLED IN...!
THRUMM

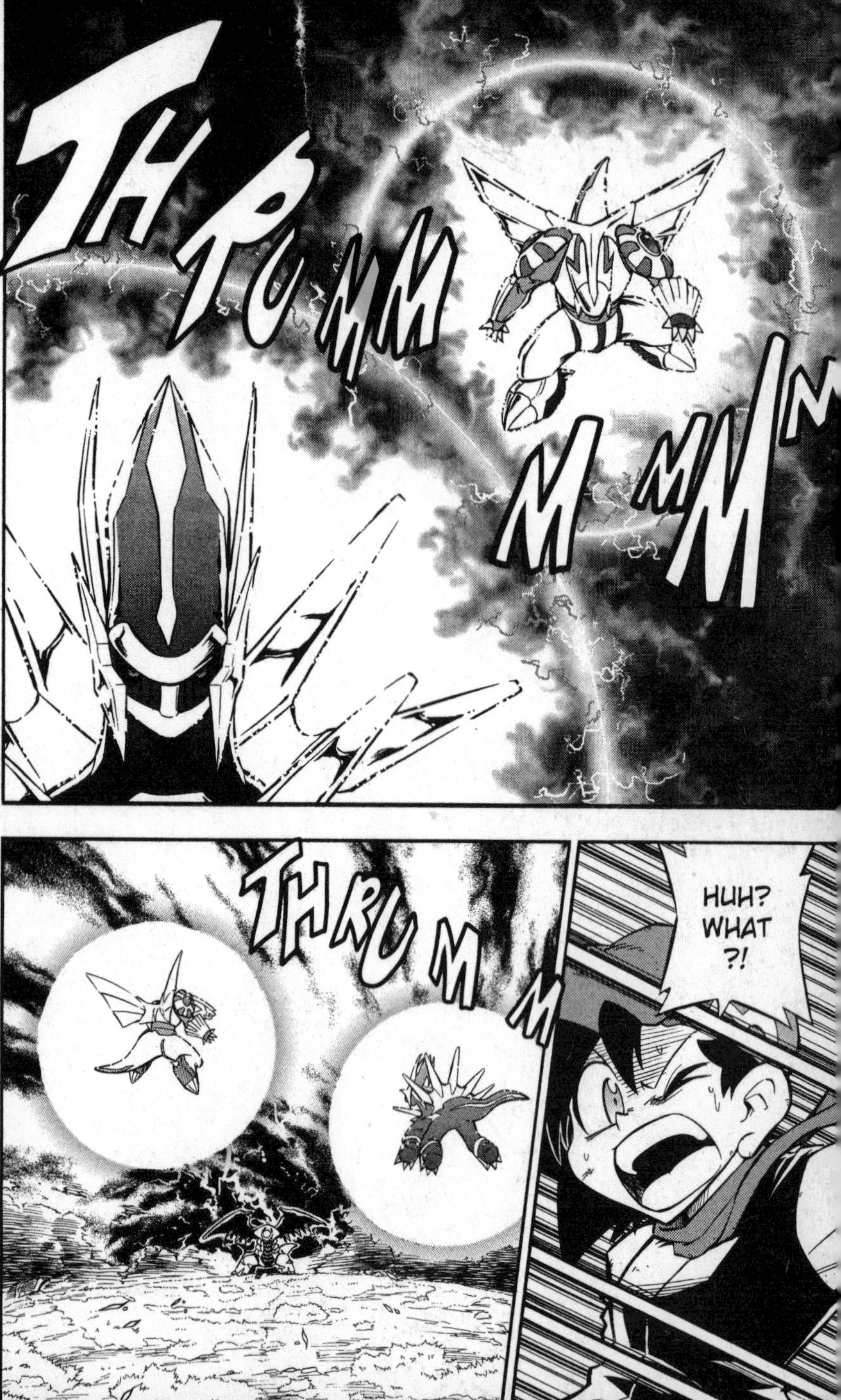
THRUMM
MMMMn
HUH? WHAT?!
THRUMM

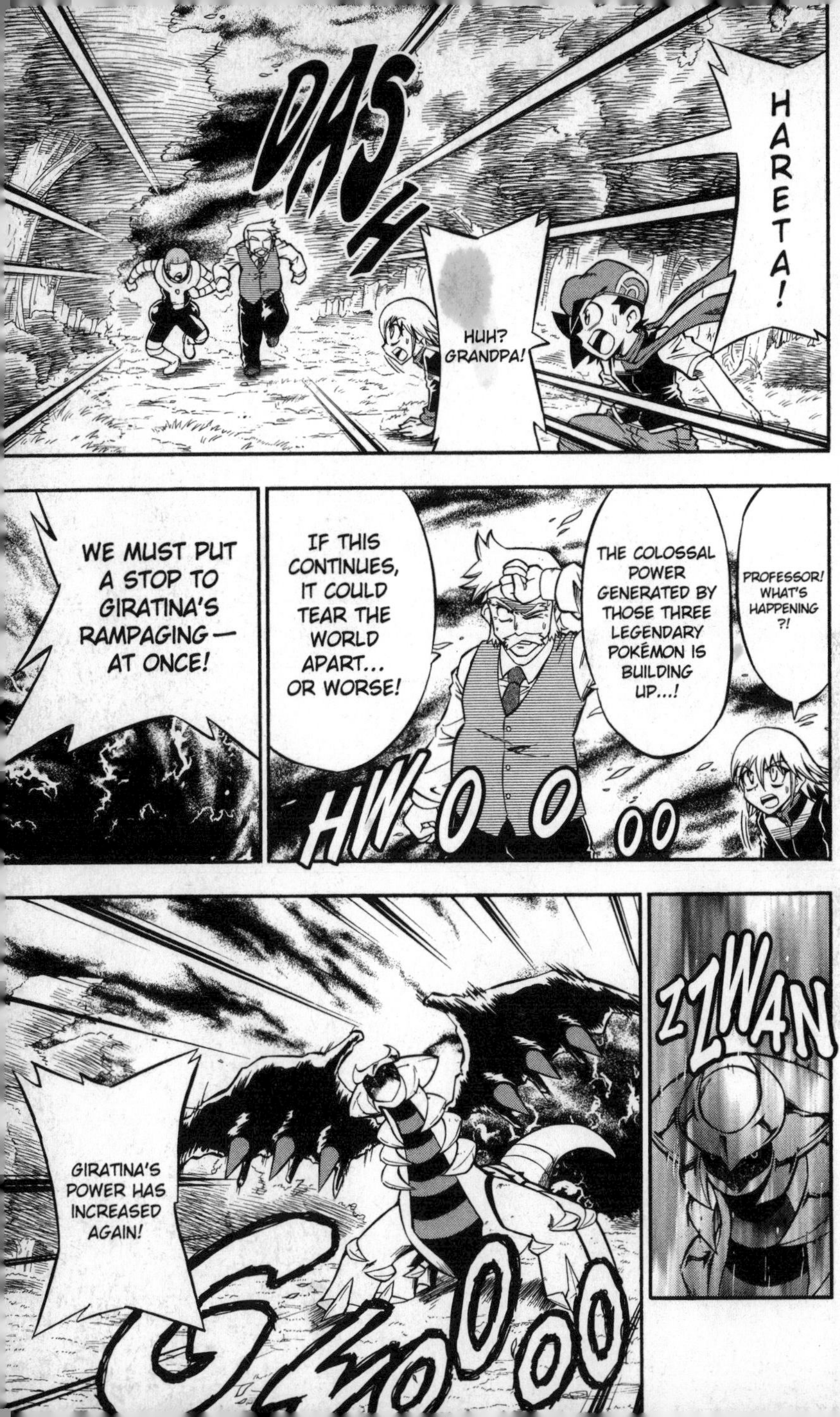
HARETA!
HUH? GRANDPA!
DASH
PROFESSOR! WHAT'S HAPPENING?!
THE COLOSSAL POWER GENERATED BY THOSE THREE LEGENDARY POKÉMON IS BUILDING UP...!
IF THIS CONTINUES, IT COULD TEAR THE WORLD APART... OR WORSE!
HWOOOOO
WE MUST PUT A STOP TO GIRATINA'S RAMPAGING— AT ONCE!
ZZWAN
GIRATINA'S POWER HAS INCREASED AGAIN!

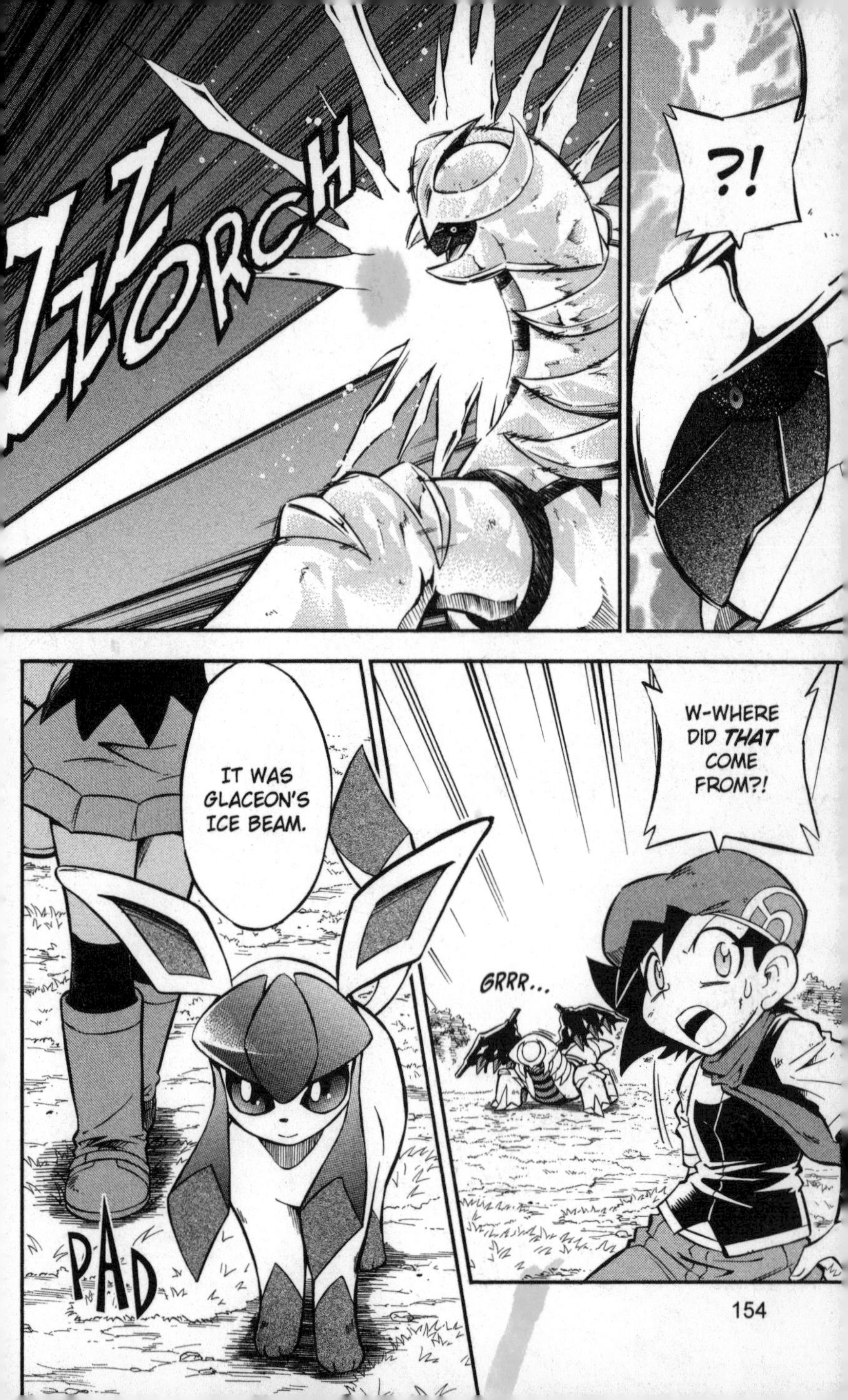
?!
ZZZORCH
W-WHERE DID THAT COME FROM?!
GRRR...
IT WAS GLACEON'S ICE BEAM.
PAD

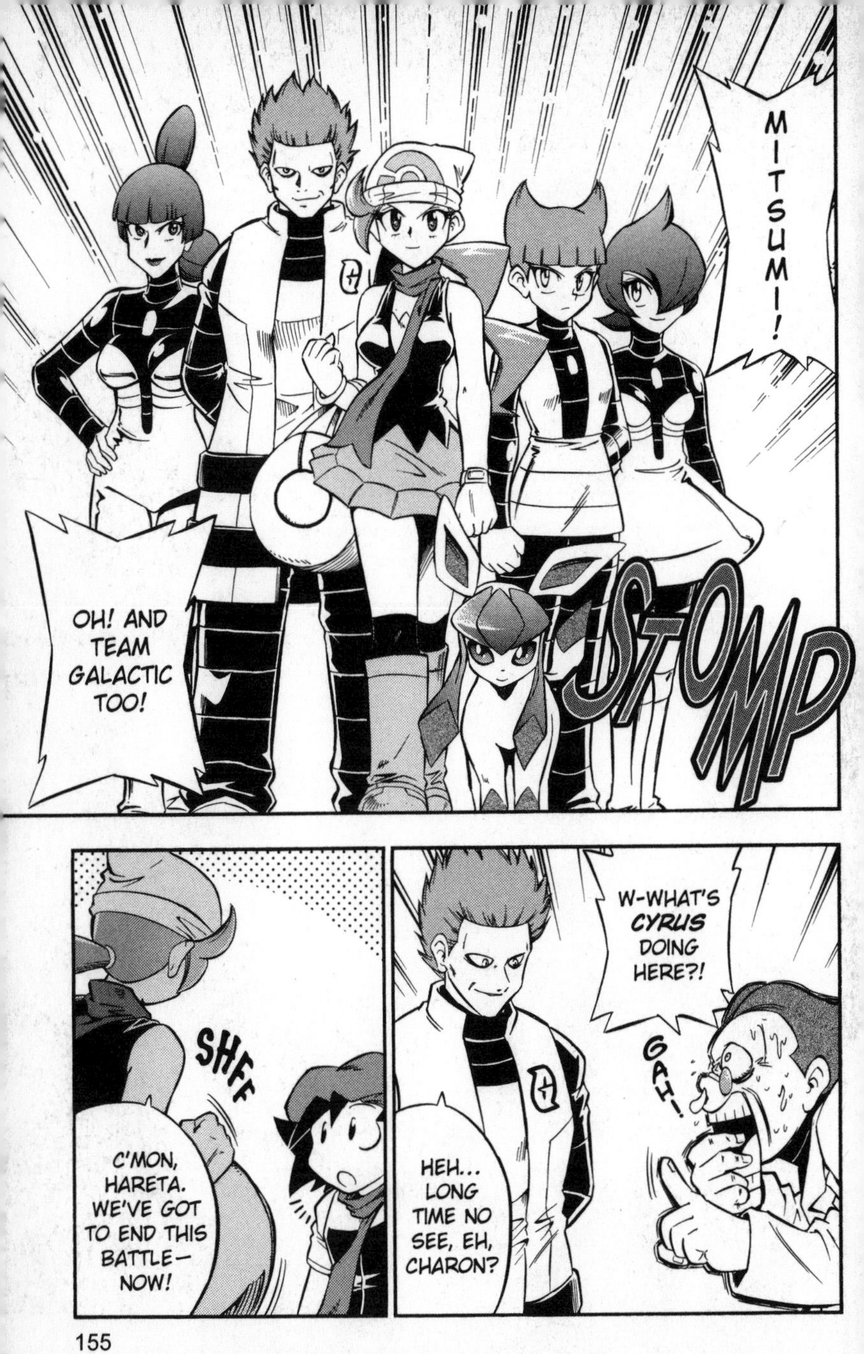
MITSUMI!
STOMP
OH! AND TEAM GALACTIC TOO!
W-WHAT'S CYRUS DOING HERE?!
GAH!
HEH... LONG TIME NO SEE, EH, CHARON?
SHFF
C'MON, HARETA. WE'VE GOT TO END THIS BATTLE—NOW!

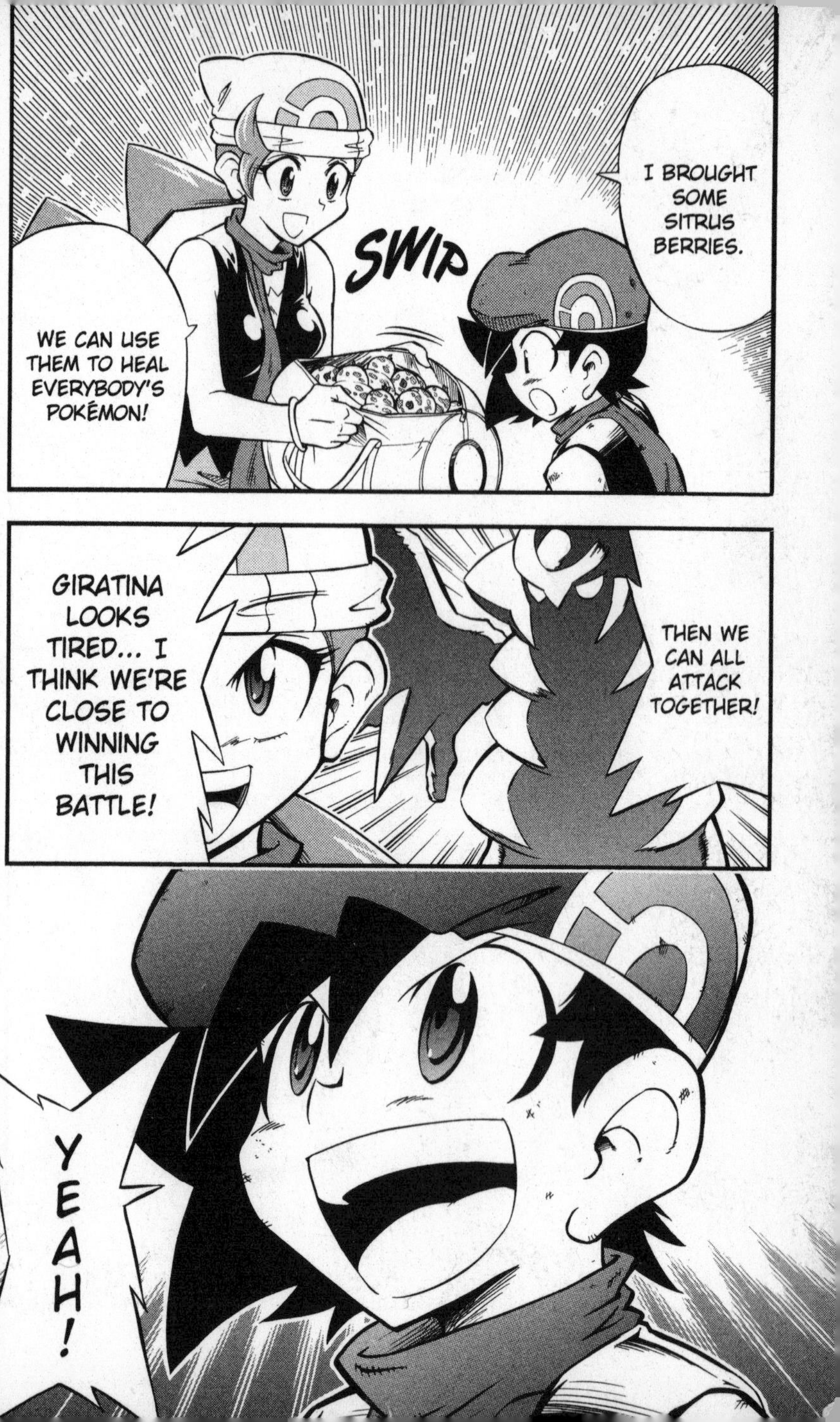
I BROUGHT SOME SITRUS BERRIES.
SWIP
WE CAN USE THEM TO HEAL EVERYBODY'S POKÉMON!
THEN WE CAN ALL ATTACK TOGETHER!
GIRATINA LOOKS TIRED... I THINK WE'RE CLOSE TO WINNING THIS BATTLE!
YEAH!

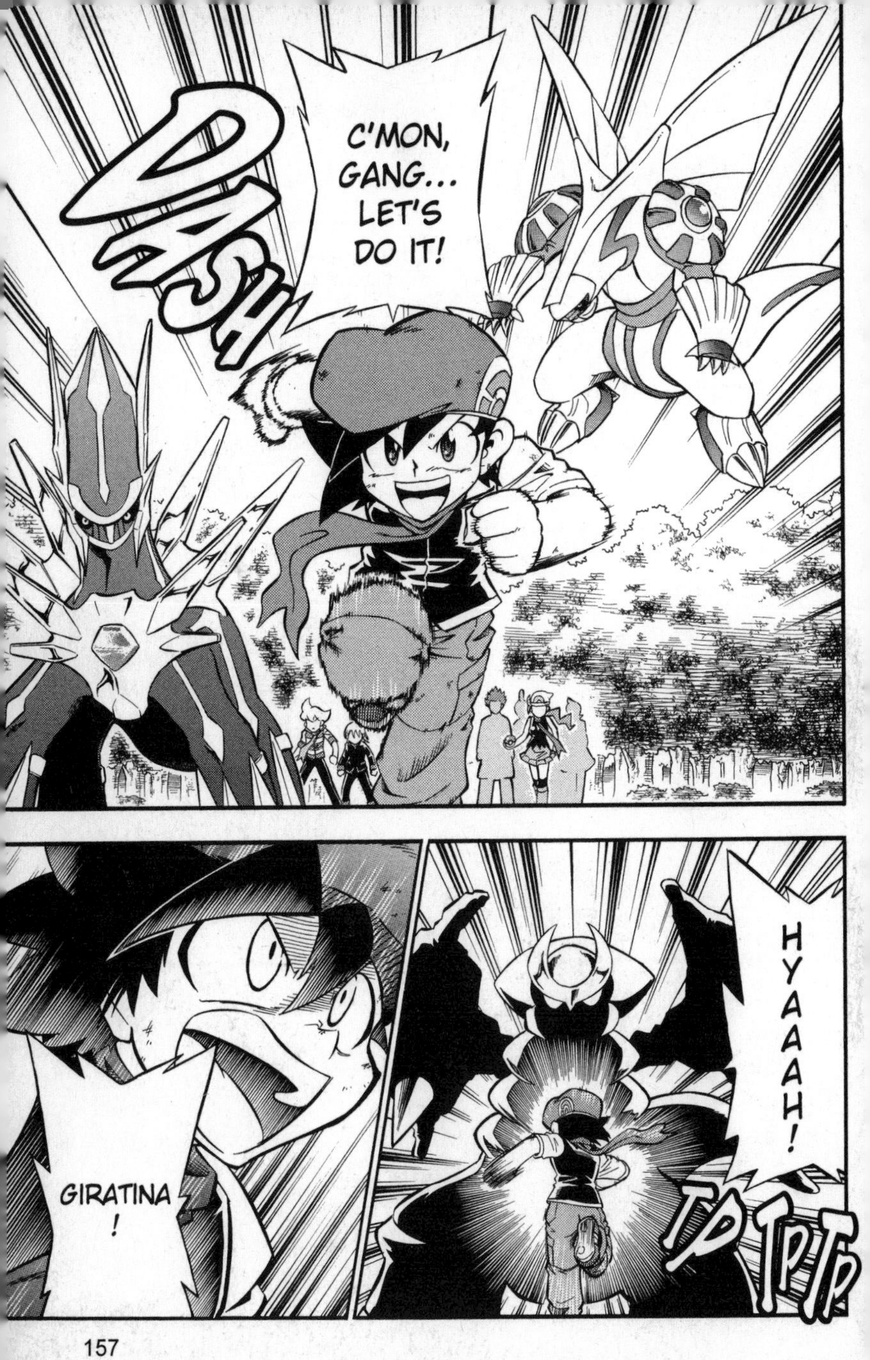
C'MON, GANG... LET'S DO IT!
DASH
HYAAAAH!
TP TP TP
GIRATINA!

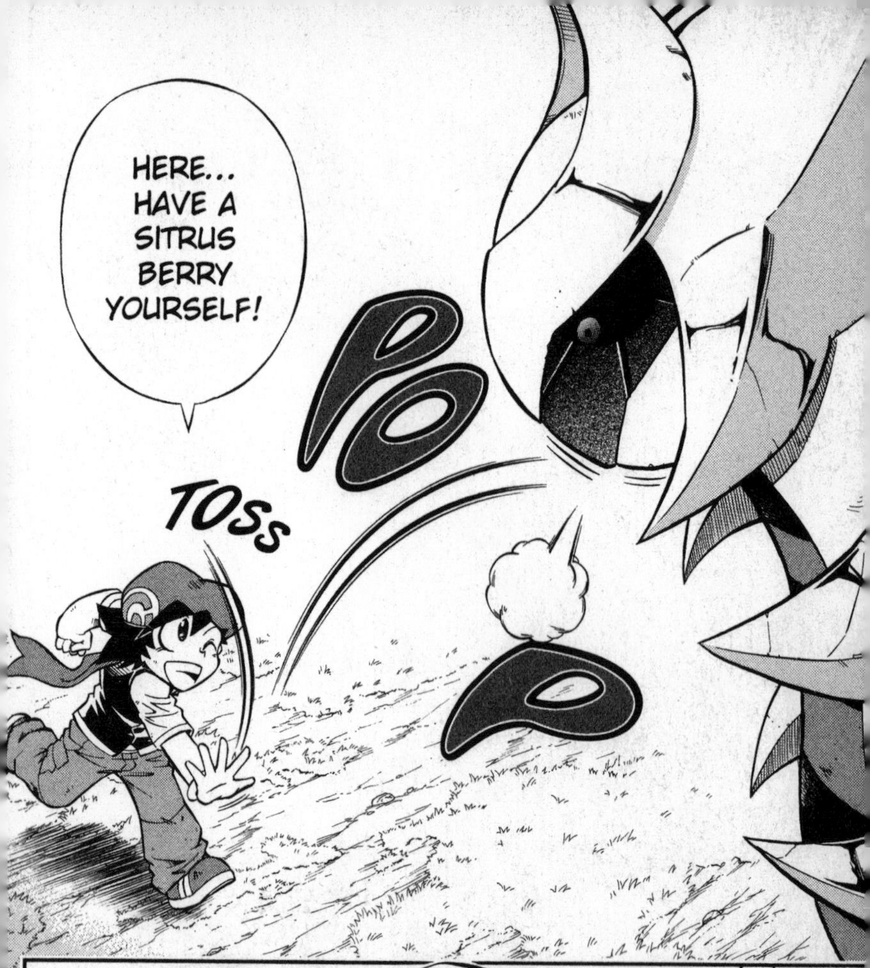
HERE... HAVE A SITRUS BERRY YOURSELF!
TOSS
POP

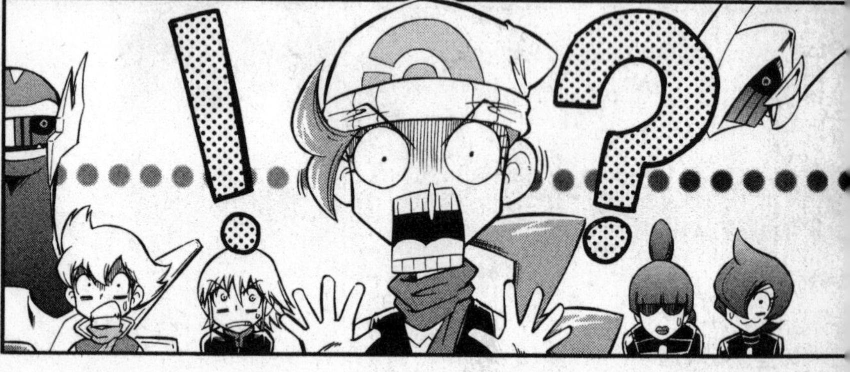
!?

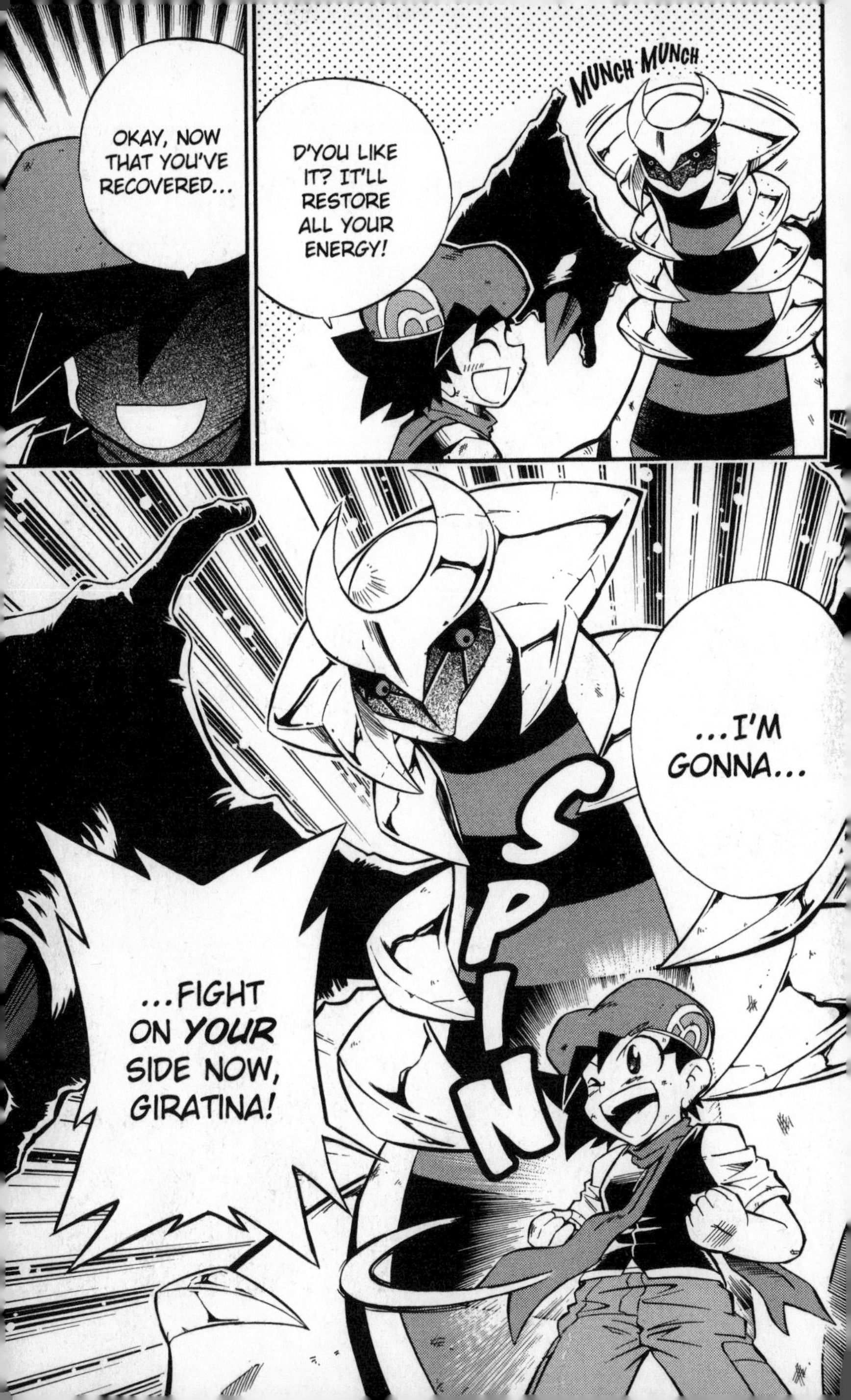
MUNCH MUNCH
D'YOU LIKE IT? IT'LL RESTORE ALL YOUR ENERGY!
OKAY, NOW THAT YOU'VE RECOVERED...
...I'M GONNA...
SPIN
...FIGHT ON *YOUR* SIDE NOW, GIRATINA!

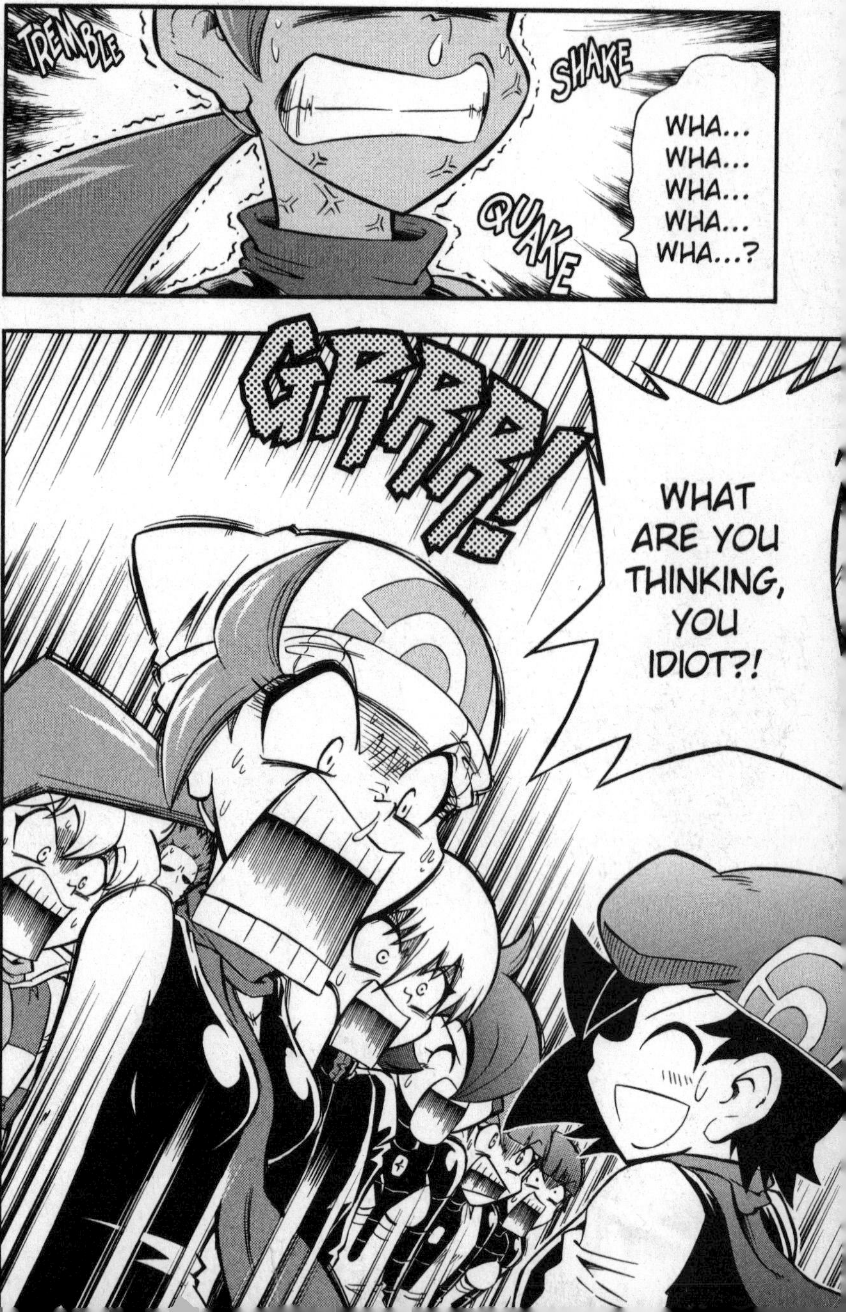
WHA... WHA... WHA... WHA... WHA...?
SHAKE
TREMBLE
QUAKE
WHAT ARE YOU THINKING, YOU IDIOT?!
GRRR!!

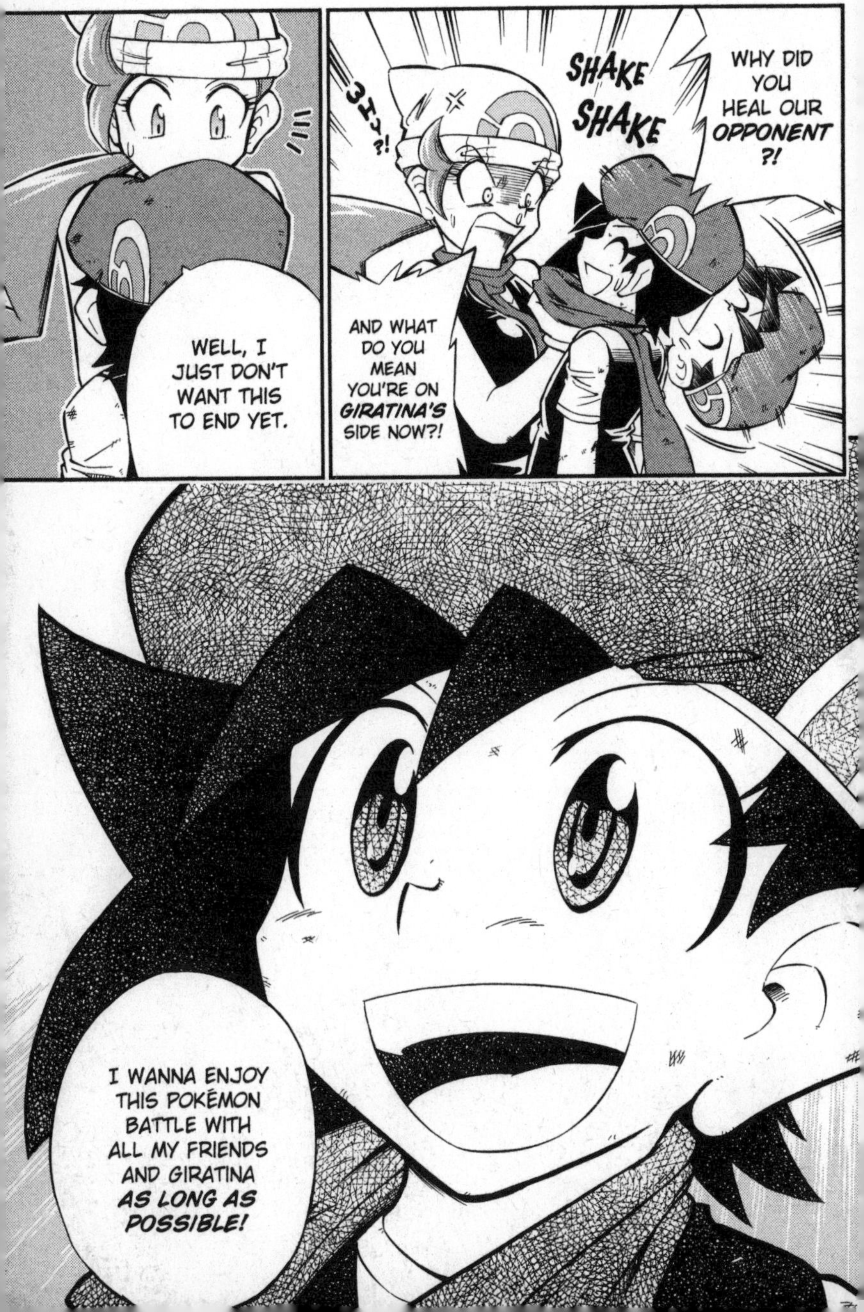
SHAKE
SHAKE
WHY DID YOU HEAL OUR **OPPONENT** ?!
AND WHAT DO YOU MEAN YOU'RE ON ***GIRATINA'S*** SIDE NOW?!
WELL, I JUST DON'T WANT THIS TO END YET.
I WANNA ENJOY THIS POKÉMON BATTLE WITH ALL MY FRIENDS AND GIRATINA ***AS LONG AS POSSIBLE!***

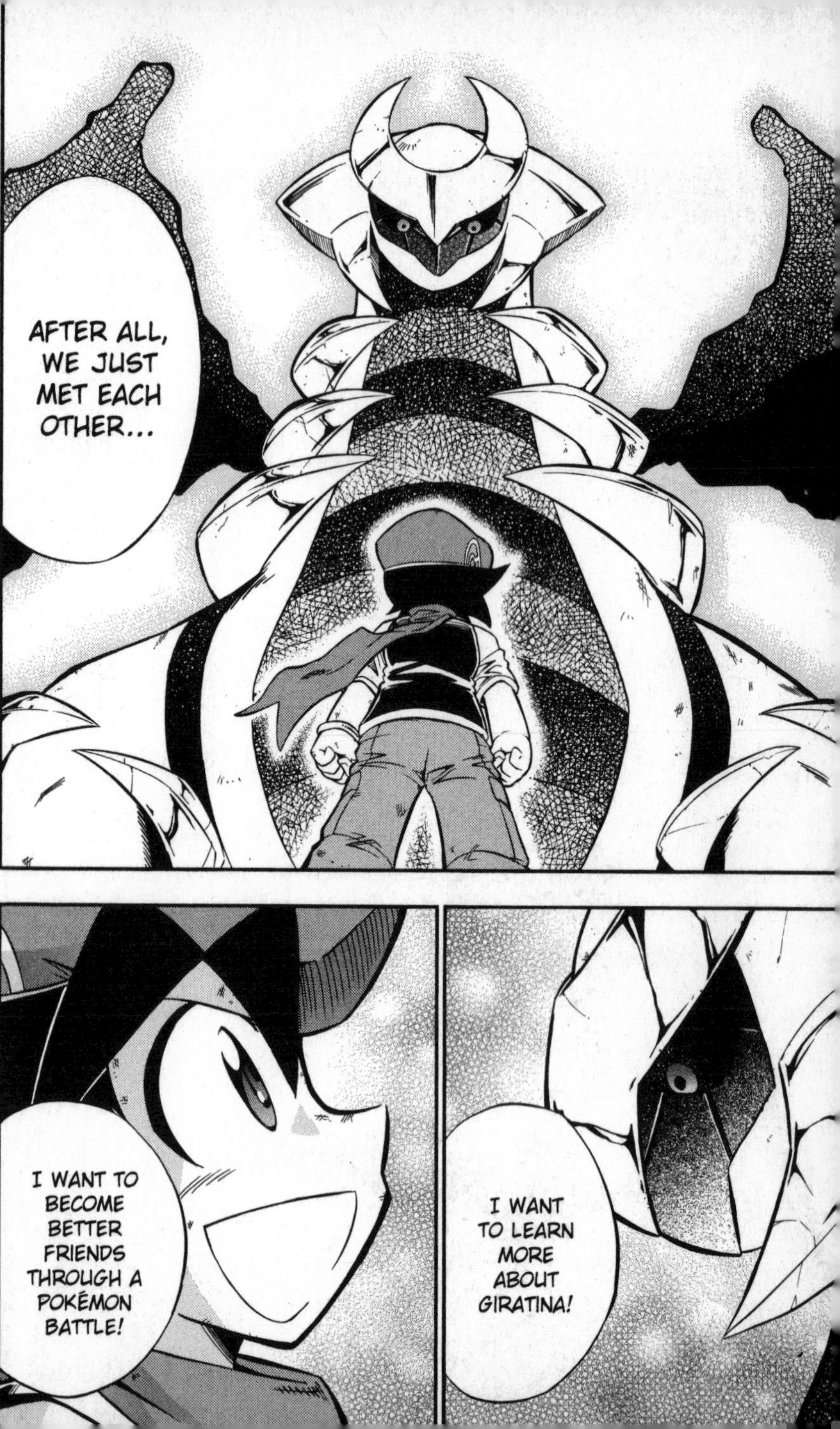
AFTER ALL, WE JUST MET EACH OTHER...
I WANT TO LEARN MORE ABOUT GIRATINA!
I WANT TO BECOME BETTER FRIENDS THROUGH A POKÉMON BATTLE!

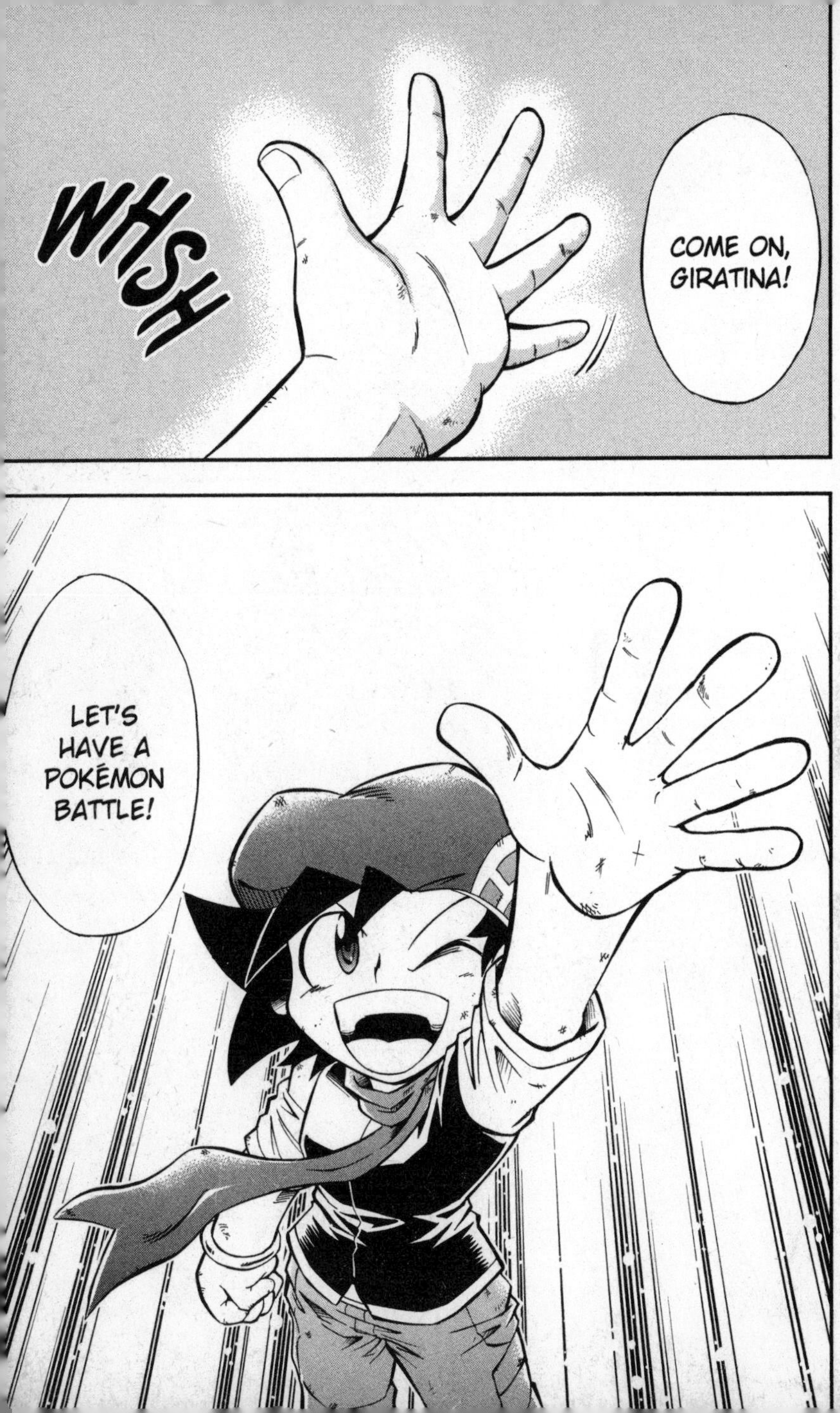
COME ON, GIRATINA!
WHSH
LET'S HAVE A POKÉMON BATTLE!

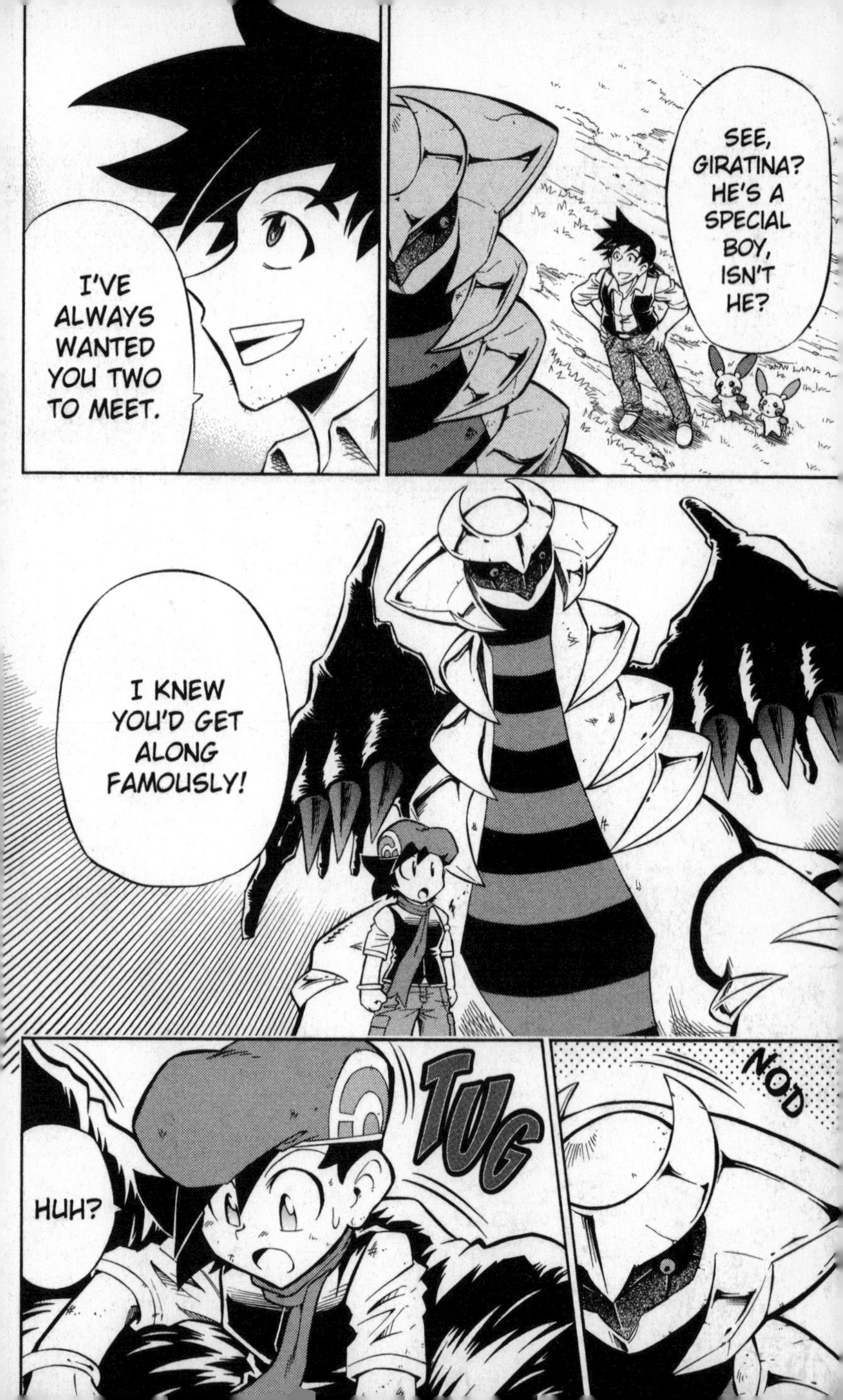
SEE, GIRATINA? HE'S A SPECIAL BOY, ISN'T HE?
I'VE ALWAYS WANTED YOU TWO TO MEET.
I KNEW YOU'D GET ALONG FAMOUSLY!
NOD
TUG
HUH?

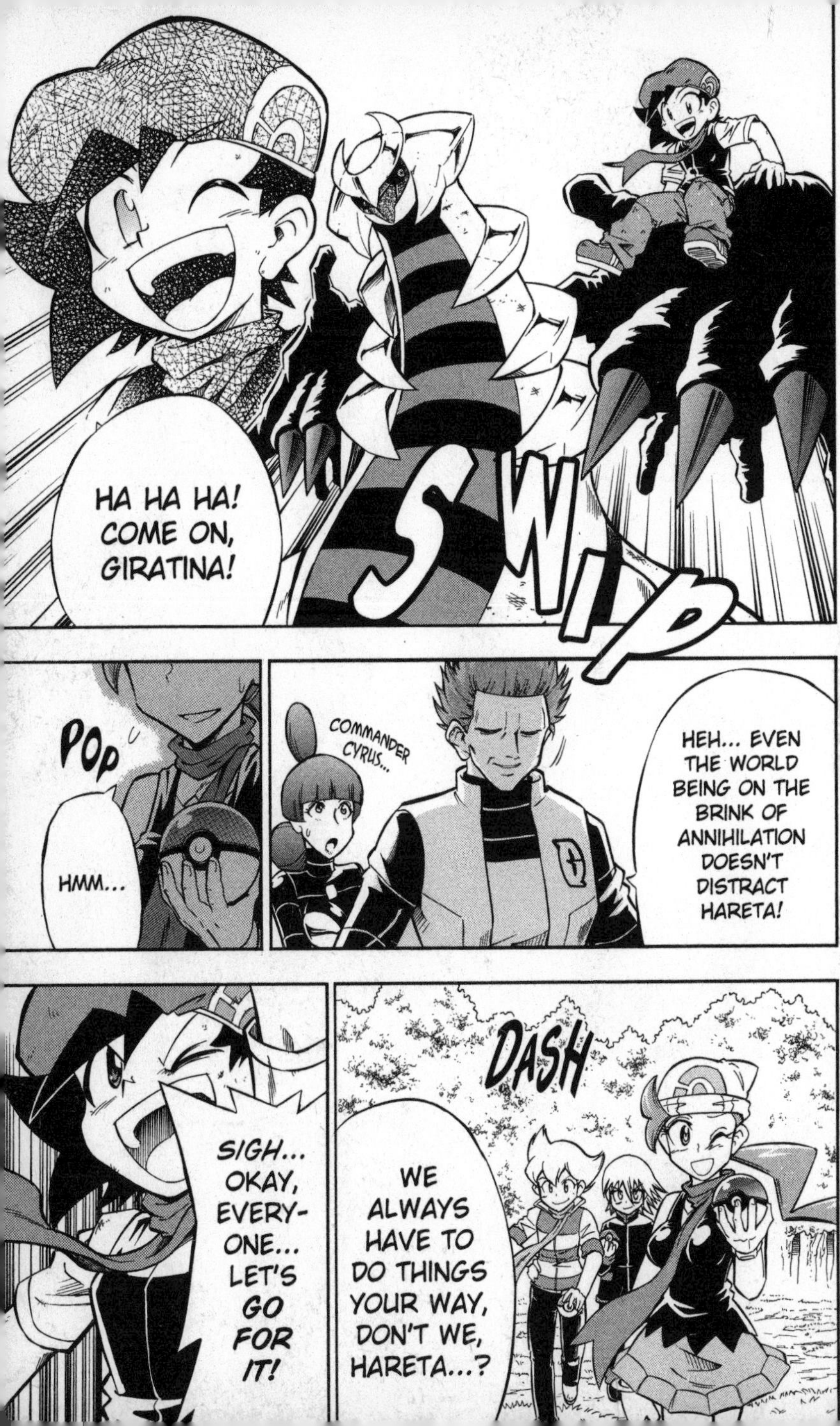
HA HA HA! COME ON, GIRATINA!
SWIP
HEH... EVEN THE WORLD BEING ON THE BRINK OF ANNIHILATION DOESN'T DISTRACT HARETA!
COMMANDER CYRUS...
POP
HMM...
DASH
WE ALWAYS HAVE TO DO THINGS YOUR WAY, DON'T WE, HARETA...?
SIGH... OKAY, EVERY-ONE... LET'S GO FOR IT!

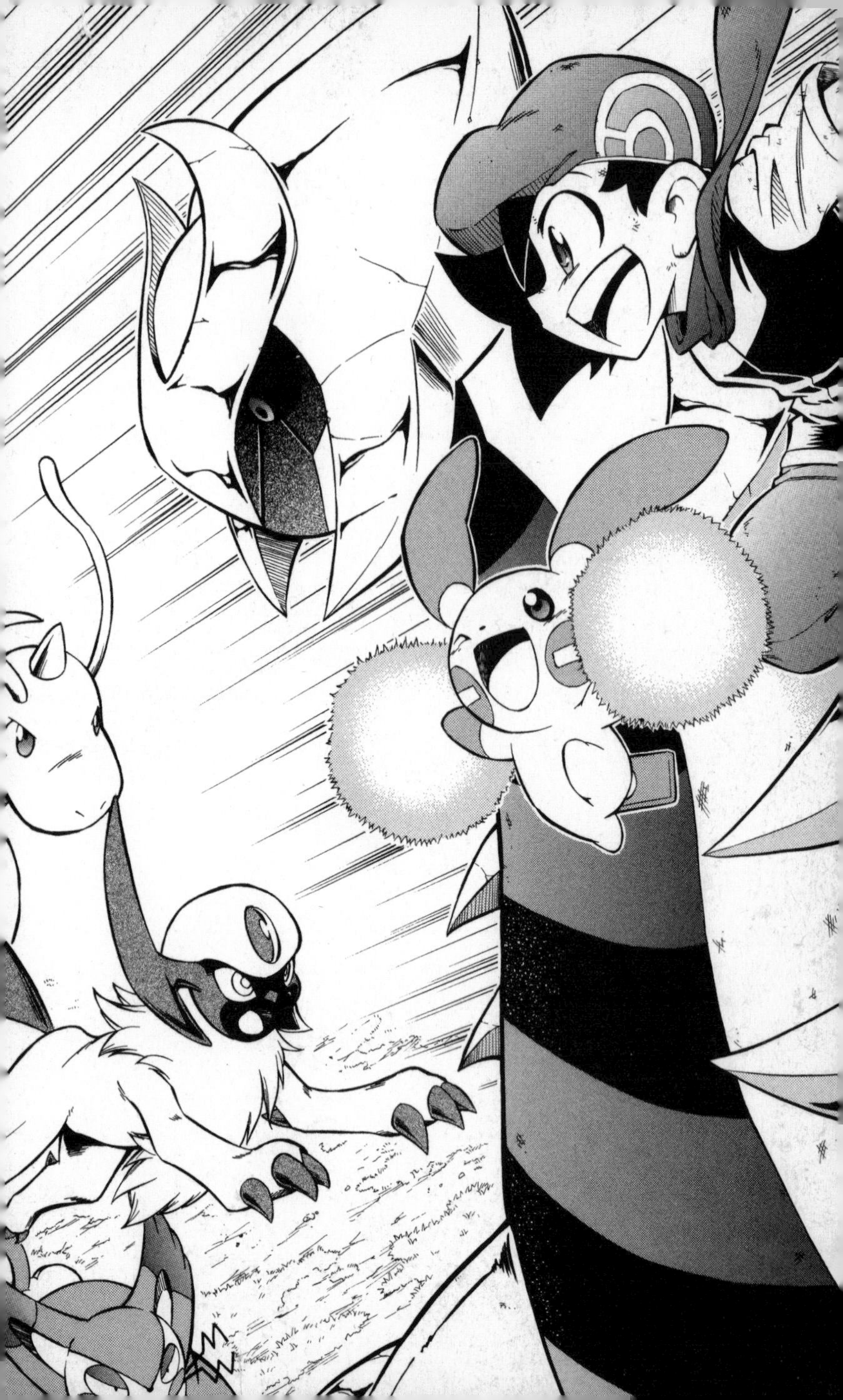

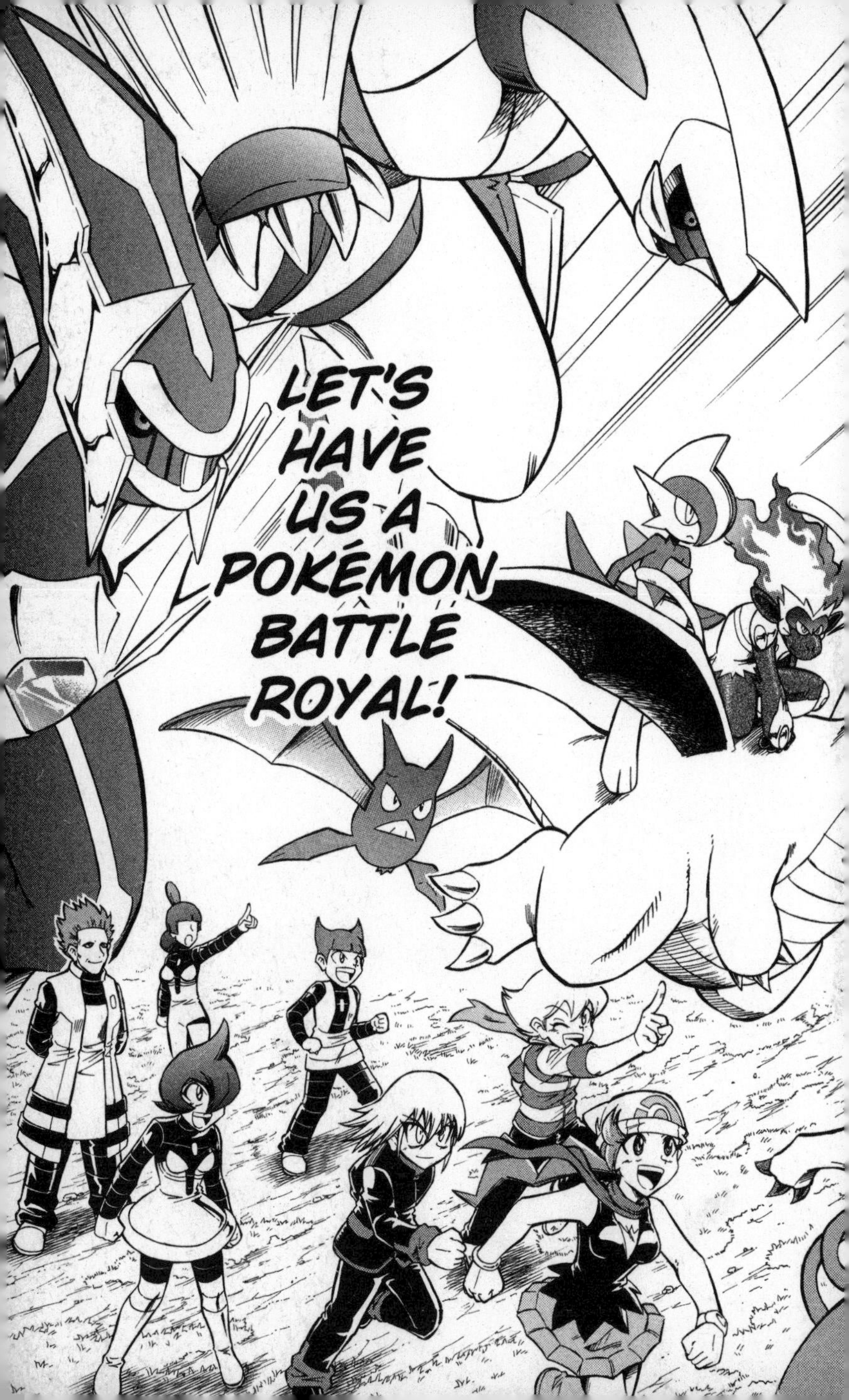
LET'S HAVE US A POKÉMON BATTLE ROYAL!

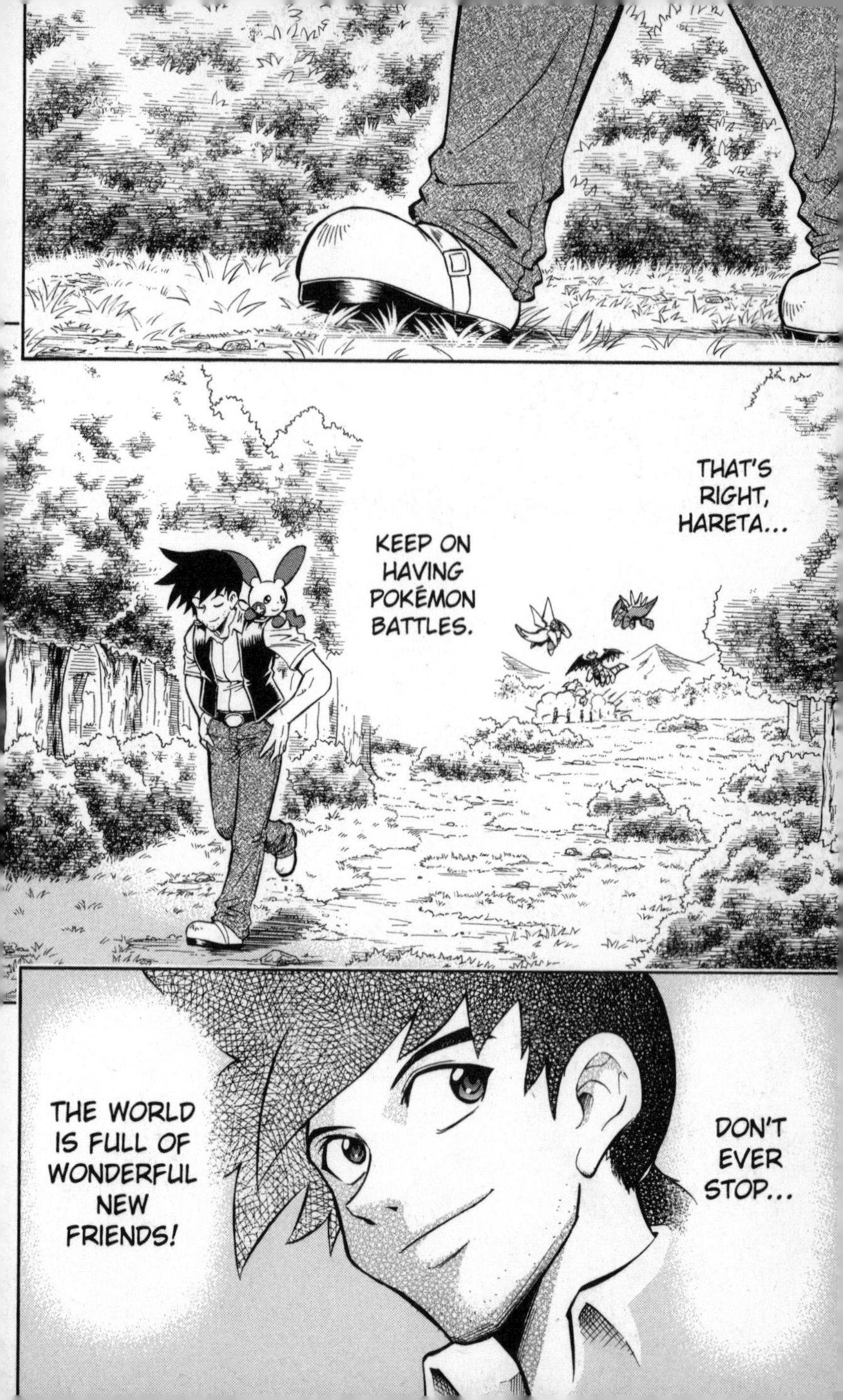
THAT'S RIGHT, HARETA...
KEEP ON HAVING POKÉMON BATTLES.
DON'T EVER STOP...
THE WORLD IS FULL OF WONDERFUL NEW FRIENDS!

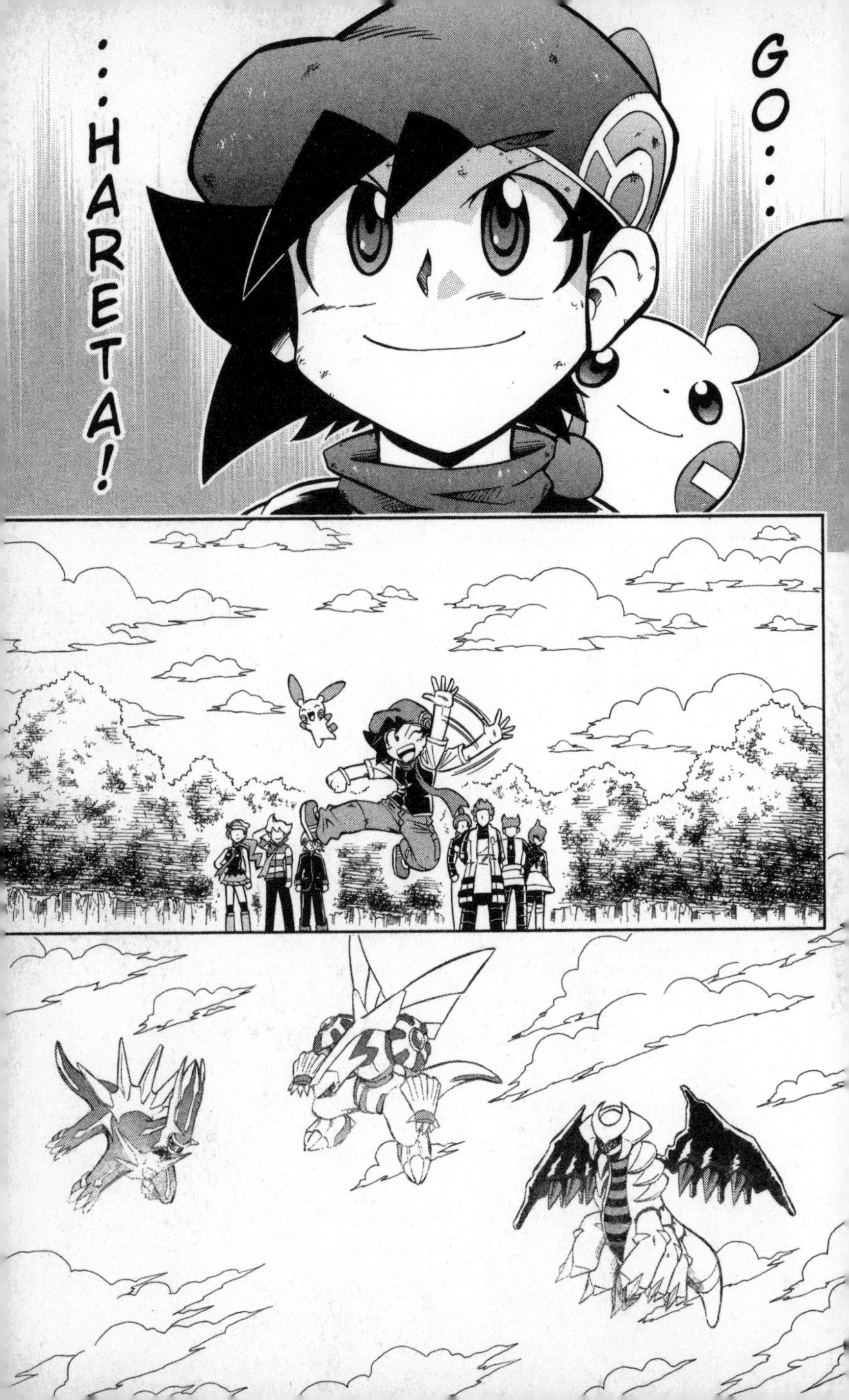
GO...
...HARETA!

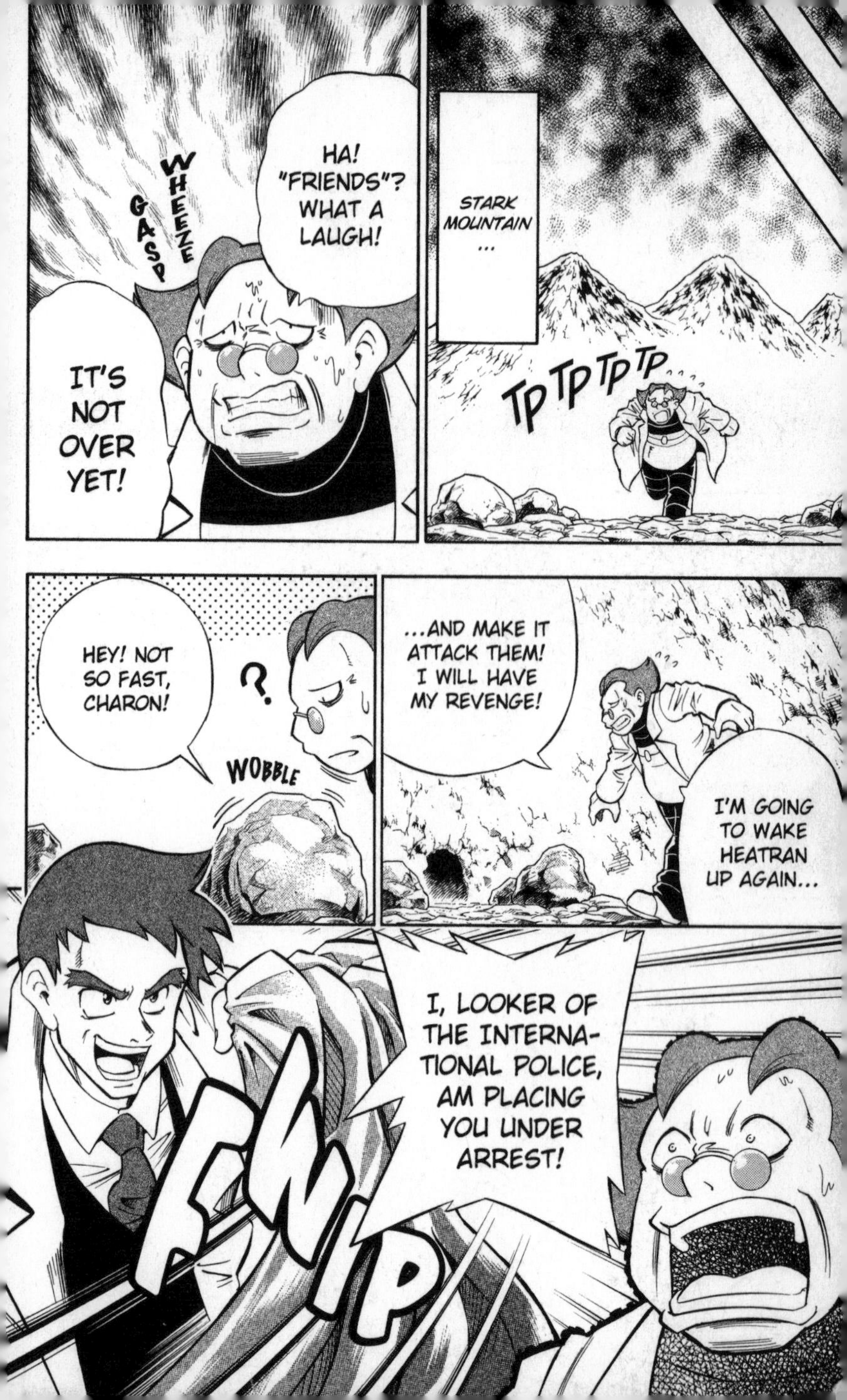
STARK MOUNTAIN ...
TP TP TP TP
HA! "FRIENDS"? WHAT A LAUGH!
WHEEZE
GASP
IT'S NOT OVER YET!
I'M GOING TO WAKE HEATRAN UP AGAIN...
...AND MAKE IT ATTACK THEM! I WILL HAVE MY REVENGE!
?
WOBBLE
HEY! NOT SO FAST, CHARON!
I, LOOKER OF THE INTERNATIONAL POLICE, AM PLACING YOU UNDER ARREST!
FWIP

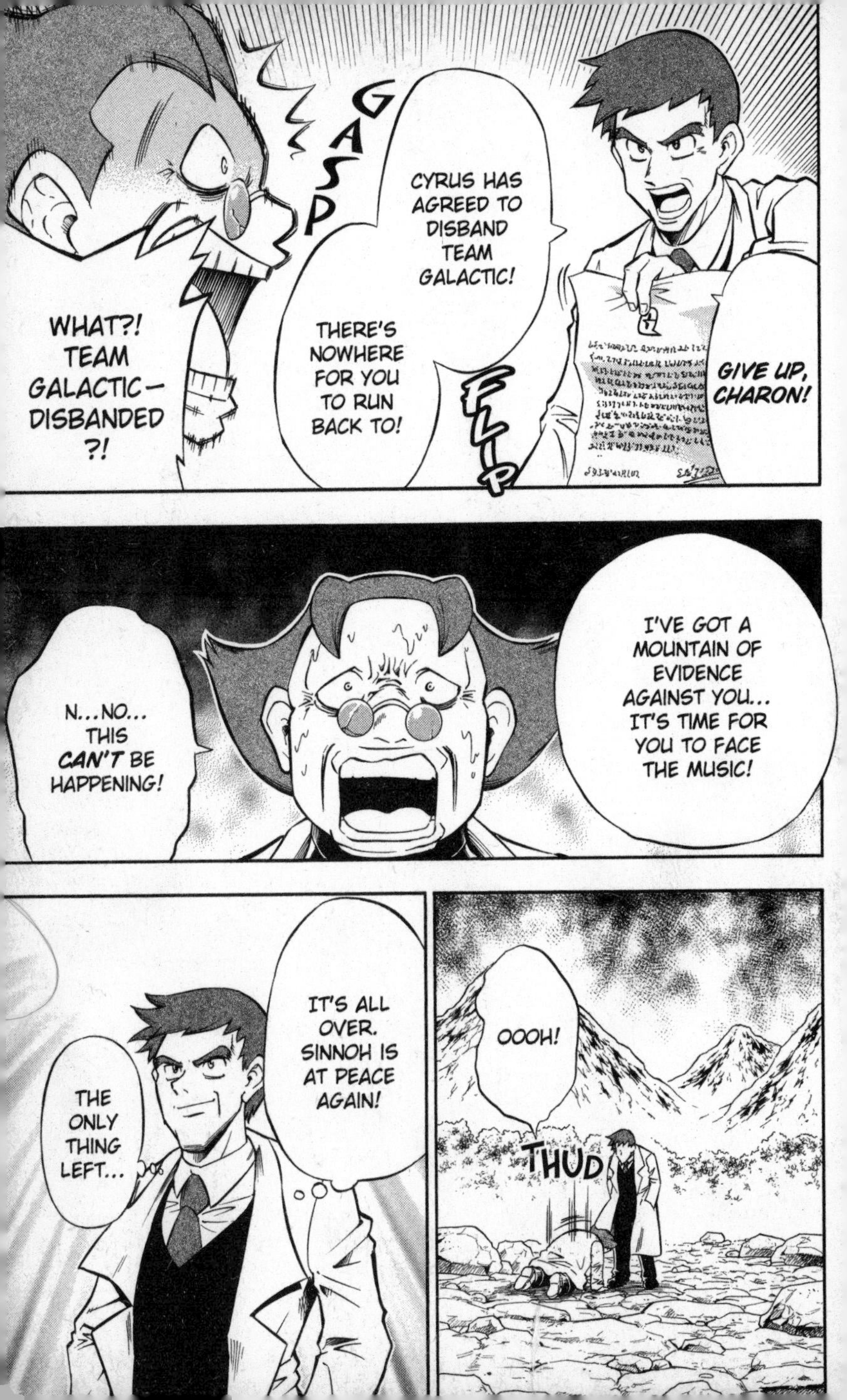
GIVE UP, CHARON!
CYRUS HAS AGREED TO DISBAND TEAM GALACTIC!
THERE'S NOWHERE FOR YOU TO RUN BACK TO!
FLIP
GASP
WHAT?! TEAM GALACTIC—DISBANDED?!
I'VE GOT A MOUNTAIN OF EVIDENCE AGAINST YOU... IT'S TIME FOR YOU TO FACE THE MUSIC!
N...NO... THIS *CAN'T* BE HAPPENING!
OOOH!
THUD
IT'S ALL OVER. SINNOH IS AT PEACE AGAIN!
THE ONLY THING LEFT...

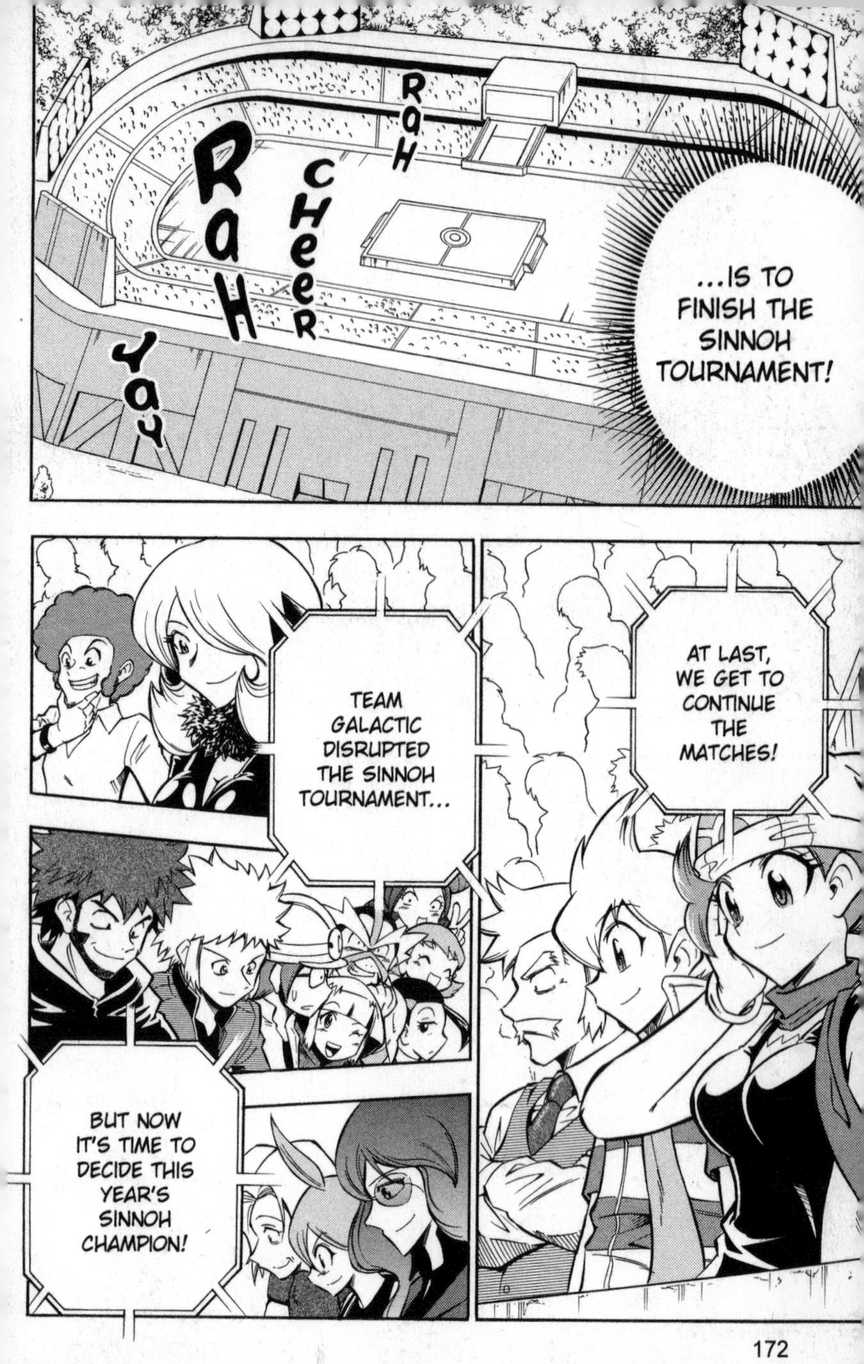
...IS TO FINISH THE SINNOH TOURNAMENT!
RAH
CHEER
RAH
AT LAST, WE GET TO CONTINUE THE MATCHES!
TEAM GALACTIC DISRUPTED THE SINNOH TOURNAMENT...
BUT NOW IT'S TIME TO DECIDE THIS YEAR'S SINNOH CHAMPION!

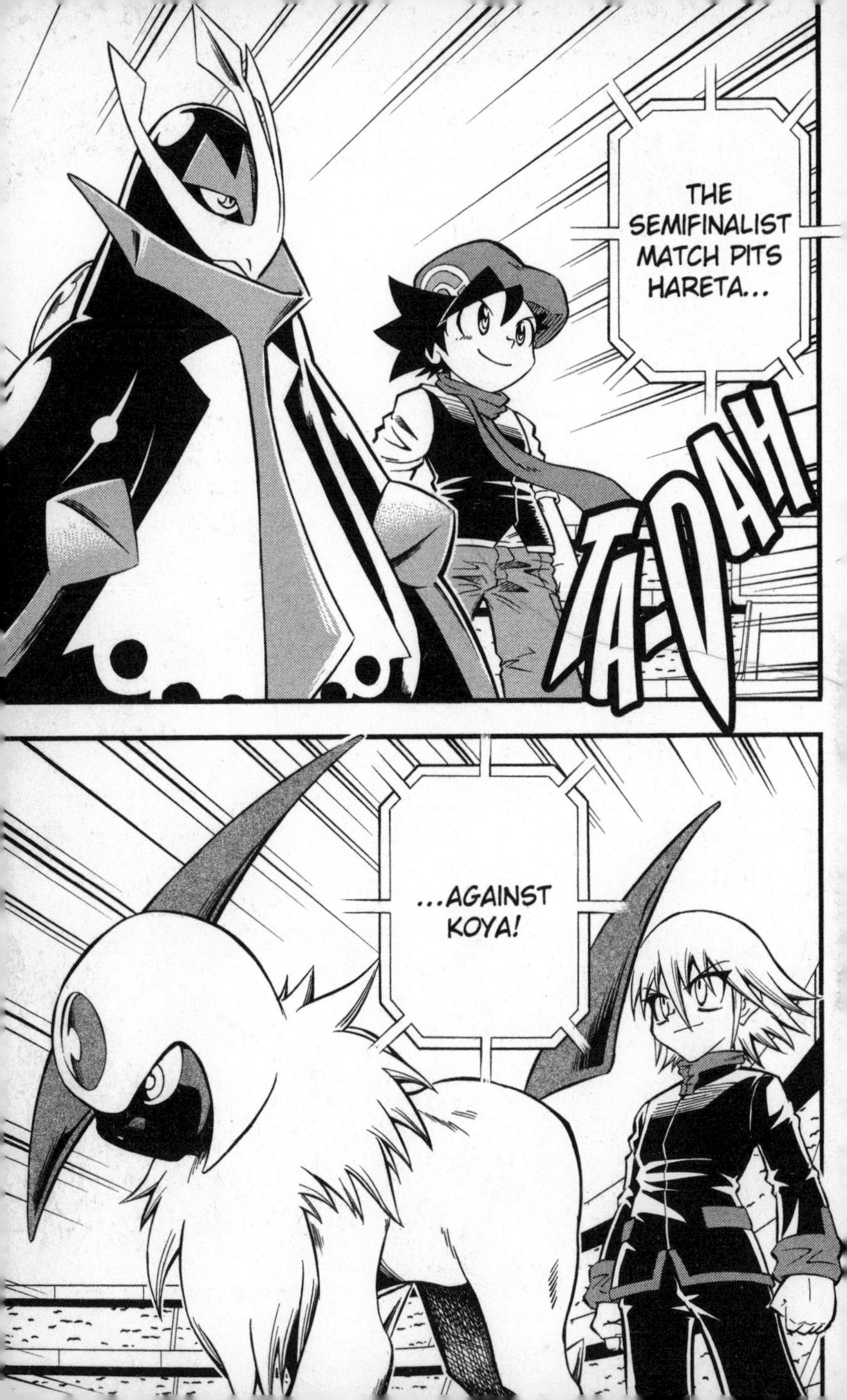
THE SEMIFINALIST MATCH PITS HARETA...
TA-DAH
...AGAINST KOYA!

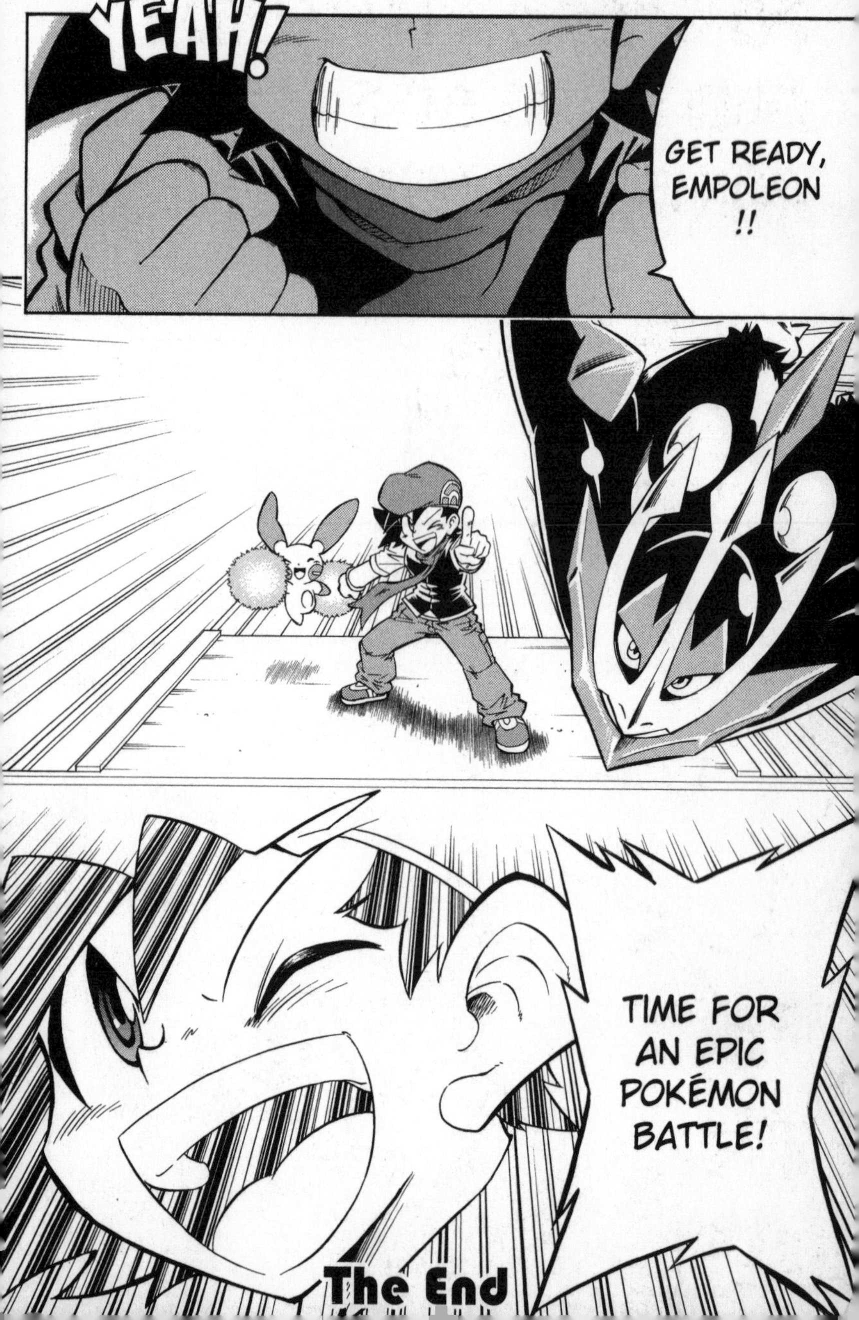
GET READY, EMPOLEON !!
YEAH!
TIME FOR AN EPIC POKÉMON BATTLE!
The End

POKÉMON DIAMOND AND PEARL BONUS STORY: HARETA'S FUTURE

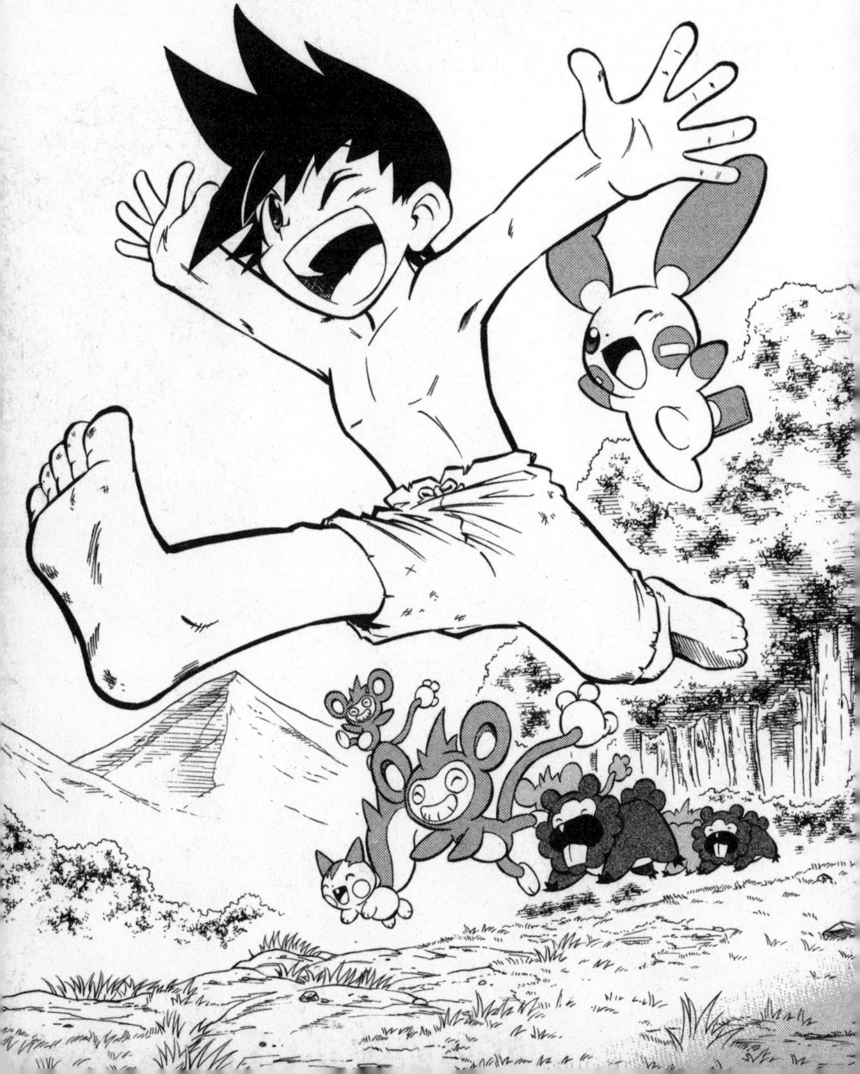

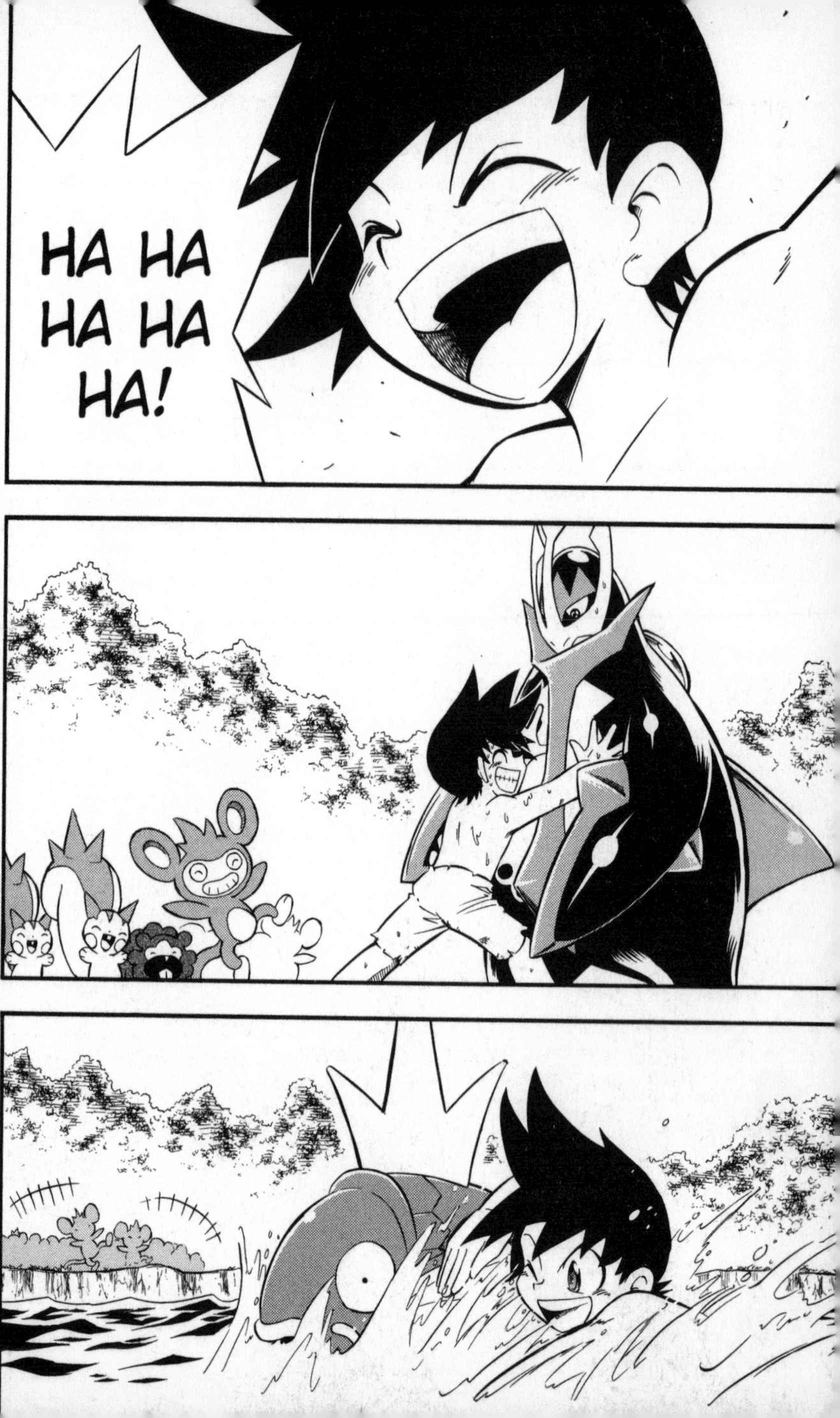
HA HA HA HA HA!

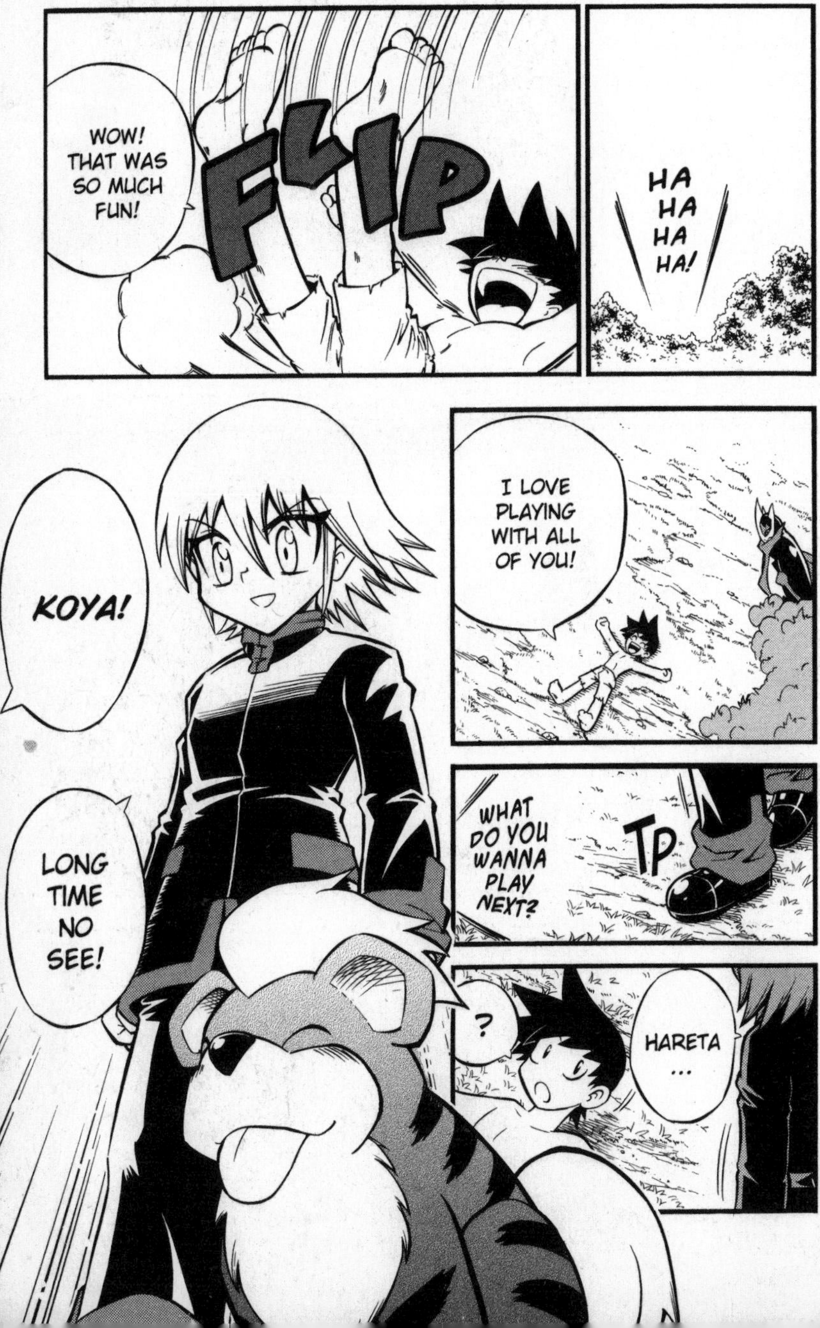
HA HA HA HA!
FLIP
WOW! THAT WAS SO MUCH FUN!
I LOVE PLAYING WITH ALL OF YOU!
TP
WHAT DO YOU WANNA PLAY NEXT?
HARETA ...
?
KOYA!
LONG TIME NO SEE!

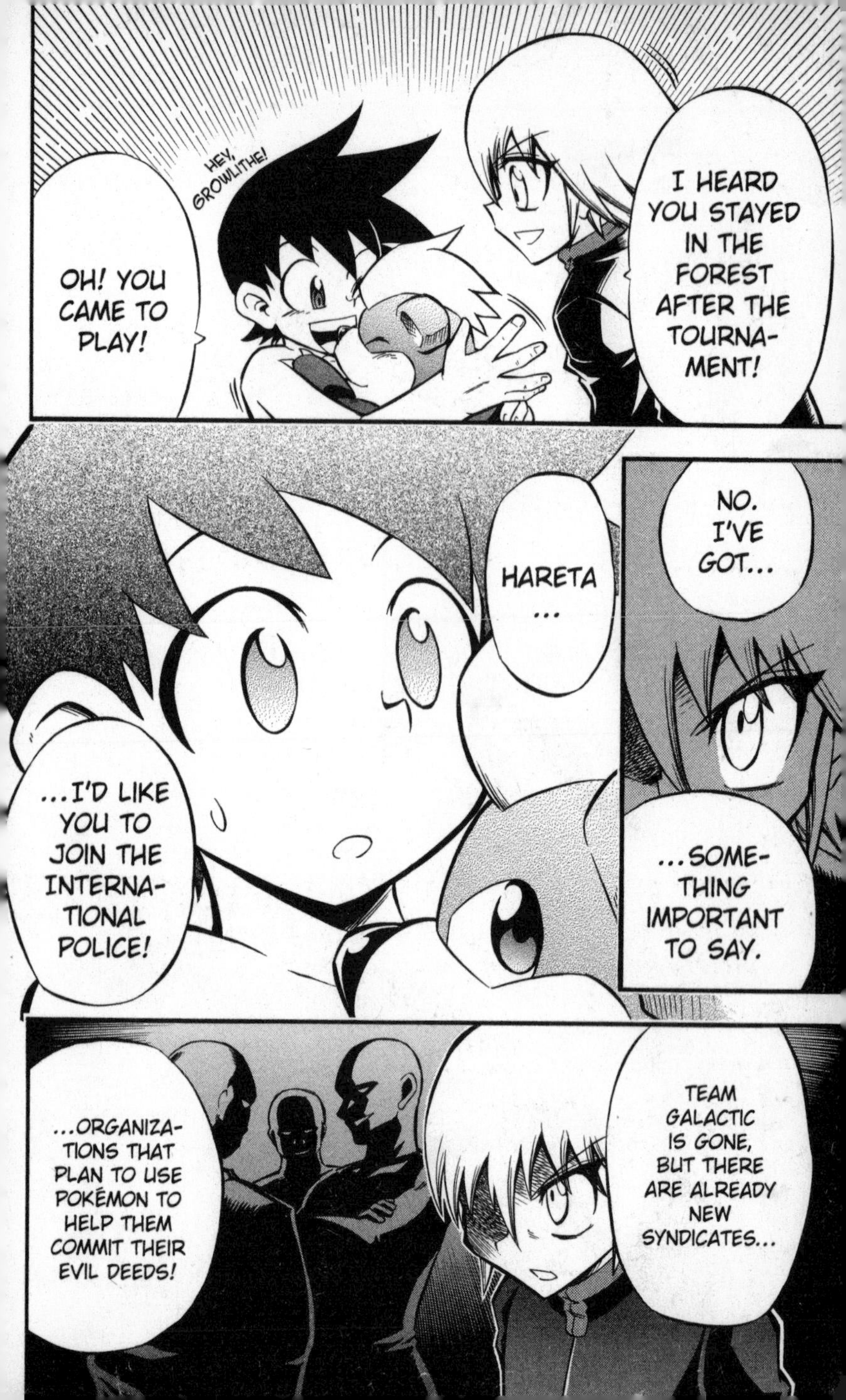
I HEARD YOU STAYED IN THE FOREST AFTER THE TOURNAMENT!
HEY, GROWLITHE!
OH! YOU CAME TO PLAY!
NO. I'VE GOT...
...SOMETHING IMPORTANT TO SAY.
HARETA...
...I'D LIKE YOU TO JOIN THE INTERNATIONAL POLICE!
TEAM GALACTIC IS GONE, BUT THERE ARE ALREADY NEW SYNDICATES...
...ORGANIZATIONS THAT PLAN TO USE POKÉMON TO HELP THEM COMMIT THEIR EVIL DEEDS!

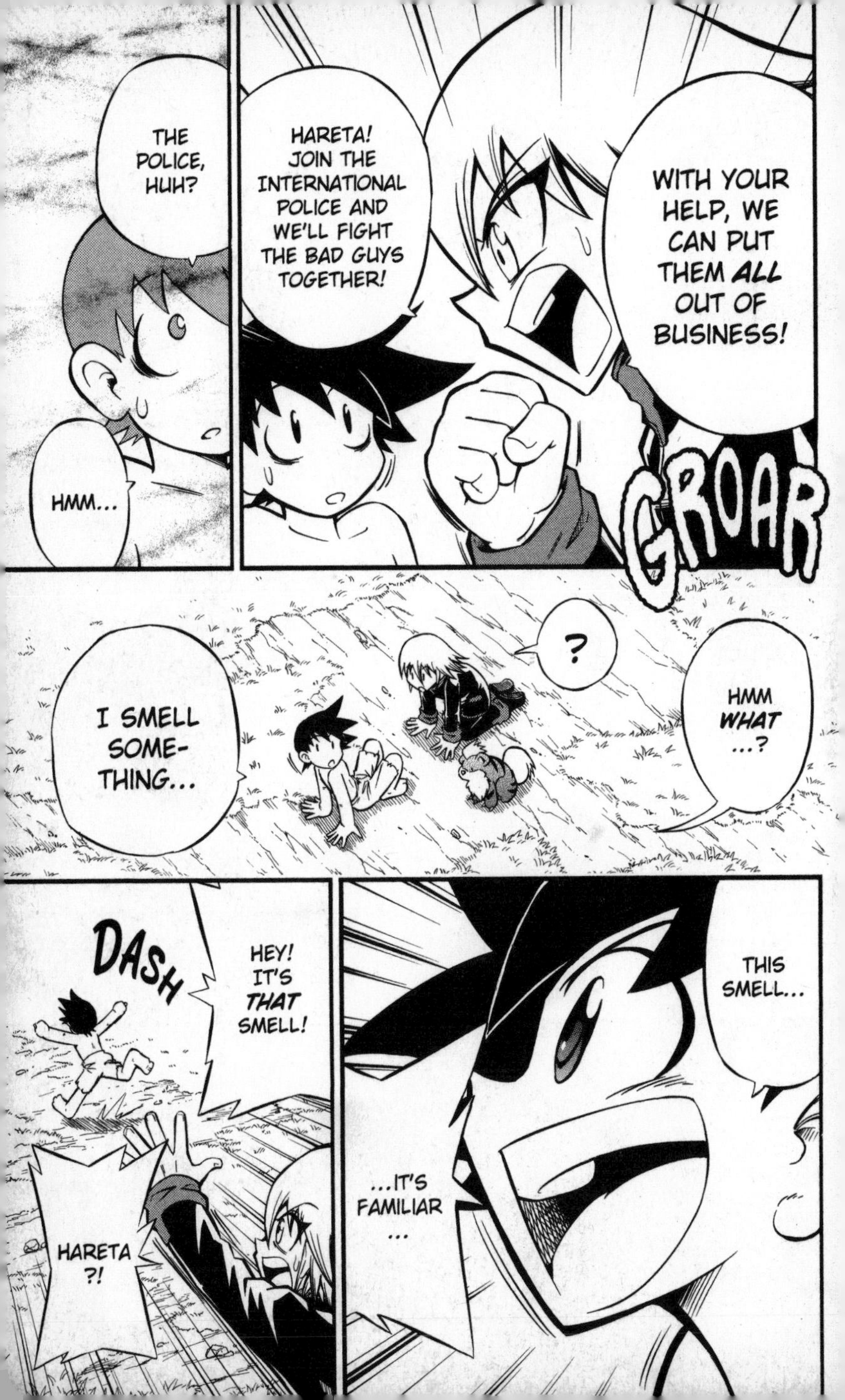
HARETA! JOIN THE INTERNATIONAL POLICE AND WE'LL FIGHT THE BAD GUYS TOGETHER!
WITH YOUR HELP, WE CAN PUT THEM *ALL* OUT OF BUSINESS!
GROAR
THE POLICE, HUH?
HMM...
HMM *WHAT* ...?
?
I SMELL SOME-THING...
THIS SMELL...
...IT'S FAMILIAR ...
HEY! IT'S *THAT* SMELL!
DASH
HARETA ?!

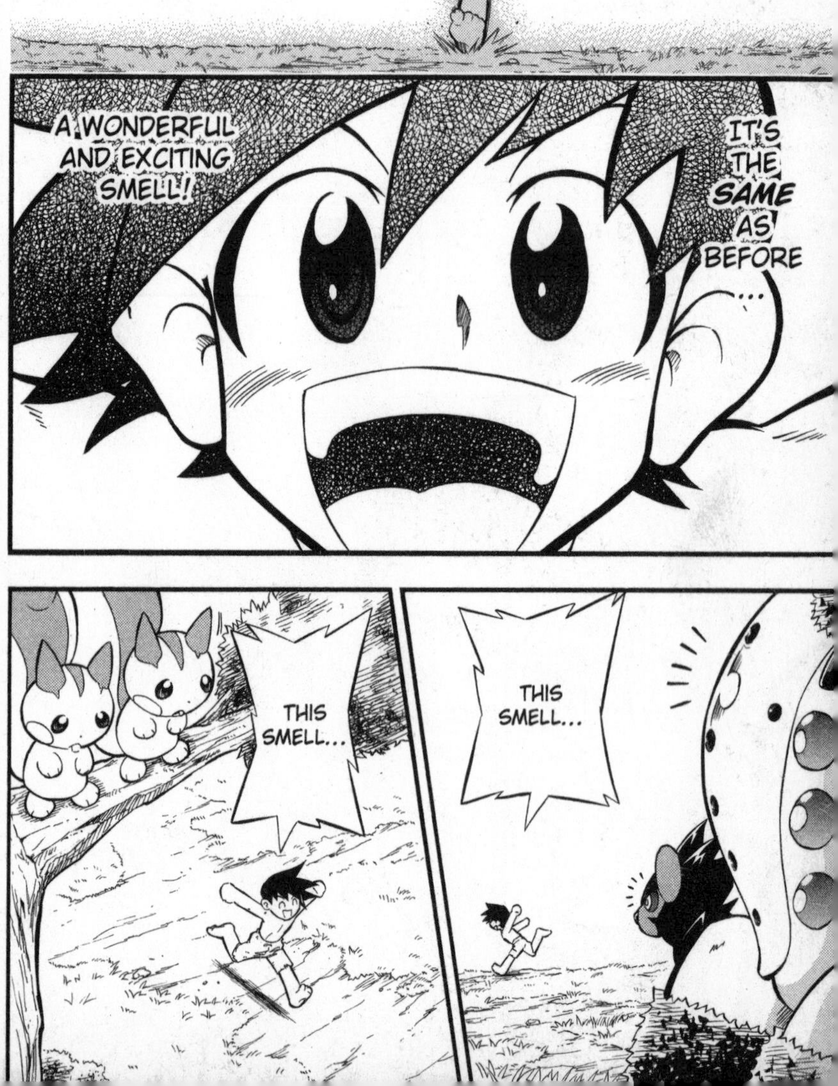
THIS SMELL...
THIS GREAT SMELL...
IT'S THE SAME AS BEFORE...
A WONDERFUL AND EXCITING SMELL!
THIS SMELL...
THIS SMELL...

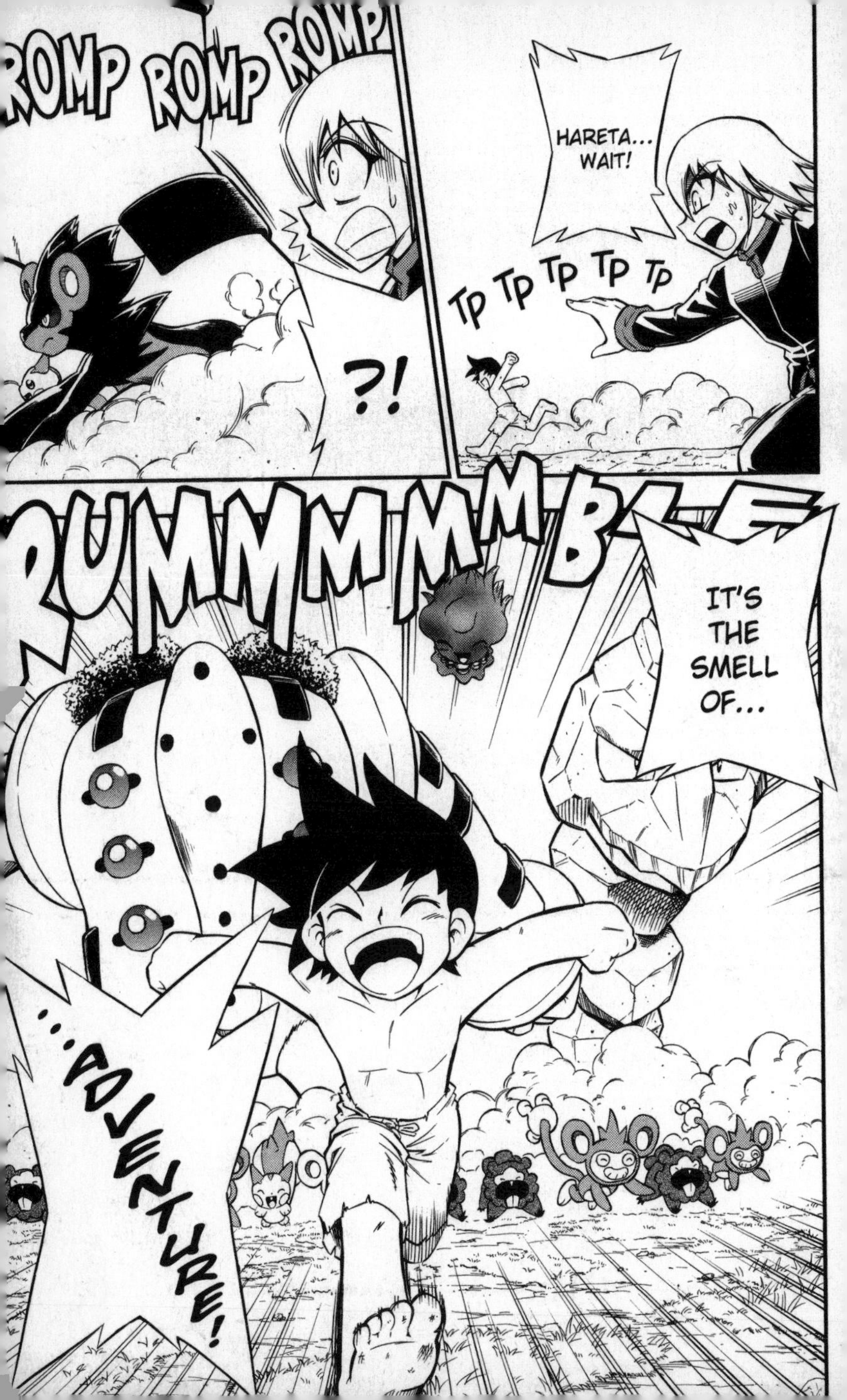
HARETA... WAIT!
TP TP TP TP TP
ROMP ROMP ROMP
?!
RUMMMMMMBLE
IT'S THE SMELL OF...
...ADVENTURE!

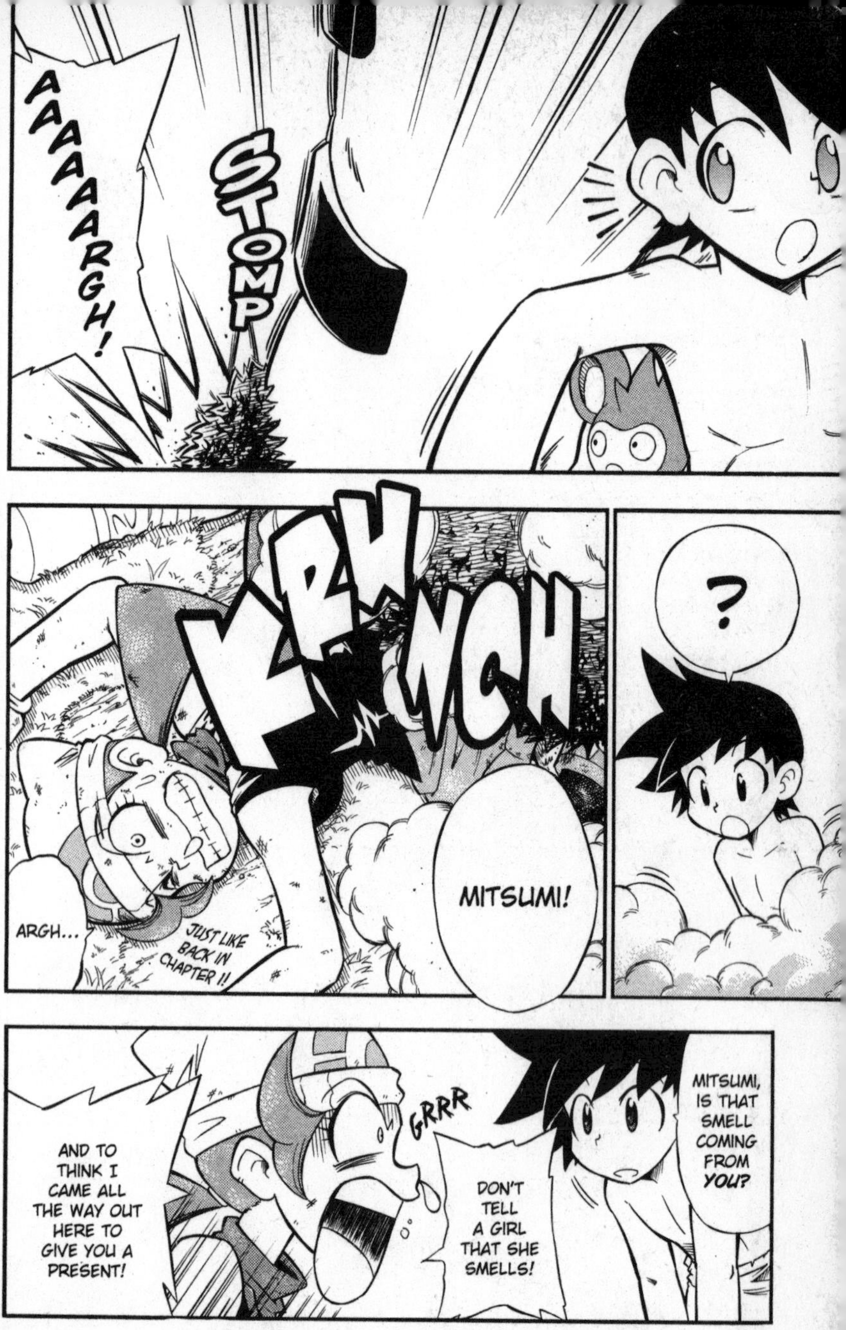
STOMP
AAAAAARGH!
?
KRUNCH
MITSUMI!
JUST LIKE BACK IN CHAPTER 1!
ARGH...
MITSUMI, IS THAT SMELL COMING FROM *YOU?*
GRRR
DON'T TELL A GIRL THAT SHE SMELLS!
AND TO THINK I CAME ALL THE WAY OUT HERE TO GIVE YOU A PRESENT!

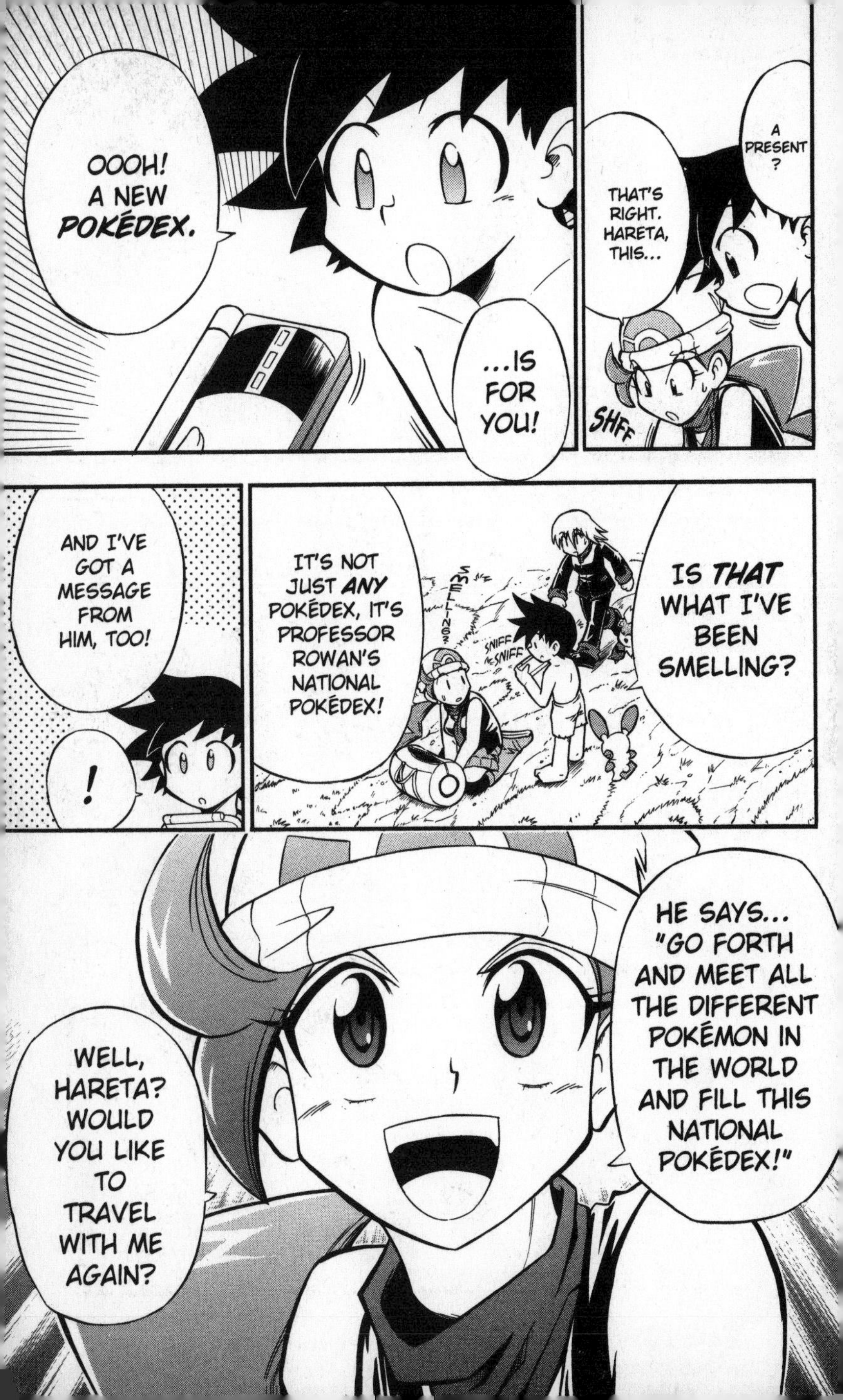
A PRESENT?
THAT'S RIGHT. HARETA, THIS...
SHFF
...IS FOR YOU!
OOOH! A NEW *POKÉDEX.*
IS *THAT* WHAT I'VE BEEN SMELLING?
SMELLING?
SNIFF SNIFF
IT'S NOT JUST ***ANY*** POKÉDEX, IT'S PROFESSOR ROWAN'S NATIONAL POKÉDEX!
AND I'VE GOT A MESSAGE FROM HIM, TOO!
!
HE SAYS... "GO FORTH AND MEET ALL THE DIFFERENT POKÉMON IN THE WORLD AND FILL THIS NATIONAL POKÉDEX!"
WELL, HARETA? WOULD YOU LIKE TO TRAVEL WITH ME AGAIN?

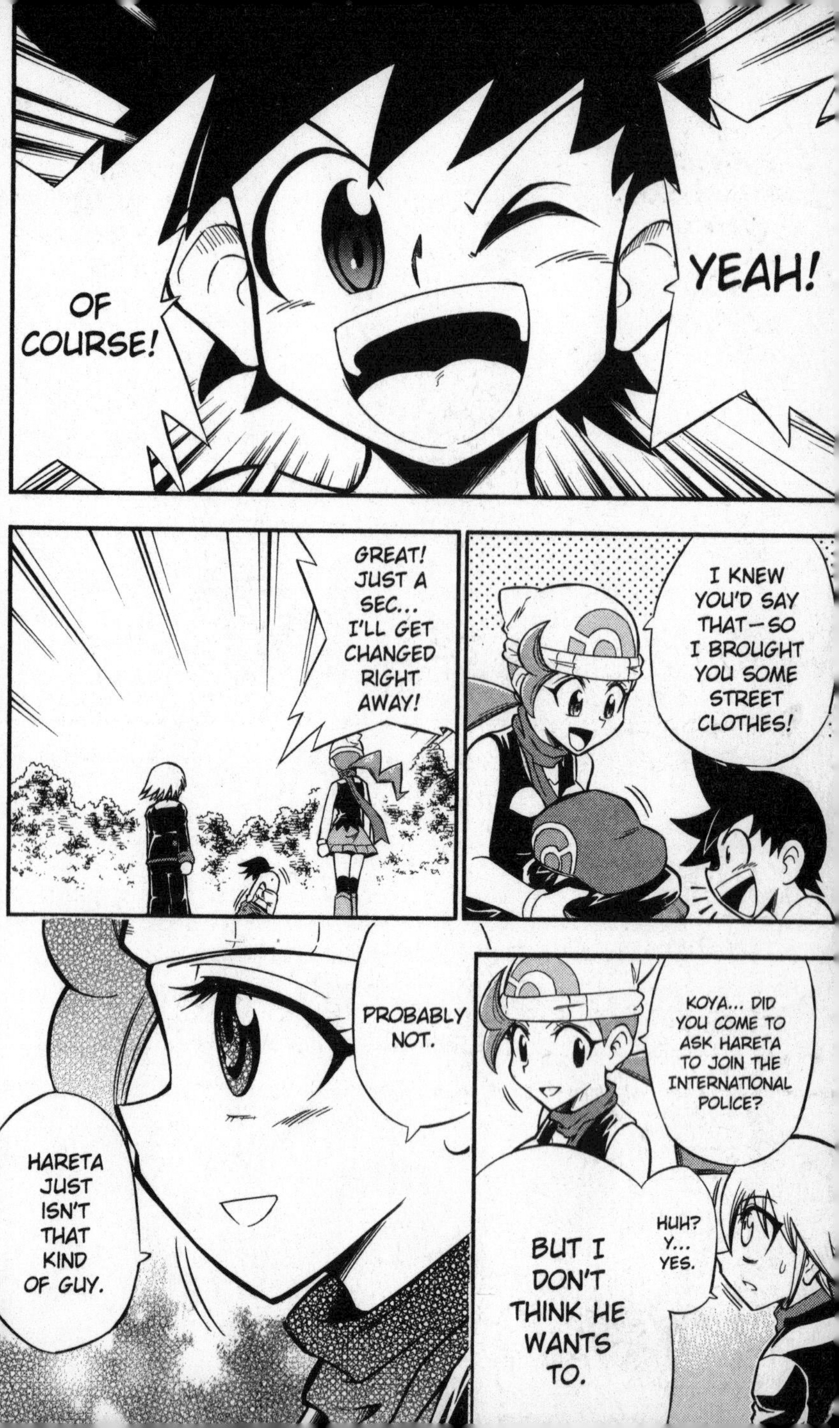
YEAH!
OF COURSE!
I KNEW YOU'D SAY THAT—SO I BROUGHT YOU SOME STREET CLOTHES!
GREAT! JUST A SEC... I'LL GET CHANGED RIGHT AWAY!
KOYA... DID YOU COME TO ASK HARETA TO JOIN THE INTERNATIONAL POLICE?
HUH? Y... YES.
BUT I DON'T THINK HE WANTS TO.
PROBABLY NOT.
HARETA JUST ISN'T THAT KIND OF GUY.

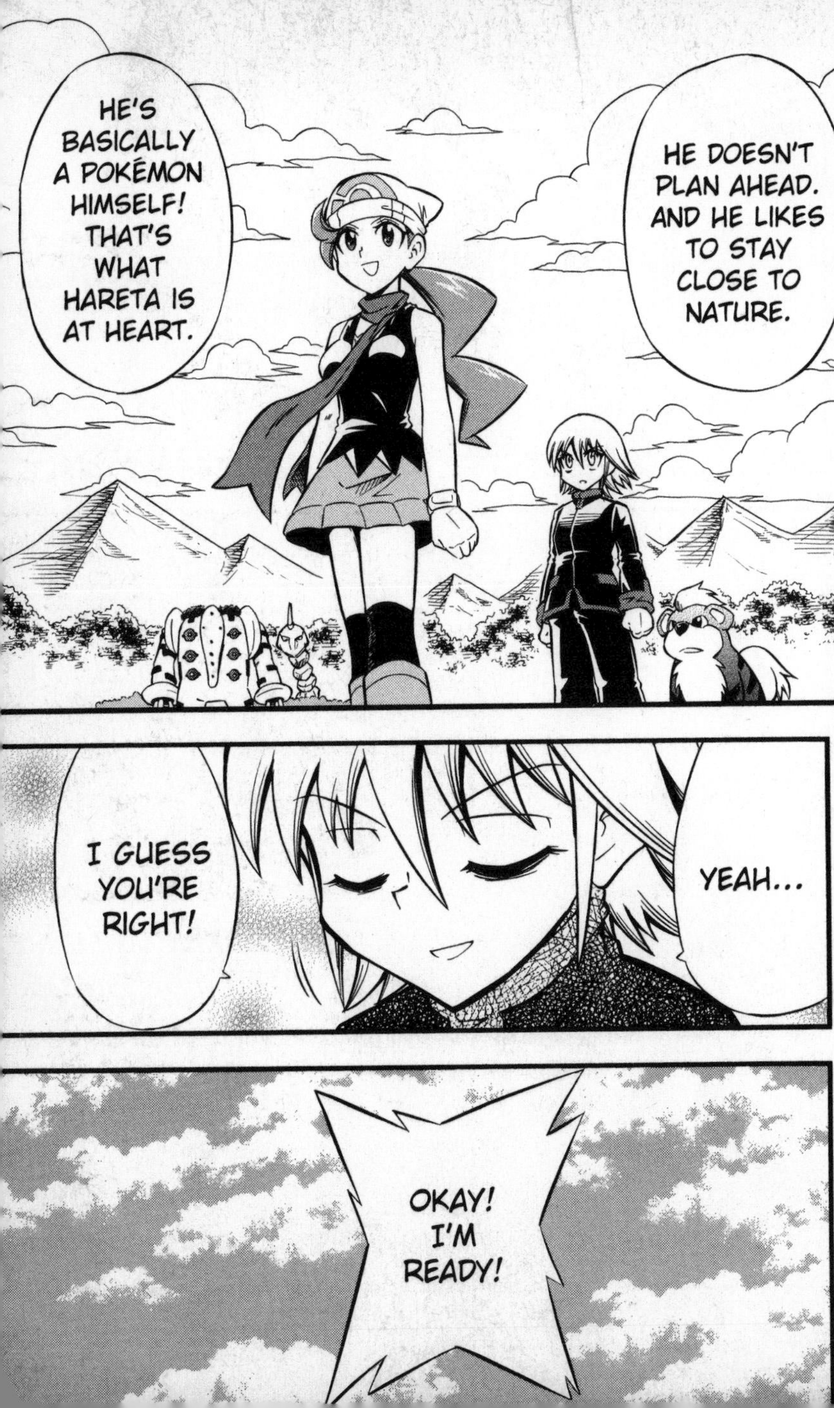
HE DOESN'T PLAN AHEAD. AND HE LIKES TO STAY CLOSE TO NATURE.
HE'S BASICALLY A POKÉMON HIMSELF! THAT'S WHAT HARETA IS AT HEART.
YEAH...
I GUESS YOU'RE RIGHT!
OKAY! I'M READY!

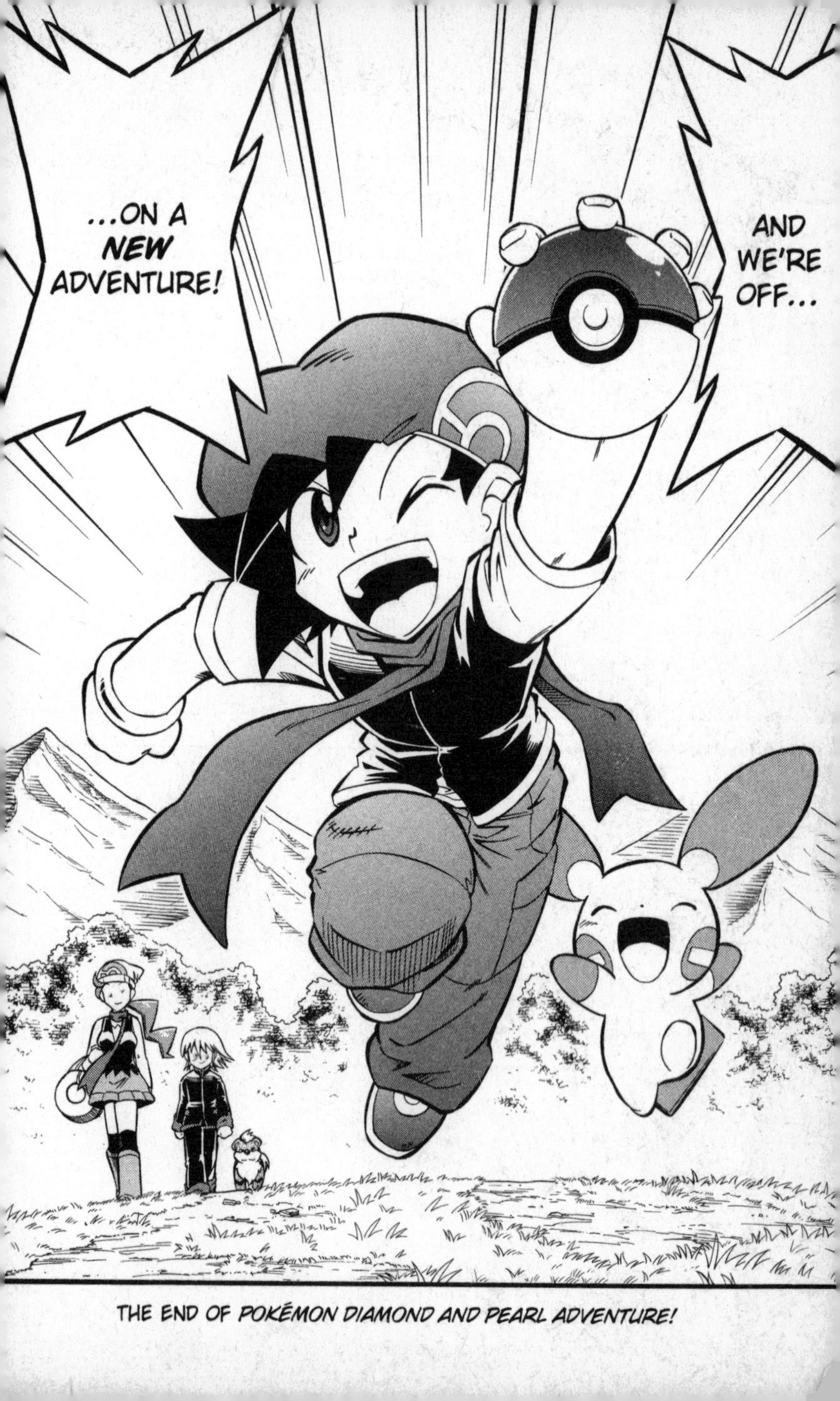
AND WE'RE OFF...
...ON A *NEW* ADVENTURE!

THE END OF *POKÉMON DIAMOND AND PEARL ADVENTURE!*

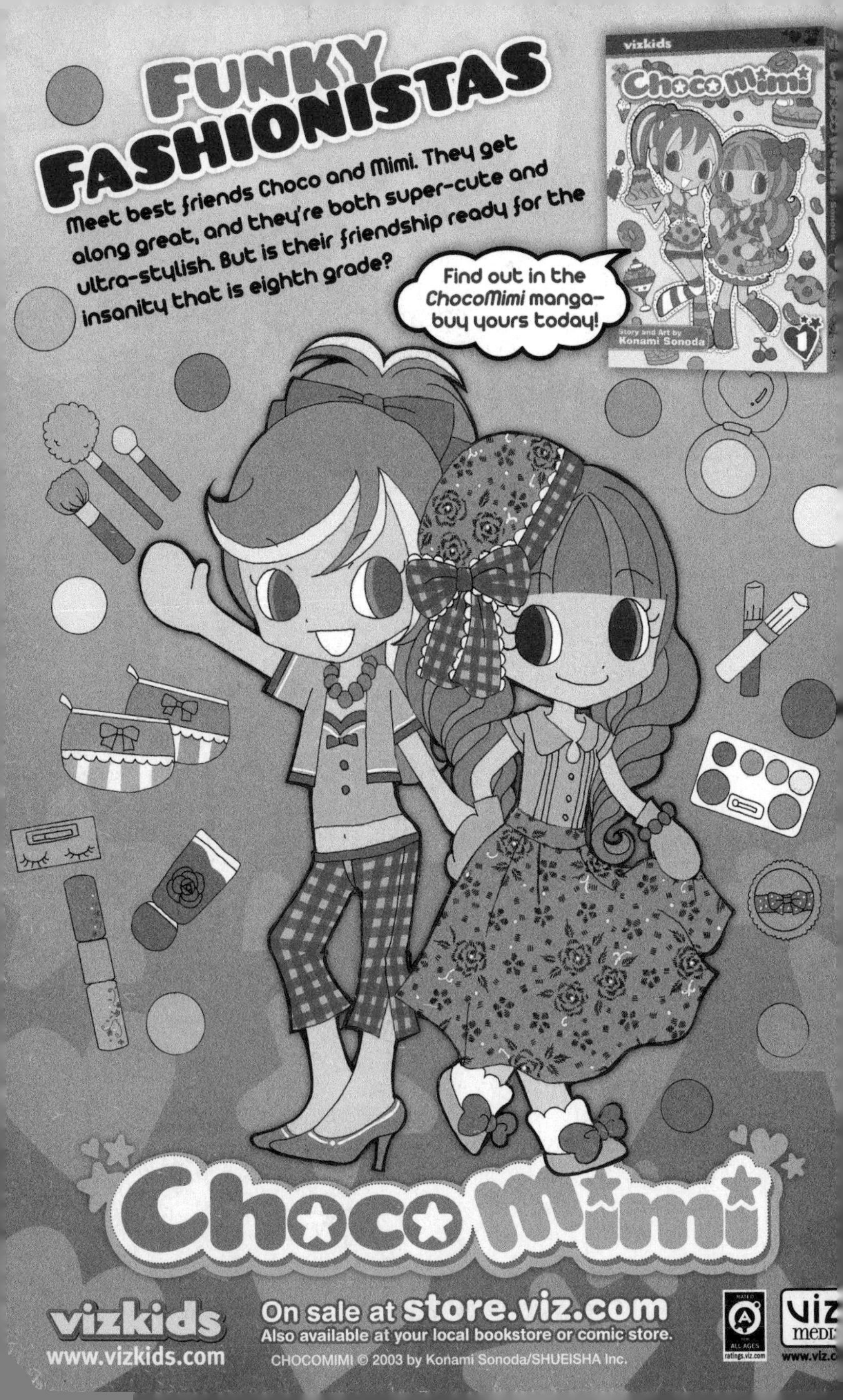
FUNKY FASHIONISTAS
Meet best friends Choco and Mimi. They get along great, and they're both super-cute and ultra-stylish. But is their friendship ready for the insanity that is eighth grade?
Find out in the ChocoMimi manga–buy yours today!
vizkids
Choco Mimi
Story and Art by Konami Sonoda
1
Choco Mimi
vizkids
www.vizkids.com
On sale at store.viz.com
Also available at your local bookstore or comic store.
CHOCOMIMI © 2003 by Konami Sonoda/SHUEISHA Inc.
RATED
ALL AGES
ratings.viz.com

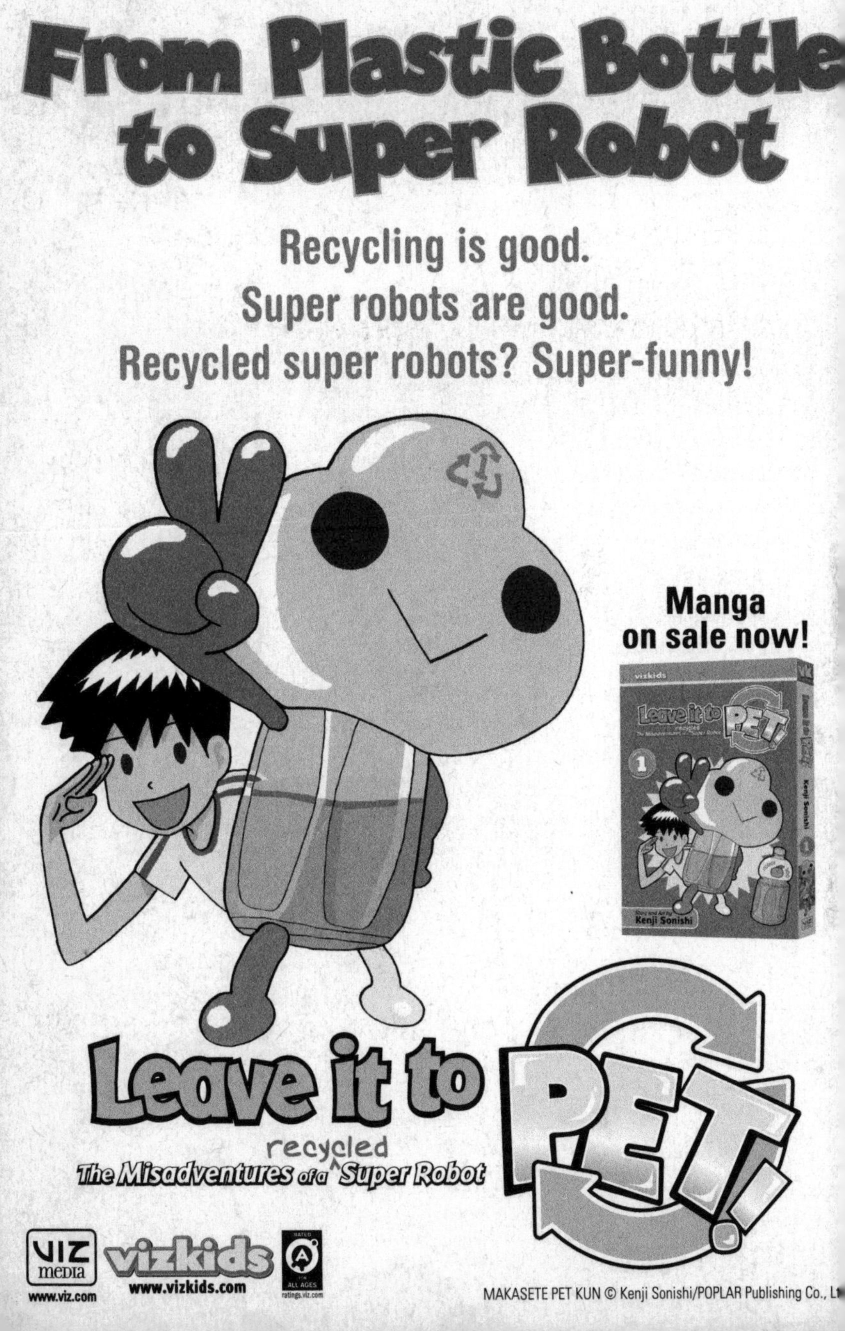

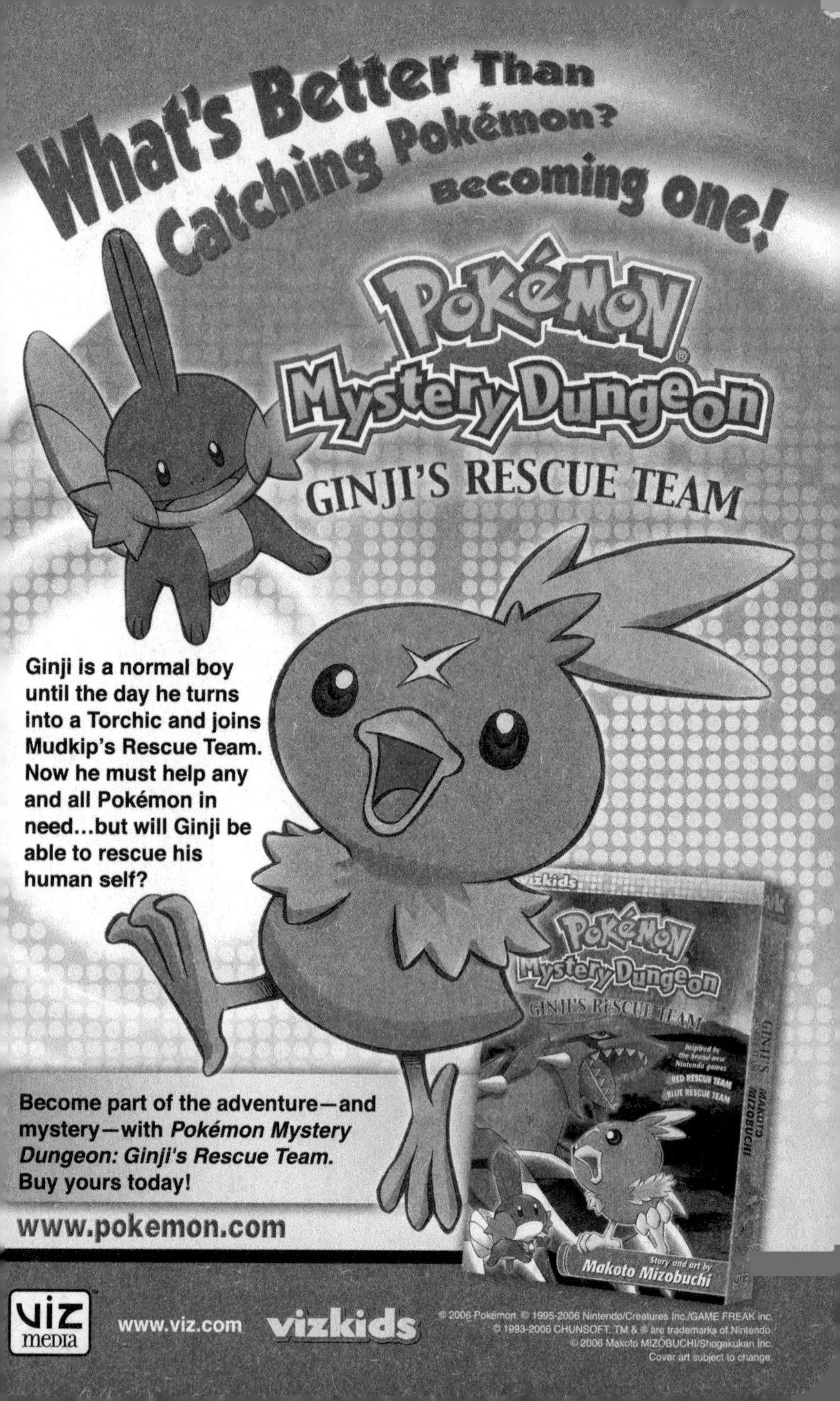
What's Better Than Catching Pokémon?
Becoming one!
POKéMON® Mystery Dungeon
GINJI'S RESCUE TEAM
Ginji is a normal boy until the day he turns into a Torchic and joins Mudkip's Rescue Team. Now he must help any and all Pokémon in need...but will Ginji be able to rescue his human self?
vizkids
POKéMON Mystery Dungeon
GINJI'S RESCUE TEAM
Inspired by the brand-new Nintendo games
RED RESCUE TEAM
BLUE RESCUE TEAM
Story and art by
Makoto Mizobuchi
Become part of the adventure—and mystery—with *Pokémon Mystery Dungeon: Ginji's Rescue Team.* Buy yours today!
www.pokemon.com
viz media
www.viz.com
vizkids
© 2006 Pokémon. © 1995-2006 Nintendo/Creatures Inc./GAME FREAK inc.
© 1993-2006 CHUNSOFT. TM & ® are trademarks of Nintendo.
© 2006 Makoto MIZOBUCHI/Shogakukan Inc.
Cover art subject to change.

JADEN YUKI WANTS TO BE THE BEST DUELIST EVER!

GRPH J IHARA
Ihara, Shigekatsu.
PokGemon.